An Isle of Surrey
A Novel

by

Richard Dowling

Double9
BOOKS

An Isle of Surrey
A Novel
by Richard Dowling

Copyright © 2024

All Rights reserved.

ISBN: 978-93-65782-54-7

Published by

DOUBLE 9 BOOKS

2/13-B, Ansari Road
Daryaganj, New Delhi – 110002
info@double9books.com
www.double9books.com
Tel. 011-40042856

This book is under public domain

ABOUT THE AUTHOR

Richard Dowling (1846–1898) was an Irish novelist, journalist, and editor, best known for his contributions to 19th-century Irish literature. Born in Clonmel, County Tipperary, he moved to Dublin, where he began his career as a journalist. He worked for The Nation and The Irish Times, writing both fiction and non-fiction. Dowling is known for his suspenseful novels and short stories, often exploring themes of mystery and supernatural occurrences. His novel The Mystery of Killard gained significant attention for its intriguing plot and vivid characterization.

Apart from his fiction, Dowling was a skilled editor, contributing to and shaping literary discourse in Dublin. He frequently incorporated Irish settings and folklore into his works, connecting deeply with the Irish cultural landscape. Though his career was cut short by his early death at age 52, his contributions to Victorian-era fiction left a lasting mark on Irish literary history.

CONTENTS

CHAPTER I
WELFORD BRIDGE

There was not a cloud in the heavens. The sun lay low in the west. The eastern sky of a May evening was growing from blue to a violet dusk. Not a breath of wind stirred. It was long past the end of the workman's day.

A group of miserably clad men lounged on Welford Bridge, some gazing vacantly into the empty sky, and some gazing vacantly into the turbid water of the South London Canal, crawling beneath the bridge at the rate of a foot a minute towards its outlet in the Mercantile Docks, on the Surrey shore between Greenwich and the Pool.

The men were all on the southern side of the bridge: they were loafers and long-shoremen. Most of them had pipes in their mouths. They were a disreputable-looking group, belonging to that section of the residuum which is the despair of philanthropists--the man who has nothing before him but work or crime, and can hardly be got to work.

One of them was leaning against the parapet with his face turned in mere idleness up the canal. He was not looking at anything: his full, prominent, meaningless blue eyes were fixed on nothing. Directly in the line of his vision, and between him and Camberwell, were Crawford's Bay and Boland's Ait. The ait, so called by some derisive humourist, lay in the mouth of the bay, the outer side of it forming one bank of the canal, and the inner side corresponding with the sweep of Crawford's Bay, formed forty feet of canal water.

The man looking south was low-sized, red-bearded, red-whiskered, red-haired, with a battered brown felt hat, a neckerchief of no determinable colour, a torn check shirt, a dark blue ragged pea-jacket of pilot cloth, no waistcoat, a pair of brown stained trousers, and boots several sizes too large for him, turned up at the toes, and so bagged and battered and worn that they looked as though they could not be moved another step without falling asunder. This man would have told a mere acquaintance that his name was Jim Ford, but he was called by those who knew him Red Jim.

All at once he uttered a strong exclamation of surprise without shifting his position.

"What is it, Jim?" asked a tall, lank, dark man by his side.

The others of the group turned and looked in the direction in which Jim's eyes were fixed.

"Why," said Red Jim, in a tone of incredulity and indignation, "there's some one in Crawford's House!"

"Of course there is, you fool! Why, where have you been? Haven't you heard? Have you been with the Salvation Army, or only doing a stretch?"

"Fool yourself!" said Red Jim. "Mind what you're saying, or perhaps I'll stretch you a bit, long as you are already." The other men laughed at this personal sally. It reduced long Ned Bayliss to sullen silence, and restored Red Jim to his condition of objectless vacuity.

"I hear," said a man who had not yet spoken, "that Crawford's House is let."

"Let!" cried another, as though anyone who mentioned the matter as news must be ages behind the times. "Let! I should think it is!"

"And yet it isn't so much let, after all," said Ned Bayliss, turning round in a captious manner. "You can't exactly say a place is let when a man goes to live in his own house."

"Why, Crawford's dead this long and merry," objected a voice.

"Well," said Ned Bayliss, "and if he is, and if he left all to his wife for as long as she kept his name, and if she married a second time and got her new husband to change his name instead of *her* changing *hers*--how is that, do you think, Matt Jordan?"

It was plain by Ned Bayliss's manner and by the way in which this speech was received by the listeners that he was looked up to as a being of extraordinary mental endowment, and possessed preëminently of the power of lucid exposition.

"True enough," said Matt Jordan humbly, as he hitched up his trousers and shifted his pipe from one side of his mouth to the other, and coughed a self-deprecatory cough. "And a snug property he has come into, I say. I only wish I was in his place."

Jordan was a squat, ill-favoured man of forty.

"Why," said Bayliss derisively, "a man with your points wouldn't throw himself away on a sickly widow with only a matter of a thousand a-year or thereabouts out of a lot of ramshackle tenement-houses and canal wharfs. You'd look higher, Matt. Why, you'd want a titled lady, any way.

With your face and figure, you ought to be able to do a great deal better than an elderly sickly widow, even if she is rich."

Jordan shifted his felt hat, made no reply, and for a while there was silence.

Crawford's House, of which the loungers on Welford Bridge were speaking, stood a few feet back from the inner edge of Crawford's Bay, about three hundred yards from the bridge. Jim Ford, the first speaker, had concluded, from seeing all the sashes of the house open, and a woman cleaning a window, and a strip of carpet hanging out of another, that a tenant had been found for this lonely and isolated dwelling, which had been standing idle for years.

"Have you seen this turncoat Crawford?" asked a man after a pause.

No one had seen him.

"He must have a spirit no better than a dog's to change his name for her money," said Red Jim, without abandoning his study of Crawford's House, on which his vacant eyes now rested with as much curiosity as the expressionless blue orbs were capable of.

"It would be very handy for *some* people to change their names like that, or in any other way that wouldn't bring a trifle of canvas and a few copper bolts to the mind of any one in the neighbourhood of the East India Docks," said Bayliss, looking at that point of the sky directly above him, lest any one might fancy his words had a personal application.

With an oath, Red Jim turned round, and, keeping his side close to the parapet, slouched slowly away towards the King William public-house, which stood at the bottom of the short approach to the steep humpbacked bridge.

"Nice chap he is to talk of changing a name for money being disgraceful!" said Bayliss, when the other was out of hearing. "He was as near as ninepence to doing time over them canvas and bolts at the East India. Look at him now, going to the William as if he had money! *He* isn't the man that could stand here if he had a penny in his rags." The speaker jingled some coins in his own pocket to show how he, being a man of intellectual resources and strong will, could resist temptation before which common clay, such as Red Jim was made of, must succumb.

Red Jim did not enter the William. As he reached the door he stopped and looked along the road. A man coming from the western end drew up in front of him and said:

"Is that Welford Bridge?" pointing to where the group of loungers stood, with the upper portions of their bodies illumined by the western glow against the darkening eastern sky.

"Yes," said Jim sullenly, "that's Welford Bridge."

"Do you know where Crawford's Bay is, here on the South London Canal? Is that the canal bridge?"

"I know where Crawford's Bay is right enough," said the other doggedly. He was not disposed to volunteer any information. "Do you want to go to Crawford's Bay? If you do, I can show you the way. I'm out of work, gov'nor, and stone broke."

"Very good. Come along and show me Crawford's House. I'll pay you for your trouble."

Red Jim led the way back to the bridge.

"Who has he picked up?" asked Bayliss jealously, as the two men passed the group.

None of the loungers answered.

"He's turning down Crawford Street," said Bayliss, when the two men had gone a hundred yards beyond the bridge.

"So he is," said another. Bayliss was the most ready of speech, and monopolised the conversation. His mates regarded him as one rarely gifted in the matter of language; as one who would, without doubt, have made an orator if ambition had led the way.

"I wonder what Red Jim is bringing that man down Crawford Street for? No good, I'm sure."

"Seems a stranger," suggested the other man. "Maybe he wants Jim to show him the way."

"Ay," said Bayliss in a discontented tone. "There's a great deal to be seen down Crawford Street! Lovely views; plenty of rotting doors. Now, if they only got in on the wharf, Jim could show him the old empty ice-house there. Do you know, if any one was missing hereabouts, and a good reward was offered, I'd get the drags and have a try in the ice-house. There's ten feet of water in it if there's an inch, so I'm told."

"It is a lonesome place. I wonder they don't pump the water out."

"Pump it out, you fool! How could they? Why, 'twould fill as fast as any dozen fire-engines could pump it out. The water from the canal soaks into it as if the wall was a sieve."

Nothing more was said for a while. Then suddenly, Bayliss, whose eyes were turned towards the bay, uttered an oath, and exclaimed, "We're a heap of fools, that's what we are, not to guess. Why, it must be Crawford, the new Crawford--not the Crawford that's dead and buried, but the one that's alive and had the gumption to marry the sickly widow for her money! There he is at the window with that girl I saw going into the house to-day."

Bayliss stretched out his long lean arm, and pointed with his thin grimy hand over the canal towards Crawford's House, at one of the windows of which a man and woman could be seen looking out into the dark turbid waters of Crawford's Bay.

CHAPTER II
CRAWFORD'S HOUSE

Crawford Street, into which the stranger and his uncouth conductor had turned, was a narrow, dingy, neglected blind lane. The end of it was formed of a brick wall, moss-grown and ragged. On the right hand side were gates and doors of idle wharves, whose rears abutted on the bay; on the left, a long low unbroken wall separating the roadway from a desolate waste, where rubbish might be shot, according to a dilapidated and half-illegible notice-board; but on the plot were only two small mounds of that dreary material, crowned with a few battered rusty iron and tin utensils of undeterminable use.

In the street, which was a couple of hundred yards long, stood the only dwelling. Opposite the door Red Jim drew up, and, pointing, said, "That's Crawford's House. I belong to this neighourhood. I'm called after the place. My name is James Ford. I'm called after the place, same as a lord is called after a place. They found me twenty-nine years ago on the tow-path. Nobody wanted me much then or since. Maybe you're the new Mr. Crawford, and, like me, called after the place too?" He spoke in a tone of curiosity.

At the question, his companion started, looking at Red Jim out of a pair of keen, quick, furtive eyes. "I told you I would pay you for showing me the place. Here's sixpence. If you want any information of me, you'll have to pay me for it. If you really care to know my name, I'll tell it to you for that sixpence." The stranger laughed a short sharp laugh, handed Red Jim the coin, and kept his hand outstretched as if to take it back.

Jim turned on his heel, and slunk away muttering.

The stranger knocked with his fist on the door, from which the knocker was missing. The panels had originally been painted a grass-green, now faded down to the sober hue of the sea.

The door was opened by a tall slender girl, whose golden-brown hair was flying in wild confusion over her white forehead and red cheeks, and across her blue eyes, in which, as in the hair, flashed a glint of gold. She smiled and laughed apologetically, and thrust her floating hair back from her face with both her hands.

"Miss Layard?" said the stranger, raising his hat and bowing. He thought, "What beauty, what health, what spirits, what grace, what youth, what deliciousness!"

"Yes," she answered, stepping back for him to enter. "Mr. Crawford?" she asked in her turn.

"My name is Crawford," he said going in. "I--I was not quite prepared to find you what you are, Miss Layard--I mean so--so young. When your brother spoke to me of his sister, I fancied he meant some one much older than himself."

She smiled, and laughed again as she led him into the front room, now in a state of chaotic confusion.

"We did not expect you till later. My brother has not come home yet. We have only moved in to-day, and we are, O! in such dreadful confusion."

On the centre of the floor was spread a square of very old threadbare carpet, leaving a frame of worn old boards around it. In the centre of the carpet stood a small dining-table. Nothing else in the room was in its place. The half-dozen poor chairs, the chiffonnier, the one easy-chair, the couch, were all higgledy-piggledy. The furniture was of the cheapest kind, made to catch the inexperienced eye. Although evidently not old, it was showing signs of decrepitude. It had once, no doubt, looked bright and pleasant enough, but now the spring seats of the chairs were bulged, and the green plush expanse of the couch rose and fell like miniature grazing-land of rolling hillocks.

The young girl placed a seat for her visitor, and took one herself with another of those bright cheerful laughs which were delicious music, and seemed to make light and perfume in the darkening cheerless room.

"My brother told me you were not likely to be here until ten; but your rooms are all ready, if you wish to see them."

She leant back in her chair and clasped her hands in her lap, a picture of beautiful, joyous girlhood.

He regarded her with undisguised admiration. She returned his looks with smiling, unruffled tranquillity.

"So," he said in a low voice, as though he did not wish the noise of his own words to distract his sense of seeing, concentrated on her face and lithe graceful figure, "you got my rooms ready, while you left your own in chaos?"

"You are too soon," she answered, nodding her head playfully. "If you had not come until ten, we should have had this room in order. As you see, it was well we arranged the other rooms first. Would you like to see them?"

"Not just now. I am quite content here for the present," he said, with a gallant gesture towards her.

"I don't think my brother will be very long. In fact, when you knocked I felt quite sure it was Alfred. O! here he is. Pardon me," she cried, springing up, and hurrying to the door.

In a few minutes Alfred Layard was shaking hands with the other man, saying pleasantly and easily, "I do not know, Mr. Crawford, whether it is I ought to welcome you, or you ought to welcome me. You are at once my landlord and my tenant."

"And you, on your side, necessarily are my landlord and my tenant also. Let us welcome one another, and hope we may be good friends."

With a wave of his hand he included the girl in this proposal.

"Agreed!" cried Layard cheerfully, as he again shook the short plump hand of the elder man.

"You see," said Crawford, explaining the matter with a humorous toss of the head and a chuckle, "your brother is my tenant, since he has taken this house, and I am his tenant, since I have taken two rooms in this house. I have just been saying to Miss Layard," turning from the sister to the brother, "that when you spoke to me of your sister who looked after your little boy, I imagined she must be much older than you."

"Instead of which you find her a whole ten years younger," said Layard, putting his arm round the girl's slim waist lightly and affectionately; "and yet, although she is only a child, she is as wise with her little motherless nephew as if she were Methuselah's sister."

The girl blushed and escaped from her brother's arm.

"You would think," she said, "that there was some credit in taking care of Freddie. Why, he's big enough and good enough to take care of himself, and me into the bargain. I asked Mr. Crawford, Alfred, if he would like to look at his rooms, but he seemed to wish to see you."

"And I am here at last," said Layard. "Well, shall we go and look at them now? You observe the confusion we are in here. We cannot, I fear, offer you even a cup of tea to drink to our better acquaintance."

Crawford rose, and the three left the room and began ascending the narrow massive and firm old stairs.

To look at brother and sister, no one would fancy they were related. He was tall and lank, with dark swarthy face, deep-sunken small grey eyes, not remarkable for their light, dark brown hair, and snub nose. The most remarkable feature of his face was his beard--dark dull brown which looked almost dun, and hung down from each side of his chin in two enormous thin streamers. His face in repose was the embodiment of invincible melancholy; but by some unascertainable means it was able to light up under the influence of humour, or affection, or joy, in a way all the more enchanting because so wholly unexpected.

Alfred Layard was thirty years of age, and had been a widower two years, his young wife dying a twelve-month after the birth of her only child Freddie, now three.

William Crawford was a man of very different mould; thick-set, good-looking, with bold brown eyes, clean-shaven face, close thick hair which curled all over a massive head, full lips that had few movements, and handsome well cut forehead too hollow for beauty in the upper central region. The face was singularly immobile, but it had a look of energy and resolution about it that caught the eye and held the attention, and ended in arousing something between curiosity and fear in the beholder. Plainly, a man with a will of his own, and plenty of energy to carry that will out. In all his movements, even those of courtesy, there was a suggestion of irrepressible vigour. His age was about five or six and thirty.

It was an odd procession. In front, the gay fair girl with azure eyes, golden-brown hair, and lithe form, ascending with elastic step. Behind her, the thick-set, firm, resolute figure of the elder man, with dark, impassive, immobile features, bold dark eyes, and firm lips, moving as though prepared to meet opposition and ready to overcome it. Last, the tall, lank angular form of the young widower, with plain, almost ugly, face, deep-set eyes, snub nose, dull complexion, and long melancholy dun beard, flowing like a widow's streamers in two thin scarves behind him. Here were three faces, one of which was always alight, a second which could never light, and a third usually dull and dead, but which could light at will.

"This is the sitting-room," said Hetty, standing at the threshold. "You said you would prefer having the back room furnished as the sitting-room, Alfred told me."

"Yes, certainly, the back for the sitting-room," said Crawford, as they entered. He looked round sharply with somewhat the same surprising quickness of glance which had greeted Red Jim's question at the door. It conveyed the idea of a man at once curious and on his guard.

His survey seemed to satisfy him, for he ceased to occupy himself with the room, and said, turning to the brother and sister, with a short laugh, "This, as you know, is my first visit to Crawford Street. I had no notion what kind of a place it was; and when I am here, two or three days in the month, and a week additional each quarter, I should like to be quiet and much to myself. I don't, of course, my dear Mr. Layard, mean with regard to your sister and you," he bowed, "but the people all round. They are not a very nice class of people, are they?" with a shrug of his shoulders at people who were not very nice.

"There are no people at all near us," answered Layard cheerfully. "No one else lives in the street, and we have the canal, or rather the Bay, at the back."

"Capital! capital!" cried Crawford in a spiritless voice, though he rubbed his hands as if enjoying himself immensely. "You, saving for the presence of Miss Layard and your little boy, whose acquaintance, by the way, I have not yet made, are a kind of Robinson Crusoe here."

"O!" cried Hetty, running to the window and pointing out, "the real Robinson Crusoe is here."

"Where? I hope he has Man Friday, parrot, and all; walking to the window, where they stood looking out, the girl, with her round arm, pointing into the gathering dusk. In the window-place, they were almost face to face. Instead of instantly following the direction of Hetty's arm, he followed the direction of his thoughts, and while her eyes were gazing out of the window, his were fixed upon her face.

"There," she said, upon finding his eyes were not in the direction of her hand.

"I beg your pardon," he said, "but I can see no one."

He was now looking out of the window.

"But you can see his island."

"Again I beg your pardon, but I can see no island."

"What you see there is an island. That is not the tow-path right opposite: that is Boland's Ait."

"Boland's Ait! Yes, I have heard of Boland's Ait. I have nothing to do with it, I believe?" he turned to Layard.

"I think not."

"O, no!" said the girl laughing; "the whole island is the property of Mr. Francis Bramwell, a most mysterious man, who is either an astrologer, or an author, or a pirate, or something wonderful and romantic."

"Why," cried her brother in amused surprise, "where on earth did you get this information?"

"From Mrs. Grainger, whom you sent to help me to-day. Mrs. Grainger knows the history of the whole neighbourhood from the time of Adam."

"The place cannot have existed so long," said Crawford, with another of his short laughs; "for it shows no sign of having been washed even as far back as the Flood. Is your Crusoe old or young?"

"Young, I am told, and handsome. I assure you the story is quite romantic."

"And is there much more of the story of this Man Friday, or whatever he is?" asked Crawford carelessly, as he moved away from the window towards the door.

"Well," said she, "that is a good deal to begin with; and then it is said he has been ruined by some one or other, or something or other, either betting on horses or buying shares in railways to the moon, and that he did these foolish things because his wife ran away from him; and now he lives all alone on his island, and leaves it very seldom, and never has any visitors, or hardly any, and is supposed to be writing a book proving that woman is a mistake and ought to be abolished."

"The brute!" interpolated Crawford, bowing to Hetty, as though in protest against any one who could say an unkind thing of the sex to which she belonged.

"Isn't it dreadful?" cried the girl in a tone of comic distress. She was still standing by the window, one cheek and side of her golden-brown hair illumined by the fading light, and her blue eyes dancing with mischievous excitement. "And they say that, much as he hates women, he hates men more."

"Ah! that is a redeeming feature," said Crawford. "A misanthropist is intelligible, but a misogynist is a thing beyond reason, and hateful."

"But, Hetty," said Layard, "if the man lives so very much to himself and does not leave his house, how is all this known?"

"Why, because all the women have not been abolished yet. Do you fancy there ever was a mystery a woman could not find out? It is the business of women to fathom mysteries. I'll engage that before we are a week here I shall know twice as much as I do now of our romantic neighbour."

"And then," said Crawford, showing signs of flagging interest, and directing his attention once more to the arrangement of the room, "perhaps Miss Layard will follow this Crusoe's example, and write a book against men."

"No, no. I like men."

He turned round and looked fully at her. "And upon my word, Miss Layard," said he warmly, "I think you would find a vast majority of men very willing to reciprocate the feeling."

Hetty laughed, and so did her brother.

"As I explained," said Crawford, "I shall want these rooms only once a month. I shall have to look after the property in this neighbourhood. I think I shall take a leaf out of our friend Crusoe's book, and keep very quiet and retired. I care to be known in this neighbourhood as little as possible. There is property of another kind in town. It, too, requires my personal supervision. I shall make this place my head-quarters, and keep what changes of clothes I require here. It is extremely unlikely I shall have any visitors. By the way, in what direction does Camberwell lie?" He asked the question with an elaborate carelessness which did not escape Alfred Layard.

"Up there," said Layard, waving his left hand in a southerly direction.

Once more Crawford approached the window. This time he leaned out, resting his hand on the sill.

In front of him lay Boland's Ait, a little island about a hundred yards long and forty yards wide in the middle, tapering off to a point at either end. Beyond the head of the island, pointing south, the tow-path was visible, and beyond the tail of the island the tow-path again, and further off Welford Bridge, lying north.

Hetty was leaning against the wainscot of the old-fashioned deep embrasure.

"Does that tow-path lead to Camberwell?" asked Crawford.

"Yes," answered the girl, making a gesture to the left.

"Is it much frequented?" asked he in a voice he tried to make commonplace, but from which he could not banish the hint of anxiety.

"O, no, very few people go along it."

"But now, I suppose, people sometimes come from that direction," waving his left hand, "for a walk?"

"Well," said the girl demurely, "the scenery isn't very attractive; but there is nothing to prevent people coming, if they pay the toll."

"O, there *is* a toll?" he said in a tone of relief, as if the knowledge of such a barrier between him and Camberwell were a source of satisfaction to him.

"Yes; a halfpenny on weekdays and a penny on Sundays."

He leaned further out. The frame of the window shook slightly. "We must have this woodwork fixed," he said a little peevishly. "What building is this here on your left?--a store of some kind with the gates off."

"That's the empty ice-house. It belongs to you, I believe."

"Ah! the empty ice-house. So it is. I never saw an ice-house before."

"It is full of water," said the girl, again drawing on the charwoman's store of local information. "It makes me quite uncomfortable to think of it."

The man, bending out of the window, shuddered, and shook the window-frame sharply. "There seems to be a great deal of water about here, and it doesn't look very ornamental."

"No," said Hetty; "but it's very useful."

Crawford's eyes were still directed to the left, but not at so sharp an angle as to command a view of the vacant icehouse. He was gazing across the head of the island at the tow-path.

Suddenly he drew in with a muttered imprecation; the window-frame shook violently, and a large piece of mortar fell and struck him on the nape of the neck. He sprang back with a second half-uttered malediction, and stood bolt upright a pace from the window, but did not cease to gaze across the head of the island.

Along the tow-path a tall man was advancing rapidly, swinging his arms in a remarkable manner as he walked.

"No, no, not hurt to speak of," he answered, with a hollow laugh, in reply to a question of Layard's, still keeping his eyes fixed on the tow-path visible beyond Boland's Ait. "The mortar has gone down my back. I shall change my coat and get rid of the mortar. My portmanteau has come, I perceive. Thank you, I am not hurt. Good evening for the present," he added, as brother and sister moved towards the door.

Although he did not stir further from the window, they saw he was in haste they should be gone, so they hurried away, shutting the door behind them.

When they had disappeared he went back to the window, and muttered in a hoarse voice: "I could have sworn it was Philip Ray--Philip Ray, her brother, who registered an oath he would shoot me whenever or wherever he met me, and he is the man to keep his word. He lives at Camberwell. It must have been he. If it was he, in a few minutes he will come out on the tow-path at the other end of the island; in two minutes--in three minutes at the very outside--he must come round the tail of the island, and then I can make sure whether it is Philip Ray or not. He will be only half the distance from me that he was before, and there will be light enough to make sure."

He waited two, three, four, five minutes--quarter of an hour, but from behind neither end of the island did the man emerge on the tow-path. There could be no doubt of this, for from where he stood a long stretch of the path was visible north and south beyond the island, and William Crawford's eyes swung from one end of the line to the other as frequently as the pendulum of a clock.

At length, when half-an-hour had passed, and it was almost dark, he became restless, excited, and in the end went down-stairs. In the front room he found Layard on the top of a step-ladder. He said:

"I was looking out of my window, and a man, coming from the northern end of the tow-path, disappeared behind the island, behind Boland's Ait. He has not come back and he has not come out at the other end. Where can he have gone? Is there some way of getting off the tow-path between the two points?" The speaker's manner was forced into a form of pleasant wonder; but there were strange white lines, like lines of fear, about his mouth and the corners of his eyes, "Is there a gate or way off the tow-path?"

"No. The man *must* have come off the tow path or gone into the water and been drowned," said Layard, not noticing anything peculiar in the other, and answering half-playfully.

"That would be too good," cried Crawford with a start, apparently taken off his guard.

"Eh?" cried Layard, facing round suddenly. He was in the act of driving in a brass-headed nail. The fervour in Crawford's tone caught his ear and made him suspend the blow he was about to deliver.

"Oh, nothing," said the other, with one of his short laughs. "A bad-natured joke. I meant it would be too much of a joke to think a man could be drowned in such a simple way. But this man hid himself behind the island and did not come forth at either end for half-an-hour, and I thought I'd ask you what you thought, as the circumstance piqued me. Good-night."

When he found himself in his own room he closed the window, pulled down the blind, hasped the shutters, and drew the curtains. He looked round on the simple unpretending furniture suspiciously, and muttered:

"He here--if it were he, and I think it was, appearing and disappearing in such a way! He cannot have found me out? Curse him, curse her; ay, curse her! Is not that all over now? She was to blame, too."

He walked up and down the room for an hour.

"If that was Philip Ray, where did he go to? He seems to have vanished. Layard knows every foot of this place. It was Philip Ray, and he did vanish! Could he have seen me and recognised me? or could he have tracked me, and is he now out on that little quay or wharf under my window, *waiting* for me? Ugh!"

CHAPTER III
THE PINE GROVES OF LEEHAM

Below London Bridge, and just at the end of the Pool, the Thames makes a sharp bend north, and keeps this course for close on a mile. Then it sweeps in a gentle curve eastward for half a mile; after this it suddenly turns south, and keeps on in a straight line for upwards of a mile. The part of London bounded on three sides by these sections of the river is not very densely populated if the acreage is considered. Much of it is taken up with the vast system of the Mercantile Docks; large spaces are wholly unbuilt on; the South London Canal, its tow-path, and double row of wharves and yards, cover a large area; and one of the most extensive gasworks in the metropolis and a convergence of railway lines take up space to the exclusion of people. There are stretches of this district as lonely by night as the top of Snowdon.

Little life stirs by day on the canal; after dark the waters and the tow-path are as deserted as a village graveyard. Along the railroad by day no human foot travels but the milesman's, and at night the traffic falls off to a mere echo of its incessant mighty roar by day. The gasworks are busy, and glowing and flaming and throbbing all through the hours of gloom and darkness, but people cannot get near them. They are enclosed by high walls on all sides except one, and on that side lies the South London Canal, which crawls and crawls unhastened and unrefreshed by the waters of any lock. The solitude of the tow-path after dark is enhanced at the point where it passes opposite the gasworks by the appearance of life across the water, and the impossibility of reaching that life, touching the human hands that labour there, receiving aid from kindly men if aid were needed. The tow-path at this point is narrow and full of fathomless shadows, in which outcasts, thieves, and murderers might lurk; deep doorways, pilasters, and ruined warehouses, where misery or crime could hide or crouch.

But of all the loneliness by night in this region which is vaguely styled the Mercantile Docks, the deepest, the most affecting, the most chilling is that which dwells in the tortuous uninhabited approaches leading from the docks to the river north and south, and east and west from Deptford to Rotherhithe.

Out of the same spirit of mocking humour which gave the name of Boland's Ait to the little island in the canal, these solitary ways are called the Pine Groves. The pine-wood which gives them their name has ceased to be a landscape ornament many years, and now stands upright about ten feet high on either side of the roads, in the form of tarred planks.

There are miles of this monotonous black fencing, with no house or gate to break the depressing sameness. By day the Pine Groves are busy with the rumble of heavy traffic from the docks and wharves; by night they are as deserted as the crypt of St. Paul's.

Between the great gasworks and the docks, and at a point upon which the canal, the main railway, and three of these Pine Groves converge, there is an oasis of houses, a colony of men, a village, as it were, in this desert made by man in the interest of trade and commerce. This patch of inhabited ground supports at most two hundred houses. The houses are humble, but not squalid. The inhabitants are not longshore-men, nor are they mostly connected with the sea or things maritime. They seem to be apart and distinct from the people found within a rifle-shot of the place. Although they are no farther than a thousand yards from Welford Bridge, to judge by their manners and speech, they are so much better mannered, civilised, and refined, that a thousand years and a thousand miles might lie between them and the longshore-men and loafers from whom William Crawford had been supplied with a guide in Red Jim. This oasis in the desert of unbuilt space, this refuge from the odious solitude by night of the Pine Groves, this haunt of Arcadian respectability in the midst of squalid and vicious surroundings, is honoured in the neighbourhood by the name of Leeham, and is almost wholly unknown in any other part of London. It will not do to say it has been forgotten, for it has never been borne in memory. The taxman and the gasman and the waterman, and the people who own houses there, know Leeham; but no other general outsiders. It is almost as much isolated from the rest of London as the Channel Islands.

It has not grown or diminished since the railway was built. No one ever thinks of pulling down an old house or building up a new one. Time-worn brass knockers are still to be found on the doors, and old-fashioned brass fenders and fireirons on the hearths within. Families never seem to move out of the district, and it never recruits its population from the outer world. Now and then, indeed, a young man of Leeham may bring home a bride from one of the neighbouring tribes; but this is not often. A whole family is imported never. It is the most unprogressive spot in all Her Majesty's dominions.

At first it seems impossible to account for so respectable a settlement in so squalid and savage a district. Who are the people of Leeham? And how do they live? When first put, the question staggers one. Most of the houses are not used for trade. Indeed, except at the point where the three Pine Groves meet, there is hardly a shop in the place. Where the East and West and River Pine Groves meet, there stands a cluster of shops, not more than a dozen, and the one public-house, the Neptune. But the name of this house is the only thing in the business district telling of the sea. Here is no maker of nautical instruments, no marine-store dealer, no curiosity shop for the purchase of the spoil of other climes brought home by Jack Tar, no music-hall or singing-saloon, no slop-shop, no cheap photographer.

Here are a couple of eating-houses, noticeable for low prices and wholesome food; a butcher's, and two beef-and-ham shops, two grocers', and a greengrocer's, two bakers', and an oil-and-colour man's. These, with the Neptune, or nucleus, form by night the brightly lighted business region of the settlement. This point is called the Cross.

Leeham repudiated the sea, and would have nothing to do with it at any price. Down by the docks the sea may be profitable, but it has not a good reputation. It is inclined to be rowdy, disreputable. Jack Tar ashore may not be worse than other men, but he is more noisy and less observant of convention. He is too much given to frolic. He is not what any solid man would call respectable.

No one ever thought of impugning the respectability, as a class, of gasmen or railway officials. In fact, both are bound to be respectable. Leeham had, no doubt, some mysterious internal resources, but its chief external dependence was on the enormous gasworks and the railway hard by. Hundreds of men were employed in the gashouse and on the railway, and Leeham found a roof and food for three-fourths of the number. There were quiet houses for those whose means enabled them to keep up a separate establishment, and cheap lodgings for those who could afford only a single room. No man living in a dwelling-house of Leeham was of good repute unless he had private means, or was employed at either the railway-yard or the gasworks--called, for the sake of brevity, the yard and the works. But it was a place in which many widows and spinsters had their homes, and sought to eke out an income from the savings of their dead husbands, fathers, or brothers, by some of the obscure forms of industry open to women of small needs and very small means.

The greengrocer's shop at Leeham Cross, opposite the Neptune, was owned by Mrs. Pemberton, an enormously fat, very florid widow of fifty. She almost invariably wore a smile on her expansive countenance, and was well known in the neighbourhood for her good nature and good temper. In fact, she was generally spoken of as "Mrs. Pemberton, that good-natured soul." The children all idolised her; for when they came of errands to buy, or for exercise and safety and a sight of the world with their mothers, Mrs. Pemberton never let them go away empty-handed as long as there was a small apple, or a bunch of currants, or a couple of nuts in the shop.

On that evening late in May when Red Jim showed Crawford the way to Crawford's House, Mrs. Pemberton stood at her shop door. She held her arms a-kimbo, and looked up and down the Cross with the expression of one who does not notice what she sees, and who is not expecting anything from the direction in which she is looking. The stout florid woman standing at the door of the greengrocer's was as unlike the ordinary Mrs. Pemberton as it was in the power of a troubled mind to make her. At this hour very few people passed Leeham Cross, and for a good five minutes no one had gone by her door.

Mrs. Pemberton had not remained constantly at the door. Once or twice she stepped back for a moment, and threw her head on one side, and held her ear up as if listening intently; then, with a sigh, she came back to her post at the threshold. There must have been something very unusual in the conditions of her life to agitate this placid sympathetic widow so much.

Presently a woman of fine presence came in view, hastening towards the greengrocery. This was Mrs. Pearse, a widow like Mrs. Pemberton, and that good lady's very good friend.

"I needn't ask you; I can see by your face," said Mrs. Pearse, as she came up. "She is no better."

"She is much worse," said Mrs. Pemberton in a half-frightened, half-tearful way; "she is dying."

"Dying!" said the other woman. "I didn't think it would come to that."

"Well, it hurts me sore to say it, but I don't think she'll live to see the morning."

"So bad as that? Well, Mrs. Pemberton, I am sorry. Along with everything else, I am sorry for the trouble it will give you."

"O! don't say anything about that; I am only thinking of the poor lady herself. She's going fast, as far as I am a judge. And then, what's to become of the child? Poor innocent little fellow! he has no notion of what is happening. How could he? he's little more than a baby of three or four."

"Poor little fellow! I do pity him. Has she said anything to you?"

"Not a word."

"Not even told you her name?

"No."

"Does she know, Mrs. Pemberton, how bad she is? Surely, if she knew the truth of her state of health, she'd say a word to you, if it was only for the child's sake. She would not die, if she knew she was dying, and say nothing that could be of use to her little boy."

"You see, when the doctor was here this morning, he told her she was dangerously ill, but he did not tell her there was no hope. So I did my best to put a good face on the matter, and tried to persuade the poor thing that she'd be on the mending hand before nightfall. But she has got worse and worse all day, and I am sure when the doctor comes (I'm expecting him every minute) he'll tell her she's not long for this world. It's my opinion she won't last the night."

"Dear, dear, dear!--but I'm sorry."

"Here he is. Here's the doctor!"

"I'll run home now, Mrs. Pemberton, and give the children their supper. I'll come back in an hour to hear what the doctor says, and to do anything for you I can."

"Thank you! Thank you, Mrs. Pearse! I shall be very glad to see you, for I am grieved and half-terrified."

"I'll be sure to come. Try to bear up, Mrs. Pemberton," said kind-hearted Mrs. Pearse, hurrying off just as the doctor came up to the door.

True to her promise, Mrs. Pearse was back at the Cross. By this time the shutters of Mrs. Pemberton's shop were up; but the door stood ajar. Mrs. Pearse pushed it open and entered.

Mrs. Pemberton was sitting on a chair, surrounded by hampers and baskets of fruit and vegetables, in the middle of the shop. She was weeping silently, unconsciously, the large tears rolling down her round florid face. Her hands were crossed in her lap. Her eyes were wide open, and her whole appearance that of one in helpless despair.

When she saw her visitor come in, she rose with a start, brushed the tears out of her eyes, and cried, seizing the hand of the other woman and pressing her down on a chair:

"I am so glad to see you, Mrs. Pearse! It is so good of you to come! I am in sore distress and trouble!"

"There, dear!" said the visitor in soothing tones. "Don't take on like that. All may yet be well. What does the doctor say about the poor soul?"

"All will never be well again for her. The doctor says she is not likely to see another day, short as these nights are. O my--O my heart! but it grieves me to think of her going, and she so young. And to think of what a pretty girl she must have been; to think of how handsome she must have been before the trouble, whatever it is, came upon her and wore her to a shadow."

"And I suppose she has not opened her mind to you even yet about this trouble?"

The question was not asked out of idle curiosity, but from deep-seated interest in the subject of the conversation. For this was not the first or the tenth talk these two kindly friends had about the sick woman upstairs.

"She has said no more to me than the dead. My reading of it is, that she made a bad match against the will of her people, and that her husband deserted her and her child."

"And what about the boy? Does the poor sufferer know how bad she is?"

"Yes; she knows that there's not any hope, and the doctor told me to be prepared for the worst, and that she might die in a couple of hours. Poor soul! I shall be sorry!"

Mrs. Pemberton threw her apron over her head and wept and sobbed; Mrs. Pearse weeping the while, for company.

When Mrs. Pemberton was able to control herself she drew down her apron and said:

"I never took to any other lodger I had so much as I took to this poor woman. Her loneliness and her sorrow made me feel to her as if she had been my own child. Then I know she must be very poor, although she always paid me to the minute. But bit by bit I have missed whatever little jewellery she had, and now I think all is gone. But she is not without money; for, when I was talking to her just now, she told me that she had enough in her work-box to pay all expenses. O, Mrs. Pearse, it is hard to hear the poor young thing talking in that way of going, and I, who must be twice her age, well and hearty!"

Again the good woman broke down and had to pause in her story.

"She told me no one should be at any expense on her account; and as for the boy, she said she knew a gentleman, one who had been a friend of hers years ago, and that he would surely take charge of the child, and that she had sent word to a trusty messenger to come and fetch the boy to this friend, and that she would not see or hear from any one who knew her in her better days. I can't make it out at all. There is something hidden, some mystery in the matter."

"Mystery, Mrs. Pemberton? Of course there is. But, as you say, most likely she made a bad match, and is afraid to meet her people, and has been left to loneliness and sorrow and poverty by a villain of a husband. She hasn't made away with her wedding-ring, has she?"

"No; nor with the keeper. But I think all else is gone in the way of jewellery. I left Susan, the servant, with her just now. She said she wished to be quiet for a while, as she wanted to write a letter. Now that the shop is shut I can't bear to be away from her, and when I am in the room I can't bear to see her with her poor swollen red face, and I don't think she is always quite right in her mind, for the disease has spread, and the doctor says she can hardly last the night. Poor, poor young creature!"

Here for the third time, kind sympathetic Mrs. Pemberton broke down, and for some minutes neither of the women spoke.

At length Mrs. Pemberton started and rose from her chair, saying hastily:

"She must have finished the letter. I hear Susan coming down the stairs."

The girl entered the shop quickly and with an alarmed face.

"The lady wants to see you at once, ma'am. She seems in a terrible hurry, and looks much worse."

Mrs. Pemberton hastened out of the shop, asking Mrs. Pearse to wait.

In a few minutes she returned, carrying a letter in her hand, and wearing a look of intense trouble and perplexity on her honest face.

"I am sure," she said, throwing herself on a chair, "I do not know whether I am asleep or awake, or whether I am to believe my eyes and my ears. Do you know where she told me she is sending the child now--to-night--for she cannot die easy until 'tis done."

"I cannot tell. Where?"

"I heard her say the words quite plainly, but I could not believe my ears. The words are quite plain on this letter, though they are written in pencil, but I cannot believe my eyes. Read what is on this envelope, and I shall know whether I have lost my reason or not. That's where she says the child is to go. This is the old friend she says will look after the little boy!"

She handed the letter she held in her hand to her friend. Mrs. Pearse read:

"Francis Bramwell, Esq., Boland's Ait, South London Canal."

CHAPTER IV
THE MISSING MAN

It was near ten o'clock that night before Alfred Layard and his sister gave up trying to get their new home into order. Even then much remained to be done, but Mrs. Grainger, the charwoman who had been assisting Hetty all day, had to go home to prepare supper for her husband, and when she was gone the brother and sister sat down to their own.

Alfred Layard was employed in the gasworks. His duties did not oblige him to be at business early; but they kept him there until late in the evening. He had a very small salary, just no more than enough to live on in strict economy. He had rented a little cottage during his brief married life, and the modest furniture in the room where the brother and sister now sat at supper had been bought for his bride's home out of his savings. Just as his lease of the cottage expired he heard of this house, and that the owner or agent would be glad to let it at a rent almost nominal on the condition of two rooms being reserved and kept in order for him.

The place just suited Layard. It was within a short distance of the gashouse, and he calculated that the arrangement would save him twenty pounds a year.

"Well, Hetty," said he, with one of his surprisingly pleasant smiles, as the supper went on, "how do you like the life of a lodging-house keeper?"

"So far I like it very much indeed, although I have had no chance of pillage yet."

"Never mind the pillage for a while. I must see if there is any handbook published on the subject of the 'Lodger Pigeon.' I am not quite sure there is a book of the kind. I have a notion the art is traditional, handed down by word of mouth, and that you have to be sworn of the guild or something of that kind. Before we had our knockdown in the world, in father's time, when I lived in lodgings in Bloomsbury, I knew a little of the craft--as a victim, mind you; but now I have forgotten all about it, except that neither corks nor stoppers had appreciable effect in retarding the evaporation of wine or spirits, and that fowl or game or meat always went too bad twelve hours after it was cooked to be of further use to me. Tea also would not keep in the insalubrious air of Bloomsbury."

"Well," said the girl, with a smile, "I suppose I must only live in hope. I cannot expect to be inspired. It would, perhaps, be unreasonable to expect that the sight of our first lodger for half-an-hour would make me perfect in the art of turning him to good account. It is a distressing thing to feel one is losing one's opportunity; but then, what is one to do?" she asked pathetically, spreading out her hands to her brother in comic appeal.

"It is hard," said he with anxiety; then brightening he added, "Let us pray for better times, better luck, more light. By the way, Hetty, now that we have fully arranged our method of fleecing the stranger, what do you think of him? How do you find him? Do you like him?"

"I find him very good-looking and agreeable."

"I hope there is no danger of your falling in love with him. Remember, he is a married man," said the brother, shaking a minatory finger at the girl opposite him; "and bear in mind bigamy is a seven years' affair."

"It's very good of you to remind me, Alfred," she said gravely. "But as I have not been married, I don't see how I could commit bigamy."

"You are not qualified *yet* to commit it yourself, but you might become an accessory."

"By the way, Alfred, now that I think of it," said she, dropping her playful manner and looking abstracted and thoughtful, with a white finger on her pink cheek, "I did notice a remarkable circumstance about our new lodger. Did you?"

"No," said the brother, throwing himself back in his chair and looking at the ceiling, "except that he has a habit of winking both his eyes when he is in thought, which always indicates a man fond of double-dealing. Don't you see, Hetty?--one eye winked, single-dealing; two eyes, double-dealing. What can be more natural? There is one thing about trade I can never make out. Book keeping by double-entry is an interesting, respectable, and laudable affair, and yet double-dealing is a little short of infamous."

"I don't understand what you are saying, Alfred," said the girl in a voice of reproach and despair. "I don't think you know yourself, and I am sure it's nonsense."

"Yes, dear."

"No; I'm not joking," she cried impatiently. "I *did* observe something very remarkable about Mr. Crawford, under the circumstances. Did you not notice he never spoke of his wife, or even referred to her, although he got all this property through her or from her?"

Layard looked down from the dingy ceiling. "Of course, you are right, child. I did not notice it at the time; but now I recollect he neither spoke of his wife nor made any reference to her. It was strange. And now that I think of it, he did not upon our previous meeting. It is strange. I suppose he is ashamed to own he owes everything to his wife."

"Well," said the girl hotly, "if he had the courage to take her money he might have the courage to own it, particularly as he is aware we know all about him."

"All about him?" said the brother in surprise. "Indeed, we don't know all about him; we know very little about him--that is, unless this wonderful wife of Grainger told you."

"No; she told me nothing about him. But we know that the money belonged to Mrs. Crawford and not to him, and that he changed his name to marry the widow, as otherwise her property would go somewhere else."

"To Guy's Hospital. But it would not go to the hospital if she remained unmarried. The fact of the matter is, I believe, that this Crawford--I mean the original one--was a self-made man, and very proud of his own achievements, and wished to keep his name associated with his money as long as possible. You see, when he married he was an elderly, if not an old man, and his wife was a young and very handsome woman. Now she is middle-aged and an invalid."

"Then," cried Hetty with sprightly wrath, "I think it the more shameful for him to make no allusion to her. But you have not told me all the story. Tell it to me now, there's a good, kind, dear Alfred. But first I'll clear away, and run up for a moment to see how Freddie is in his new quarters. He was so tired after the day that he fell asleep before his head touched the pillow."

She found the boy sleeping deeply in his cot beside her own bed. She tucked him in, although the clothes had not been disarranged, and then bent down over him, laying her forearm all along his little body, and, drawing him to her side, kissed him first on the curls and then on the cheek, and then smoothed with her hand the curl she had kissed, as though her tender lips had disturbed it. After this she ran down quickly, and, entering the sitting-room, said, as she took her chair, "He hasn't stirred since I put him to bed, poor chap. I hope he won't find this place very lonely. He will not even see another child here. And now, Alfred," she added, taking up some work, "tell me all you know about our lodger, for I have heard little or nothing yet."

"Well, what I know is soon told. His old name was Goddard, William Goddard. He came to live at Richmond some time ago, and lodged next door to Mrs. Crawford's house. She was then an invalid, suffering from some affection which almost deprived her of the use of her limbs. She went out only in a carriage or Bath-chair. He met her frequently, and became acquainted with her, often walking beside her in her Bath-chair. Her bedroom was on the first floor of her house; his was on the first floor of the next house. One night the lower part of her house caught fire. He crept on a stone ledge running along both houses at the level of the first floor window. He had a rope, and by it lowered her down into the garden and saved her life, every one said. The shock, strange to say, had a beneficial effect upon her health. She recovered enough strength to be able to walk about, and-- she married him."

The girl paused in her work, dropping her hands and her sewing, and falling into a little reverie, with her head on one side.

"So that he is a kind of hero," she said softly.

"Yes; a kind of hero. I don't think his risk was very great, for he could have jumped at any time, and got off with a broken leg or so."

"A broken leg or so!" cried she indignantly. "Upon my word, Alfred, you do take other people's risks coolly. I don't wonder at her marrying him, and I am very sorry I said anything against him awhile ago. The age of chivalry is not gone. Now, if she was young and good-looking--but forty, and an invalid----"

"And very rich," interrupted the brother, stretching himself out on the infirm couch and blowing a great cloud of smoke from his briar-root pipe.

"Your cynicism is intolerable, Alfred. It is most unmanly and ungenerous, and I for one have made up my mind to like, to admire Mr.----"

A knock at the door prevented her finishing the sentence.

"Come in," cried Layard, springing up and moving towards the door.

"I am afraid it is a most unreasonable hour to disturb you."

"Not at all," said Layard, setting a chair for the lodger. "My sister and I were merely chatting. We are not early people, you must know. I haven't to be at the works until late, so we generally have our little talks nearer to midnight than most people. Pray sit down."

Crawford sat down somewhat awkwardly, winking both his eyes rapidly as he did so. He gave one of his short, sharp laughs.

"You will think me very foolish, no doubt," he said, looking from one to the other and winking rapidly, "but, do you know, what you said about that man going into the canal has had a most unaccountable and unpleasant effect upon me. I feel quite unnerved. As you are aware, I am not acquainted with the neighbourhood. Would it be asking too much of you, Mr. Layard, to go out with me for a few minutes and ascertain for certain that no accident has befallen this man--that is, if Miss Layard would not be afraid of being left alone for a little while? If my mind is not set at rest I know I shall not sleep a wink to-night."

"Afraid? Afraid of what, Mr. Crawford? Good gracious, I am not afraid of anything in the world," cried the girl, rising. "Of course Alfred will go with you."

Layard expressed his willingness, and in a short time the two men were out of the house in the dark lane, where burned only one lamp at the end furthest from the main road.

"I do not know how we are to find out about this man," said Layard, as they turned from the blind street into Welford Road; "could you describe him?"

Layard thought Crawford must be a very excitable and somewhat eccentric man to allow himself to be troubled by a purely playful speech as to the pedestrian on the tow-path; but he felt he had been almost unjust to Crawford when talking to his sister, and he was anxious for this reason, and because of a desire to conciliate his lodger, to gratify him by joining in this expedition, which he looked on as absurd.

"Yes; I can describe him. He wore a black tail-coat, a round black hat, a black tie, and dark tweed trousers. He was nearer your height and build than mine. The chief things in his face are a long straight nose, dark and very straight brows, and dark eyes. He has no colour in his cheeks."

Layard drew up in amazement.

"Do you mean to say," he asked with emphasis, "that you could see all this at such a distance?"

"I," the other answered with a second's hesitation--"I used a glass."

"O!" said Layard; and they resumed their walk, and nothing further was said until they came to the bridge, on which they stood looking up the tow-path, along which the pedestrian ought to have come.

Layard broke the silence.

"Unless we are to make a commotion, I don't see what we can do beyond asking the toll-man. The gate is shut now. It must be eleven o'clock, and this place owns an early-to-bed population."

He was now beginning to regret his too easy participation in his lodger's absurd quest.

"Do not let us make any commotion, but just ask the toll-man quietly if such a man went through his gate," said Crawford hastily. "I know my uneasiness is foolish, but I cannot help it."

They turned from the parapet over which they had been looking, and Layard led the way a little down the road, and, then turning sharp to the right, entered the approach to the toll-house.

As they emerged from the darkness of the approach, the toll-taker was crossing the wharf or quay towards the gate. He passed directly under a lamp, and opened the gate which closed the path at the bridge.

Crawford caught Layard by the arm, and held him back, whispering:

"Wait!"

From the gloom of the arch a young man stepped out into the light of the lamp. He wore a black tailed-coat, a black tie, a black round hat, and dark tweed trousers. His nose was straight, and his brows remarkably dark and straight. Upon the whole, a young man of rather gloomy appearance.

"It's all right," whispered Crawford quickly into Layard's ear; "that's the man. Come away."

He drew his companion forcibly along the approach back to the road.

"It's well I didn't make a fool of myself," he whispered. "Come on quickly. I am ashamed even to meet this man after my childish fears."

They were clear of the approach, and retracing their steps over the bridge, before the pedestrian emerged from the darkness of the approach. When he gained Welford Road he went on straight--that is, in a direction opposite to that taken by the two.

"I am greatly relieved," said Crawford, rubbing his perspiring forehead with his handkerchief.

"I am not," thought Layard. "I am afraid there is something wrong with Crawford's upper storey."

CHAPTER V
A SECOND APPARITION

When Alfred Layard got back to the house he was far from easy in his mind about his lodger. In appearance Crawford was the least imaginative man in the world. His face, figure, and manner indicated extreme practicalness. No man could have less of the visionary or the seer about him. One would think he treated all things in life as a civil engineer treats things encountered in his profession. And yet here was this man giving way to absurd and sentimental timidity about nothing at all.

Of course, Layard himself would have been greatly shocked if he thought any harm had come to that solitary pedestrian on the tow-path; but not one man in a thousand would have allowed the circumstance of the man's non-appearance and the jesting words he himself had used to occupy his mind five minutes, to say nothing of suffering anxiety because of the circumstance, and sallying out to make inquiries and clear it up.

He did not bargain for such eccentricity as this when he agreed to live for a few days a month under the same roof with William Crawford. He would say nothing to Hetty of his fears, or rather uneasiness; but it would be necessary for him to suggest precautions.

When Crawford had bidden the brother and sister good-night finally, and the two were again alone in the front sitting-room, and Alfred had told Hetty, with no alarming comment, what had occurred since they left the house, she cried, "Now, sceptic, what have you to say? Could anything be more humane or kind-hearted than the interest he took in that unknown man, a man he could absolutely have never seen once in all his life? You were in the act of implying that he saved the widow because she was rich, and married her because she was rich, when, lo! Sir Oracle, down comes Mr. Crawford to see what had happened to that man, the unknown man! Tell me, was *he* rich? Is *he* going to marry *him*?"

"I confess things look very black for my theory," said the brother, from the couch, where he lay smoking placidly.

"I do believe," she cried with animation, "that you are rather sorry he turned out so nobly. I do believe you would rather he showed no interest in that man on the tow-path."

"Candidly, Hetty, I would."

"It is all jealousy on your part, and you ought to be ashamed of yourself. Are you?"

"No--o--o," he said slowly, "I can't say I am much ashamed of myself on that account."

"Then," she said, "it is worse not to repent than to sin, and your condition is something dreadful. Now, my impression is that Mr. Crawford never thought of money at all when he married his wife. I believe he married her for pure love, and the fact of her being an invalid was a reason for his loving her all the more. To me he is a Bayard," cried this enthusiastic young person with flushing cheek, and eyes in which the gold glinted more than ever.

"He's too stout, my dear," said the brother placidly from his couch.

"What!" cried she indignantly. "Too stout to marry for love! You are outrageous!"

"No; not to marry for love, but to be a Bayard. You know as well as I do our lodger would not cut a good figure on horseback," said the brother with calm decision.

"You are intolerable, Alfred, and I will not speak to you again on the subject. Nothing could be in worse taste than what you have been saying," said the girl, gathering herself daintily together and looking away from him.

"Besides, you do an injustice to our lodger."

"I wish, Alfred, if you find it necessary to refer to Mr. Crawford, that you would do so in some other way than by calling him our lodger. It is not respectful."

"Not respectful to whom?"

"To me," with a very stately inclination of the gallant little head.

"I see. Well, I will call him Mr. Bayard," said the brother with provoking amiability.

"I am sure, Alfred, I do not know how you can be so silly."

"Evil communications, my dear."

"The gentleman's name is Crawford, and why should you not call him Crawford?"

"Just to avoid the monotony."

"And, I think, Alfred, to annoy me."

"Perhaps."

"Well, I must say that is very good-natured of you."

"But I aim at an identical result."

"I don't understand you."

"To avoid monotony, too. You are always so good-humoured and soft-tempered it is a treat to see you ruffled and on your dignity. But there, Hetty dear, let us drop this light-comedy sparring----"

"I'm sure I don't think it's light comedy at all, but downright disagreeableness; and I didn't begin it, and I don't want to keep it up, and I am sure you have a very clumsy and unkind notion of humour, if talking in that way is your idea of it."

"Remember, Hetty," he said, holding up his hand in warning, "you are much too big a girl to cry. You are a great deal too old to cry."

"A woman is never too old to cry--if she likes."

"She is, and you are, too old to cry for anything a brother may say to you. According to the usage of the best society, you are too old to cry because of anything I may say to you. It will be your duty to repress your tears for your lover. According to good manners you ought not to shed a tear now until you have your first quarrel with your lover; and then, mind you, I am to hear nothing about it, or it would be my duty to call the scoundrel out, when there is no knowing but he might injure or even kill me, and then you couldn't marry him, for he would be your brother's murderer; and if I killed him you couldn't marry him, because I should be his murderer; and I don't see of what use we could be to any one, except to write a tragedy about, and that is about as bad a use as you can put respectable people to."

The girl's face had been gradually clearing while Layard spoke, and by the time he had finished, all trace of annoyance had vanished from it, and she was bright and smiling once more.

"You are a queer old Alfred, and I am a fool to allow myself to grow angry with you or your nonsense. I of course said too much. I did not mean quite that I thought him a Bayard."

"He's much better-looking than the only portrait of the Chevalier I ever saw. I must say the knight, by his portrait, is a most repulsive and unchivalrous brute, more fit for the Chamber of Horrors than the Hall of Kings. I assure you, Hetty, Mr. Crawford is a much better-looking man."

How was he to warn his sister without alarming her? To say he thought the man was not quite right in his mind would terrify Hetty, and it would not do to leave her without any caution. At last he could think of nothing but a most simple and most matter-of-course caution--that of locking the door of the room in which she and the child slept. "For," thought Layard, "if there is anything wrong with his head, although it may now be in the direction of excessive humanity, later it may change to be dangerously homicidal."

As they were saying "good-night," he remarked, as carelessly as he could:

"Remember, Hetty, although we are in our own house, it still it is not all our own."

"Of course I know that, Alfred."

"And if Fred cries, you must quiet him as quickly as possible."

"So that Mr. Crawford may not be disturbed?"

"Yes; and you may as well lock your door?"

"I will."

And thus they parted, and he felt at rest; for even if a paroxysm seized Crawford in the night, he could do no serious hurt without making noise enough to wake the others.

At the time that Layard was providing against a possible maniac in William Crawford, there was not a saner man within the four corners of London.

That night passed in perfect peace under the roof of Alfred Layard. So far as Layard knew, Crawford had slept the sleep of mental and bodily health, and little Freddie had not awakened once, as his aunt certified when she came down to breakfast.

Mrs. Grainger, the charwoman whose services were to be enlisted all the time Mr. Crawford was in the house, brought up his breakfast, and carried down news that the gentleman was arranging his papers and the rooms generally, as was only natural and to be expected upon a gentleman taking up his residence in a new lodging. Mr. Crawford she found very civil, but not inclined at all for conversation. He told Mrs. Grainger he should ring for her when he wanted her, and she took the liberty of explaining to the gentleman that he could not ring for her, because there was no bell. Upon this the gentleman said he should put his head over the balustrade and call to her, if she would be good enough to favour him with her name; which she accordingly did, giving her Christian name and married name, and adding with a view to defying fraud or personation, her maiden name (Wantage) also. The only piece of information he had volunteered to Mrs. Grainger, *née* Wantage, was that he had no intention of stirring out that day.

Layard did not renew the conversation of the night before. He was extraordinarily fond of his beautiful, sprightly, gentle-hearted sister, and he knew that his badinage had reduced her almost to tears. He was grave and tender, and devoted himself through most of breakfast to his lusty, restless, yellow-haired boy of three, little Freddie.

Alfred Layard's duties lay at the works, not the office, of the great Welford Gas Company. Hence, although his functions were those of a clerk, he had not the hours of a clerk. Years ago the Layards had been in a position very different from that occupied by them now. Then their father had been a prosperous merchant in Newcastle, but a series of disasters had come upon him: a partner failed in another business, a bank broke, and the father's health gave way utterly, and he died leaving absolutely nothing behind him. Alfred was at Cambridge at the time of the crash. He left the University at once, and for some time failed to get anything to do. At length an old friend of his father's found him a situation worth a hundred and twenty pounds a year in the great Welford Gasworks. In a couple of years his salary was increased ten pounds a year, upon which joyful encouragement he married Lucy Aldridge, the penniless girl he had, before the downfall of his father's house, resolved to make his wife.

For a little while he and his wife and sister lived very happily and contentedly on his modest hundred and thirty pounds a year. Then came little Freddie, and although it was an additional mouth to feed, any one of the three would have been without meat and butter from year's end to year's end rather than without baby Freddie. And when Freddie was a year old and could just syllable his mother's name, the ears of the poor young well-beloved mother were closed for ever in this life to the voice of her only sweetheart, Alfred, and her only child.

The brother and sister put her to rest with other dead in a great cemetery, and never once mentioned her name after that, although often when their loss was fresh upon them they would sit hand in hand by the widowed hearth, weeping silently for the ease of their full and weary hearts.

The day following that on which the brother and sister took possession of Crawford's House, Layard felt less anxious about their lodger's condition of mind than he had the evening before. In the darkness of night and the strangeness of a new house and the loneliness of this deserted neighbourhood it had seemed as though Crawford was insane--might, in fact at any moment develop into a dangerous maniac. In the sweet sunlight of a bright May morning the fears of the night before looked preposterous, and at very worst the lodger appeared to be no more than a fidgety, nervous, excitable man, with whom it would be a bore to live all one's life.

When his usual time came, Layard kissed his little son and his sister, and went off to his business at the great gasworks with no fear or misgiving in his heart.

Mr. Crawford gave no indication of being a troublesome lodger. He had a simple breakfast, consisting of eggs and bacon and coffee, and in the middle of the day a simple dinner, consisting of a chop and potatoes, with bread-and-cheese and a bottle of stout. At tea he hadn't tea, but coffee again, and a lettuce and bread-and-butter. For a man with his income he was easily pleased, thought Hetty. He had found fault with nothing. In fact, he had said no word beyond the briefest ones that would convey his wishes, and when Mrs. Grainger asked if the food had been to his liking he had said simply, "It was all right, thank you." To that good lady he had imparted the impression that he was too much occupied with matters of the mind to give much heed to matters of the body, and he had answered all her questions in a preoccupied and absent-minded manner.

After tea Mr. Crawford showed no sign of going out. He drew an easy-chair to the window, and sat down at the right-hand side of the embrasure, so as to command a view of the head of the island across which he had seen the man pass the evening before.

He heard Layard's knock and his voice below-stairs, but still he did not stir. From the place where he sat, any man coming along the tow-path at a walking pace would be in view a minute or a minute and a half before passing out of sight behind Boland's Ait. Crawford did not remove his eyes from that tow-path for any thirty consecutive seconds.

"I knew him at once," he whispered; "I knew him the minute I saw him. I knew his build, his figure, his walk, the way he swings his hands--ay, his face, far off as he was--ay, his face, his accursed vengeful face."

He leaned forward. He judged, by the dying of the light and the shrouded rose-tint on the chimneys and upper walls of the houses in view, that it was growing near the hour at which the solitary man had appeared on the tow-path last evening.

"I wonder, if he saw me, would he recognise me? He thinks I am not in this country. He is not on the look-out for me. I am much changed since I saw him last." He passed his hand over his close-shaven face. "I had a beard and moustache then, and taking them off makes a great difference in a man's appearance--puts him almost beyond recognition. Then I have grown stouter--much stouter. I daresay my voice would betray me; and then there is that St. Vitus's dance in my eyelids. That is an awful drawback. I am horribly handicapped; it isn't a fair race. And the worst of that jumping of my eyelids is that it always comes on me when I am most excited and least want it, and, moreover, when I am mostly unconscious of it until the excitement is over. Confound it! I *am* heavily handicapped."

He rested his elbow on the arm of the chair, and dropped his chin into his palm, keeping his eyes all the while fixed on that section of the tow-path visible beyond the head of the island.

"I," he went on in a voice so low as to be almost inaudible to himself, "was on the look-out for him when I recognised him. I knew he lived in Camberwell, and that Camberwell was in the neighbourhood; and when I knew that this tow-path goes to that place, I had a presentiment he would come along that tow-path into my view. It might be called a superstition, I know, but I had the feeling, and it came true. He did come along that tow-path--he the man of all others on this earth I dread. But where did he delay? Where did he linger? Where did he hide himself? Layard said there was no place but in the canal, and I can see that the fence is too high for any man to scale without the aid of a ladder."

He rose and stood at the window, to command a better view of the scene.

"It seems unnatural, monstrous, that I should fear this Philip Ray more than Mellor. If I ought to be afraid of any one, it is Mellor; and yet I stand in no dread of him, because, no doubt----"

He paused with his mouth open. He was staring at the tow-path.

A tall slender man had come into view beyond the head of Boland's Ait. He was walking rapidly north, and swinging his arms as he moved.

"It is he!" whispered Crawford in a tone of fear.

He stood motionless by the window for a while--five, ten, fifteen minutes. The man did not reappear.

Crawford wiped his forehead, which had grown suddenly damp.

"At any cost I must find out the explanation of this unaccountable disappearance."

He went from the house and into the blind lane at the front of the house.

CHAPTER VI
CRAWFORD'S INVESTIGATIONS

William Crawford ascended the lane until he reached the high road; then, turning sharply to the left, he went at a more leisurely pace towards the Welford Bridge.

He kept his eyes fixed ahead, and in every action of his body there was that vital alertness which characterised him in motion and even in repose. This alertness was more noticeable now than it had been before. Frequently, when he put down his foot in walking, he seemed dissatisfied with the ground upon which it had alighted, and shifted the foot slightly, but briskly and decisively, while resting on it, and stepping out with the other leg. He touched one thigh sharply with one hand, then the other thigh with the other hand, as though to assure himself that his hands and legs were within call, should he need their services for some purpose besides that upon which they were now employed. He rapped his chest with his fist, and thrust his thumb and forefinger into his waistcoat pocket and brought forth nothing. In another man this would be called nervous excitement, but in William Crawford it did not arise from any unusual perturbation, but was the result of unutilised energy.

As he approached the bridge his pace fell to a saunter. He subdued his restlessness or manifestations of repressed activity. Nothing but his eyes showed extraordinary alertness, and they were fixed dead ahead. The houses on his left prevented his seeing the tow-path, and the humpbacked bridge prevented his seeing where the approach from the toll-house joined the main road.

On the bridge lounged a group of loungers similar to that of the evening before. When Crawford had got over the middle of the bridge, and the road began to dip westward, he approached the parapet and looked up the canal. The long straight line ran off in the distance to a vanishing point, seeming to rise as it receded, but not a soul was visible from the spot at which he stood to the point at which the path disappeared.

Red Jim sidled up to where the stranger had paused, and after drawing the back of his hand across his mouth, by way of purifying himself before speaking to a man of property, said deferentially:

"Good-evening, guv'nor."

"Good-evening," said Crawford briskly, sharply, in a tone which implied he would stand no familiarity or nonsense.

Red Jim pushed his hat over his eyes in token of acknowledging a rebuff; but he remained where he was in token of cherishing hope of a job, or anyway of money.

Crawford took a few paces further down the slope of the bridge. He did not care to speak in the hearing of all these men. Then he beckoned to Red Jim. The man came to him with alacrity.

"How long have you been here this evening?"

"Most of the evening. I'm out of work."

"You have been here half-an-hour?"

"Yes. A good bit more."

"Have you seen any one pass along the tow-path this way (pointing) in the last half-an-hour?"

"No."

"Did you see any one come along the path in that time?"

"Ay, I did."

Crawford paused a moment in thought. He laughed and said, "I have a little bet on. I betted that a man did come along the tow-path, but did not come off it at the bridge here. I was looking out of a window and saw him. My friend said it was impossible, as the man otherwise must go into the canal."

It was plain Crawford did not appear anxious about the man himself. It was only about the wager he cared.

"The man went across the canal."

"Across the canal!" cried Crawford in astonishment. "Do you mean over the bridge?"

"No."

"Then how did he get across the canal?"

"How much have you on it?" asked Red Jim. He was afraid his own interests might suffer if he gave all the information he possessed before making terms.

"Confound you! what is that to you?" cried Crawford angrily.

"Well, then, I'll tell you how he went across," said Red Jim, looking up straight over his head at the sky.

"How did he get over?" cried the other impatiently, as Jim showed no sign of speaking.

"He flew," said Jim, suddenly dropping his full prominent blue eyes on Crawford. "He flew, that's the way he got across the canal." And, thrusting his hands deep into his wide-opened trousers pockets, he began moving slowly away.

For a moment Crawford looked as if he could kill Ford. Then, with a sudden quick laugh, he said:

"Oh, I understand; I will make it worth a tanner for you."

Red Jim was back by his side in a moment. He stretched out his arm, and, pointing towards the tail of the island, said:

"Do you see that floating stage?"

"Floating stage? No. What is a floating stage?"

"Two long pieces of timber with planks across. Don't you see it at the tail of Boland's Ait?"

"Yes, I do."

"Well, that's the way he got over. That was drawn by a chain across the canal to the tow-path. He got on it and then drew it back to the Ait, do you see? So you've won your money, guv'nor."

Crawford's face grew darker and darker, as the explanation proceeded. He handed Jim the promised coin in silence, turned back upon the way he had come, and began retracing his steps at a quick rate. His eyes winked rapidly, and he muttered curses as he walked.

"Can it be--can it possibly be that Philip Ray is my next-door neighbour? Incredible! And yet that was Philip Ray, as sure as I am alive, and he went to this island! Can this Robinson Crusoe be Philip Ray? If so, I cannot keep on here. I must find some other place for my--business. This is not exactly Camberwell, and I heard Ray lives in Camberwell; but this is very near it-- very near Camberwell!"

When he reached Crawford Street he diminished his speed. It was plain he did not want to seem in a hurry. As soon as he gained the house he ascended the stairs at once to his own room. He closed the door, and began walking up and down, hastily muttering unconnected words. After a while he went to the window and looked out on Boland's Ait with an expression in which hatred and fear were blended.

The buildings on the island consisted of an old sawmill, from which the machinery had been removed, now falling into ruin; a couple of dilapidated sheds, with tarred wooden roofs; a yard in which once the timber had been piled in stacks higher than the engine-house itself; and a small four-roomed house, formerly used as the dwelling-place of the foreman. These buildings and the wall of the yard rose between Crawford and the tow-path. The island itself was on a level with the ground on which Crawford's House stood; and William Crawford's sitting-room, being on the first floor, did not overpeer even the wall of the yard: hence the view of the tow-path was cut off except at the head and the tail of Boland's Ait.

William Crawford bit his under lip and gnawed the knuckle of his left forefinger, and plucked at his shaven cheek and upper lip as though at whiskers and moustache. At last he dropped his hand, and remained motionless, as though an idea had struck him and he was considering it. Suddenly he raised his head like one who has made up his mind, and walked with a quick step to the door, and, opening it, went out on the landing. He leaned over the balustrade and called out:

"Mrs. Grainger, will you come up, please? I want to speak to you for a minute."

Mrs. Grainger hastened from the kitchen. She had the sleeves of her washed-out lilac cotton dress rolled up above her arms, and an enormous apron, once white, now mottled and piebald with innumerable marks and stains.

"Will you sit down a moment?" Crawford said, pointing to a chair. He walked up and down the room during the interview.

Mrs. Grainger sat down and threw her apron over to her left side, by way of qualifying herself for the honour of a seat in Mr. Crawford's room and in Mr. Crawford's presence.

"Miss Layard told me last evening some interesting facts you mentioned to her about a--gentleman who lives on this island here in the canal."

"Yes, sir. A Mr. Bramwell, who lives all alone on Boland's Ait."

"Exactly. Do you know anything about him? The case is so remarkable, I am interested in it merely out of curiosity."

"I know, sir; and he is a curiosity, certainly," said Mrs. Grainger, settling herself firmly on her chair, and arranging her mind as well as her body for a good long chat, for every minute devoted to which she would be receiving her pay.

Crawford caught the import of her gesture and said sharply:

"I do not wish to keep you long, Mrs. Grainger; I have only a few questions to ask, and then you may leave me."

"Yes, sir," said the charwoman, instantly sitting upright and on her dignity.

"Have you ever seen this strange man?"

"Only twice."

"Would you know him again if you saw him?"

"O, yes, sir, I should know him anywhere."

"Tell me what he is like."

"Quite the gentleman, sir, he looks, but seems to be poor, or he wouldn't live in such a place all by himself and wear such poor clothes."

"His clothes are poor, then?"

"Very. But not so much poor as worn shabby, sir."

"Ah," said Crawford thoughtfully. (He had not been near enough to that man on the tow-path to tell whether his clothes were greatly the worse of wear or not.) "Is he dark or light?"

"Dark. Very dark. His hair is jet-black, sir. I was as close to him on Welford Road as I am to you now."

Philip Ray was dark. "Did you notice anything remarkable about him?"

"Well, as I said, he is very dark, and he has no colour in his cheek."

"H'm!" said Crawford in a dissatisfied tone. Ray had no colour in his cheek. "Did you remark anything peculiar in his walk?" No one could fail to observe the way in which Ray swung his hands.

"No, I did not."

Crawford drew up in front of the woman, and stood gnawing his knuckle for a few seconds. Then he resumed his pacing up and down.

"Was the gentleman walking fast at the time?"

"No."

Philip Ray, when alone, always went at an unusually rapid pace. He was a man quick in everything: quick in speech, in the movements of his limbs, quickest of all and most enduring also in his love and--anger.

"Is he a tall man?"

"No."

"What!" cried he in astonishment, drawing up again in front of the charwoman, now somewhat cowed by Crawford's abrupt, and vigorous, and abstracted manner. "Don't you call six feet a tall man? Have you lived among Patagonians all your life?"

"No, sir; I can't say I ever lived with any people of that name," she said, bridling a little. She did not understand being spoken to by any one in that peremptory and belittling way, and if all came to all it wasn't the rich Mr. Crawford who paid her and supplied the food she had eaten, but poor Mr. Layard, who gave himself no airs, but was always a pleasant gentleman, though he was not in the counting-house of the great Welford Gas Company, but in the works, where her own husband was employed.

"Why, don't you consider a man four inches taller than I a tall man?" cried Crawford, drawing brows down over his quick furtive eyes, and looking at the woman as if he was reproaching her with having committed a heinous crime.

"Four inches taller than you!" said the woman with scornful asperity. "I never said he was four inches taller than you, sir. He isn't four inches taller than you, Mr. Crawford."

"He is."

"Excuse me, sir; if you tell me so, of course I have nothing more to say," said Mrs. Grainger, rising with severity and dignity. "The gentleman that lives on Poland's Ait is a *shorter* man than you, sir."

"Are you sure?" said Crawford, standing for the third time in front of the woman.

"Quite certain."

"*Shorter* than I?" said he, in a tone of abstraction, as he gnawed his knuckles, unconscious of her presence--"*shorter* than I?" he repeated, lost in thought. "Then he can't be Philip Ray," he cried in a tone of relief. The words were uttered, not for Mrs. Grainger's hearing, but for his own. He wanted to have this pleasant assurance in his ear as well as in his mind.

"I never said he was, sir; I said he was Mr. Bramwell--Mr. Francis Bramwell," said Mrs. Grainger, making a mock courtesy and moving towards the door.

With a start Crawford awoke from his abstraction to the fact of her presence. "Bless my soul! but of course you didn't! Of course you didn't! You never said anything of the kind! You never said anything of any kind! Ha, ha, ha, ha!" He laughed his short and not pleasant laugh, and held the door open for Mrs. Grainger.

When she was gone he walked up and down the room for some time in deep cogitation. Then he went to the window and looked out on the scene, now darkening for the short night. His eyes rested on Boland's Ait, and he muttered below his breath:

"Whoever my next-door neighbour may be, it is not Philip Ray, and I am not afraid of any one else on earth. But who is this Francis Bramwell that Philip Ray visits? Who can he be?" Crawford paused awhile, and then said impatiently as he turned away from the window, "Bah, what do I care who it is? I fear no one but Philip Ray."

CHAPTER VII
A VISITOR AT BOLAND'S AIT

On the evening that Crawford arrived for the first time at the house called after his name, and saw the man he recognised as Philip Ray hastening along the tow-path, the man of whom he expressed such fear was almost breathless when, having passed the head of the Ait, he was hidden from view. As soon as he got near the tail of the island he suddenly stopped, bent down, and seizing a small chain made fast to an iron ring below the level of the tow-path and close to the water, drew heavily upon it, hand over hand. Gradually a long low black floating mass began to detach itself from the island, and, like some huge snake or saurian, stretch itself out across the turbid waters, now darkening in the shadows of eve. This was the floating stage of which Red Jim had told Crawford.

When the stage touched the bank Philip Ray stepped on it, walked to the other end, stooped down to the water, and, catching another chain, drew the stage back. Then he stepped ashore on Boland's Ait.

He paused a moment to gather breath and wipe his forehead, for in his wild haste he had run half the way from Camberwell. With rapid steps and arms swinging he strode to the door of what had once been the foreman's cottage, and knocked hastily. Then he made a great effort, and forced himself into an appearance of calm.

There was the sound of some one rising inside. The door swung open, and a man of thirty slightly under the middle height stood facing the failing light of day.

"Philip," he said. "Philip, I did not expect to see you so soon again. Come in."

On a table littered with papers a reading-lamp was already burning, for even at the brightest hour the light in the small oblong room was not good. By the table stood a Windsor armchair; another stood against the wall furthest from the door. There was a tier of plain bookshelves full of books against one of the walls, a few heavy boxes against another, and absolutely nothing else in the place. The cottage stood at the head of the island, and the one window of the occupant's study looked up the canal in the direction of

Camberwell. "At work, as usual," said Ray, pointing to the papers on the table as he shut the door.

"My work is both my work and my play, my meat and my rest. Sit down, Philip. Has anything unusual happened? I did not expect to see you until Sunday," said the solitary man, dropping into his chair, resting his elbows on the arms of it and leaning forward.

"I am out of breath. I ran most of the way," said Ray, avoiding the question.

"Ran!" cried the other in faint surprise. "Your walking is like another man's running. Your running must be terrific. I never saw you run. What made you run this evening?" He smiled very slightly as he spoke of Ray's walking and running.

"I am out of breath," said the other, again shirking the question. "Give me a minute."

It was not to gain breath Philip Ray paused, but to put in shape what he had to say. He had come from Camberwell at the top of his speed because he was burning with intelligence which had just reached him. He had been so excited by the news that he had never paused to think of the form in which he should communicate it, and now he was in great perplexity and doubt.

Francis Bramwell threw himself back in his chair in token of giving the required respite. He was a pale broad-browed man, with large, grave, unfathomable, hazel eyes His hair and moustache were dark brown; his cheeks and chin, clean-shaven.

Ray fidgeted a good deal in his chair, and acted very badly the man who was out of breath.

"You must have run desperately hard," said Bramwell, at length, in a tone half sympathy, half banter.

"Never harder in all my life," said the other, placing his hand on his side, as though still suffering from the effects of his unusual speed.

After a while he sat up and said, "I was pretty tired to begin with. I had been wandering about all the afternoon, and when I found myself near home I made up my mind not to budge again for the night. I found a letter waiting for me, and I have come over about that letter." He ceased to speak, and suppressed the excitement which was shaking him.

"A letter!" said Bramwell, observing for the first time that something very unusual lay behind the manner of the other. "It must have been a letter of great importance to bring you out again, and at such a rate, too." He looked half apprehensively at his visitor.

"It was a letter of importance."

A spasm of pain shot over the face of Bramwell, and his brows fell. "A letter of importance that concerned me?" he asked in a faint voice.

"Well," after a pause, "partly."

Bramwell's lips grew white, and opened. He scarcely breathed his next question: "From *her*?"

"O, no!" answered Ray quickly.

"About her?"

"No."

Bramwell fell back in his chair with a sigh of relief. "I thought the letter was about her. I thought you were preparing me to hear of her death," said he tremulously, huskily.

"I am sorry to say you were wrong. That would be the best news we could hear of her," said Ray bitterly.

"Yes, the very best. What does the letter tell you that affects me?"

"It is about *him*," answered Ray, with fierce and angry emphasis on the pronoun.

"What does the letter say?"

"That he is in England."

"Ah! Where?"

"In Richmond."

"So near!"

"Who saw him?"

"Lambton."

"Beyond all chance of mistake?"

"Beyond all chance of mistake, although he has shaved off his whiskers and moustache. Lambton saw him on the railway platform, and recognised him at once. Lambton had no time to make any inquiries, as his train was just about to move when he recognised the villain standing alone. But *I* have plenty of time for inquiries, and shall not miss one. I'll shoot him as I would a rabid dog."

"The atrocious scoundrel!"

"When I read the letter I only waited to put this in my pocket."

He took out a revolver and laid it on the table.

Then for a while both men sat staring at one another across the table, on which lay the weapon. At length Bramwell rose and began pacing up and down the room with quick, feverish steps. Ray had not seen him so excited for years--not since his own sister Kate, the solitary man's wife, had run away, taking her baby, with that villain John Ainsworth, whom Edward Lambton had seen at Richmond. After the first fierce agony of the wound, the husband had declined to speak of her flight or of her to his brother-in-law. He plunged headlong into gambling for a time until all his ample means were dissipated, unless Boland's Ait are enough to keep body and soul together. Then his grief took another turn. He was lost to all his former friends for months, and at last took up his residence, under an assumed name--Francis Bramwell instead of Frank Mellor--on Boland's Ait, in the South London Canal. To not a living soul did he disclose his real name or his place of habitation but to Philip Ray, the brother of his guilty wife, and the sworn avenger of her shame and his dishonour.

Ray watched Bramwell with flashing, uneasy eyes. By a desperate effort he was calming his own tumultuous passions.

At last Bramwell wound his arms round his head, as though to shut out some intolerable sight, to close his ears to some maddening sounds, to shield his head from deadly, infamous blows.

"Bear with me, Philip!" he cried huskily, at length. "Bear with me, my dear friend. I am half mad--whole mad for the moment. Bear with me! God knows, I have cause to be mad."

He was staggering and stumbling about the room, avoiding by instinct the table on which the lamp burned.

Ray said nothing, but set his teeth and breathed hard between them.

"I did not think," went on Bramwell, unwinding his arms and placing his hands before his face, as he went on unsteadily to and fro, "that anything could break me down as this has done. I thought I had conquered all weakness in the matter. I cannot talk quite steadily yet. Bear with me awhile, Philip!"

The younger man hissed an imprecation between his set teeth.

Bramwell took down his hands from his face and tore the collar of his shirt open.

"What you told me," he resumed in a gentler voice, a voice still shaken by his former passion of wrath, as the sea trembles after the wind has died away, "brought it all back upon me again. How I worshipped her! How I did all in my power to make her love me! How I hoped in time she would forget her young fancy for him! I thought if she married me I could not fail to win her love, and then when the child was born I felt secure. But the spell of his evil fascination was too strong for her feeble will, and--and--and he had only to appear and beckon to her to make her leave me for ever; and to go with *him*--with such a man as John Ainsworth! O God!"

Ray drew a long breath, brought his lips firmly together, but uttered no word. His eyes were blazing, and his hands clutched with powerful strenuousness the elbows of his chair.

"I am calmer now," resumed Bramwell.

"I am not," breathed Ray, in a whisper of such fierceness and significance that the other man arrested his steps and regarded the speaker in a dazed way, like one awakening from sleep in unfamiliar surroundings.

"I am not calmer now," went on Ray, in the same whisper of awful menace, "unless it is calmer to be more than ever resolved upon revenge."

"Philip----"

"Stop! I must have my say. You have had yours. Have I no wrongs or sorrow? Am I not a partner in this shame thrust upon us?"

"But----"

"Frank, I will speak. You said a while ago, 'Bear with me.' Bear you now with me."

Bramwell made a gesture that he would hear him out.

"In the first wild burst of your anger you would have strangled this miscreant if you could have reached his throat with your thumbs--would you not?"

He was now speaking in his full voice, in tones charged with intense passion.

"I was mad then."

"No doubt; and I am mad still--now. I have never ceased to be mad, if fidelity to my oath of vengeance is madness. You know I loved her as the apple of my eye, and guarded her as the priceless treasure of my life; for we were alone--she was alone in the world only for me. Him I knew and loathed. I knew of his gambling, his dishonourableness, his profligacy. I knew she was weak and flighty, vain and headlong, open to the wiles of a flatterer, and I shuddered when I found she had even met him once, and I forbade her ever to meet him again. She promised, and although my mind was not at rest, it was quieted somewhat. Then you came. I knew you were the best and loyalest and finest-souled man of them all. Let me speak. Bear with me a little while."

"My life is over. Let me be in such peace as I may find." Bramwell walked slowly up and down the room with his head bowed and his eyes cast on the floor.

"And why is your life over--at thirty? Because of him and his ways of devilish malice; he cared for her really nothing at all. When he came the second time, a year after the marriage, he set his soul upon ruining you and her. He thought of nothing else. Do not stop me. I will go on. I will have it out for once. You would never listen to me before. Now you shall--you shall!"

He was speaking in a loud and vehement voice, and swinging his arms wildly round him as he sat forward on his chair.

"Go on."

"Well, I liked you best of all; you had everything in your favour: position, money, abilities, even years. You were younger than the scoundrel, and quite as good-looking. You had not his lying smooth tongue for women, or his fine sentiment for their silly ears. I thought all would be well if she married you. She did, and all went well for a year, until he came back, and then all went wrong, and she stole away out of your house, taking your child with her."

"I know--I know; but spare me. I have only just said most of this myself."

"No doubt; but I must say what is in my heart--what has been in my heart for years. Well, we know he deserted her after a few months. He left her and her child to starve in America, the cowardly ruffian! What I have had in my mind to say for years, Frank, is that of all the men in this world, I love and esteem you most; that I love and esteem you more than all the other men in this world put together, and that it drives me mad to think shame and sorrow should have come upon you through my blood."

"Do not speak of her, Philip. What has been done cannot be undone."

"No; but the shame which has come upon you through my blood can be washed out in his, and by----, it shall! and here I swear it afresh."

With a sudden movement forward he flung himself on his knees and threw his open right hand up, calling Heaven to witness his oath.

Bramwell paused in his walk. The two men remained motionless for a moment. Suddenly Bramwell started. There was a loud knocking at the door.

CHAPTER VIII
FATHER AND SON

Ray rose to his feet and bent forward.

"I did not know you expected any visitor," said he in a tone of strong irritation.

"I do not expect any visitor. I never have any visitor but you," said Bramwell, looking round him in perplexity, as though in search of an explanation of the sound. He was beginning to think that his ears must have deceived him, and that the knock had not been at the door. "Did you," he asked, "draw back the stage when you got here?"

"Yes, but I did not fasten it. Any one on the tow-path might have pulled it across again. I hope no one has been eavesdropping."

"Eavesdropping! No. Who would care to eavesdrop at *my* door?"

"HE!"

"Philip, you are mad? If you trifle with your reason in this way you will hurt it permanently. I do not believe there was any knock at all. It may have been a stone thrown by some boy from the tow-path."

"Well, open the door and see. There can be no harm in doing that."

Ray stretched out his hand to recover the revolver which he had placed on the table. Bramwell snatched it up, saying:

"What folly, Philip! I will have no nonsense with such tools as this. We are in England--not the West of America." He dropped the revolver into the pocket of his jacket.

The minds of both men had been so concentrated on the idea of John Ainsworth during this interview that neither would have felt much surprise to find him on the threshold. Bramwell had repudiated Ray's suggestion that Ainsworth was there, but in his heart he was not sure of his own assertion. Nothing on earth could be more monstrously improbable than that Ainsworth would come and knock at *that* door; but then neither of the men in the room was in full possession of his reasoning powers. While Bramwell had lived on Boland's Ait no caller but Philip Ray had ever knocked at that door before, and now--now there came a knock while Philip Ray was sitting in the room, and as they had heard of Ainsworth's presence in England, and at the very moment Philip Ray was swearing to take that reprobate's life. Reason said it was absurd to suppose Ainsworth could be there. Imagination said he might; and if he were found there while Philip was in this fury, what direful things might not happen? Now that Bramwell had the revolver in his possession he felt more assured.

He moved to the door, opened it, and looked out.

No figure rose between him and the deep dusk of night. The light from the lamp on the table passed out through the doorway, and shone upon the wall of the old engine-house opposite.

"There is no one. It must have been a stone," said Bramwell, relieved, and drawing back.

"A stone cannot hit twice. There were two knocks. I heard two quite distinctly. Go out and look around. Or stay, I'll go. Give me back my revolver."

"No, no. Stay where you are. I will see."

He was in the act of stepping forth, when, looking down, he suddenly perceived the figure of a little child in the doorway. With a cry, "What is this?" he sprang back into the middle of the room.

Ray shouted, "Is the villain there? I told you it was Ainsworth!"

Ray was about to pass Bramwell at a bound, when the latter seized him and held him back, and, pointing to the child in the doorway, whispered, "Look!"

Ray peered into the gloom, and then came forward a pace warily, as though suspecting danger. "A child!" he cried in a whisper. "A little child! How did he come here? Do you know anything of him?"

"No." Bramwell shuddered and drew back until he could reach the support of the table, on which he rested his hand.

Ray advanced still further, and, bending his tall thin figure, asked in a muffled voice, "Who are you, my little man? and what have you got in your hand?" The child held something white in a hand which he extended to Ray.

The child did not answer, but crossed the threshold into the full light of the lamp, still offering the white object, which now could be seen to be a letter.

"What is your name, my little man?" repeated Ray, with a look of something like awe on his face.

"Don't!" whispered Bramwell, backing until he reached his chair. "Don't! Can't you see his name?"

"No. I am not able to make out what is on the paper at the distance. Give me the paper, my little lad."

Bramwell knew what the name of the child was, and Ray had a tumultuous and superstitious feeling that the coming of this child across the water in the night to the lonely islet and this solitary man had some portentous significance.

Ray took the letter from the child, and read the superscription with dull sight. Then he said, turning to Bramwell, "This does not explain how you know his name. There is nothing on this but,

'Francis Bramwell, Esq.

Boland's Ait,

South London Canal.'

What is your name? Tell me your name, my little man."

"Frank," said the child in a frightened voice.

"Yes. What else?"

"Mellor."

"What!" shouted Ray, catching up the boy from the floor and holding the little face close to the lamp.

"Did not you see his name on his face? Look! Is it not her face? Philip, I am suffocating!"

Ray gazed at the child long and eagerly. Bramwell, swaying to and fro by his chair, kept his eyes on the rosy face of the boy. The boy blinked at the light, and looked from one man to the other with wide-open, unconcerned eyes. At length Ray put the little fellow on the floor. The boy went to the table and began looking at the papers spread upon it. From his self possessed, unabashed manner, it was plain he was well accustomed to strangers.

"Who brought you here?" asked Ray again. The other man seemed bereft of voice and motion, save the long swaying motion, which he mechanically tried to steady by laying hold of the arm of the chair.

"A man," answered the child, running his chubby young fingers through some papers.

"Where did you come from?"

"Mother," answered the child.

"Who is mother?"

The boy looked round in smiling surprise.

"Mother *is* mother," and he laughed at the notion of grown-up people not knowing so simple a thing as that his mother was mother. He was thoroughly at his ease--quite a person of the world.

"You had better open the letter," said Ray, holding it out to Bramwell. "I did not recognise the writing. It is not like what I remember, and it is in pencil."

Bramwell took the letter. His face worked convulsively as he examined it. "I should not recognise the writing either, and yet it could be no other than hers, once you think of her and look at it." He turned the unopened envelope round and round in his hand. "What is the good of opening this, Philip? It will make no difference in me. I shall never look at her of my own free-will again."

"How can you judge the good of opening it unless you know what it contains? You cannot send it back by this messenger. My little lad," he said, turning to the child, who was still moving his dimpled fingers through the confused mass of papers on the table, "where is the man that brought you here?"

"Gone away," answered the child, without suspending his occupation.

"He left you at the door and knocked and went away?"

The boy nodded.

"He brought you across the water and set you down and knocked, and went back across the water?"

"Went back across the water," repeated the boy.

"What did he do then?"

"Ran off."

"You see, Frank," said Ray to the other man, "you cannot send back the letter by the messenger who brought it."

"Shall I throw it into the canal? I made up my mind never to know anything about her again in this life," said Bramwell.

Ray put his hand on the child's head and said, "Where did you leave your mother?"

"At home."

"Where?"

"A long way."

"Do you know where?"

"Yes; in bed."

Bramwell tore open the envelope, read the letter, handed it to Ray, and flung himself into his chair. The note, written in pencil like the address on the cover, ran:

"May 28.

"Frank,--I have found out where you are after long search. I ask nothing for myself--not even forgiveness. But our child, your little son, will be alone and penniless when I die, which the doctor tells me must be before morning. I have enough money to pay all expenses. It is not his money, but money made by myself--by my singing. You may remember my voice was good. I shall be dead before morning, the doctor tells me. There will be money enough for my funeral, but none for my child. He is very young--I forget exactly how old, for my head is burning hot, and my brain on fire. He is called after you, for you used to be kind to me when I was at Beechley before I was married to Frank Mellor. You remember him? This is a question you can never answer, because I hear in my ears that I shall die before morning. The money for my funeral is in my box. I am writing this bit by bit, for my head is on fire, and now and then I cannot even see the paper, but only a pool of flame, with little Frank--my baby Frank--on the brim, just falling in, and I cannot save him. I am writing my will. This is my will. I think I have nothing more to say. I wish I could remember all I have said, but I am not able; and I cannot read, for when I try, the paper fills with fire. It is easier to write than to read.... I am better now. My head is cooler. It may not be cool again between this and morning, and then it will be cold for ever. [I have money enough for myself when I am dead.] Take my boy, take our child. Take my only little one--all that is left to me. I do not ask you to forgive me. Curse me in my grave, but take the child. You are a good man, and fear and love God. My child is growing dim before my dying eyes. I could not leave him behind when I fled your house. I cannot leave him behind now, and yet I must go without him. I know you are bound in law to provide for him. That is not what I mean. Take him to your heart as you took me once. I love him ten thousand times more than I ever loved myself, or ever loved you. I can give you nothing more, for I am not fit to bless you. The pool of flame again! But I have said all.

"Kate."

Ray had read the letter standing by the table, and with his back to the chair into which Bramwell had sunk. When he finished he turned slowly round and fixed his gaze on the child. A feeling of delicacy and profound sympathy made him avoid the eyes of the other man. The dying woman was his sister, but she was this man's wife. A little while ago he had said that death would well befit her; and yet now, when, as in answer to his words, he read her own account of the death sentence passed upon her, he felt a pang of pity for her and remorse for his words. For a moment his mind went back to their orphaned childhood, and his love and admiration of his sister Kate's beauty. He had to banish the pictures ruthlessly from his mind, or he would have broken down. Silence any longer preserved would only afford a gateway to such thoughts; so he said, as he placed his hand once more on the head of the boy:

"She was delirious, or half-delirious, when she wrote this."

"Philip, she was dying."

"Yes. What do you propose to do?"

"Nothing. The boy said he came a long way, and that whoever brought him ran away. It is plain she has taken precautions to conceal her hiding-place. Let things be as they are. They are best so."

He spoke like a man in a dream. He was half stunned. It seemed to him that all this had passed in some dreary long ago, and that he was only faintly recalling old experiences, not living among words and facts and surroundings subsisting to-day.

"And what about----?" Ray finished the sentence by pointing with his free hand at the boy.

"Eh? About what?"

Bramwell's eyes were looking straight before him far away.

"About our young friend here?"

"She has been careful to remind me of my legal responsibility. I have no choice. Besides, putting the question of legality aside, I have no desire to escape from the charge, though I am ill-suited to undertake it, and do not know how I shall manage. He is, of course, a stranger to me. He was a mere baby when last I saw him. I cannot think of this matter now. I am thick-blooded and stupid with memories and sorrows."

Ray groaned, and began pacing up and down the room. The child, always self-possessed, had now gathered courage and was slowly making the circuit of the table, holding on by the rim, and now and then turning over some of the papers: plainly a child accustomed to amuse himself.

Neither of the men spoke. Bramwell sat stupefied in his chair. Ray strode up and down the room with hasty steps.

The child pursued his course round the table. On the table was nothing but papers, and the lamp inaccessible in the middle, the pens and an ink-bottle unattainable near the lamp. When the circuit of the table was completed, and was found to afford nothing but dull papers, with not even one picture among them, the little feet ceased to move. One hand laid hold of the leaf, the white blue-veined temple was rested on the soft pad made by the plump tiny hand, and the young voice said with a weary yawn, "Frank's tired. Frank wants to go to mother." As the boy spoke he sank down to the floor, overcome by drowsiness and fatigue.

Ray hastened to the child and raised him from the ground, and held him tenderly in his arms. "Poor little man! Poor tired little motherless man!"

"Mother!" murmured the boy, "I want to go to mother!" The child smiled, and nestled into the breast of the tall powerful man. "Frank wants mother and wants to go to bed."

"Hush, my boy: Frank has no mother."

Then a sudden impulse seized Ray. He crossed the room with the little lad in his arms, and placed him in the arms of Bramwell, saying to the child:

"You cannot go to your mother: you have no mother any longer. But you have a father. Take him, Frank; he is not to blame."

Bramwell caught the boy to his breast, and stooped and kissed his round soft young cheek, and pressed him again to his bosom, and then all at once handed him back to Ray, saying, in a choking voice:

"I am distracted, overwhelmed. I cannot stand this. What do I want here--alive?"

He rose and began stumbling about the room as if on the point of falling. Suddenly something heavy in his coat struck the table and shook it. A gleam of joy shot over his face, illumining it as though he stood within the light of deliverance.

Swift as thought he drew the revolver from his pocket and placed it against his forehead. With a cry of horror, Ray struck his arm up, dropped the child, and seizing Bramwell's wrist, wrenched the weapon from his grasp.

"It is *you* who are mad now!" he cried angrily. "What do you mean? Does all your fine morality vanish at the contact with pain and disgrace? For shame, Frank! for shame! You were always a man. What unmans you now? This," he added, dropping the revolver into his own pocket, "is safer in my keeping than in yours. I intended to do only justice with it; you would commit a crime."

"I am calmer now," said Bramwell; "it was only the impulse of a moment. Forgive me, Philip! forgive me, Heaven! I was frenzied. I hardly remember what passed since--since the boy came and I read that letter, and saw her ruin and death, and tasted the ashes of my own life upon my lips. I am calm--quite calm now. I will do my duty by the child. Trust me, I will not give way again; although I am not much safer without the revolver than with it. I have as deadly a weapon always at hand."

"What is that? I did not know you kept any weapon in the place."

"I keep no weapon in the place; but," he went to the window looking south along the canal, "all around me is--the water."

Shortly after this Philip Ray left, promising to call next evening. It was after this interview that Layard and Crawford saw him emerge from the gloom of the arch of Welford Bridge, the night that Crawford entered upon the tenancy of his rooms in Crawford's House, on Crawford's Bay, opposite Boland's Ait, and hard by the flooded ice-house, Mrs. Crawford's property.

CHAPTER IX
CRAWFORD'S HOME

The third and last day of William Crawford's visit to Welford was devoted to the business of his wife's property. The rents had not been collected for a couple of months, and before he returned in the evening he had upwards of a hundred pounds in his possession. Some of the tenants paid quarterly; the rents of the smaller ones were due weekly, but it had been the custom of the estate not to apply for the latter until four weeks outstanding. The neighbourhood, though poor, was for a place of its class eminently solvent, owing to the gas-house and the railway. Of course these was no difficulty with the stores, or wharves, or yards, or better class of houses; and even the poorer tenants could not afford to get into arrears or treat a landlord unjustly, for such matters might come to the ears of either of the great companies, and do the delinquent harm.

It was almost sundown when Crawford reached his lodgings. Layard had come in and gone out again, and Hetty was alone in their sitting-room. She had just come down from little Freddie, who, after a valiant fight against Billy Winkers, had at last succumbed. Crawford saw Hetty at the window, and motioned that he wished to speak with her.

"Mr. Layard out?" asked he, after greetings.

"Yes," said the girl; "the evening was so lovely, he said he'd go for a walk."

"The evening is lovely, no doubt," said he; "but is there such a thing as a tolerable walk within reasonable distance?"

Hetty had opened the sitting-room door, and now stood on the threshold.

"There is no nice walk quite close, but Alfred often goes for a stroll to Greenwich Park. That is not far off, you know, and the air there is so sweet and pure after the heat and unpleasantness of the works all day."

She thought he was speaking merely out of politeness, and, believing he wished to be gone, drew back a little into the room.

He was in no great hurry to go upstairs. He knew what her movement indicated, but he construed it differently.

"Am I invited to enter?" he asked suavely, bowing slightly, and making a gesture of gallant humility with his arms and shoulders.

"Certainly," she said, smiling and making way for him. He did look a powerful man, she thought, who could dare danger, and rescue and carry out of the flames an invalid woman. He was not very handsome, it was true, and there was something unusual about his restless eyes. But perhaps that might be quite usual with heroes. She had never before met a man who had rescued any one from death. She had not, that she could remember, ever met a man, either, who had married a widow. According to plays and satirists, the man who married a widow had more courage than the man who would do no more than face death in a burning house.

"I am sorry to have to trouble you about a little business matter--no, thank you, I will not sit down, I shall run away in a minute--but, as your brother is out, I fear I must intrude on your good nature, if you will allow me."

His voice and manner were exceedingly soft and pleasant and insinuating; not in the least like his voice and manner of the former evening, when his manner was abrupt and his voice hard, if not harsh. This speech somewhat disconcerted the girl. She felt sure he was going to ask her to do something altogether beyond her abilities.

"Anything in my power, Mr. Crawford, I shall be very happy to do for you."

"Thank you extremely. It is exceedingly kind of you to say so." He spoke as though weighed down by a sense of his own unworthiness.

The girl began to feel embarrassed. Such profuse thanks rendered in anticipation placed the obligation of gratitude on her shoulders. His words and manner and gestures had already thanked her more than sufficiently for anything she could do for him.

"I am going out this evening," he said, "and shall not be back until very late--an hour too late even to mention to any well-ordered person--and I do not wish to disturb any one when I come back."

"We, Alfred and I, always sit up very late."

"My dear Miss Layard, you could have no conception of the time at which I may return. It may be three, four, five o'clock. I have to go to see an old friend in the West End, and he will, in all likelihood, keep me until the cocks have crowed themselves hoarse in full daylight."

"Well," said she, gathering her brows and looking very uncomfortable as she felt how helpless she was in a case of such mystery and difficulty, "what can Alfred or I do for you?"

The grave aspect and manner of apology left his face and gestures all at once, and he smiled, and with a light airy, humorous manner said, "If there is such a thing as a latchkey, and your brother hasn't it with him, will you lend it to me?"

The girl burst out laughing, partly from relief and partly from enjoyment of this elaborate joke, and, going to the chimney piece, handed him from it a key. "We had to get a new latch. Alfred has one key. This is for you."

"Thank you. Good-night." And he went, shutting the door softly after him.

William Crawford went to his own room and took off the quiet, sedate, and somewhat shabby clothes in which he had arrived at Welford. He washed, put on a fresh shirt and elegant laced boots, of much finer make and more shiny than he had worn all day. He substituted a coloured tie for the one of sober black, a blue frock-coat of exquisite make, and over this a dark summer topcoat. When he surveyed himself in the glass he looked ten years younger than when he came in after the arduous labours of the day.

Of the money he had collected that day most was in notes or gold. He dropped all the notes and gold into his pocket, and, having locked a few cheques in his portmanteau, left the house quietly, as though not wishing to attract attention.

When he reached Welford Road he looked up and down for a minute, and muttering, "Pooh! No hope of a hansom in this place, of course!" turned his face west, and began walking rapidly with his quick step. Now and then he twitched his shoulders with suppressed energy; constantly he swung his eyes from left to right, as though it would not suit him to miss seeing anything on either side.

After a quarter-of-an-hour's walking he came to the beginning of a tram line. He got into a car about to move. He took no notice of the destination of the car. The car was going west--that was enough for him.

In half-an-hour he reached a busy crossing where hansoms were plentiful. He alighted here, hailed a cab, and was driven to a quiet street off Piccadilly. He got down here, and proceeded on foot to a still quieter cross street, finally entering a modest, unpretentious house, the home of the Counter Club, a club which had nothing whatever to do with the yard-stick or scales and weights, but where members might amuse themselves at games in which no money changed hands at the table, and was therefore blameless. All a member had to do before beginning to play was to provide himself with counters, to be obtained of the secretary for--a consideration. The reason why these counters were used and not money, was because the games played here were games of chance, and it is illegal to play games of chance for money. Very elaborate precautions were taken by the committee to avoid any confusion between the counters whose use, after the formality of paying, was sanctioned by the secretary, and counters not issued by him.

It was, as Crawford had predicted, long after sunrise when he opened Layard's door with his latchkey. A good deal of the briskness and energy of his manner a few hours ago was abated. When he found himself in his sitting-room he flung his overcoat and hat on the table. "Cleaned out, by Heavens!" he cried. "Is this accursed luck to last for ever?"

Then he changed his clothes, putting on those he had worn the day before, and took a chair at the open window of his sitting-room, overlooking the canal.

Here he remained motionless, brooding gloomily until six o'clock. Then he got up, wrote a line to Layard saying he had to go away early, and would be back again on June 27. He left the house noiselessly, and made his way partly on foot, partly by tramcar (for here the tramcars run early), and partly by cab to Ludgate Hill, whence by train he reached Richmond.

It was still early, about eight o'clock, when Crawford gained his own home and let himself in. The servants were stirring. "Tell Mrs. Crawford when she rings," said he to the housemaid, "that I have been up all night, and have gone to lie down. Do not call me for breakfast." Then he went to his dressing-room, kicked off his boots with a curse, threw himself on the bed, and was asleep in five minutes.

Noon came and went, and still he slept peacefully. Just as one o'clock struck he awoke with a start, and sprang from the bed, threw off his coat and waistcoat, rolled up his shirt-sleeves, washed his face and hands, brushed his hair, and, when his coat and waistcoat were once more on, opened the door leading to his wife's room and went in.

Mrs. Crawford was sitting in an armchair by the open window. She was a pale, fragile, beautiful woman of seven-and-forty. Her eyes were large, luminous, violet, and full of gentleness and love. Her lips were remarkably beautiful and red for an invalid of her years. Her smile was the softest and most engaging and endearing in all the world. Nothing could exceed the tender loveliness of her face, or the sweet cheerful resignation of her disposition. The mitigation of her symptoms following the shock at the fire had not been permanent, and, although on the day of her second marriage she had been well enough to walk up the whole length of the church, she was now once more incapable of moving across the room without help.

Upon the entrance of Crawford she turned her head quickly and smiled, holding out her hands, saying:

"O, William, I am glad you're back! I am glad to see you once more. I have been lonely. This is the longest time we have been separated since our marriage."

He went to her and kissed her affectionately, first her lips and then her forehead, and then her hair, now thickly shot with grey, but abundant still. He drew a chair beside hers, and sat down, taking one of her thin transparent hands in both his, and stroking it as though it was made of the most fragile and precious material.

"And how has my Nellie been since?" he asked in a low caressing voice, very different from the one Red Jim or Alfred Layard had heard, but somewhat akin to the one in which he had apologised to Hetty the evening before.

"Well--very well; but lonely. I hoped you would be able to get home, dear, last night," she said, lying back in her chair and looking at him out of her gentle violet eyes with an expression of absolute rest and joy.

"So did I. So, indeed, I should, only for my ill luck. I am greatly put out by my first visit to Welford, Nellie," he said, lowering his brows and looking troubled.

"Put out, dear! Put out by your visit to Welford! What put you out, William? I am very sorry you went. I am very sorry I let you go. I am sorry we ever got rid of Blore, if the thing is going to be a bother to you." Blore had been the agent before the advent of William Crawford.

"O, no! You need not be sorry. I was not put out on account of myself, but on account of you." He said this very tenderly, and with a gentle pressure on the transparent wax-like fingers between his hands.

"On my account, William?" she said, with a smile rich in love and satisfaction. "Why on my account, dear?"

"Well, because I have been disappointed in the results of my own efforts. I could get very little money. Out of over two hundred pounds overdue, upwards of a hundred of which is arrears, I got no more than twenty pounds." He said this ruefully, keeping his gaze fixed out of the window, as though ashamed to meet her eyes.

His wife laughed.

"Is that all? I thought you had met some unpleasantness to yourself there. My dear William, don't let that trouble you. They will pay next month or the month after. They are excellent tenants, taking them all together."

"I daresay they *will* pay next month. But I could not help feeling disappointed and depressed in having to come back to you almost empty-handed. This is all I succeeded in getting--twenty-seven pounds ten."

He held out a little bundle to her.

With a laugh she pushed it away.

"It is yours, William, not mine. What have I to do with money now? You know more about money than I do. You take care of me and of the money for us. No, no; I will not touch it! Put it in the bank, or do what you like with it. I and all that was mine is yours, love."

There was a rapture of self-sacrifice and devotion in the woman's voice and manner. There was a prodigal richness of love and faith in her eyes. She had not loved her first husband when she married him, and during the years they had spent together no passionate love had arisen in her heart, though she was fond of her husband and an excellent wife. She had passed not only the morning, but the zenith of life when she met this man; but to him she had given all that remained to her of love and hope and all her faith, never shaken by any shock.

Crawford winced slightly. Even he drew the line somewhere. He would rather battle stubbornly against odds for his way than sit still and be overwhelmed with free and lavish gifts. He liked to win, but he also liked to contend. He was passionately fond of money, and would sacrifice almost anything to get it. He would not work for it, but he would rather win it at cards than get it for nothing. If he had not gambled away those eighty pounds last night, she would have given them to him now. He felt a perverse gratitude that he was not beholden to her for the eighty pounds. He had, as it were, earned those eighty pounds by the deceit he had practised. But this money, which she had refused to receive, burnt his fingers.

He took the money, however, and kissed her thin fragile hand, and pressed it against his broad powerful chest.

"You are the best woman in the world, Nellie, and the dearest. These fellows will, no doubt, pay next month. I wonder, if I asked Blore about them, would he give me some information?"

"I always found Mr. Blore the most courteous and honest and straightforward of men. If I were you I should see him."

"I will. And now let us drop business and talk about something more interesting. Tell me to begin with, all that my good wife has been doing while I have been away." He slipped his arm round her waist and drew her head down upon his shoulder. His ways with men and women were widely different. With the former he was quick, or abrupt, or peremptory, or combative. He seemed to value his time at a price so high that the speech of other men caused him an intolerable loss, by reason of his having to listen to it.

With women he was soft and gentle, and even quietly humorous at times. He never was restless or impatient. His manner was that of one who had found out the condition of existence in which life could be most delightfully passed, that of his companion's society; and if he did not absolutely make love to a woman when alone with her, and this was but seldom with one under fifty, he invariably implied that he would rather have her society than the society of all the men on this earth. He varied the details of his style according to the age, condition, and disposition of his companion.

He could adopt the melancholic, the enthusiastic, the poetic manner, according as circumstances and the subject demanded. Without any striking physical advantages, he was a most fascinating man to women. There was no false polish, no lacquer about him. He had no airs and graces. He did not groan or simper. He never laid aside his manhood for a moment. He did not beg so much as expostulate for love. His love-making took the form of an irresistible argument. He thought no mere about women than he did about hares or rabbits, or flowers. He liked most women when they were not a trouble to him. They amused him. He liked their graceful ways and their simple loyal hearts. He liked their dainty raiment and their soft delicate hands. He liked the perfumes they used and the flowers they wore. He liked most women, but he had a contempt for all of them.

He hated all men.

He did not repudiate or despise principles, but he had none himself. He nourished no theories as to what a man ought or ought not to do. He troubled himself about no other men at all. He always did exactly what he liked best, or believed to be best for his own interest. He had banished everything like religion from his mind long ago. He did not bother himself to ask whether there might or might not be a Hereafter. He was quite certain there was a Here, and he had made up his mind to make the best of it. In some senses of the word, he was no coward. He would face a danger, even a risk, so long as he could see his way, and all was in the full light of day and commonplace. But he was afraid of the unseen: of the dagger or the bullet, of ghosts and supernatural manifestations. He was a gambler, and, like all gamblers, superstitious.

Twenty years ago he had been placed in the counting-house of a first-class Liverpool place of business. His mother was then dead, his father living. John Ainsworth--that was the name with which he started in life--was an only child. His father had saved a few thousand pounds as manager of a line of steamboats.

Young Ainsworth went to the bad before he was twenty-five, and was kicked out of his situation. The shock killed his father, who was an old man. There was no will, and young Ainsworth got his father's money and went betting on the turf, and when there were no races he devoted his energies to cards. It was on his way back from a great Sussex race-meeting that he came upon the quiet little town of Beechley, and first met Kate Ray. He was then past thirty years of age, and had been moderately successful on the turf and on the board of green cloth. In Beechley he concealed the nature of his occupation, stayed there a month or two, and won the giddy heart of the beautiful Kate Ray. But her brother would not listen to him, and Kate, who would have a little money when she came of age, was a minor and in the hands of guardians, who would have nothing to do with him either. So Ainsworth, being by no means insensible to the money Kate would come into at twenty-one, drew off for a while, promising Kate to come back later.

Two whole years passed before John Ainsworth again appeared at Beechley. By this time the flighty and beautiful girl had married Frank Mellor, who had just inherited a considerable fortune upon the death of an old miserly bachelor grand-uncle, that had lived all his life in London, and made money in the Baltic trade.

Then, out of a spirit of pure revenge, Ainsworth secretly pursued Kate, and worked upon her fickle and weak nature until she fled with him, taking her baby boy, Frank Mellor's child.

After three years that child had been restored to his father, while the mother lay dying at good Mrs. Pemberton's, a rifle-shot from Boland's Ait and the office of John Ainsworth, who had assumed the name of Crawford.

CHAPTER X
FATHER AND SON

Of all the men in London, there was scarcely one less qualified to take charge of a young child than Francis Bramwell, living alone on his tiny island in the South London Canal. He was not used to children. He had had only one sister, and no brother. His sister, twelve years older than himself, had married and gone away to Australia before he was eight years of age. His father had been a successful attorney in Shoreham, where he died ten years ago, when his son was just twenty years old. His mother had been dead many years at that time.

When his grand-uncle was buried a few years later, Bramwell became rich and left Shoreham. He had been reading for the Bar in a half-hearted and dilatory way.

He gave up all thought of the profession, and resolved to lead a life of lettered ease and contemplation, to be summed up later, probably in a book of one kind or another. In fact, as soon as he found himself independent he determined to devote his attention to poetry, and, as he did not feel certain of possessing a strong vein of genius, he determined to confine himself to translations by way of a beginning.

For quietness he moved out of Shoreham to a cottage a few miles from the dull little town of Beechley, and in Beechley, after the first visit of John Ainsworth, he made the acquaintance of Philip Ray and his beautiful sister Kate.

When he fell in love he threw his books to the winds, and, beyond verses addressed to his mistress, had no dealings with the Muse.

He was then a man to all outward appearance of singularly unemotional temperament. But under a placid demeanour he concealed a sensitive and enthusiastic nature, a nature of fire and spirit, subject to raptures and despairs, and desiring rapture almost as a necessity. Prose would not satisfy him; he must have the wine of poetry. To love was not enough for him; he must adore. Devotion was too tame; he must immolate himself.

He had lived most of his years since adolescence apart, and had never tried to make himself agreeable to any girl, until he told himself that life without Kate Ray would be simply intolerable. After marriage he treated his wife more like the goddess of a temple than the young, pretty, vain, foolish, flighty mistress of a home.

Kate, who loved flattery and fine clothes, and trivial gaiety, could not understand him. She thought him cold and formal at one time; a wild man, a lunatic at another. He did not stoop to flattery, or condescend to simulation. He was worshipful, not gallant. He praised her spirit and her soul, possessions to which she did not attach much importance. He said little about her eyes, or her figure, or her hair, which she knew to be beautiful, and of which she was inordinately vain.

She could not comprehend him. She did not try very hard. She never tried very hard to do anything, except dress well and look pretty. He was, no doubt, very grand, but she loved John Ainsworth all the while. John's ways and manner were perfectly intelligible to her, and when he came to her the second time secretly, and threw a romantic light upon their stolen meetings--when she heard his flattery and sighs and oaths--her weak will gave way, and she fled with him, taking the boy with her.

Now, after three years, and when Bramwell had made up his mind he should never see wife or child again, the boy had come from his wife's death-bed to his door. What was he to do with this helpless being?

He had decreed in his own soul, beyond the reach of appeal, that he would never see his wife again. It was plain she had not contemplated a meeting with him. It was plain she had put such a thing beyond her hopes--beyond, most likely, her desires. For had she not known where he lay hidden? and had she not refrained from seeking him, refrained even from letting him know she was alive? But when she found herself on the point of dissolution, when she had been told she had only a few hours to live, when the delirium of death was upon her, she had sent the child to him. She had at least the grace to feel her shame, and sufficient knowledge of him to be certain that no consideration on earth would induce him once more to look on her, the woman he had loved, who had betrayed his honour and laid his life in ruin.

But the boy? What was to be done with him?

The night before he had been too stupefied to think. When Philip left him he had taken the child to his own room and put him in his own bed, and the little fellow, overcome by fatigue and the lateness of the hour, had fallen asleep.

Now it was bright, clear, unclouded morning, the morning after the boy's advent. The little fellow still slept, but the father was broad awake. He had risen at five, and was sitting in the room where Philip had found him the evening before. His elbows rested on the table; his head leaned upon his hands.

What should he do with the boy? Her child?--the child of the woman who had brought infamy on his name, who had taken the heart out of his life; leaving nothing but a harsh and battered husk behind?

The child was like her, too. He had known the first moment he looked on the little face that this was the baby she had stolen away from his home when he thought she was gradually growing to love him, when he thought she had forgotten for ever the villain who had induced her perfidy!

Like her! Good heavens! was this child to live with him always? Was this child, day after day, hour after hour, to remind him by the look in his eyes of all his youthful dreams of love and happiness, and the wildering blow that for a time drove his reason from him and wrecked his life before the voyage was well begun?

That would be intolerable. No man could bear that. Heaven could not expect him to endure such a hell on earth.

He rose with a groan, and began pacing the room up and down.

He was a man slightly below the middle height, somewhat uncouth and awkward in his motions. His shoulders were broad, his figure thin almost to emaciation. He had large and powerful hands, not handsome and soft, but muscular and knotty, like those of a man who had done much physical labour, although he had never performed a day's manual work in all his life. His nose was long and blunt at the end. His cheeks were sunken. There were odd grey streaks in his long, straight hair. He stooped slightly, and was slovenly in his carriage and dress. The colour of his face was dark, almost dusky. His forehead was high and pale.

The mere shell of the man was poor, almost mean. He did not look as though he could fight or work. Beyond the breadth of his shoulders there was no suggestion of bodily strength about him. When he walked his tread lacked firmness. He looked as though the push of a child would knock him down.

But when you had formed a poor opinion of the man, and set him down as a weed, and were prepared to make short work of him morally, or mentally, or physically, and came close to him face to face, and he looked up at you and spoke, you felt confused, abashed. His eyes were dark hazel, large, deep-set, luminous. They seldom moved quickly, they seldom flashed, they seldom laughed. They rarely seemed concerned with the people or things immediately in front of him. They had the awful sadness and far-away look of the Sphinx. They saw not you, nor through you, but beyond you. You became not the object of their gaze, but an interruption in their range. They made you feel that you were in the way. You seemed to be an impertinence interposing between a great spirit in its commune with supernatural and august mysteries.

His voice was slow, deliberate, low in ordinary speech. It was not musical. It had a breathlessness about it which fixed the attention at once of those who heard. It suggested that the words spoken were read from the margin of some mighty page, and that the speaker, if he chose, could decipher the subject of the scroll.

If he raised his voice above this pitch it became uncertain, harsh, grating, discordant. It suggested the unwilling awakening of the man. It seemed to say that he lived at peace, and would that he were left at peace, and that you came unnecessarily, undesired, to rouse and harass him.

But it was when excited beyond this second stage, it was when not only awakened but lifted into the expression of enthusiasm, that the wonderful qualities of his voice were displayed. Then it became full and rich and flexible and organ-toned, at once delicate and powerful. It sounded as though not only the words, but the music also, were written on the great scroll before his eyes, and he was reading both with authority.

It was the spirit in the eyes and the spirit in the voice Philip Ray worshipped. He knew the heart of this man was made of gold, but in the eyes and the voice he found the spirit of a seer, a hero, a prophet.

The spirit of this man Kate Ray never knew, never even perceived. She was too busy with the thought of her own physical beauty to notice anything in the man but his plain appearance and unusual ways. He had more money than ever she had hoped to share with a husband, but he cared nothing for the things she liked or coveted. He would not take a house in London: he would not move into even Beechley. The only value he set upon a competency was because of the power it gave him over books, and because of the privilege it afforded him of living far away from the hurly-burly of men. His union with Kate Ray was an ill-assorted marriage, and the greatest evil that can arise out of an ill-assorted marriage had come of it.

From the day Kate left his house he never opened a volume of verse. At first he plunged into a vortex of excitement, from which he did not emerge until he had lost in gambling everything but Boland's Ait, which brought in no revenue, and an income of about a hundred a year from some property in the neighbourhood of the island.

When he regained his senses, and resolved upon retiring into solitude, he recognised the importance, the necessity of finding some occupation for his mind. He would have nothing which could remind him of the past, nothing which could recall to his mind the peaceful days at Shoreham or the joy and hope that his sweetheart and wife had brought into his life. All that was to be forgotten for ever. His life was over. It was immoral to anticipate the stroke of death. Between him and death there lay nothing to desire but oblivion, and work was the best thing in which to drown thought. He would devote the remainder of his life to history, philosophy, science.

Although he had been on the island now more than two years, he had still no definite idea of turning his studies to practical account. He read and read and made elaborate notes and extracts from books. But his designs were vague and nebulous. He called it all work. It kept his mind off the past: that was the only result of all his labours. He had no object to work for. He shuddered at the bare idea of notoriety or fame, and he did not need money, for his means were sufficient for his simple wants. Work was with him merely a draught of Lethe. He numbed his brain with reading, and when he could read no longer he copied out passages from his books or forced himself to think on subjects which would not have been bearable three years ago. He was not so much conquering himself as dulling his power to feel.

Now, in upon this life had come the boy, bringing with him more potent voices from the past than all the verses of all the poets; and, worst of all, bringing with him the face of his disgraced, dead wife!

What should he do? Either madness or death would be a relief, but neither would come. The two things of which men are most afraid are madness and death, and here was he willing to welcome either with all the joy of which his broken heart was still capable.

When that baby was born he had felt no affection for it on its own account. It seemed inexpressibly dear to her, and therefore it was after her the most precious being in all the world to him. Up to that time he knew his wife's heart had not gone out to him in love as his heart had gone out to her. He believed that the child would be the means of winning his beautiful wife's love for him. He had read in books innumerable that wives who had been indifferent towards their husbands in the early days of marriage grew affectionate when children came. For this reason he welcomed with delight the little stranger. This baby would be a more powerful bond between them than the promises made by her at the altar. It would not only reconcile her to the life-long relations upon which they had entered, but endear him to her.

But she broke her vow, broke the bond between them, and in fleeing from his house took with her the child, the creature that was dearer to her than he! Here was food for hopelessness more bitter than despair.

Now, when hope was buried for ever, and she was dead, the child had come back to remind him every hour of the past, to neutralise the cups of Lethe he felt bound to drink, that his life might not be a life of never-ending misery, to torture him with his wife's eyes, which had closed on him for ever three years ago, and which now were closed for ever on all things in death.

What should he do? Would not merciful Providence take his reason away, or stop these useless pulses in his veins?

He threw himself once more in his chair, and covered his face with his hands.

From abroad stole sounds of the awakening world. The heavy lumbering and grating of wagons and carts came from Welford Road, and from the tow-path the dull heavy thuds of clumsy horses' feet.

The man sat an hour in thought, in reverie.

At length Bramwell took down his hands and raised his large eyes, in which there now blazed the fire of intense excitement. "Light!" he cried aloud; "God grant me light!"

He kept his eyes raised. His lips moved, but no words issued from them. An expression of ecstasy was on his face. His cry had not been a cry for light, but a note of gratitude-giving that light had been vouchsafed to him. He was returning thanks.

At length his lips ceased to move, the look of spiritual exaltation left his face, his eyes were gradually lowered, and he rose slowly from his seat.

He stood a minute with his hand on his forehead, and said slowly, "I was thinking of myself only. I have been thinking of myself only all my life. I have, thank God, something else, some one else to think of now! Who am I, or what am I, that I should have expected happiness, complete happiness, bliss? Who am I, or what am I, that I should repine because I suffer? Who am I, or what am I, that I should murmur? My eyes are open at last. My eyes are open, and my heart too. Let me go and look."

He crept noiselessly out of the room to the one in which the boy lay still sleeping.

The chamber was full of the broad full even light of morning in early summer. The window stood open, the noise of the carts and wagons came from Welford Road, and the dull heavy thuds of the clumsy horses' hoofs from the tow-path. The sparrows were twittering and flickering about the cottage on the island. Dull and grimy as the place usually appeared, there was now an air of health and brightness and vigorous life about it which filled and expanded the heart of the recluse.

For years he had felt that he was dead, that his fellowship with man had ceased for ever. His heart was now opened once more.

Who should cast the first stone, the first stone into an open grave, her grave, Kate's grave? His Kate's grave! Not he; O, not he! His young, his beautiful, his darling Kate's grave! His young Kate's grave!

He turned to the bed on which rested the child.

Yes, there lay young Kate, younger than ever he had known her. The beautiful boy! There was her raven hair, there the sweet strange curve of the mouth, there the little hand under the cheek, as Kate used to lie when she slept.

"God give me life and reason for him who is so like what I have lost!" he cried; and circling his arm round the little head, he kissed the sweet strange curve about the little mouth, and burst into tears, the first he had shed for a dozen long years. In his great agony three years ago he had not wept.

The child awoke, smiled, stretched up his little arms, and caught his father round the neck.

"I want to go mother," whimpered the boy when he saw whom he held.

"You cannot go just now, child. But you and I shall go to her one day--in Heaven."

CHAPTER XI
"CAN I PLAY WITH THAT LITTLE BOY?"

Hetty Layard was not sorry when, upon the morning of Mr. William Crawford's return from the Counters Club, she found a note for her brother Alfred, explaining that he had gone out for an early walk, the weather was so lovely, and that he would not be back until next month, when he hoped to find her and Mr. Layard very well; and thanking her and him for the entertainment afforded him. He, moreover, left her a cheque--one collected the previous day--for a couple of sovereigns, out of which he begged her to take whatever his food had cost and half-a-crown which she was to present from him to Mrs. Grainger.

Miss Layard uttered a little sigh of relief when she put down the note. Every one knows that men are a nuisance about a house, especially men who have no fixed or regular business hours of absence. Men are very well in their own way, which means to the housewife when they are not in her way. A man who is six, eight or ten hours away from home every day, and goes to church twice on Sunday and takes a good long walk between the two services, may not only be tolerated, but enjoyed. But a man who does not get up until ten o'clock and keeps crawling or dashing about the house all day long is an unmitigated and crushing evil. It does not matter whether he wears heavy boots or affects the costume of a sybaritic sloven, and wanders about like a florid and venerable midday ghost in dressing-gown and slippers.

A woman's house is not her own as long as there is a man in it. While enduring the presence of male impertinence she cannot do exactly as she likes. There is at least one room she may not turn topsy-turvy, if the fit takes her. There is no freedom, no liberty. If the man remain quietly in one room, there is the unpleasant feeling that he must be either dead or hungry. A man has very little business to be in the house during day-time unless he is either dead or hungry. If the man does not confine himself to one room he is quite certain to go stumbling over sweeping-brushes and dust-pans in passages where he has no more right to be than a woman behind the counter of a bank or on the magisterial bench. From, say, the o'clock in the morning till four in the afternoon you really can't have too little of a man about a house.

Very practical housekeepers prefer not to see their male folk between nine and seven. Undoubtedly, strong-minded women believe that two meals a day and the right to sleep under his own roof of nights is as much as may with advantage to comfort be allowed to man.

But Hetty Layard was not strong-minded at all. She was not over tender-hearted either, though she was as tenderhearted as becomes a young girl of healthy body and mind, one not sicklied over with the pale cast of sentimentalism. She was as bright and cheerful as spring; but all the same, she was not sorry when she found her lodger had fled, and that they were to have the place to themselves for a month.

That day Hetty was to enjoy the invaluable service of Mrs. Grainger from breakfast to tea-time. From that day until Mr. Crawford's next visit Mrs. Grainger was to come only for a couple of hours in the forenoon every day to do the rough work. Mrs. Grainger was childless, and could be spared from her own hearth between breakfast and supper, as her husband took his dinner with him to the works, and had supper and tea together.

"So the unfortunate man has succeeded in getting out of your clutches," said Alfred Layard at his late breakfast, when Hetty told him the news.

"Yes; but he left something behind him. Look." She handed her brother the cheque. "I am to take the price of all he has had out of this, and give half-a-crown to Mrs. Grainger."

Alfred Layard shook his head very gravely. "Hetty, I had, I confess to you, some doubts of this man's sanity; I have no longer any doubt. The man is mad!"

"Considering that we are obliged to find attendance, I think he has been very generous to Mrs. Grainger."

"As mad as a hatter," said the brother sadly.

"If, Alfred, I tell you how much to take out of this, will you send him the change, or is the change to remain over until next time?"

"The miserable man is as mad as a March hare."

"See! This is all I spent for him--twelve and threepence, and that includes a lot of things that will keep till he comes again."

"To think of this poor man trusting a harpy, a lodging-house keeper, with untold gold! O, the pity of it!"

"There are candles and lamp-oil, and tea and soap, and sugar, and other things that will keep, Alfred. You can explain this when you are sending him the change. I suppose it will be best to send him the change. You have his Richmond address?"

"Freddie," said the father, addressing his flaxen-haired, blue-eyed little son at the other side of the table, "when you grow up and are a great big man, don't lodge with your Aunt Hetty. She'd fleece you, my boy. She'd starve you, and she wouldn't leave you a rag to cover you." He shook a warning finger at the boy.

"I shall live always with Aunt Hetty," said the boy stoutly, "and I want more bread-and-butter, please."

"See, my poor child, she is already practising. If she only had her way, she would reduce you to a skeleton in a week."

"Alfred, I wish you'd be sensible for a minute. This is business. I really don't know what to do, and you ought to tell me. Will you look at this list, and see if it is properly made out?" she said pouting. She had a pretty way of affecting to pout and then laughing at the idea of her being in a bad humour.

Her brother took the slip of paper and glanced at it very gravely.

"May I ask," said he, putting down the slip on the breakfast cloth, "whether this man has had his boots polished here?"

"Of course he had; twice--three times I think."

"And had he free and unimpeded use of condiments, such as salt, pepper, vinegar, mustard?"

"Yes. You don't think he could eat without salt, do you?"

"Perhaps--perhaps he even had PICKLES?"

"I think he had some pickles."

"Then, Hetty"--he rose, and, buttoning up his coat, made signs of leaving--"I am going to find an auctioneer to sell up the furniture. We are ruined."

"Ah, Alfred, like a good fellow, help me!" she pleaded, coming to him and putting her hand on his arm. "What do you mean by asking all these silly questions about blacking and vinegar?"

"Not one, Hetty, not one of the items I have named is charged in the bill, and I am a pauper, pauperised by your gross carelessness, by the shamefully lax way in which you have kept my books. What do you think would become of the great corporation I serve if our accounts were kept in so criminally neglectful a manner? Why, the Welford Gas Company would be in liquidation in a month! Suppose we treated ammonia lightly; suppose we gave all our coke to the Mission to the Blacks for distribution among the negroes; suppose we made a present of our tar to the Royal Academicians to make aniline colours for pictures to be seen only by night; suppose we gave all our gas to aeronauts who wanted to stare the unfortunate man in the moon out of countenance; suppose we supplied all our customers with *dry meters*, Hetty; suppose, I say, we supplied all our customers with *dry meters*, where should we be? Where on earth should we be?"

"Perhaps not on earth at all, Alfred, but gone up to heaven with the aeronauts. Do be sensible for a moment. I want you to tell me if we are to keep the change until next time or send it after him?"

"Have you given that half a-crown to Mrs. Grainger?"

"Yes."

"O, you prodigal simpleton! What need was there to give it? Why did you not keep it and buy a furbelow? No doubt you were afraid that when this man came back he would find out all about it. Nonsense! Why, we could dismiss Mrs. Grainger, and if she came loafing about the place, nothing in the world could be easier than to push her into the canal. I like her husband, and it would please me to do him a good turn."

There was a knock at the door, and the charwoman put in her head.

"Come in, Mrs. Grainger. What is it?" said Hetty, going towards the door.

Mrs. Grainger, in her lilac cotton dress and large apron, advanced a step into the room. Her sleeves were rolled up above the elbows of her red thick arms. She was a stout, fair-faced woman of fifty. She had not a single good feature in her face. But her expression was wholly honest and not unkindly.

Layard could not help looking from her to Hetty and contrasting the joyous youth and grace, the fresh colour and golden-brown hair of the girl, and the dull, dead, unintelligent drab appearance of the woman.

"I beg your pardon, Miss Layard," said the charwoman, "but you were talking to me yesterday and the day before about the poor lonely gentleman that lives on Boland's Ait."

"Yes. Well, what about him? Have you found out anything fresh?" said Hetty with interest.

"Only that he isn't alone any longer."

"You don't mean to say he has got married and has just brought his wife home," said Layard, affecting intense astonishment and incredulity.

An Isle of Surrey | 83

"No, sir," said the woman, somewhat abashed by his manner. "Not a wife, sir, but a child; a little boy about the size of Master Freddie there."

"Bless my soul, wonders will never cease! But I say, Hetty, I must be off. If the Cham of Tartary and the great sea-serpent came to live on that island, and had asked me to swim across and have tiffin and blubber with them, I couldn't go now. I must be off to the works. Hetty, we'll resume the consideration of the cruet-stand when I come back this evening. Let all those matters stand till then. The delay will give us an opportunity of charging interest for the money in hand."

He hastened from the room, and in a minute was out of the house and hastening up Crawford Street, with the long streamers of his beard blowing over his shoulders.

"Where did you see the child from, Mrs. Grainger?" asked Hetty, when her brother disappeared up the street. "From Mr. Crawford's room?"

"No, miss; you can't see into the timber-yard on the island from Mr. Crawford's room on account of the wall. But you can see over the wall from your own room, miss; and 'twas from your own room I saw the child. And he was carrying on, too, with that child, miss," said the woman, coming further into the room, and busying herself about clearing away the breakfast-things.

She was not exactly idle or lazy; but no living woman would rather scrub and scour than chat, particularly when paid by time and not by piece.

"What do you mean by 'carrying on?' What was he doing?"

"Well, he was kissing, and cuddling, and hugging the child, more like a mother with her baby than a man with a child. The boy is quite as big as little Master Freddie, there, and the poor gentleman seemed to be pretending the great boy couldn't walk without help, for he led him by the hand up and down the yard, and when he did let go of him for a moment he kept his hand over the little chap's head, like to be ready to catch hold of him if he was falling or stumbled. A great big boy, as big as Master Freddie there; it's plain to be seen he's not used to children," said Mrs. Grainger scornfully; for, although she had no children of her own, she was sympathetic and cordial with little ones, and often looked after a neighbour's roomful of babies while the mother went out marketing or took the washing, or mangling, or sewing home.

"Perhaps it is his own child," said Hetty, as she helped to put the breakfast-things on the tray.

"His own child? Of course it isn't. How could it be? Why, if it was his own child he'd be used to it. He'd know better than to go on with such foolery as guiding it with his hand along a level yard. He doesn't know anything about children, no more than the ground they are walking on."

"Perhaps he is afraid it might fall into the water. I'll wash up the breakfast things myself, Mrs. Grainger."

"Very well, miss. Afraid it might fall into the water! Why, the child couldn't. They're in the timber-yard, and there's a wall all around it, and neither of the gates is open."

"Well," said Hetty, as the woman left the room carrying the tray, "maybe he is looking after the child for some friend; perhaps the child has only come on a visit to him."

"Look after a child for a friend! Is he the sort of man to look after a child for a friend?" Mrs. Grainger called out from the kitchen. "What friend would ask a man like him to mind a child? I'd as soon ask a railway-engine or a mangle to look after a child of mine, if I had one. Besides, if the child belongs to a friend, what does he mean by kissing and cuddling it?"

"I give it up," said the girl. "I own I can make nothing of it. What do you think, Mrs. Grainger? You know more about this strange man and his strange ways than I do."

"I think," said Mrs. Grainger, in the voice of one uttering an authoritative decision, "the whole thing is a mystery, and I can make nothing of it. But you, miss, go up and look. If you want to see him, he is in the timber-yard. Go to your room, miss, and have a peep. You may be able to make something of it; I can't."

"I will," said the girl; "I shall be down in a few minutes." And she ran out of the sitting-room, upstairs with a light springy step, and the murmured burden of a song on her lips.

She went to the open window of her own room and looked out.

It was close on noon, and the blazing light of early summer filled all the place beneath her. The view had no charms of its own, but the fact that she was above the ground and away from immediate contact with the sordid earth had a purifying effect upon the scene. Then, again, what place is it that can look wholly evil when shone upon by the unclouded sun of fresh May?

In front and to right and left the canal flamed in the sunlight. At the other side of the water lay a sloping bank of lush green grass, beyond that a road, and at the other side of the road a large yard, in which a great number of gipsy-vans, and vans belonging to cheap-Jacks and to men who remove furniture, were packed.

So far, if there was nothing to delight, there was nothing to displease the spectator. In fact, from a scenic point of view the colour was very good, for you had the flaming canal, the dark green of the grassy bank, and the red and yellow and blue caravans of the gipsies and the cheap-Jacks and the people who remove furniture.

Beyond this yard there spread a vast extent of small, mean, ill-kept houses which were not picturesque, and which suggested painful thoughts concerning the squalor and poverty of the people who lived in them.

To the right stretched the tow-path leading to Camberwell, to the left a row of stores, and only a hundred yards off was the empty ice-house. To the right lay Leeham, invisible from where the girl stood, and nearer and visible a row of stores and a stone-yard.

In front of her was Boland's. Ait, and in the old timber-yard of the islet Francis Bramwell walking up and down, holding the hand of a boy of between three and four in his hands, as though the child had walked for the first time within this month of May.

Mrs. Grainger was right. This man, whose face Hetty could not see, for he bent low over the child, was treating the boy as though he were no more than a year or fifteen months old. He was also displaying towards him a degree of affection altogether inconsistent with the supposition that the youngster was merely the son of a friend.

The two were walking up and down the yard, the right hand of the child in the left hand of the man, the right hand of the man at one time resting lightly on the boy's head, at another on the boy's shoulder. The man's whole mind seemed centred on his charge. He never once raised his head to look around. No doubt the thought that he might be observed never occurred to him. For two years he had lived on that island, and never until now arose a chance of any one seeing him when he was in the yard; for the only windows that overlooked it were those of Crawford's House, and that had been unoccupied until three days ago.

Suddenly it occurred to Hetty that she was intruding upon this stranger's privacy. Of course she was free to look out of her own window as long as she liked; but then it was obvious Bramwell thought there was no spectator, or, at all events, he had not bargained in his mind for a spectator.

A faint flush came into her cheek, and she was on the point of drawing back when a loud shrill voice sounded at her side:

"Aunt Hetty, Aunt Hetty, I want to see the little boy!"

The girl started, and then stood motionless, for the recluse below had suddenly looked up, and was gazing in amazement at the girl and child in the window above him.

The man and boy in the yard were both bare-headed. Bramwell raised his open hand above his eyes to shield them from the glare of the sky, that he might see the better.

Hetty drew back a pace, as though she had been discovered in a shameful act. Her colour deepened, but she would not go altogether away from the window. That would be to admit she had been doing something wrong.

"Aunt Hetty," cried Freddie, in the same shrill loud voice, "can I play with that little boy down there? I have no one to play with here."

The upturned face of the man smiled, and the voice of the man said, "Come down, my little fellow, and play with this boy. He is just like yourself--he has no one to play with. You will let him come, please? I will take the utmost care of him."

"I--I'll see," stammered Hetty, quite taken aback.

"You will let him come? O, pray do. My little fellow has no companion but me," said the deep, full, rich pleading voice of the man.

In her confusion Hetty said, "If it's safe. If he can get across."

"O, it's quite safe. I will answer for the child. I'll push across the stage in a moment, and fetch the child. There is plenty of room for them to play here, and absolutely no danger."

CHAPTER XII
PHILIP RAY AT RICHMOND

Once Philip Ray started on any course he was not the man to let the grass grow under his feet. All his time was not at his disposal. He was in the Custom House, and for several hours a day he was chained to his desk.

No sooner were his duties discharged on the day following the arrival of the boy at Boland's Ait than he hastened to Ludgate Hill railway station and took the first train to Richmond.

He had not worked out any definite plan of search. His mind was not a particularly orderly one. Indeed, he was largely a creature of impulse, and in setting out he had only two ideas in his head. First, to find the man who had caused all the shame and misery; and, second, to execute summary vengeance on that man the moment he encountered him.

He did not seek to justify himself morally in this course; he did not consider the moral aspect of his position at all. When his blood was up he was impulsive, headlong. He had made up his mind three years ago that John Ainsworth deserved death at his hands for the injury done, and neither during any hour of these three years nor now had he the slightest hesitancy or compunction.

He had sworn an oath that he would kill this man if ever he could get at him, and kill him he would now in spite of consequences. People might call it a cowardly murder if they pleased. What did he care? This man deserved death, and if they chose to hang him afterwards, what of that? He was quite prepared to face that fate. Kate was dying or dead; the honourable name of Ray had been disgraced for ever; the life of the man he loved best in all the world had been blasted by a base, vicious scoundrel, and he would shoot that scoundrel just as he would shoot a mad dog or a venomous snake. He was inexorable.

No thought of seeking his sister entered his mind. She was, doubtless, dead by this time. From the moment she left her husband's roof she had been dead to him. In the presence of Frank, and with that letter before him, he had held his tongue regarding her. But his mind was completely unchanged. The best thing that could happen to her was that she should die. A woman who could do what she had done deserved no thought of pity, had no place in the consideration of sane people; a woman who could leave Frank Mellor, now known as Francis Bramwell, for John Ainsworth, deserved no pity, no human sympathy. She had sinned in the most heinous way against loyalty; let him show that all the blood of the family was not base and traitorous. He would sin on the other side to make matters even.

He knew that such forms of vengeance were not usual in this time and country. So much the worse for this time and country. What other kind of satisfaction was possible? The law courts? Monstrous! How could the law courts put such a case right? By divorcing those who had already been divorced! By a money penalty exacted from the culprit! Pooh, pooh! If a man shot a man they hanged him, put him out of pain at once. But if a man was the cause of a woman's lingering death from shame and despair, and imposed a life of living-death on an innocent human being, they let the miscreant go scot-free; unless, indeed, they imposed a fine such as they would inflict for breach of an ordinary commercial contract. The idea that treatment of this sort had even the semblance of justice could not be entertained by a child or an idiot!

Before setting out from Ludgate Hill and on the way down to Richmond nothing seemed more reasonable than that he should take the train to that town, and without any serious difficulty find John Ainsworth. The town was not large, and he could give any one of whom he asked aid the man's name and a full description of his appearance. He possessed, moreover, the additional fact that Ainsworth had shaved his face, taken off his beard, whiskers, and moustache. He should be on his track in an hour, and face to face with Ainsworth in a couple of hours at the outside.

He stepped briskly out of the train at Richmond, and waited until the platform was cleared of those who had alighted. Then he spoke to the most intelligent porter he could find. First of all he gave the man a shilling. He said he was in search of a Mr. John Ainsworth, a gentleman of about thirty-five or thirty-seven years of age, five feet eight or thereabouts, with a quick restless manner, a clean-shaven roundish face, dark hair and dark eyes, in figure well made, but inclining to stoutness.

The porter knew no gentleman of the name, he was sorry to say, and recalled a great number of gentlemen who corresponded in some respects with the description, but none that corresponded with all. As far as he was aware, there was no man of the name in Richmond--that is, no gentleman of the name. He knew a Charles Ainsworth, a cab-driver, but Charles Ainsworth was five feet eleven or six feet, and no more than twenty-five years of age. Perhaps the stationmaster might be able to help.

The stationmaster knew no one of the name--that is, no one named John Ainsworth. He knew Charles Ainsworth the cabdriver. He could not identify any one corresponding to Ray's description, but the interrogator must remember that a great number of gentlemen passed through that station from week's end to week's end. Why not look in a directory and find out his friend's address at once?

Of course. That was an obvious course. It had not occurred to Ray before.

Accordingly he left the station, and turned into an hotel and asked to see the local directory.

No John Ainsworth here.

Another disappointment. But this was not disheartening; for Ainsworth in all likelihood was not a householder. At the hotel they suggested that the post-office would be the place to learn the address of his friend.

Ray smiled grimly as he noticed that the three people of whom he had inquired all referred to Ainsworth as his "friend."

His luck at the post-office was bad also. Nothing was known there of any Ainsworth but Charles, the cabdriver.

This was becoming exasperating. The man he sought could not have vanished into thin air. Edward Lambton, who saw Ainsworth, was quite sure of his identity. When a man recognises another who has taken off his beard, whiskers and moustache, there is not the slightest room for doubt of the identification, particularly if the identification is casual, not suggested, spontaneous.

Ray felt more than exasperated now. He was furious. He walked about the town for an hour, asking here and there, but could find no trace of John Ainsworth. He was no more known in the place than if he had never been born.

Suddenly he stopped with an exclamation of surprise and anger. "I am a lunatic!" he cried in a low voice, "I'm a born lunatic! Is it because Lambton saw Ainsworth on the platform of this place that he must live here? Might not ten thousand people have seen me on the platform of this place an hour or so ago, and do I live here? Indeed I do not think any human being out of Bedlam could be so hopelessly idiotic as I have been to feel sure he lived here."

He found his way back to the station and returned to town. He got out at Camberwell, and walked from there to Boland's Ait. It was upon this occasion that Crawford, sallying from Layard's, learnt from Red Jim how the man who had come along the tow-path had failed to emerge from the cover of the island.

"And what have you been doing all day?" asked Ray, when he was seated in one of the armchairs in the study or dining-room of the cottage.

The boy was seated on the floor, turning over the leaves of a book full of pictures.

"We have been busy and playing," said Bramwell, nodding towards the child. "I was putting the place to rights, getting in order for my new lodger. I thought you would have come sooner." For the first time in three years Francis Bramwell spoke in a cheerful tone and looked almost happy. There had always been a great deal of reserve in this man, but now he seemed more open and free than he had ever appeared even before his marriage. Suffering had purified, and the presence of his son, whom he had taken into his heart, had soothed and humanised the recluse.

Ray paused in doubt as to whether he should tell the other of his visit to Richmond. He had taken no notice of the boy upon his entrance, but he was pleased and grateful that Bramwell showed an awakened interest in life. The child had done this, and his heart softened towards the little fellow. Anything that brought light to his brother-in-law was an object of thankfulness. If his friend, his brother, as he called him, were in better spirits, owing to the coming of the child, why should he dissipate them by telling him of his search of vengeance. He answered the question of the other by saying:

"I was delayed. I had to attend to something."

Bramwell's face darkened. Philip had no secret from him. He was a man who could keep nothing from a friend. Why did he not say what had detained him? There could be only one explanation: the delay had been caused by something in connection with the letter Philip had received the evening before. It was plain to Bramwell what had detained Kate's brother. Bramwell said very gravely:

"You have been to Richmond?"

Philip nodded.

"Ah," Bramwell sighed heavily, "I thought so! Did you find out anything?"

"Nothing. Absolutely nothing. He is not known there. I tried at the railway station, in the directory, at the post-office, in a dozen shops. No account or trace was to be found of the scoundrel."

"Thank Heaven!"

"I do not believe he lives there. He must have been only in the town a little while, visiting some one, or passing through, on some new devil's work, I will swear."

"It was a mercy for you that he was not to be found."

"A mercy for him, you mean."

For a few minutes Bramwell seemed plunged in gloomy thought. The two men were silent. At length the elder shook himself, rose, and said:

"Come, see the arrangements I have made for the boy. He is to sleep in my room. I am going to give him my bed. The stretcher will do excellently for me. I have spoken to Mrs. Treleaven--you know the woman who brings me what I want every morning. She is to come for an hour or two a day and keep matters right for us. Up to this she has never been on the Ait, but I could not myself keep the place as tidy as I should like now that I am not alone. Early impressions are lasting, and I must do the best I can to brighten up this hermitage for the sake of the new young eyes. Come!"

The two men went to the bedroom.

"See," said the father, with a sad smile; "I have laid down this bit of old carpet, and hung up these prints, and put the stretcher close to the bed, so that I may be near him, and also that it may serve as a step when he is getting in and out of his own bed. Children, I have often read, should sleep in beds by themselves; and, above all, it is not wholesome for them to sleep with grown-up people. You don't think this place is unhealthy for a child, Philip?"

"O, no! You have enjoyed very good health here."

What a change--what a blessed change had come over this man! He had been reborn, re-created by the touch of those chubby fingers and young red lips; by the soft, silky hair and the large dark eyes; by the fresh, sweet clear voice, and the complete dependency and helplessness of the boy.

"But I am a man in the vigour of life," said the father anxiously; "and am therefore able to resist influences of climate or situation which might be perilous to one so young and delicately formed, eh? You don't think there is any danger in the place?"

"Certainly not."

"But so much water that is almost stagnant? You are aware that there is hardly any current in the canal, and that there are no locks on it?"

"O, yes; but I never heard any complaints of insalubrity, and you know the neighbourhood of a gas-house, although it does not make the air bright or sweet, purifies it."

"I know; I thought of that. I know that a still more unsavoury business--that of candle-making--is a preventive to pestilence; at least, it was in the days of the Plague, and chandlers had immunities and privileges on that account. But it is the water I fear for him. None of your family, Philip, had delicate chests?"

"No, no; I think you may make your mind easy. I am sure the boy will thrive marvellously here."

"I am glad to hear you say so. Let us go back. The poor little chap must not be allowed to feel lonely. You did not take any notice of him when you came in. Philip," he put his hand on his brother's arm, "you are not going to visit any anger on the desolate orphan? Remember, he is an orphan now; and you must not bear ill-will towards the dead, or visit the--the faults of the parent on the child."

"Tut, tut!" said Philip, as they left the room and returned to the study; "I am not going to do anything of the kind. I took no notice of the child when I arrived because my head was full of other things."

He went to the boy and raised him in his arms, and pinched his cheek, and patted his hair and kissed him.

"Thank you," said Bramwell. "I feel new blood in my veins and new brains in my head, and a new heart in my body. I intend giving up dreaming for ever. I am now going to try to make a little money. Presently the child will have to be sent to school--to a good school, of course."

"My dear Frank," cried Philip, with tears in his eyes and voice, "it is better to listen to you talk in this way than to hear you had been made a king."

"I am a king," cried the father in a tone of exultation. "I am an absolute monarch. I reign with undisputed sway over my island home, and my subject is my own son, whom I may mould and fashion as I please, and whom no one will teach to despise me."

CHAPTER XIII
AN INVITATION ACCEPTED

"And so," said Alfred Layard to Hetty the evening of the day little Freddie, now in bed, had made his first visit to the island, "you have absolutely spoken to this Alexander Selkirk. Tell me all about it."

She began, and told him how she went up to her own room and saw Bramwell and the boy in the yard on the island, and how Freddie's cry had betrayed her presence, and in the confusion at being found out she had consented to let their youngster go to play with the other youngster.

"You are not annoyed with me, Alfred, for allowing him, are you?" she asked in some suspense. The little fellow had never before been so long from under her charge.

"Annoyed? Not I. What should I be annoyed at, so long as the people are all right, and there is no danger of Freddie tumbling into the water?"

"O, there is no danger whatever. A wall runs all round the yard, and Mr. Bramwell was in and out all day looking after the boys."

"How did Freddie get across? Swam?"

"Don't be absurd, Alfred." She knew very well her brother did not ask her seriously if the child had swum across the waters of Crawford's Bay. And she knew equally well that he was not reproaching her for letting the boy cross the water. At an ordinary time she would have passed by such a question from him in silence, disregarded, but there lingered in her mind a vague feeling that she stood on her defence about the expedition of the morning, and she felt timid under anything like levity. "No; when we got down and out by the back door to the wharf we saw Mr. Bramwell pulling a great long floating thing made of timber through the water. He pushed this over to where we stood. It reached across the water. He told us he had another of the same kind on the canal side of the island."

"I know. A floating stage."

"I daresay that is what they call it. I should call it a floating bridge. Well, he walked across this and took little Freddie in his arms and carried him over. I was a good deal frightened, for the thing rocked horribly, but he told me there was no danger."

"Of course, there was no danger while the child was carried by a careful man. We had two of these stages at the works, but we had to get rid of them, for the men were always either going out for drink or getting drink brought in for them."

"And, do you know, Freddie did not cry or seem a bit afraid of the water."

"Hetty, take my word for it that from what you tell me there is the making of a great naval hero in that boy of ours."

"I wish you would try to be sensible for a while."

"I think I shall call him from this date Frederick Nelson Layard."

"Don't be ridiculous, Alfred."

"Or Frederick Cochrane Layard."

"O, don't, please, Alfred."

"It is well to be prepared for fame, and we should always take care that our children are prepared for fame and what more simple and inexpensive preparation can a man have for fame than to be suited, clothed, I may say, in a name becoming fame? Hetty, my dear, remind me in the morning to decide which of these names I shall finally adopt; it is a matter that admits of no delay. I would not think of calling him Frederick Drake Layard for all the world, because in the first place the name Drake in connection with water suggests a whole lot of frivolous jests, always an abomination to me; and in the second place, there was too much of the buccaneer about Drake. Hetty, don't forget to remind me of the matter in the morning. The boy wasn't sea-sick, I hope?"

The girl only sighed this time. She had now lost all sense of uneasiness about the part she had played in the affair of the morning.

"You know," he went on in a tone of pleasant reverie, "I think something ought to be done with the surname too. It would be well to be ready at every point. All you have to do is to write in an *n*, and you have a distinctly nautical flavour. How do you like Frederick Nelson Cochrane Lanyard? But there--there--my girl, don't answer me now. It is, you would naturally say, too important a question to be decided offhand. Think of the matter to-night. Sleep on the idea, my dear Hetty, and let me have your decision in the morning. If in the dead waste and middle of the night any difficulties which you think I could solve arise in your mind, do not fail to call me. I shall be happy to give you any assistance in my power."

"Are you out of breath, Alfred? I hope you are."

"No, but I am out of tea. Another cup, please, and let us dismiss business from our minds. Let us unbend. It weakens the bow to keep it always bent. Tell me, what is this man, our next-door neighbour, like? I have a theory myself that he is a coiner."

"Well, if he is a coiner you must not think he uses much of his ill-gotten gold in buying clothes. He's dreadfully shabby. But, whatever else he may be, he is a gentleman."

"Good-looking, of course?"

"No, but remarkable-looking. When you see him you could never take him for a common man. He seems awfully clever."

"Well, as some philosopher, whose name has escaped me, says, we must take him as we find him, though I must say it seems to me that it would be very difficult to take him as we do not find him, or as we find him not. To be serious, Hetty----"

"O, thank goodness! at last!" cried the girl, with a sigh of relief, and raising her eyes in gratitude.

"If you don't take great care," he said, shaking a long thin forefinger at her, "you can't tell what may happen. I am not the man to submit to bullying at your hands. What I was going to say when you threatened me is this, that while I have no objection to Freddie going over now and then to play with this boy----"

"He promised to go over again to-morrow," interrupted Hetty.

"All right; let him go over to-morrow. But for two or three reasons he must not go over every day. This young--By the way, what's his name?"

"Bramwell. The man told me he was his son, his only child."

"Very good. This young Bramwell must come over, turn and turn about, and play with Freddie here. In the first place, I think one of the upstairs rooms is a safer place for these young shavers than the island, though there is a wall; and in the next place, this Bramwell is at work on coining, or whatever it is, all day, and can't be expected to look after two mischievous boys of their age. Of course you can't have the two of them here when we have Crawford; but that will not be for four weeks more. That reminds me: he said he should like to see Freddie. Did he ask afterwards for the boy?"

"No. You see he was busy tidying, or rather untidying, his room all one day, and he was out a good deal of the time, and went away early in the morning."

"Just so. My sister, you are very quick with excuses for your hero, your Bayard."

"I still say what I said before."

"Naturally you do. Women always do stick to what they say. They are the unprogressive sex. But we will let him go by. I confess, from the little I have heard of this Bramwell--solitary now no longer--I am interested in him. A man who has kept himself to himself for years must, if there ever was anything in him, have something to say worth listening to when he speaks. We are solitary enough ourselves, goodness knows. Who can tell but this Zimmermann may be induced to cross the Hellespont, or, to be more near the situation, cross over from his Negropont to the mainland? When you meet him to-morrow, say I should be very glad if he would come to us and have a chat and smoke a pipe."

"I will, but I'm sure he doesn't smoke."

"Why are you sure of that, my sister?"

"Because he has quite an intellectual look."

"Thank you, Hetty. Very neat indeed. I shall not forget that thrust for a while. Now" (he raised his warning finger again and shook it at her with a look of portentous meaning) "mind, this is the second man you have fallen in love with during the past three days, and the horrible part of the matter is that both of them are married."

Whatever might be forgotten next morning, one thing was sure to be recollected in Crawford's House. It is a fact that Hetty did not remember to draw her brother's attention to the change of name projected for Freddie the evening before. Nor, strange to say, did her brother revert to the contemplated alteration.

But what was remembered beyond all chance of forgetting was that Freddie had promised to go across to the island again to-day. If the father and aunt happened by any means to lose sight of the fact, they were not allowed to remain a moment in doubt about it. The first thing the boy said when he opened his eyes was, "I'm to go to play with Frank again to-day, amn't I, Auntie Hetty?"

At breakfast he had most of the talk to himself, and all his talk was about Frank and the island, and the boat by which he had gone across, and Frank's father, who had given them both sugar on bread-and-butter, and the old barrow which was in the yard, and which served them with great fidelity as a cab, and a tramcar, and a steamboat, and a house, and a canal-boat, and a horse, and a great variety of other useful appliances and creatures.

"Are there wheels to that barrow?" asked the father as he got up to leave the house for the works.

"No, no wheels. But we play that there are."

"So much the better there are none. And now, my young friend," said the father, catching up the boy and kissing him, "take care you do not fall out of that barrow and cut your nose, and take care you don't hurt the other little boy; for if you do you shall never, never, never go over to the island again. Remember that, won't you?"

"Yes," said Freddie, struggling out of his father's arms in order to get on a chair and see through the kitchen window if the other little boy's father was already coming to fetch him on that long narrow boat across those wide waters to the haven of joy, the old timber-yard beyond.

Alas! the little boy's father was not there, and to the young eyes the place looked desolate, forlorn.

"Will Frank's father come soon, Mrs. Grainger?" asked Freddie, in a tone of despair.

"Of course he will. He'll be here in a few minutes," said that good woman, who knew absolutely nothing of Hetty's promise of the previous afternoon, as she had left the house long before Freddie came back and the undertaking for another visit was given. But Mrs. Grainger was fond of children, and, if she had had any of her own, would have spoiled them beyond hope of reformation.

"Frank said he'd be up very early," said the boy in pensive complaint.

"And very early he'll be," said Mrs. Grainger, as she polished the fender with resolute vigour. "He'll be here, I warrant, before you have time to say Jack Robinson."

The phrase which Mrs. Grainger used to indicate a very little while was new to the boy, and he took it literally, and murmured softly, in a voice that did not surmount the sound of Mrs. Grainger's conflict with the fender, "Jack Robinson, Jack Robinson, Jack Robinson!" and then, finding the soothsaying unfulfilled, he lapsed into a spiritless silence, keeping his eyes fixed on the point where he knew Bramwell must come round the corner of the yard-wall.

Presently he raised a great shout and clapped his hands, and, getting down from the chair on which he had been standing, tore, shouting through the house, to discover his Aunt Hetty, and tell her the joyful news and fetch his hat.

He found Hetty, and in quick haste the aunt and nephew were out on the little quay or wharf, and stretching towards them, drawn by Francis Bramwell, was the long, low, black floating stage.

Little Frank was not visible. His father had left him safe behind the wall of the yard. It would be unsafe to trust him on the edge of Crawford's Bay, and dangerous to carry two boys of so young an age across that long, oscillating, crank raft.

Hetty stood at the edge of the water holding the boy in her arms.

"How do you do, Mrs. Layard?" said Bramwell, lifting his battered billycock hat as he landed. "I am indebted to your little nephew for your name."

He spoke gravely, with an amelioration of the subdued and serious lines of his face that was almost a smile. During the past two or three days he had not only re-inherited the power of smiling, but had absolutely laughed more than once at some speech or action of his son's, or when his thoughts took a pleasant turn about the boy. But he had been so long out of use in smiling or laughing that he could not yet exercise these powers except in connection with the child.

Hetty in some confusion said she was very well, and thanked him. Freddie's summons had been sudden, and, at the moment, unexpected, so that she felt slightly embarrassed.

"I am sure," the man said, keeping his large, luminous, sphinx-like eyes on her, "it is very good of you to allow your little fellow to come to play with mine. You do me a great kindness in lending him to me. I shall take the utmost care of him, I pledge you my word."

In these few seconds the girl had regained her self-possession, and said, with one of those bright sunny smiles of hers, in which golden light seemed to dance in her blue eyes, "Understand, I allow him to go as a favour."

"Undoubtedly," he said, bowing, and then looking at her with a faint gleam of surprise in his eyes.

"And you will repay favour for favour?"

"If I can."

"Well, my brother is a very lonely, home-keeping man, who hardly ever has any one to see him, and he told me to ask you if you would do him the kindness of coming in this evening for a little while, as he would like to meet you, now that our young people are such friends. That is the favour I ask. I ask it for my brother's sake. Will you come, please?"

The man started, drew back, and looked around him half-scared. The notion of going into the house of another man had not crossed his mind for two years. The invitation sounded on his ears as though it were spoken in a language familiar to him in childhood, but which he had almost wholly forgotten. He had come across the water in order to secure a companion for his little son: but that any one should think he would come across that water and speak to people for an object of his own was startling, disconcerting, subversive of all he had held for a long time: since his arrival at the Ait.

Hetty saw that he hesitated, and, having no clue to his thoughts, fancied her invitation had not been pressing enough.

"You will promise?" she said, holding Freddie out to him. "You said you would do me a favour in return for the loan of the boy. You will not withdraw. It would really be a great kindness, for my brother is alone in the evenings except for me, and he seldom goes out."

"But Mrs. Layard----" said the man, in discomposure and perplexity, as he took Freddie in his arms, and hardly knowing what he said.

"Ah," said the girl, shaking her head, and pointing up to the unclouded sky, "she went when Freddie was a tiny little baby."

"Dead?" whispered the man, as a spasm passed over his face.

"Yes, more than three years."

"I beg your pardon. I am very stupid. I am afraid I have caused you pain. Believe me, I am extremely sorry."

"No, no; you must not say anything more of that. But you will come?"

"It is strange," said he in a tone of profound abstraction; "it is strange that the two little motherless boys should take such a liking to one another, and that both should come to this district--this place--at about the same time."

He had forgotten the girl's presence. Like most men who have lived long in solitude, he had contracted the habit of talking aloud to himself, and he was now unconscious that he had a listener.

"We may count on you?"

He awoke with a start: he did not know exactly to what the question referred. He was aware that he had been keeping the girl waiting for an answer, and that she had asked him for a favour in return for the loan of a companion for his boy. He blurted out "Certainly," and was back on the Ait once more before he realised the nature of the promise he had made.

CHAPTER XIV
THE FIRE AT RICHMOND

A more devoted husband was not in all Richmond than William Crawford. A more trusting and affectionate wife could not be found in all England than Ellen, his wife, whom in tones of great tenderness he always called Nellie. To her first husband, old Thomas Crawford, whom she had married in the zenith of her maiden beauty twenty-five years ago, when she was twenty-two, she had ever been Ellen. Her name in his mouth had always seemed cold and stately; at home she had always been Nellie. But the dignity of marriage, and of marriage with a man forty years older than herself, had elevated her into Mrs. Crawford among outsiders and Ellen among her own relatives and in her own house.

Her husband, father and mother, and only brother had been dead some time before her present husband came to live next door to her at Singleton Terrace, Richmond. She was a confirmed invalid, and had been unable to move about freely for four years. She had always been the gentlest of the good, and rested quite resigned to her fate. She never repined, never grumbled, never murmured. Except while in the throes of pain, her face wore a placid look, which changed into a smile when any one spoke to her or came near her.

Her doctors had told her all along that her case was not beyond hope. They spoke of it generally as loss of nerve-power. In hundreds of such affections there had been complete cures, and in thousands partial and important improvements. They traced her condition to a carriage accident, in which the horses ran away, and she had been heavily thrown, shortly after her marriage. The injury then received lay dormant until developed by the sudden and horrible death of her husband.

He was past eighty at the time, but hale and hearty. He ate a good breakfast on the day of his death, and had gone out to look at some new machinery a friend of his had got in a sawmill.

An hour after leaving his own door he was carried back over the threshold, a palpitating, bleeding mass, torn and ground and mangled out of all human shape. His coat had caught in the machinery, and he had been drawn in among the ruthless wheels and killed. His wife happened to be looking out of the dining-room window as the bearers came along the road and up the front garden. Owing to brutal thoughtlessness, no one had been sent on to break the awful news to her. She rushed into the hall as the four men bearing the stretcher entered.

They had placed a cloak over the body. She knew by the face being covered that all was over.

"Is he dead?" she shrieked, and raised the cloak before any one could stay her. She saw the mangled horror which an hour ago had been sound and hearty and--whole.

Without a sound she sank to the floor in a swoon. When she recovered consciousness she could not stand without aid. The strength of her lower limbs was gone. A double blow had fallen on that house, and although people expressed and felt sorrow for the old man, and horror at his sudden and terrible death, all the tears were for the lovely soft-mannered wife, who seemed to think less of herself than another woman of her own shadow.

After the awful death of her husband followed years of lonely widowhood, in which she was as helpless to get about as a little child Then came this suave and low-voiced man to lodge next door. He made no advances to her whatever. To do anything of the kind would have been revolting. It would have been plain to the most credulous that he sought her money, and not herself. He was not even a friend. He did not affect to be on terms of intimacy with her. He comported himself as an acquaintance who had great interest in her and sympathised much with her in the unhappy condition of her health.

Later occurred the fire and the rescue. The cause of the fire had never been ascertained. It arose in the kitchen under Mrs. Crawford's room, and in the back of the house. Because of her malady, the widow occupied a room on the first floor, the kitchen being a sunken story.

At that time Mrs. Crawford had a companion--a widow also--who usually slept in the same room with the invalid, but who on the night of the fire was absent from the house. The companion went for a day and a night every month to visit her brother at Rochester. All the other nights the lady companion had been away the cook passed in her mistress's room. But at this time a change of the two servants, cook and housemaid, had just taken place, and both being strangers, Mrs. Crawford decided to have neither in her room that night; she resolved to sleep alone. Mrs. Farraday on her way to the station had met the next-door lodger and told him these facts, expressing a sincere hope that Mrs. Crawford would pass a comfortable night, and adding that though the poor lady often found a great difficulty in going to sleep, once she went off she never woke till morning, and required no help in the night, but had some one in her room merely for companionship.

All this Mrs. Farraday told the sympathetic next-door lodger, who joined with her in the expression of a hope--nay, a conviction--that the invalid would pass a peaceful and untroubled night.

The sympathetic lodger next door was not, of course, then called William Crawford. He took that name when some months later he married the widow. He was not known by the name of John Ainsworth either. For a very simple and sufficient reason he wished to forget John Ainsworth. Philip Ray had sworn never to forget John Ainsworth, and had, moreover, sworn to shoot John Ainsworth if ever they met.

John Ainsworth had as many names as a royal prince. He cared very little for names. He cared a great deal for pretty faces just for a while; or, rather, he cared for pretty faces always, but liked change. Better even than pretty faces, he cared for money. The older he grew the more enamoured he became of money. When a man of spirit cares greatly for pretty faces, and still more greatly for money, what matters how people may call him so long as he may gaze on beauty and rattle guineas in his pocket? One of the most useful qualities of a pretty face is that you can turn your back upon it when you are tired of it. One of the most delightful qualities of money is that you can, if you only know where to seek, always find men willing to gamble with you.

When John Ainsworth left Beechley suddenly and not alone three years ago he and the companions of his flight changed trains at Horsham. At the same time he altered his name. He became of his own free action, unchallenged by any one, Mr. George Hemphill. When he left the train and went on board the steamer for New York he described himself and his party as Mr. and Mrs. Edwin Plunkett and child. When he took steamer back to England he travelled alone as Mr. Walter Greystones.

Mrs. Crawford's sympathetic next-door lodger was known to her and to Richmond as Mr. William Goddard.

In Mrs. Crawford's house the only servants, the cook and housemaid, slept in a front top room.

At about four o'clock in the morning, after Mrs. Farraday's departure for Rochester, Mrs. Crawford was awakened by an awful sense of suffocation. The room was full of smoke. She could see this by the night light. She called out as loudly as she was able, but there were two doors, three floors, and three pair of stairs between her and the maids. She rang the little handbell placed at the side of her bed by Mrs. Farraday before setting out for the train. The voice was very thin and weak, and the bell no better than a toy. The voice could be heard no further off than the next room and hall. The sound of the bell might reach the kitchen and the drawing-room overhead, no farther.

The smoke in the room increased. It had a thick, oppressive, oily taste and smell, something like the smell of paraffin. Mrs. Crawford was not aware of any paraffin being in the house. She had a horror of paraffin, and none could be in the house with her approval.

She lay in her bed perfectly helpless. It was awful to lie here awaiting the approach of death, seeing the great clouds of smoke rise thicker and thicker every minute, and know that soon insensibility would fall upon her, and then death.

If she could but get to the window and fling herself out, she might be maimed for the remainder of her days, still she would be almost certain to escape with life. But she could not move from that bed to save her life. Her arms were as strong and capable as ever; but her lower limbs were as much beyond her control as the limbs of the dead.

She had often pictured to herself the horrors of being buried alive. She had often fancied to herself the soul-distracting awakening in the tomb, the confined space, the damp cerecloths, the cold planks, the stifling air, the maddening certainty that above were space and sunshine and warmth, the songs of birds and the voices of kindly people going blithely to and fro.

Her own situation was as bad, nay worse. In the tomb there would be no light to show the sombre robes of death gradually closing down upon her. There would be no danger of the fierce fiery agony of flame before all was over. There would be from the first no hope of deliverance.

Here she was helpless, and could see the smoke growing denser and denser every moment, the weight upon her chest increasing with every tumultuous inspiration. Around her head, across her brow, a band of burning hot metal seemed gradually tightening and bursting in upon her brain.

She could hear the sound of the flames flapping and beating in muffled distant riot below, and yet she could not move.

She had read once of a man buried up to the head in the sand of the seashore for scurvy, powerless to stir, and so left by his companions while they went away for an hour. Towards this miserable man presently glides a serpent out of some sedges above high-water mark. That situation had filled her mind with ineffable horror. Her case now was still more terrible, for there was no companion who might chance to return in time. Besides, until the last moment the man in the sand might hope the serpent would not strike, that the reptile was not hungry. Here the fire would strike infallibly; flames were always hungry, voracious, in satiable.

The oppression grew more suffocating. She was lying on her back, and she felt as though an intolerable mass of lead were crushing in her chest. The band across her forehead tightened, and she could not persuade herself that the bone of her skull had not been driven in upon her beating brain. Her hands seemed as though they were swollen to ten times their size. She could no longer move her arms with ease.

At length she felt as if the inexorable hand of death had seized her throat and was squeezing and closing up her windpipe.

She kept her eyes fixed on the light. This was the only thing that told of life. She could see nothing else.

It was not a light now, but a blue blur upon the darkness. It faded to a patch of faintly luminous smoke. She closed her eyes for a moment to clear her sight. The motion of the lids pained her exquisitely, and made the redhot band across her beating forehead burn more fiercely, more crushingly than ever into her brain.

With a groan she opened her eyes.

All was dark! The light had gone out, extinguished by the smoke.

She knew that where lights went out life soon followed This light had illumined dimly the way to the tomb. This bed was her grave.

She summoned all her courage, and drew a long breath. She summoned all her strength, and uttered one cry:

"Help!"

There was a loud crash, a sound of breaking glass, a rush of fresh cool air. She fainted.

When she recovered consciousness she was out of the burning house, in her own garden, and standing by her was William Goddard, who had rescued her from the burning house.

That was the beginning of close acquaintance between the man and the widow. She regarded him as one who had delivered her from death, and all Richmond and all the world who read an account of the fire looked upon him in the same way. There was no doubt in the mind of any one that had not this William Goddard crept along the ledge running round both houses and taken the helpless woman out of the burning house that night, she would never have seen the dawn of another day.

Before the fire had time to spread beyond the kitchen and Mrs. Crawford's room, help had arrived, and the maids were roused and taken to a place of safety.

When Mrs. Farraday came back she received nearly as great a shock as if she too had been in that threatened room the night before. She loved the gentle, kindly Mrs. Crawford as she loved no other living woman. Her first impulse was to fall on her knees and give thanks that her life had been spared. She kissed and embraced the invalid, and vowed that not to see all the relatives in the world would she ever leave her dear friend alone again.

"Every one is too good to me," said Mrs. Crawford, kissing the other woman, with tears in her eyes; "and, for all we know to the contrary, the terror of last night may have been designed by Heaven for my good only."

"Your good only! How could such an awful fright and such awful suffering have been only for your good? You are not one who needs to be made pious by terror. You are a saint!"

"Hush! Do not say such a foolish thing, Mrs. Farraday. I am nothing of the kind. I am only weak clay. But I was not speaking of spiritual benefits, but of bodily."

"Bodily benefits! Why, I wonder you did not die. If I had gone through what you suffered last night I do believe I should lose the use of my reason."

"And, owing to the fright I got last night, I have recovered the use of my limbs. Look!"

And she rose and walked across the room.

"Merciful Heavens!" cried the other. "This is indeed a miracle!"

The house in which the fire had occurred was Mrs. Crawford's own property, so she did not leave it, but had the requisite repairs done while continuing to occupy it. The widow now no longer required a room on the first floor. She was able to go up and down stairs. She could not walk so fast or so far as before the day her husband was carried in dead, but for all the purposes of her household she was as efficient as ever. The very fact that she was obliged to walk more slowly than other women added a new gentleness, a new charm to her graciousness. Her gratitude for deliverance from the fire and the thraldom of her wearying disease added a fresh softness to her smile and manner. It seemed as though youth had been restored to her. The whole world was beautiful to her, because it had been given back to her after she had made up her mind she should see it no more. All the people she met were her friends; for had not one of them snatched her from death, and restored her to the holy brotherhood of mankind?

And what more natural than that among all the brotherhood of mankind she should look with most favour and gratitude on the man who had risked his life for hers, and restored her again to intimacies with the sunshine and the birds and the flowers?

That surely was enough for one man to do for any mortal.

But this man had done more for her. He had performed a miracle, wrought a charm. Doctors might say it was the shock which had cured her. All she knew was that when she lay there in the throes of death she had been helpless, that she had been helpless for years; that he came and snatched her from the choking deadly vapour, and that when she awoke to consciousness she was healed.

She had no more thought of love or marriage then than she had of wearing the Queen of England's crown.

But William Goddard had thoughts of marriage, and although he fancied he managed very skilfully to hide his designs, they were plain enough to Mrs. Farraday long before he did more than offer what might pass for considerate courtesies to Mrs. Crawford.

It was not without pain that Mrs. Crawford found she had no longer any need of Mrs. Farraday. But the pain was more than compensated for by the invigorating knowledge that she who had been a helpless invalid was now able to look after her own house. It is doubtful if she would ever have been able to suggest the idea of her companion's leaving. But the other woman began by seeing that she was not wanted, and ended by feeling that she was in the way. Accordingly, she anticipated what she perceived to be inevitable, and dismissed herself. She was sincerely attached to the amiable woman with whom she had lived so long, and whom no one could know well without loving dearly. But she felt it would be an injustice for her to tarry longer; and besides, she had duties of her own to look after in Rochester, for her brother living there had just lost his wife, and had asked her to come to him and keep house for him and look after his little children.

"If ever you have any need of me, you know where to send; and although I suppose I must consider myself as belonging to my brother, I will come to you for all the time I can. I hope and trust and pray that your health may never make you want any one in the house such as I have been. Who knows but you may soon find a more suitable *companion* than I could ever make."

The other blushed like a girl, and said:

"You are very, very kind, and you must come to see me often. Rochester is not so far away."

"No, not so far. I will come, you may be sure."

They embraced and kissed and wept; and so these two good women parted with mutual love and respect.

By this time William Goddard's attentions had become unmistakable. Mrs. Crawford could not deny that something was going on between her and her hero, her rescuer, the quiet-mannered, low-voiced, kind-hearted man who lived next door.

Mrs. Crawford was as simple as a child. She had not married her first husband for love. She married him because he had asked her and had treated her with respectful admiration and with a kind of rough gallantry, and, above all, because her father had told her that if she did marry Thomas Crawford it would relieve him of dire distress and put him on the high road to fortune. But, alas! for him, although he was somewhat relieved by Crawford on his marriage with Ellen, he never touched fortune. There was nothing like buying the girl on Crawford's side or compulsion on the father's. The girl was heart-whole and fancy-free, and would have laid down her life for her father.

She had never, in the romantic sense of the phrase, loved her husband; but from the day she was married until he died he was the first of all men in her consideration and esteem. She did her duty by him to the utmost of her power without having any irksome feeling of duty. He was a good, kind, indulgent husband--a man who, although hard in business, was amiable and good-natured at home, and who had aroused her enthusiastic gratitude, not by what he gave her, but by the services he had willingly rendered her father.

We read little of such lives in books. No doubt the beauty and sacredness that inhabit them make writers loth to invade their holy peace.

CHAPTER XV
HOW WILLIAM GODDARD
CHANGED HIS NAME

This gentle woman, who had long since left youth behind her, was experiencing for the first time the influence of romantic love. She was in her forty-seventh year, a widow who had been a faithful and devoted wife, and yet her heart was the heart of a girl. The age of passion was passed. The fact that up to the time of her marriage she had had no sweetheart, had never once found her heart dwelling on any young man of her acquaintance, may prove that she was never capable of the passion of love. There was at present no passion in her soul. But the overpowering and self-annihilating sentiment of love filled her now, and for the first time in her life she felt that she lived.

With her, as in all true love worthy of the name, she wished to get nothing; the desire, the insatiable desire, to give was paramount, with no rival feeling near its throne. There was no coquetry of concealment in her words or manner. When this man asked her to be his wife she took him tenderly by the hand and placed before him all the reasons why she was not worthy of him.

She was, she told him, older than he by many years. She was a widow. She had suffered long ill-health, was not now quite recovered, and had been cautioned by the doctors that her extraordinary respite from helplessness might be ended any moment. She could never hope to be an active woman again. She could not go about with him as his wife should. He was a young man. A man of five-and-thirty was young enough to marry a girl thirty years younger than she was. He had told her he had found a wonderful plant in South America, a plant which would yield a fibre of inestimable value, a fibre that one day might be expected to supersede cotton and wool. He had told her that as soon as he had secured his patent and got up a company he should be one of the richest men in England, in the world. Why should he, whose star was rising, link himself to her, whose star was sinking fast, who could not hope to live very long, and who must not expect that even the short span allowed to her would be unbroken by a return of infirmity and helplessness? If he wanted money to carry out his great scheme, if he wanted not to share the harvest of his discovery with strangers, she was not without means, and every penny she could command was most heartily and humbly at his service.

He listened to her without any show of impatience, without a single interruption. When she had done he went on as though she had said nothing.

"I have everything on earth I want but one, and that one is more important to my happiness than all the rest put together. I want you for my wife. Will you marry me, Nellie?"

She smiled, and gazed at him out of eyes that told him he was unspeakably dear to her. "If you will have me you may," she said, and smiled again. Her husband had never in all their joint lives called her anything but Ellen. It touched her tender and confiding heart to be, as it were, drawn by that dear and familiar form of her name into the heart and nature of this man.

"I must and will," he said, and kissed her.

"If you care for me," she said, taking one of his hands in both her own, "I am yours to take by reason of my love for you, and by reason of your having restored my life when I had given it up. When I gave it up it was no longer mine. It became yours when you gave it back to me. What is left of it is yours, and everything else I have. Even my very name must be yours if you claim me."

"I do claim you, and no power on earth shall take you from me."

"Or you from me?"

"Or me from you, I swear."

He kissed her again. That was the betrothal.

There was nothing violent in the scene. Except for the two kisses and the beautiful light in the eyes of the woman and the clasping hands, any one seeing it and hearing nothing would have had no reason to suspect that it was a love scene. He was calm, firm, persistent, grave. He did not smile once. He indulged in no heroics, no extravagances, no transports. She admired him all the more for this. Anything of the kind would have been out of place, shocking. She was no young girl, to be won by rhapsodies or carried away by transports. She knew that although her youth had left her all her good looks were not yet gone. But he never said a word about her beauty. He was too sensible, and too noble, and too chivalrous, she told herself, to think she, a woman of forty-seven and in weak health, could be pleased by flippant flattery.

They sat hand in hand for a while, she in a dream of contented happiness. To her this was not the aftermath of love gathered off an autumn land; it was the first growth, which had never come above the soil until now, because no sun had shone on the field before.

There came no let or hindrance in the course of William Goddard's wooing. He had only been a few months in Richmond, but during that time his conduct there had been above reproach. At first, it is true, he had not been a regular attendant at church on Sunday. He had gone now and then, but not every Sabbath. From the beginning of his love-making he never missed the forenoon, and often attended the evening, services. He kept much to himself, and made no friends. He was a strict teetotaler, and frequented no such profitless places as clubs or billiard-rooms. When people heard of the engagement between Mrs. Crawford and William Goddard they said she was a lucky woman, and that her second husband would be even better, if such a thing were possible, than her first. If there had been in the whole town a rumour to his disadvantage it would have swelled into a howl, for those who knew the gentle widow felt a personal interest in her, a love for her, as though she had been a mother or sister.

When Mrs. Farraday went finally to take the head of her brother's (Edward Chatterton's) house at Rochester she naturally told him all the news of Richmond, of the fire, the rescue, the love-making, the engagement or understanding between the widow and the heroic next-door lodger. She told him everything she knew, and minutely described the two people and the two houses.

Her brother seemed interested. He was a florid, well conditioned, good-humoured, shrewd man of fifty, not averse from gossip in the evening when he sat in front of his own fire, with his legs stretched out before him, smoking his pipe.

"What is known of this man? You say he has been only a few months in Richmond?"

"That is all. I believe he has spent most of his life in South America. For a while he was in a gold mine, and he was for a while a farmer, I think."

"And what brought him back to England? South America is a fine place--that is, parts of it--if you are any good and have an opening. What did he come back to England for? Has he made his fortune?"

"I don't think he has made his fortune. He is not an old man, not even middle-aged. He is almost young--not more than thirty-five or so."

"Then *why* did he come back, and what is he losing months of his time in England for--at his time of life, too, when he ought to be working his hardest?"

"I don't know exactly. I think he has found some plant in the llanos out of which he can make cloth, and has come over about starting a company and taking out a patent. He says the plant is more valuable than flax or wool or cotton."

"Or all together?"

"Yes, I think he said that, but I am not sure. I haven't a good memory for this sort of thing."

"Kitty?"

"Well?"

"I have a fixed idea that every man who wants to take out a patent and start a company, and is months about the job, is either a born idiot or a consummate rogue. I have a very poor opinion of this Mr. Crawford Number Two."

"Good gracious, John! aren't you very hard on a man you never saw?"

He nodded his head gravely at the fire, but took no other notice of her question. He puffed at his pipe a minute in silence, blowing the smoke straight out in front of him, as if in pursuit of some design. Then he took his pipe out of his mouth with one hand, waved away the banks of smoke lying before him with the other, and turning round to her, said:

"And, Kitty, I should not be at all surprised to find that he set fire to the house and then rescued the fool of a woman for reasons best known to himself."

Mrs. Farraday started to her feet aghast.

"Do you know, John, that you are saying the most awful things a man could say? You horrify me!"

"I mean," he went on, looking once more lazily into the fire, "that I think he set fire to the house and rescued the woman in order that he might have a claim upon her, and that he doesn't care a ---- for her, and that all he wants, or ever thought of, is her money."

"John, you do not know the man, and it is shameful of you to say such things, and you could be put in prison for saying them; and then to think of your calling the dearest creature alive 'that fool of a woman,' is worse than any libel you could speak of think of!"

The tears were in Mrs. Farraday's eyes, and she could hardly command her voice.

"Think over the matter. He knows this fool of a woman is a helpless invalid. He knows from you that you are coming here. He learns from you that there are two strange servants who sleep in the top of the house; and on the very night you are away, and the first night for years this elderly woman is sleeping alone, the house next door to which he lives takes fire; the kitchen over which she sleeps takes fire, and there is a great smell of paraffin oil in the place, although no one knew of any being in the house. And lo and behold you! when the woman is just dead, he comes, bursts in her window, and rescues her, and makes love to this well-off invalid woman--he who has come back to England at the age of thirty-five, without a fortune, and with a cock-and-bull story about a patent and a fibre."

"Good-night. I will listen to no more such awful talk."

"Good-night, Kitty; yet, take my word for it, he set fire to that house."

But then, as Mrs. Farraday had remarked, her brother did not know the man; nor, moreover, did he live at Richmond.

No one suggested that there was any reason for delaying the marriage between Goddard and the widow. He had not yet secured his patent, and therefore could not start his company. Now and then he had to go up to London for a day or two to see the artificers who were carrying out his designs for the machines to be employed in converting his plant into cloth. When he returned to Singleton Terrace after these brief absences, he made up for lost time by increased tenderness and devotion.

He never came back empty-handed, and he never brought any splendid present; always a book, or a bouquet, or a basket of fruit--nothing more. He had bought her a ring, of course; but even that was inexpensive and simple--three small diamonds in a plain gold band.

"I shall be poor, Nellie, until I am rich; and I shall not be rich in money until my patent and my company are all right."

"But when you get your patent and your company, you will not want to go away again to America?" she asked anxiously. "I do not think I could face so long a voyage."

"O, no! There will be no need for me to go out again. I have all arranged over there. I have an intelligent and energetic agent there. I will remain at home attending to the interests of the company (of which I shall, of course, be chairman), and hunting up markets for my fibre. We shall very likely have to leave this place and live in town, take a good house in Bayswater or Kensington, for we must do a little entertaining. You would not mind changing Richmond for Bayswater or Kensington?"

"Nothing could please me better than to be of any use I can to you; and if my health keeps good, as good as it is now, I could manage the entertaining very well indeed."

"You grow stronger every day. I have not a particle of fear on the score of your health. I dare not have any fear of that, Nellie. You must not even refer to such a thing again. When we have taken that new place I lay you a bunch of roses you will dance at our house-warming, ay, out-dance all the young girls in the place."

She sighed, and took one of his hands in both hers and smiled. She had never dreamed of a lover, but if she had dreamed of one in her latter years he surely would be such a one as this. How sensible and considerate and affectionate he was! If he had been more ardent, more enthusiastic, she might fear his displays were insincere, that although he loved her then, he would tire of her soon after they were married, and, she being so much older than he, take his ardours and transports to the feet of younger and more beautiful goddesses.

But with such as he there could be no such fear. Raptures might please a girl, and be excused in a young man towards a girl, but from any man to her they would be absurd and repulsive. It would be impossible to believe them sincere, and the mere idea that a lover's words and actions were not the outcome of candid feeling would be shocking, destructive of all sympathy and self-respect.

But William, her William, as she now called him, was perfect in all he said and all he did; and of one thing she felt quite sure: that if ever a cloud came between them in their married life, it would arise from some defect in her nature, not in his.

When old Crawford made his will a couple of years before his death he did not wish to place any restraint upon her as to marriage after he had gone, except that she was to keep his name. He had made all his money himself; he had worked hard for it, allowing himself no luxuries and little comfort for the best part of life, and deferring marriage until he was well on in years and had given up active business. He had no child, no relative he knew of in the world. He would have welcomed a son with joy. Nothing would have pleased him more than to think that the name which he had raised up out of poverty into modest affluence would survive and flourish when he was no more.

But a son was denied to him. All hope of an heir was gone. He loved his wife in his own way, and he would not fetter her future with an imposed lifelong widowhood. She was to be left free to wed again if her choice lay that way. She had been a true and tender wife to him, the one source of peaceful happiness in his old age. She should not feel the dead hand of a niggard; she should have all his money, but she should keep his name. His name should not die out wholly even when she ceased to be. He should leave her all the income from his property for her life, or as long as she retained the name he had given her. If she changed that name the name should not die. His money should go to Guy's Hospital, and be known, while that great handmaiden of the sick poor survived, as the Crawford Bequest. When she followed him to the grave the money should go finally to the hospital, and be of bounteous service to the indigent sick and a perpetual living monument to his name.

"Mrs. Crawford," said Mr. Brereton, her lawyer, when he came to draw up the necessary documents in connection with the marriage of the widow and Goddard, "has only a life interest in the estate. It goes to Guy's Hospital upon her death."

"Is it necessary for us to take further into consideration that remote and most melancholy contingency?" asked Goddard.

"No, no," said Mr. Brereton hastily. "But business is business, and I thought it only right to mention the matter to you."

Goddard merely bowed, as though dismissing the horrible thought from amongst them.

Goddard settled upon her ten thousand pounds.

"I did not know you had so much money, William," said she, "but surely it is a waste of law expenses to settle anything on me? In the course of nature, even if I were not ailing, I must go first."

When he told her of the settlement he had made they were alone.

"I haven't the money now, but it will come as a first charge on my general estate when the company is floated. As to my outliving you, we do not know. Who can tell? It is well always to be prepared for the unforeseen, the unforeseeable. And as to which of us shall live the longer, let us speak or think no more of that. Let us tell ourselves that such a consideration belongs to the remote future. Let us devote ourselves to the happy"--he kissed her--"happy present."

At the time William Crawford, lately William Goddard, returned from his first visit to Welford they had been about three months married, and Mrs. Crawford's old affliction had gradually been stealing back upon her.

CHAPTER XVI
AT PLAY

When Francis Bramwell, on the morning Crawford left Welford for Richmond, found himself with little Freddie in his arms inside the gate of the timber-yard he set the child down, and having closed the gate, fetched little Frank out of the cottage.

The two children ran to one another. If they had been girls they would have kissed; being boys, they had things too weighty on their minds to allow of wasting time over such a frivolous and useless thing as kissing.

"Come into the van," cried Frank, leading the way at a trot to the old wheelless barrow.

"It's not a van, but a boat," said Freddie, as they scrambled into it.

"It's a van," said the host, who was dark and small, and wiry; while the other was tall and fair, and rounded. "Look at the horse," pointing between the shafts or handles at nothing.

"But a boat has a horse, too," cried Freddie, "and this is a boat. Look at the smoke coming up the funnel!" He held his arm erect to do duty as a funnel.

"It's a van and a boat together," said Frank, trying to compromise matters in any way so that they might get on, and not keep vegetating there all day.

"But if it's a van," said Freddie, lowering the funnel, "it will sink in the water, and we shall get drowned in the canal; and I'm not allowed to get drowned. Aunt Hetty says I mustn't, and Mrs. Grainger says I can't, for it is only dead dogs that get drowned in the canal." Freddie knew more about boats and the canal than he did about vans. They had lived near the canal before coming to their new house.

Frank, on the other hand, knew very little of boats or canals. "Well, let us play it's an elephant," suggested he, making a second attempt to arrange matters and get to work. Time was being wasted in a barren academic dispute, and time was precious.

"But you can't get into an elephant."

"Well, a whale." He was desperate, and drew on his memory of a Scripture story-book with coloured plates.

"What's a whale?" Freddie's library did not contain that book.

"A great big fish, with a roar as big as a steamboat whistle." Frank was combining imagination and experience of a voyage across the Atlantic.

"Hurrah!" cried Freddie wildly. "It's a steamboat; and I'm the man that whistles," and he uttered a shrill scream.

"We're off!" shouted the other boy, frantically seizing his cap and waving it like mad. The fact that you ought to shriek, and shriek frequently, when playing at steamboat, and that there was no satisfactory precedent for shrieking when you were in a whale's inside, overcame Frank completely, and he at once handselled his new craft with a shriek of overwhelming vigour and piercing force.

Bramwell leaned against a wall at the further end of the yard, and watched the children at play. He had no fear or concern for their safety. No danger could befall them here; the walls were high, and he had seen that the doors were firm and secure. He was experiencing the birth of a new life. Every word and shout and cry of his boy seemed to put fresh strength and motive into his body and brain.

A week ago he had had absolutely nothing to live for.

Now he was gradually recovering the zest of life. He felt that he had not only to eat and breathe, but to work and plan as well. He had regarded that islet as a graveyard, and that cottage as a tomb. The islet had now become the playground of his child, and the cottage the home and sanctuary of his boy.

A week ago he had had nothing to think of but his miserable and wrecked self. Now he had nothing to think of but his young and innocent and beautiful son. Himself and his own wretched life had died and been buried, and from the ashes of his dead self had risen the child full of youth and health and vital comeliness.

A week ago he had felt old beyond the mortal span of man, and worn beyond the thought of struggle, almost beyond the power of endurance. Now he felt less old than his years, with dexterity and strength for the defence of his child, an irresistible athlete.

He had not begun to plan for the future yet, but plans seemed easy when he should will to consider them. His spirit was in a tumult of delight and anticipation. He did not care to define his thoughts, and he could not express them in words. He had been raised from a vault to a hilltop; and the magnificence and splendour of the prospect overcame him with joy. He sat upon his pinnacle, satisfied with the sense of enlargement and air. He knew that what he contemplated was made up of details, but he had no eye for detail now. It would be time enough to examine later. The vast flat horizon and the boundless blue above his head, and the intoxicating lightness and purity of the atmosphere, were all that he took heed of now.

A week ago the present had been a dull, dark, straight, unsheltered road, leading nowhere, with no spot of interest, no resting-place, no change of light. His thoughts had been an agony to him. The present then weighed him down like a cope of lead. To-day he dallied in a land of gardens and vineyards, and arbours and fountains, and streams and lakes, and statues and temples, where the air was heavy with perfumes and rich with the waverings of melodious song. Through this land he would wander for a while, healing his tired eyes with the sight of the trees and the flowers and the temples, soothing his weary travel-worn feet with the delicious coolness of the water of the streams, and drinking in through his hungry ears the voices of the birds and the tones of the harpists and the words of the unseen singers in the green alleys and marble fanes.

He had eschewed poetry as an art; he was enjoying it now as a gift.

At last he awoke from his reverie, shook himself, and went up to the old barrow, in which the children were still playing with unabated vigour.

"Well," he said, "where is the steamboat going now?"

"'Tisn't a steamboat now," said Freddie, who was the more ready and free of speech; "it's a gas-house, and I'm charging the retorts. Frank never saw them charging the retorts, but I did often with my father."

"Then Frank shall go one day and see."

"I'll take him," said Freddie, "I know Mr. Grainger and nearly all the men. When they draw the retorts they throw water on the coke, and then such steam! Aunt Hetty won't let me throw water on the fire. If she did, I could make as good steam as the men, and then we'd have plenty of gas. Shouldn't we?"

"Plenty, indeed. It seems to me your Aunt Hetty is very good to you."

"Sometimes," said the boy cautiously. "But she won't let me make gas. Mrs. Grainger let me throw some water on the fire last night before I went to bed."

"And did you get any gas?"

"Lots, only it all went up the chimney and about the kitchen; and there are no pipes for it in our new house. There were in the old house. If you haven't pipes there's no use in making gas, for it gets wet and won't burn. Have you pipes?"

"No."

"If you had pipes I'd make some for you. They make tar at the works, too."

"Indeed!"

"I can make tar."

"Can you? And how do you make tar, Freddie?"

"With water, and blacklead and soap. Only Aunt Hetty won't let me. I'll show Frank how to make tar."

"I'd be very much obliged to you if you would."

"I can make lots of things, and I'll show Frank how to make all of them. Have you got a cat?"

"I'm sorry to say we have not. Perhaps you could make one for us?"

"Make a cat! No; I couldn't. Nobody could make a cat."

"Why not?"

"Because they scrape you awfully. We had a cat in the other house, and we took it to this house and it ran away, and Mrs. Grainger says it will never come back. And it needn't have run away, because when I grow big I am going to fish in the canal and catch fish for it. Cats like fish."

"And can you make fish?"

"I never tried. The water in our house is clean water, and no use for making fish. You can only make fish out of canal water."

"O, I see."

"Have you a canary?"

"No."

"We had; but Jack, that was our cat's name, ate the canary's head off, and then he couldn't fly, although his wings were all right. Jack never ate his wings. I think Jack is gone back to eat the wings."

"He must have been a wicked cat to eat the poor bird!"

"No, he wasn't wicked, for he was all black except his nose, and that was white; and Mrs. Grainger says a black cat isn't wicked when he has a white nose."

"And did you cry when Jack went away?"

"No, I didn't; but I often cried when we had him, for he used to scrape me when I wanted to make a horse or him to tow my Noah's ark."

"And did you ever get him to tow it?"

"Only once, and then he towed it only a little bit. And then he jumped out of the window with it, and we could not find my Noah's ark ever again. And father said he must have eaten the Noah's ark as well as the canary, and that was how he got his nails!"

"But he scraped you before he ate your ark?"

"Yes, but there was a toy-shop near our other house, and Jack would steal anything. I told Mrs. Grainger, and she said that she once knew a toy-shop cat, and the toy-shop people gave it away, and it wouldn't eat anything but monkeys on sticks and hairy lambs, and the people had to choke it, as they were too poor to get it its proper food."

"Mrs. Grainger seems to be a very remarkable person."

"She isn't; she's Mr. Grainger's wife. Grainger has no clothes on him when he's at the works, and Mrs. Grainger has a wart on her forehead. Mrs. Grainger told me the reason Mr. Grainger doesn't wear any clothes, or hardly any, when he's at the works is because he's so proud of his skin; he doesn't wear suspenders, but keeps his trousers up with a belt when he's not at the works. But at home, you would think he's an African black; but Mrs. Grainger says he isn't. Father gives Mrs. Grainger his old boots----"

"That is very good of your father."

"When they're worn out."

"Well, is the retort charged?"

All this time the boy was working hard at filling an imaginary scoop with coal, and pouring the coal from it into imaginary retorts. Frank was sitting on the edge of the barrow watching him intently.

"O, yes. They're all charged now."

"Well, I must leave you for a little while. You will be good boys when I am away. Take care of yourselves."

"O, yes!"

"And, Freddie, you will teach Frank to be a good boy?"

"Oh, yes, I'll teach him that, too! But I must have a book."

"Must have a book? You don't mean to say you know how to read?"

"No, but the way to be a good boy is to sit down on a chair at a table and look at pictures in a book. I hate books. Frank, it's Noah's ark now and we're the beasts."

The man moved away, and entered the cottage. He felt elated to an extraordinary degree.

For more than two years he had been dwelling alone with blighting memories. Yesterday and to-day he was experiencing sensations. Something was now entering his life. Formerly everything had been going out, going out from a life already empty.

That day he had been confused and put out by so simple a thing as that girl's invitation to spend an hour in a house not a hundred yards from his own. It was the first invitation of the kind he had received since his voluntary exile from the world. The world had been dead to him. He had almost forgotten there was such a state of existence as that in which ordinary people live. All his own experience seemed no more real than the memory of a dream, out of which the light and colour were fading slowly but surely.

The invitation to Crawford's House had for him made the fading half-forgotten world spring out of its dim retirement into light before his eyes. It suddenly forced upon his mind the fact that there were bright and happy people still moving about in the streets and fields. She, for instance, the girl who had spoken to him, was bright and seemed happy; very bright and very happy, now that he recalled her face and words and manner.

There were thousands in the world as bright and happy as she. Thousands, nay, millions.

Were there millions in the world as bright and happy as she? Hardly; for she was as bright a being as he had ever met in his life. No doubt he thought this because hers was the first sunny face of woman he had seen for a long time. For a time, that looking back now seemed immemorial: he had been dwelling in the gloomy caverns of Pluto; the voice of his boy called him forth from the hideous bowels of the earth, and, lo! no sooner did he emerge from darkness than the first being he saw was this Hebe.

But stay! What was this she had said to him? He had been confused and dull-headed at the time. She had confused him by asking him to do her a favour. Of late he had not been asked by any one to grant a favour. He had lost all intercourse with gracious ways.

O, yes! he remembered now. She had invited him to go over and spend an hour with her brother. And what folly! he had promised. He must have been stupid when he told her he would go. Why, if he went, who would mind Frank? The child could not be left in the cottage by himself.

In due time, Mrs. Grainger, whose services had been engaged for that day, called for young Freddie. Bramwell bore the boy along the stage and placed him gently in that good woman's arms. While crossing the bay he left Frank in the timber-yard; but when he came back he took his own son in his arms and carried him into the cottage.

CHAPTER XVII
THE POSTMAN'S HAIL

What had formerly been the dwelling of the foreman of Boland's Ait consisted of four rooms, all on the ground floor. It stood at the southern extremity of the islet, the end windows looking south, in the direction of Camberwell. There were three of these windows: one in what had been the kitchen, now used by Bramwell as a sitting-room, dining-room and study; another in what had been the sitting-room, now empty; and one in what had been and was a bedroom. The present study and the room now unfurnished ran right through the cottage, were oblong, and comparatively large. The room used as a bedroom was small, being only half the depth of the cottage and the same width as the study and empty room, and only half the length. The other half of the length was occupied by what had been a bedroom, now used by Bramwell as a kitchen.

There was no passage in the house. The door from the study opened directly upon an open space lying between the cottage and the old sawmill. Out of the study a door opened into the unfurnished room, and from that one door opened into the kitchen, another into the bedroom. Thus the two larger rooms ran side by side from north to south, and the two smaller, each being half the size of one of the larger, lay at the western end.

Up to this time Bramwell had spent nearly all his waking hours in the study. Now and then he went into the yard, and there, concealed from observation, walked up and down for exercise. Once in a month, perhaps, he left the islet to buy something he needed. Otherwise he lived in the study from month's end to month's end, retiring to the bedroom to rest, when sleep overcame him, far in the night.

This was the last day of May. The sun had risen in a cloudless sky, and shone out of a heaven of nameless blue from dawn to dusk.

When Bramwell entered the cottage with his boy in his arms it was getting late in the afternoon. The Layards did not breakfast early, and Hetty and the boy had dinner at three o'clock. It was to assist at that indispensable function that Freddie had been recalled from the timber-yard. Bramwell had not thought of dinner until Mrs. Grainger had summoned Freddie to his. Then the father was seized with sudden panic at his own forgetfulness, and the possible peril to his son's life. He knew from books that young children should eat more frequently than grown-up people; but whether a child of his son's age should be fed every hour, or every two hours, or every half-hour, or every four, he could not decide. In the kitchen was an oil-stove which he had taught himself to manage. Mrs. Treleaven left everything ready for dinner on a small tray. All he had to do was to light his stove and wait half-an-hour, and dinner would be ready for him and the child. A tray stood on the kitchen table, and on the tray all things necessary for the meal, saving such as were awaiting the genial offices of the stove.

Mrs. Treleaven never carried that tray to the study. She had orders not to do so, lest she might reduce the papers on the table to irretrievable confusion.

There was the half-hour to wait, and Bramwell, having ascertained by inquiry that the boy was in no immediate danger of death from hunger, cast about him to find something to do which would fill up the time and interest Frank, who was hot and tired after his harassing labours in the yard.

"It is fine to-day," he thought, "but it will not be fine every day, all the year round. On the wet days, and in the winter, where are Frank and Freddie to play? In this room, of course." He went into the empty one next his own. "Here they will be under cover, and will not interfere with my work. I can look in on them now and then, and in case they want me I shall be near at hand."

"Frank," said he aloud to the child, "I shall make this room into a play-room for you."

"What's a play-room?" asked the boy. He had had no experience of any kind of life but that spent in poor lodgings.

"Where you and little Freddie can play if the weather is wet or cold."

"And may we bring in our steamboat?" asked the boy anxiously.

"We shall see about that. You would like a ball to play with in this room and in the yard?"

"O, yes! I have a ball at home."

"Frank, my boy, this is your home. You are to live here now. You are not going back."

"But I want my ball, and I want mother."

"You shall have a ball; but your mother is gone away for ever."

"Will the ball be all red and blue?" His own had been dull white, unrelieved by colour.

"I think so," said the father gravely, and grateful for the suggestion contained in the boy's words. He had forgotten that splendid balls such as are never used in fives, or tennis, or cricket, or racket could be got in the toy-shops.

The boy was satisfied.

Then Bramwell took a brush and began sweeping the empty room with great vigour and determination, chatting all the while to the boy about the wonderful adventures encountered by Frank and Freddie that day in their many journeys by sea and land.

By the time the room was swept the dinner was ready, and Bramwell, who had learned to wait upon himself, carried in the tray, cleared away half the table of papers, spread the folded-up cloth, and the two sat down.

Moment by moment the father was waking up to a sense of his new position. He felt already a great change in the conditions of his life. He was no longer free to read and muse all day long, eating his solitary meals when he pleased. He must now adopt some sort of regularity in his management. The hours of breakfast, dinner, and tea should be fixed; and it would be advisable to tell Mrs. Treleaven to bring all things necessary and advantageous for children Mrs. Treleaven had a large family, and would know what was proper to be done.

When dinner was over, he gave Frank the run of the house, carried the tray back to the kitchen, and sat down in his chair to think.

Yes, he should have to work now in earnest. He would no longer dawdle away his time in fancying he was preparing for the beginning. He would begin at once. He should add to his income by his pen. When he had more money than he needed years ago, he had always told himself that he would write a book--books. Now, perhaps, he could hardly spare time for so long an undertaking as a book. He should write articles, essays, poems, perhaps; anything to which he could turn his hand, and which would bring in money.

The change of name he had adopted two years ago would be convenient. He had then used it to obliterate his identity; he should now use it to establish a new identity. He had no practical experience of writing for magazines or newspapers, but he believed many men made good incomes by the pen of an occasional contributor. Of course, he could take no permanent appointment, even if one offered, for it would separate him from his boy.

The afternoon glided into evening. Philip Ray had been at the island every night of late. He was coming again this evening.

Between the news of Ainsworth and the arrival of the boy he could not keep away. He was strangely excited and wild. Philip was the best fellow in the world, but very excitable--much too excitable. No doubt he would quiet down in time.

If it should chance Philip met a good, quiet, sensible girl, it would be well for him to marry. The sense of responsibility would steady him. He was one of those men to whom cares would be an advantage. Not cares, of course, in the sense of troubles. Heaven keep Philip from all such miseries! but it would do Philip good to be obliged to share his confidences and his thoughts with a prudent woman whom he loved, and upon whose disinterested solicitude for his welfare he could rely.

"Yes; it would be well for Philip, dear, good, unselfish Philip, to marry, even if he and his wife had to pinch and scrape on his small income."

Some one was drawing the stage across the canal. Here was Philip himself.

"I was just thinking of you, Philip," said Bramwell. "I want you to do something for me."

The other looked at him in blank astonishment. This was the first admission for two years made by Bramwell that anything could be done for him.

"What is it?"

He was almost afraid to speak lest he should make the other draw back. He would have done anything on earth for Frank--anything on earth except forgive John Ainsworth, otherwise William Goddard, otherwise William Crawford.

The *aliases* of Mrs. Crawford's husband were known to neither of these men. These two *aliases* were unknown as *aliases* to any one in the world.

"You need not be afraid. It is not anything very dreadful or very difficult."

"If it were impossible and infamous, I'd do it for you, Frank."

"Fortunately it is neither. To-day that little boy came to play with Frank again, and his aunt asked me to go over to-night and chat for an hour with her brother. In a moment of thoughtlessness and confusion I promised to go. Of course I can't, and I want you to walk round and apologise, and explain matters to the aunt and father of Freddie. You see, I would not like to seem rude or inconsiderate. I don't know what I should do if they withdrew their leave from the coming over of their boy."

"But why won't you go?" asked Philip eagerly. "It would do you all the good in the world."

"My dear Philip, I am astonished at you. Out of this place I have not gone into a house for two years."

"So much the more reason why you should go. I suppose you do not intend living the same life now as during those two years?"

"No. I intend making a great change in my manner of life. But I can't do it all at once, you know."

"But surely there is nothing so terrible in spending an hour with a neighbour. That would seem to me the very way of all others in which you might break the ice most easily. Do go."

"I can't, for two reasons."

"When a man says he has two reasons, one of them is always insincere. He advances it merely as a blind. The likelihood is that both those he gives are insincere, and that he keeps back the real one. What are your two reasons for not going?" Ray did not say this in bitterness, but in supposed joy. It delighted him beyond measure to see how alert and bright Bramwell's mind had become already after only a few days' contact with the boy. In his inmost heart he had come to believe that his brother-in-law's emancipation from the Cimmerian gloom in which he had dwelt was at hand, and would be complete.

"Which reason would you like to have: my real or invented one? Or would you like both, in order that you may select?" asked Bramwell, with a look of faint amusement.

"Both," said Ray.

"In the first place, Frank can't be left alone."

"I'll stay here and see that he is all right; so that needn't keep you here. Number two?"

"Look at me; am I in visiting trim? and I have no better coat."

"You don't mean to say that *you* care what kind of a coat you wear. This is grossly absurd--pure imposture. It does not weigh the millionth of a grain in my mind. *You* care about your coat?"

"But they may. How can I tell that they are not accustomed to the finest cloth and the latest fashion?"

"And live in that ramshackle old house down that blind alley? O, yes! I am sure they are fearfully stuck-up people. Does the aunt take in washing or make up ladies' own materials? Ladies who look after their brothers' children generally wear blue spectacles or make up ladies' own materials, when they live in a place like Crawford's House."

"Besides, Philip, I'd rather not leave the child behind me. I feel I could not rest there a moment. I should be certain something had happened to him."

"What did I tell you a moment ago about men with two reasons? You see I was right. It wasn't because you won't leave Frank alone, since my offer obviates that, and it wasn't because you aren't clothed in purple and fine linen. Your real reason for not going is a woman's reason--you won't go, because you won't go."

"Well, let it stand at that, if you will."

"But really, Frank, you must change all this."

"I engage to reform, but you do not expect a revolution. You will call and apologise for me, Philip? I can't go, and I don't want to seem ungracious to them. You need only say that when I promised to see them this afternoon I completely forgot that there would be no one here with the boy. Of course, I could not have foreseen your offer to stay with him."

Ray muttered and growled, but on the whole was well satisfied. Bramwell had not been at any time since he came to the islet so lively as this evening. If he progressed at this rate he would soon be as well as ever--ay, better than ever.

He said he would take the message round to Crawford's House.

As he was leaving the room Bramwell said gravely:

"Don't be unkind to little Freddie's aunt, even if she does make up ladies' own materials and wear glasses. All people have not their fate in their own hands."

"Pooh!" cried Ray scornfully, as he disappeared.

Bramwell got up and began pacing the room. Of old he used to sit and brood over the past, when he could no longer busy himself with his papers and books. This evening he walked up and down and thought of the future.

"Now that I recall the girl to my mind, Miss Layard is very beautiful. I do wish Philip would get married. That would get all this murderous vengeance out of his head. A single man may be willing to risk his own neck to avenge a wrong; but a man with a wife whom he loved would think twice before handing himself over to the hangman, and leaving the woman he loved desolate.

"I do hope he will fall in love with this girl. I know his present contempt for the sex, and I know the source from which that contempt springs. But all women are not alike. I have known only my mother and my sister and another, and out of the three, two are the salt of the earth and the glory of Heaven. A good woman is life's best gift, and there are a thousand good women for the one bad. It was my misfortune to--But let me not think of that.

"I know Philip would scout the idea of falling in love and marrying. Two facts now keep him from any chance of love or marriage. First, his revulsion from the whole sex because of the fault of one; and, second, because he does not meet any young girl who might convert him to particular exemption from his general scorn.

"And yet, although I have had little opportunity of judging, for I saw this girl only twice, perhaps she is not exactly the kind of wife that would be best for him. She is bright and gay, and beautiful enough, in all conscience. What a brilliant picture she made at that window! I seem to see her now more distinctly than I did at the time. There is such a thing as the collodion of the eye. And now that I think of the day, of the time she brought down the little fellow to the brink of the bay and handed him to me, how charming she looked! There was such colour in her face and hair, and such light in her eyes, and her voice is so clear and sympathetic! Ah, there are many, many, many good women in the world who are beautiful, supremely beautiful also, and she, I am sure, is one of them!

"But I fancy the wife for Philip ought to be more sedate. He is too excitable, and this Miss Layard is bright and quick. His excitement almost invariably takes a gloomy turn; hers, I should fancy, a gay direction. They would be fire and tow to one another. He ought to marry a woman of calm and sober mind, and she a man of sad and melancholy disposition like----"

He did not finish the sentence, even in his mind. He had almost said "like me."

"No, I don't think she would be the wife for him. But there! How calmly and solemnly I am disposing of the fate of two people! I had better do that thing which our race are so noted for doing well--mind my own business."

His meditations were broken in upon by a voice hailing the island from the tow-path.

"Boland's Ait, ahoy!" sang the voice.

Bramwell rose and left the cottage by the door from the study. Abroad it was growing dark. "Philip has been gone a long time," he thought. "But this cannot be he, for he knows how to come over."

In the dusk he saw a man on the opposite side of the canal, with a canvas bag thrown over his shoulder. The man wore a peaked cap, and was in uniform.

"A newspaper for you, Mr. Bramwell," sang out the man.

Bramwell, in great surprise, hastened to the floating stage, and, seizing the chain, pulled the stage athwart the water.

He took the newspaper from the postman's hand. It was too dark to read the superscription.

He hastened back to the study, where the lamp was burning.

He examined the cover in the light of the lamp.

He could not recognise the writing. He had never seen it before.

He broke the cover and spread the paper out before him. It was a copy of the *Daily Telegraph*, dated that day.

On the front page a place was marked. It was in the column devoted to births, marriages, and deaths. The mark was against an item among the deaths.

With a shudder and a sick feeling of sinking, he read:

"On the 28th inst., at her residence, London, Kate, wife of Francis Mellor (*née* Ray), late of Greenfield, near Beechley, Sussex."

He raised his head slowly from the table, threw himself into a chair, and burst into a passion of tears and sobs.

CHAPTER XVIII
PRIVATE THEATRICALS

While the owner of Boland's Ait was weeping over the brief announcement of his wife's death in the newspaper, the owner of a house in Singleton Terrace, Richmond, was sitting in his wife's drawing-room in a comfortable easy-chair, reading a novel. Mrs. Crawford, in her invalid's wheeled chair, sat at the other side of the table, languidly looking over a newspaper.

Mr. Crawford was a model of domestic virtue. He spent most of his time in the house, and the greater part of the hours he was at home were passed in the society of his wife. He did not drink, or smoke, or swear, or indulge in any other vice--in Richmond. As to gambling, or anything worse, the good people of the town would as soon think of hearing the rector accused of such practices. He went to church once on Sunday regularly; but made not the least claim to piety, not to say anything of godliness. The few claims that charity or religion had made upon his purse had been responded to with alacrity and modest gifts; but the most censorious could not accuse him of ostentation.

In fact there was a complete absence of anything approaching ostentation in the man. He seemed to care nothing for society, except the society of his elderly ailing wife. The conduct of the man was inexpressibly meritorious. He afforded many estimable matrons with an exemplar of what a good husband ought to be.

"*He* never goes out anywhere," they said. "He does not even want company at his own house (though that is not only harmless, but advantageous), for the society of the woman he loves is enough for *him*. Of course, he has to go up to town every now and then to see the workmen who are preparing his wonderful machine for making cotton out of dock-leaves, or something of that kind; but, then, that is only for a day, and when he returns does he come empty-handed? Not he! He always thinks of his wife even in the little while he is away, and brings her some pretty present to show his love. Ah, if every husband were only like *him!*"

Of course, an inventor who is taking out a patent and getting models of machinery made must often see the artificers employed, and before, as well as after, his marriage, Crawford ran up to London for one day in the week; that is, he went up on the evening of one day, and returned in the morning of the next. Indeed, it was not, when put together, quite a whole day of four-and-twenty hours; for he did not leave until late in the afternoon, and was back next morning.

Now, an inventor is known to be a dreadful bore, for he is always trying to explain how the machine works, and no woman that ever lived could take a particle of interest in machinery, or even understand how one cogwheel moves another, or how a leather band can make an iron wheel revolve. Crawford did not make his house odious with plans of his models and disquisitions on his plans. If you asked him a question he answered it in the most explicit and kindest manner possible, and said no more about the thing, but told you that the moment it was in working order you should come and see his model at work. The kindness of the man's manner almost made people think they understood him.

On the table between the husband and wife lay a lot of papers, but they had nothing to do with the great invention. They related to the Crawford property in the neighbourhood of the South London Canal. Some of them were in Mr. Blore's handwriting, some of them in Crawford's. Mrs. Crawford had, at her husband's request, been looking over them before taking up the newspaper. She had glanced at the sheets, and when her brief inspection was finished put them down, and, seeing him deeply absorbed in his book, said nothing, but took up the newspaper to look at it, so that he might not think she had been waiting for him.

At last his chapter was finished. He put away his book and glanced across the table. "Well, Nellie, isn't it very extraordinary these people were so backward in paying?"

"It is a little strange," she said with a gentle smile; "but you must not be disheartened by it. They are sure to pay next month." She took up the list of the tenants and ran her eyes over it, that he might not fancy she under-estimated his efforts and anxiety respecting the rents.

"I'll tell you what I think, Nellie. I fancy that, although we issued the circular about my collecting instead of Blore, and although I had full credentials with me, they did not believe they would be quite safe in paying me."

"But they knew you were my husband," she said softly, "did they not? Was not that enough for them? It is more than enough for me." There were infinite confidence and tenderness in her voice and look.

"Of course, dear. But they could not be certain of my identity. How were they to be sure the man who called on them was the William Crawford of the notice. The man who called upon them might be an impostor, who obtained the credentials by fraud. Don't you see?"

"O, yes. That's it. Quite plainly they were afraid to pay you, lest there might be something wrong about you. Fancy something wrong about *you*, William!" and she leaned back in her chair and laughed with her eyes closed, as if the thought was too deliciously droll to be contemplated with open eyes. After a brief period of enjoying the absurdity of these people, she looked at her husband and said, "But I hope you are not angry with those people, William? They are mostly poor and ignorant."

"Angry with them! Good gracious, no! The only thing that put me out was that I could not bring the money home to you, dear."

"But I don't want any money just now."

"You never want anything for yourself, dear," he said in a tone of affectionate admiration; "yet a little money would be very handy at present. We have only a few pounds at the bank."

"But we don't want more than pocket-money until next month. There is nothing of any consequence to pay; the monthly bills have been all settled as usual." It was a great comfort to her to feel that he need not bother himself about anything so insignificant as money.

"Yes, but----" and he paused, and a look of pain and perplexity came over his face. He leaned his elbow on the table and his head upon his hand.

For a moment there was no word spoken, but a dull, heavy, low, continuous noise filled the room.

The noise ceased, and then her infinitely sympathetic voice said, "Dear, what is it?"

She was at his side. She had wheeled her invalid's chair round to him and had taken his hand in hers.

"Those workmen," he said. "They have swallowed up all I had." He did not take down his hand. He sighed heavily.

"But you are not grieving about that? It will all come back a hundredfold one day."

"Ay," he said in a tone of oppression and care, "a thousandfold--ten thousandfold. But there is the present----" He paused.

Suddenly a light broke in upon her.

"O," she cried, "how stupid I was not to guess! Why did you not speak out at once? William, dear, excuse me for not guessing. You will pardon me, dear, won't you, for not seeing what depressed you? If you want money, and there is none at the bank, why did you not sell out Consols? Mr. Brereton told me that all my Consols were as much my own as the income of the property, since they are my savings."

"No, no! I could not think of doing such a thing as take your savings."

"But yes, William, dear, yes. For my sake sell out whatever you want. Why not? They are not mine. They became yours on our marriage, dear. Why did you not sellout?"

"No, they were yours, and are yours. There is a new law."

"Then it is a bad law. Take down your hand and look at me and say you will sell what you want to-morrow. Do it to oblige me--for my sake. I cannot bear to see you in this state. I'll sign anything this foolish law obliges me to sign. If they are mine I surely can give them to you. You must take what you want if you won't take all. If they are mine I surely can give them to my husband as well as to any other person. If you do not consent to take what you want, I'll sell all out and give you the money."

She was pleading for the highest favour he could do her--to let her help him.

"No," he said in a tone of authority, "I will not allow you to do *that*."

"Well, take what you want. How much do you want?"

"Two hundred would be enough. But I can't--I can't."

"I'll write to Mr. Brereton to-morrow and ask him to sell out two hundred for myself, and tell him I want the money for a private purpose of my own. Take down your hand, dear, and let us go on with the accounts. I have looked over the list and the remarks." She cared nothing for the accounts, but she wanted the husband whom she loved to be his old self again.

He took down his hand and pressed hers, and stroked her smooth hair.

"I am sorry and ashamed," he said, "but I am awfully hard pressed, and you have delivered me."

"Let us go on with the list now, William, and say no more of this matter. Give me the list."

He handed her the papers without a word. Before sitting down he bent over and patted her hair and kissed her forehead.

"I know nearly all the names," she said, "but, of course, I have never seen any of the people."

"You have not missed much by that, Nellie," he said in tremulous tones, as though rendered almost tearful by her generosity. "They are a rough lot."

At the same time he was thinking how much more delightful it would be to have Hetty Layard, with all her buoyant youth, sitting by his side than this faded elderly invalid. But then Hetty had no money. A man ought to be allowed two wives: one with money, who need not be young or beautiful, and one with beauty, who need not be rich.

Mrs. Crawford ran her finger down the names of her tenants, and the houses which were tenantless, commenting as she went, and trying to make her own remarks bear out his theory that the tenants did not pay because they were not sure he was her husband.

"Mrs. Pemberton has not paid, I see. I don't wonder at all at that. Poor soul, she has had a great struggle for years, ever since her husband's death. She has tried to help herself along by letting lodgings, Mr. Blore told me, but that won't come to much in such a poor neighbourhood. I'm sure I don't know what could induce any one to lodge in such a district."

"People are often obliged to lodge near their place of business, no matter how objectionable their place of business may be," said he sententiously. Then he added with a smile, "Why, recollect, Nellie, that I myself am a lodger for business purposes in the locality."

"Of course you are, dear. I quite forgot that. And what kind of people are you lodging with?" she asked cheerfully, anxious to get his mind as far away as possible from those wretched Consols and rapacious artificers.

"O, they seem to be quiet respectable people enough. A little slow, you know, but perhaps none the worse for that when they have for a lodger such a gay young spark as I." He smiled.

She looked lovingly at him, and laughed at the enormity of the joke of his calling himself gay and fancying any society could harm *him*. "And now you must tell me what your landlord and landlady are like." He seemed to have forgotten about the wretched Consols and rapacious artificers.

"Well, Layard is a man who has something to do in the gas-house. The chief thing about him is a long beard. He's rather like a monkey with a beard."

"And what is Miss Layard like?"

"She's like a monkey without a beard," he said, with one of his short quick laughs. "As I thought before I went there, she's about ten or twelve years older than he. She's one of those dowdy little women, don't you know, dear, whose new clothes always look second-hand." Again came his short quick laugh. "She belongs to what geologists would call the antimacassar era. There's a dreadful Phyllis, or somebody else, in tapestry, framed over their sitting-room mantelshelf. She told me she worked it when she was young. But I ought not to laugh at the worthy soul. It is ungrateful of me; for I never tasted a more delicious omelette than she made for my breakfast. I must get her next time to give me the recipe for you, Nellie." He put his arms round his wife's shoulder and pressed his lips upon her smooth hair.

"I think, William," said she, "we are the happiest couple in England."

"And I'm sure of it," said he in a tone of full conviction.

She sighed a sigh of perfect contentment.

He sighed, thinking of Hetty Layard and her golden hair and luminous blue eyes, and her lithe round figure, and her fresh young voice, and the sweet red young lips through which that voice came to make sunshine and joy in the air.

"Shall I go on with the list, dear?" she asked.

She took no interest on her own part in this list; but then the interest of him and her was bound together in it, and there was a charm for her in the bond--not the thing binding them.

"Yes, dear," he answered, wishing the list at the bottom of the Red Sea among the chariots of Pharaoh.

She ran threw a few more items on the paper, and then paused, and said with a laugh:

"Here is one store, I see, from which you got neither money nor promise."

"What is that?"

"Ice-house, Crawford's Bay."

"O, ay. I examined the place with much interest. I believe it is in ruins. The gates are off, the lower part of it is full of water. I am told there are eight or ten feet of water in it."

"The place has not been let for ever so many years. I never saw an ice-house. I wonder what one is like."

"I'll tell you. It's exactly like a huge room of brick, lined with thick boards, and one-third below the ground. I examined this one very closely, thoroughly. There are no floors in it but the one at the bottom of the tank-- no ladders--nothing. It is like a great empty tank lined with wood."

"And you say the one at Crawford's Bay is full of water?" she asked.

"Yes."

She shuddered and drew the light shawl she wore tightly round her shoulders.

"How dreadfully dark and cold it must be there, William?"

"Yes; but bless me, Nellie, no one *lives* in an ice-house, and this one isn't even let!" he cried in surprise.

"I know. But suppose some one should fall into it? Don't you think the doors ought to be put up?"

"My dear Nellie, there isn't the least occasion to waste money on a useless place like that. Of course if we should let it we would be only too happy to put it into good repair. But what is the good of throwing money away?"

"But the danger?"

"Well, as far as that goes, you may make your mind perfectly easy. No one has access to the little quay or wharf but the people in Crawford's House. The rest of the property is lying idle, and from what I have seen of the Layards they are not the people to go wandering about on the wharf after dark. Besides, they know that the ice-house is full of water. It was Layard's maiden sister first told me."

He laughed at the idea of calling blooming young Hetty Layard's maiden sister.

"But the child, William--the child!" persisted the invalid. "Suppose by some misfortune the child should stray that way and fall in?"

"Nellie, no person with an atom of sense would think of permitting a child out on that wharf. Why, the canal, the waters of Crawford's Bay, are only a few steps from the back door of Crawford's House, and who would let a child play on the banks of a canal? I mean, of course, no people like the Layards would allow their child to play there."

"But this awful dark huge tank you tell me of is a thousand times worse than the open canal. If a child fell into the open canal people would see him, but if he fell into that dreadful tank he would be drowned, poor little fellow, before any one missed him. I do wish, William, you would get the doors put up. You see, as you tell me, there was no danger up to this, for no one could get near it; but now there is a child."

She pleaded with gestures and her eyes and her voice, as though a child of her own were menaced.

He held out his hand to her and took hers in his.

"There, Nellie, I will. I'll see the place made quite safe. Of course I'll go down and arrange about it if you wish it."

She raised the hand she held and kissed it.

He thought what a chance this would give him of meeting the Layards--Hetty--before the month was out!

"Shall I roll you round to your own place now, and you can go on with your paper and I with my book?"

"Thank you, dear."

He took up the volume, but he did not read. He fell into a profound reverie. First of all, he began to think of how pleasant it would be to tell Hetty that he had become alarmed for the safety of her little nephew, and had come back before his time to see about putting doors upon the ice-house. Hetty and he would go out on the quay, and look at the place and talk the matter over.

There was one good thing, the quay on which the icehouse stood was not visible from the tow-path, so that even if Philip Ray should chance to pass by he could not be seen.

Then his thoughts took another turn, and became concentrated on Philip Ray. He mused a long time upon his sworn enemy. Suddenly he shook all over, as if a chill had struck him. His blood seemed to thicken in his veins. His eyes stood in his head, staring straight out before him, perceiving nothing present in that room, but seeing a ghastly awful sight in that dim dark ice-house.

On the surface of the cold secret waters of the huge tank he saw a hideous object: the upturned face of a dead man, the face of Philip Ray.

Crawford's breath came short, and he panted. His mouth opened, his eyes dilated.

Philip Ray, lying drowned in that hideous lonely water where no one would ever think of looking for him! It was a perfect way out of the terror of Philip Ray's anger which beset him. It was a thing to think upon for ever. *A thing that might come to pass!*

"William," said the sweet low voice of his wife, "here is a strange thing in the paper to-day. You remember the awful nightmare you had, in which you thought two of your schoolfellows long ago were going to shoot you?"

"Yes," he answered hoarsely, but he did not know what she had said. He knew she had asked a question, and he answered "Yes." He was in a trance.

"Well, here in to-day's *Telegraph* are the two names together. Listen: 'On the 28th inst, at her residence, London, Kate, wife of Francis Mellor (*née* Ray), late of Greenfield, near Beechley, Sussex.'"

"Eh?" he cried, suddenly starting up from his chair and looking wildly at his wife. "Read that again."

In dire alarm at his manner she read again: "'On the 28th inst, at her residence, London, Kate, wife of Francis Mellor (*née* Ray), late of Greenfield, near Beechley, Sussex.'"

"What is the good of your playing with me, you fool Her death is no good to me. I am done with her. It's his life I want, and, by ----, I shall have it too!"

"William!" cried the terrified wife. "My William! Come to me. I cannot go to you. What is the matter? You look strange, and you are saying dreadful things, and you have sworn an awful oath. What is the matter? Are you unwell? Come to me."

A sudden tremor passed through him, and with a dazed expression he looked round him.

With his short laugh he said, "I hope I didn't frighten you, Nellie, dear. I was only going over a passage of a play we used to act at school. I was always good at private theatricals."

CHAPTER XIX
THE TOW-PATH BY NIGHT

It was now the second week in June. The weather had been without a flaw. From dawn to evening the sun had moved through almost cloudless skies. It was a splendid time for children to enjoy themselves out of doors, and every day Freddie was carried from the back door of Crawford's House by his Aunt Hetty, handed into the arms of Francis Bramwell, and borne across to Boland's Ait, there to spend his time in riotous fancy and boisterous play with Frank Bramwell till the dinner hour.

The two boys got on famously together. Freddie was the taller and lustier of the two, with plenty of animal spirits and enterprise in him, full of indulgent good-humour and patronising protection for his companion. Frank was more sedate and thoughtful. He had a closer and a keener mind, and as such minds are generally fascinated by the gifts of physical exuberance and mental intrepidity, he gave in to his gayer and more adventurous playmate. Each was the complement of the other. Freddie took after his Aunt Hetty in person and mind, and Frank after his father in disposition and his mother in appearance.

The fortnight had wrought a marvellous change in Francis Bramwell. In his youth he had been a dreamer, a poet. When he met Kate Ray he became a lover of her, at times austere and lofty, at times tempestuous. When he married he remained the lover still. After the flight of his wife he plunged headlong into all the fierce excitement of gambling, and led a completely reckless life. Then all at once he rushed into the direct opposite, took up his abode on the last rod of his property, Boland's Ait, and lived there the severe life of an anchorite, lived face to face with the ruins of the past and possessed his soul in silence, and mused upon the ways of Providence, and broke his spirit to the Christian law of patient endurance.

Now, for the first time in his life, he was confronted with material duties which had to be performed with his own hand. His income he now considered inadequate, and it could be increased only by his own labour. He had already planned and partly written a few articles which he hoped to get accepted by papers or magazines. He had been ashore twice and made some simple additions to the furniture of the cottage, and bought toys for Frank and Freddie to play with. He had levelled and smoothed and swept the old timber-yard for the boys, and put the play-room in order against a rainy day. For the two years he had dwelt alone on the Ait he had lived most frugally, and had not used up all his slender income, so that these little expenses did not come out of revenue.

It cheers the heart to have anything to do, and it soothes and sustains the heart when we have the result of our activity always at hand under our eyes.

Of mornings he had to dress Frank, an operation he at first executed with clumsiness and in despair. He had to get the boy his breakfast and watch him while he ate it. After that he had to fetch Freddie, set the two young people safely in the timber-yard, and, having secured the gate, go back to his sitting-room and write or meditate his articles until it was time for Freddie to go home. The boy's dinner had to be got ready, and then after the departure of Mrs. Treleaven he shut the outer door, gave Frank the run of the house, and sat down to his papers once more till tea. This meal he prepared without the aid of Mrs. Treleaven, and shortly after tea he had to undress little Frank and put him to bed.

He had been a dreamer, a poet, a lover, a gambler, a recluse. Now he was becoming a man. His duties were humanising him. When he lay down at night it was not, as of old, to live over again the hideous past with its vast calamity; but to dwell on the events of the day with restful complacency, and to contemplate with gentle satisfaction the cares and duties of the morrow. In the old days of his isolation his veins seemed filled with acrid juices, with vinegar and gall. In these nights, as he lay feeling the balm of slumber coming down upon him through the bland summer air, the milk of human kindness beat within his pulses.

In the old days his prayers were for deliverance and for a spirit of charity. But he prayed for that spirit of charity because charity was enjoined by the Great Teacher. He did not pray for deliverance in the form of death now. He prayed that he might be spared to look after his boy. He had no need to pray for charity now; for was not his child lying there beside him safe and sound and full of rosy health, and was not the child's mother forgiven by him and by a Greater, and in Heaven?

He never thought of Ainsworth. Why should he? Kate was dead, and he had his child, and what was all the rest of the world to him? Nothing.

To himself he admitted the situation was anomalous, and that he was ill-qualified to take care of so young a child. Of course it would be worse than folly to think of his sister in Australia. She had her husband and her own children, and was prosperous there. It never occurred to him once to send his boy to her. The idea that she might come over to take charge of his Frank had only arisen to his mind in dreams, to be laughed at upon waking. Of course a woman, not a man, was the natural guardian of a child of little Frank's age. Look at the care Miss Layard took of Freddie. What a lucky fellow Layard was to have such a sister to mind his boy!

Then in a dream, just as he had the idea of his sister travelling all the way from Australia to rear Frank, the idea came to him that it would be a good thing if Miss Layard would take charge of Frank; this, too, was only to be laughed at upon waking. Miss Layard was not a servant whom he could employ, or a sister of whom he could expect such a service. The thing was an absurdity worthy of midsummer madness, but what a pity it should be absurd!

He had dreamed the dream only once about his sister. He had dreamed the dream more than once about Miss Layard. This would be accounted for, no doubt, by the fact that he saw and spoke to Miss Layard every day.

The thought of leaving the Ait and taking a lodging ashore had presented itself to his mind, only to be dismissed after a few moments' consideration. By this time, after his two years of solitude, he had become accustomed to attending upon himself, and felt no more awkwardness in this respect than a sailor. He could cook his food and light his fire and make his bed as though he had been accustomed to shift for himself all his life. For two years he had been accustomed to all these services, and now he had the advantage of Mrs. Treleaven's daily visit, which relieved him of much of the drudgery. A lodging such as his present means could command would be unbearable. All his life, until the beginning of his reckless year, he had been accustomed to elegance and refinement. And all his life, until his retirement to the islet, he had lived in comfort, and part of his life in affluence. He could not endure the thought of contact with vulgar grasping landladies, and above all, he could not entertain the idea of exposing this child to the dulling and saddening intercourse with the unrefined folk to be found in such houses. He should be able to afford but one room, and how could he pursue literary studies or labours with little Frank at his very elbow? To let the child consort with those around them would be worse than all the inconveniences of this place.

No. He must stay where he was until he had mended his fortunes with his pen. The old timber-yard was a capital playground for Frank and Freddie in the fine weather, and when it rained there was the room he had prepared for them in the cottage. Besides----

Besides, if he went to live ashore Frank would no longer have so suitable a playmate as Freddie. He himself should certainly miss the cheerful, vivacious little chap who lived at Crawford's House, and--yes, and the brief meetings morning and afternoon with the gay and beautiful and sympathetic girl, Miss Layard. Let things be as they were.

Miss Layard had more than once repeated her brother's invitation to Bramwell that he should go over for an hour in the evening. He always pleaded in excuse the reason given for him by Philip Ray on the occasion of his hastily and unthinkingly accepting the first invitation. He could not leave the boy. Then she asked him to bring the boy. This could not be done either. Why? Well, because it would be giving them too much trouble. Nothing of the kind. They would be only too delighted to have Frank. Well, then, if that reason would not serve, it would not be good for the child to keep him up so late; he was always in bed a little after seven o'clock.

But Philip Ray had gone over often, and brought back word that they were very nice people, and he liked to talk a great deal about them, particularly the brother, to Bramwell, and Bramwell thought that when Philip came back from Crawford's House he was always more cool and rational, and so he was always glad when his brother-in-law went.

It is one of the curious regulations of the South London Canal that, while you have to pay toll if you wish to walk along the tow-path by day, you are free to use it by night for nothing. This rule would seem to be made out of a benevolent view to suicides. A more dreary and dangerous and murderous-looking place there is not in all London than that tow-path by night. To think, merely to think, in the daytime of walking under one of those low arches in the dark is enough to make one shudder.

The distance from the base of the arch to the edge of the water is not more than six feet. If you keep near the wall you have to bend towards the water; if you keep near the water it seems as though some hideous and terrifying influence will draw you into the foul, dark, stagnant, sinister flood. It appears to be waiting for you, passively waiting there for you, with the full knowledge that you must come, that you are coming, that you are come. It seems to have a purpose apart from all other things about it, and that purpose is to draw you. It seems to say in an unuttered voice, "I am Death and Silence."

If, as you stood under one of those odious arches, you stooped slowly, slowly until your hand touched the brink, you would have to thrust your fingers down an inch further to touch the water itself. And then you would find it was dead--that it had no motion; that by the sense of touch alone you could not tell which way the canal flows, the current is so slow--so deadly slow. In the plutonian darkness under the bridge you could see nothing, and from the dead water a peculiar and awful silence seems to rise like an exhalation.

You would not utter a word there to save your life. You would feel you had no life to save, that it already belonged to the water. If, then, as you stooped you slipped, you would roll into the water without a splash, for you would be on a level with the surface. You could not utter a cry, for the terrible, the odious influence of the place would be upon you. Even if you called out your voice would be of no avail, for no human being could hear you, and it would only infuriate the obscene genius of the place. Then, if the terror did not kill you instantly, the waters would--slowly--surely, for there is nothing to lay hold of but those flat slippery stones, and you would be in the stagnant water against a perpendicular wall. The sharp pains of the most perfect torture-chamber ever designed would not be equal to dying there alone upright against that wall, holding on by those smooth slippery flat stones on a level with your chin, and as you were gradually pulled down, down, down, inch by inch, by the loathsome genius of these waters.

But the horrors of this place are seldom invaded at night by human foot. Often from summer dark to summer dawn no tread of man beats upon that forlorn tow-path. After nightfall the place has an evil reputation in the neighbourhood. More than a dozen times in the memory of living people cold and clammy things, once men and women, have been drawn slowly, laboriously, with dripping clothes, out of these turbid waters. No man but one sorely pressed by necessity would think of taking that path at midnight: and even when in dire haste he would have need of strong nerves to face it, to set out upon it, to plunge into it. For, unlike the streets and roadways that go by the dwellings of kindly men, once upon it there is no way from it, no crossroad or byway until the stretch of half-a-mile or a mile is accomplished. If any supreme terror or danger menaced the traveller on that path, he has only one refuge, one means of escape, one sanctuary to seek--the canal itself.

In the ditch, on the inner side of the path, you cannot know what may be crouching. Shapes and forms and monsters too hateful for sanity to endure may be lurking in that ditch, and may spring out on you, on your unprotected side, at any moment as you walk along. If this should happen would not it be better for you to seek blindness and extinction in the waters?

Or may there not lie in wait some shapes in human form more appalling than gorgon or chimera dire, some human ghouls who have committed crimes never dreamt of by the soul of affrighted man? May not these come forth and whisper at your ear as you go by, and tell you what they have done in tombs and charnel houses until the flesh falls off your bones with dread, and you take these waters of forgetfulness at your side to be not a river of Orcus, but of blissful deliverance?

And what a place is this for a woman by night!

She has crept cautiously out of Leeham and struck the canal at Leeham Bridge. At that time all Leeham is asleep in bed or at work in the great gasworks. Not a soul is abroad but two or three people moving to or from the Neptune at the end of the Pine Groves.

The woman creeps cautiously from the road down the approach leading to the canal. There is not a soul on the tow-path; the place is as still as a cave. She can hear the beating of her own heart distinctly as she walks along, keeping in the shadow.

But she will have to come out of the shadow in a moment, or rather she will have to enter the sphere of light, for on the tow-path to her left there is a gas-lamp.

She darts quickly through the patch of light and into the cavernous darkness of the bridge.

In that brief period of illumination all that could be seen was that she did not exceed the average height of woman, might be a little below it; that she was poorly clad; that she wore a bonnet and thick impenetrable veil; that she was covered from neck to heel with a long dark cloak, and that the ungloved hand which grasped the cloak in front and held it close was thin and white.

She did not seem conscious of any of the horrors of that dismal arch; while under it she was more free from the chance of observation than on the road or approach. She drew herself more upright, and slackened her pace for a moment. Then with another shudder she walked swiftly from under the arch and set off for Welford Bridge.

On her right lay a ditch neither wet nor dry; on her left the voiceless waters of the canal, and beyond the canal a line of mute, uninhabited, inscrutable wharves which looked like dead parts of a living city which had drifted away, leaving this rack behind.

She sped on, unheeding her surroundings. She did not look to left or right. She kept the edge of the canal, as though the water were the best friend she had there. Now and then with her white ungloved hand she drew her cloak closer round her, rather as though to preserve her own resolution within it, to prevent her purpose from escaping, than to protect her from observation from without.

She came within the shadow of the mighty gas-house, which, too, was silent, save now and then a startling and alarming clamour of metal, as though the summons of Titan to witness some overwhelming disaster. Against the blue sky and pallid stars of early summer the huge chimneys, and cranes, and pillars, and tanks, and viaducts, and scaffolding, and shoots, and the enormous and towering masses of the gasometers, stood up in a piece like some prodigious engine of one motive, some monstrous machine used in the building of mountains or hollowing out of seas. Now and then, through apertures low down in this prodigious engine, small living things, no bigger than insects in comparison with the mass, came and stood clearly visible, pricked out in the darkness against the glow within. These were men flying for a moment from the fiery heat of the huge instrument to cool their bodies and their lungs in the open air.

The woman took no more note of all this wonderful work of man than to draw her cloak to her on that side, lest it might distract her from her purpose.

At length, as she kept on her way undismayed, she approached a black mass of shadow, stretching across the canal and tow-path, as though to bar her further progress.

As she drew nearer, an arc of light appeared in the centre of this dark barrier, and beyond, or rather in the middle of the arc a speck of brighter light still.

The dark barrier was Welford Bridge; the larger and duller light in the middle of it was the eye of the bridge; and the central ray, like the light on the pupil of an eye, was the lamp in the bedroom of Boland's Ait.

The woman paused when she saw this latter light, and, leaving the margin of the canal, crossed the tow-path to a low warehouse and leaned against the wall in the shadow to rest.

From the point at which she now stood resting against the wall she could see the light in the open window of the cottage.

Presently the spark formed by the lamp waved. The lamp had been removed from the window-sill. The sash of the window was allowed to remain up. There was a sudden flicker of light, and then all in the cottage was dark. The lamp had been extinguished.

The woman withdrew her shoulder from the wall, gathered her cloak round her, and resumed her way along the edge of the tow-path, going south. She walked more slowly now, as if in thought or to give time. She walked as though she must, because of her inclination, make progress, but must not for some reason make too quick an advance.

Presently she stepped into the profound gloom under Welford Bridge, and in a few seconds emerged upon the other side. Here she made another pause.

Not a soul was in sight. She had met no one since taking the tow-path at Leeham. The night was perfectly still. She looked around at the bridge, and then moved rapidly along the path, as though wishing to get beyond the point at which she might attract the attention of any one looking over the parapet.

When about two hundred yards from the bridge she paused once more. Here was no building against which she could lean, but instead a sharply sloping bank surmounted by a wall. Opposite where she stood a large log of wood reclined against the slope. She crept over and leaned against the bank beside the log. In this position she would be perfectly invisible to any one looking over the parapet, or even passing along the tow-path carelessly. Here the horse-track was more than twice its ordinary width, and between the trodden part of the path and the bank spread a space of grass-grown waste of equal width.

Directly opposite to her stood Crawford's House, and a little further to the left Boland's Ait. She put her hollowed right hand behind her ear, leaned her head towards the islet, and listened intently. Not a sound. She closed her eyes and concentrated all her faculties in the one of hearing. The tranquillity of the cloudless night was unbroken by any murmur but the dull dead murmur that always hangs over the city, and is faintly perceptible even here.

Suddenly a soft gentle sound stole upon her ears, but not from the desired quarter. The voice of a woman singing reached her. She opened her eyes. A light burned now in the top room of Crawford's House.

The wayfarer on the tow-path could make nothing out, owing to the distance and to the light being behind the singer, save that a woman was standing at the open window and humming in a very low voice an old lullaby song. The light of the lamp came through the hair of the singer, and the listener saw that the colour of the hair was golden.

The watcher leaned back against the bank, closed her eyes, and put her hands over her ears. She remained so a considerable time. When she opened her eyes the light had been extinguished. She took her hands down from her ears--all was still once more.

She looked up and down the track carefully, and strained her ear to catch footfalls; but no one was in view, and no noise of feet broke the frozen monotony of the silence. Gathering her cloak around her, she left her resting-place, and, having gained the edge of the water, resumed her way at a rapid rate in a southerly direction until she got opposite the tail of Boland's Ait.

Here she reduced her pace, and kept on with her eyes fixed eagerly on the ground at her feet. She bent forward, and as low as she could. Apparently, she was looking for some mark.

There gleamed the full light of unclouded June night and unsullied faint blue June stars, but no moon aided her search.

At length she stopped and examined the ground very closely. Then she stooped lower still and thrust her hand down, passing it outside the bank until it touched the water.

She seized some object first with one hand, and then with both, and drew back from the bank softly, cautiously, as though her very life depended on the care she took. Something stretched from her hands--a line, a chain. It was fast to the bank, and reached from her hands out into the water a few feet from where she stood.

She had in her hands the chain by which the floating stage was drawn from Boland's Ait across the canal when any one wanted to go from the tow-path to the island. The chain yielded with her a little, and then would come no more. She drew upon it with all her might, but it simply rose out of the water at a slightly increased distance from the bank. She became desperate, and pulled with all her might and main. She dug her heels into the ground, and threw the whole weight of her body backward. To no avail.

She tore off her cloak and flung it on the ground that she might have greater freedom. She dragged at the chain, now pulling it from one side, now from the other. The stage did not move. Her hands were cut and bleeding.

She stooped low and got the chain over her shoulder, and flung the whole weight of her body over and over again into the loop.

The harsh ragged chain tore the skin and flesh of her soft delicate shoulder until it too bled. But the stage remained motionless.

She sank down on the ground half insensible from despair and pain.

She rose up and put the chain on the uninjured shoulder, and wrenched and tore and struggled at it, whispering to herself, "I will--I must--I tell you I must see my child once more before I die. I only want to see him asleep, through the window, any way, once. Do you hear me? I *will* see my child before I die. A mother has a right to see her child before she dies. Mercy, mercy, mercy! One look, only one before I go away for ever!"

She sank to the ground again. The chain slipped from her shoulder, and with a moan she spread out her torn and bleeding hands on the rugged ground and lay still.

The first faint streaks of dawn were in the sky before she recovered consciousness. She rose, put on her cloak, and with dejected head and tattering steps turned her back upon the Ait and walked in the direction of Leeham.

CHAPTER XX
A HOSTAGE AT CRAWFORD'S HOUSE

The failure of Philip Ray's expedition to Richmond had dispirited him in the pursuit of the man whom he called John Ainsworth, but whom Richmond knew as William Crawford. He was an impulsive man in action, but when action was denied to him, he could make little or no progress. He was a man of devices rather than plans. In the heat of action he could invent, but he needed the stimulus of present necessity or expediency before he could design. He could carry out a plan, not invent one. He was a good captain, but no general.

Hence, when he found himself baffled at Richmond, he did not know in what direction to turn for a clue to Ainsworth. He chafed under his impotency; but he could not remove it. The conclusion to which he came was that Ainsworth did not live at Richmond, and he hated that town because of the disappointment he had experienced in it. His determination to take vengeance on Ainsworth was still unshaken; but he felt that, having missed his man once, the likelihood of encountering him again was diminished. Say, according to the law of chances, they should be fated to meet twice in ten years: one of those meetings had been missed, owing to the ill-luck of his not being in Richmond the day Lambton saw Ainsworth there. This, of course, was not logical, but then no one who knew Ray ever expected him to be influenced by pure reason. It was not according to the law of chances, for he had had no chance of seeing Ainsworth in Richmond, since he himself had not been in the town that day.

On the evening of his return from Richmond he had been asked by Bramwell to go and apologise to Layard for the postponement or abandonment of his brother-in-law's visit. Layard had opened the door for him, and, seeing a young man he did not know, and having heard from Hetty that Bramwell had promised to call, he concluded that this was the promised visitor; held out his hand, and had drawn Philip inside the door before the latter could explain. As soon as Ray had told Layard he was not the expected man, and that he was only a relative of the desired guest,

"Well," said Layard with one of his unexpected bright smiles on his homely face, "since you have ventured into the bandit's cave, I must hold you as hostage until he comes to release, or reclaim, or redeem you. Sit down."

"But he will not come. He cannot come, he expects me back. He is unable to come because he cannot leave the boy alone," said Ray, somewhat disarmed and drawn towards this ugly man with the kind voice and surprising smile.

"Well, now, you cannot plead the same excuse. You are here, in the first place, and, in the second place, the boy's not alone now. Do sit down, pray. I do not make a new acquaintance once in a year, and I haven't a single companionable neighbour. You won't miss half-an-hour out of your life, and I should take it as a favour if you gave me one."

What could Ray do but sit down?

"Do you smoke?" asked Layard.

"Yes.

"For," said Layard, as they lit their pipes, "my sister says she is certain Mr. Bramwell doesn't smoke; and her reason for thinking so is because he seems not to be a fool."

"Then," said Ray, putting down his pipe, "perhaps Miss Layard objects to smoking."

"Not she," said Layard; "it is only her disagreeable way of rebuking me. Please go on with your pipe."

"Old maids," thought Ray, "invariably do object to smoking. I'm sorry I sat down, and now I can't in decency get up for a while. An elderly female edition of this man would be a dreadful sight."

His own handsome face, with its straight brows and straight nose, was reflected behind Layard's back in the little mirror of the chiffonier.

"You do not live in this neighbourhood?" asked Layard, when Ray had resumed his pipe.

"No. I live in Camberwell."

Layard straightened himself in his chair, and looked hard at the other for a few seconds.

"That receding forehead," thought Ray, "indicates a weak intellect. I hope I am not face to face alone with a madman. What on earth is the ape looking at! I wish this gorgon sister, however hideous she may be, would come in."

The door opened, and, in response to his thought, the gorgon entered.

"My sister, Mr. Ray. Hetty, Mr. Ray has called to say that Mr. Bramwell cannot come this evening; he must not leave his little boy alone, and I have impounded Mr. Ray."

Ray bowed, and took in his hand the slender hand that was held out to him with a smile, took in his eyes the smile and the beauty of the girl, and said to himself, "Are they real?"

He was disposed to think some trick was being played upon him, for, from what Frank said, he had been prepared for age and ugliness; and what Layard had said about the smoking had prepared him for sourness and sarcastic eyes, and here----!

Hetty sat down quite close to Philip, and he felt very strangely at this, because still he had the feeling that there must be some trick in the affair; since he was prepared for blue spectacles, and a blue nose, and a front, perhaps, and prominent teeth. And here, instead, were the brightest and bluest and most cheerful eyes he had ever seen, instead of spectacles; and a lovely delicate, shapely nose, with the least suggestion of an aquiline curve in it, and of the colour of the petal of a white rose that lies over the petal of a red rose, and hair that was like amber against the sun, and teeth as even as a child's and as white as a fresh cut apple. Was it all real?

"Won't you go on smoking, Mr. Ray?" said the apparition at his side.

"I will," said Ray, not knowing what he said, but putting the pipe mechanically into his mouth. He didn't even say "Thank you." He had still some notion of unreality in his mind. Was it a dream, if it wasn't a trick? Anyway, it would be best to be on his guard, so he only said "I will," without even "Thank you." He was waiting to see what would happen next.

The next thing that happened was nothing to astonish an ordinary mortal, but it filled Philip Ray with such a feeling of at once disappointment and joy that he was afterwards certain he must have spoken incoherently for a few minutes.

Said Layard to Hetty, "I was just on the point of saying to Mr. Ray when you came in that if, by any misfortune, another quarter of an hour went by without my getting food, all would be up with me."

With a laugh Hetty rose and left the room.

Ray thought, "That strange look I saw in his eyes must have been the bale fire of cannibalism. He must have been thinking of eating me!"

Then in a few minutes the strangest thing in this dream happened before Philip's eyes. The girl of whose reality he had such doubt carried in the supper-things like the simplest maiden that ever ministered to man. Philip rose and stood with his back against the mantelpiece, looking on, while Layard helped his sister to spread the feast and kept up a running commentary on the various articles as they were placed on the table.

When all was ready they sat down, Philip still feeling dull and heavy, like one in a dream. Could it be that this incomparable being was no more in that household than the sister of the host? Could it be that she busied herself with plates and knives and forks, and beef and salad and cress, just like other girls he had seen? Incredible! And yet if he had not been dreaming, so it was.

"Pepper, mustard, vinegar, oil! I see only four cruets, Hetty," said Alfred Layard reproachfully. "What is the meaning of only four cruets? Where is the fifth?"

"There are only four bottles. What do you want, Alfred?"

"I do not want anything, but Mr. Ray does. Mr. Ray, do you take your arsenic with your beef or in the salad?"

Philip looked from one to the other with a stupid smile. He felt more than ever that the whole thing was unreal, notwithstanding the fact that he was eating and drinking.

"When you know Alfred better, you won't mind anything he says," said the girl, addressing the guest.

"Speak for yourself," said Layard solemnly and in a warning voice. "Listen to me! Just as you came into the room, Hetty----"

"O, I know! You told us that before. You were on the point of fainting from hunger."

"No! That was only my way of putting it. What I really meant was that I did not feel myself able to face the discovery I had made without the aid of food instantly applied, and in ample quantities."

"But what about the arsenic?" she asked, with a look of perplexed amusement.

"I'm coming to the arsenic."

"I thought you intended it for Mr. Ray. What has he done?"

"Hetty, you are flippant. What has he done? Why, do you know that he lives at Camberwell?" cried Layard, putting down his knife and fork, and glaring at his sister with a horrified expression.

"Is that a capital offence at Welford?" asked Ray, trying to rouse himself.

"In the present connection it is ten thousand times a worse crime than slaying the sacred Ibis. You live at Camberwell. You walk along the tow-path. You get by a floating-stage from the tow-path to Boland's Ait. Confess! You may as well confess. I see it all now. Were you on Boland's Ait within the past week?"

"Certainly; I confess I was. Is that a still greater offence than living at Camberwell?"

"It makes parts of the stupendous crime."

"And what is the stupendous crime?"

"Our sometime lodger, Mr. Crawford, saw you come along the track, saw you disappear behind the head of the island, and saw you did not reappear at the other end. Being thus unable to make head or tail of you, he thought you were drowned, and insisted on my going out at a most untimely hour in order that we might make certain of your fate. As we just got under Welford Bridge you stepped out from under it, looking not a penny the worse; I say you deserve death for these abnormal aquatic habits of yours, by which you disturb a quiet household, and take a peaceful citizen like me away from his warm fireside into the bleak winds of December close on midnight."

"I'm very sorry, I'm sure," said Ray, with a smile, "and I am very much indebted to Mr. Crawford for the interest he took in me. He must be a very kind-hearted man."

"He's a hero!" cried Hetty enthusiastically. "A Bayard!"

"But, as I told you before, rather fat for the part," said her brother. "Mr. Ray, he is our lodger and our landlord, and hence he must be above all reproach. Our association with him would put him all right if he was a Thug. But my sister is really too much carried away by her admiration for this Bayard because he married a rich woman----"

"Who is a hopeless invalid," broke in Hetty.

"Who owns a good deal of property in this neighbourhood----"

"And is ever so much older than he. I call him a most heroic man."

"And large savings out of her income."

"Mr. Ray, don't mind Alfred. He is only joking. In his secret heart he admires Mr. Crawford as much as I do; but he will not give in. This man saved Mrs. Crawford from being burned in her house. She is ever so much older than he, and he married her out of a wish to make her happy after saving her life at the risk of his own." The girl became quite excited as she spoke. Her lips quivered, her cheeks flushed, the golden light blazed in her blue eyes.

Her brother looked at her with admiration.

Philip Ray looked at her, and for the first time in his life realised ecstasy. He had never tasted the wine of love before, and now he was drinking the most potent and intoxicating of all kinds--love at first sight.

"I consider," he said, at last fully awake, "Mr. Crawford a very lucky man." He meant in having so beautiful an advocate.

"So do I," said Layard, meaning in a worldly sense.

"And does he live with you always?" asked Ray, who had some confused memory of the phrase, "sometime lodger."

"No," said Hetty. "He is to come to us for only a couple or three days a month. He has his offices for the property upstairs."

"O, I see," said Ray, much relieved. He did not want this object of her admiration to be near her. He was now interested no more in Mr. Crawford. To keep the conversation going, he said, "And where does Mr. Crawford live the rest of the time?"

"At Richmond."

He started. The name of the town was a harsh, discordant note; but he said nothing, and shortly after took his leave, promising to call again.

From that night he visited almost every evening at Crawford's House. When he was not there he pitied himself with a pathetic, desperate pity. When he was there he wondered how all the rest of the world could be content to dwell so far apart from her.

CHAPTER XXI
CRAWFORD SELLS A PATENT

A few days after William Crawford's return from Welford, and the scene in which he gave his wife a specimen of his quality as the player of a part in private theatricals, he went up to London with one of the hundred pounds in his pocket. He told her he could not dream of taking the money from her except to pay the men working on the models and machines for his great patent, and in the interest of their joint worldly welfare.

He set off, as usual, in the afternoon, taking with him half the money. He was a gambler, but no plunger. He played for the excitement of the game, rather than for the sake of gaining. He had no idea that he should win a fortune. His luck was usually bad, but this did not keep him back; nor did he play on in the hope or expectation that it would turn so as to recoup him. Every gambler is entitled to curse his luck, and Crawford cursed his with no bated breath. But he would rather have bad luck than no play. He was not a mean man with money when he had it, but he was a desperate man when he wanted it.

Cards and pretty faces were his weaknesses. With regard to cards, he recognised the laws of honour; with regard to pretty faces, he regarded no law but the law of his wishes. He had never been in love in his life. He admired pretty women, and made love to every pretty woman he met, if occasion served. But he was completely wanting in any feeling of self-sacrifice or devotion. He was, as he told his wife, good at private theatricals. He could play the heroic, or romantic, or sentimental lover, according as circumstances demanded, to the utmost perfection; but his heart was never once touched. He looked on women as inferior creatures, the natural prey of man. With them he had no mercy or compunction. He made love automatically to the owner of every pretty face he came across, provided there was no great risk from male friend or relative; for, though he could assume the air and words of a hero in the presence of a woman, he fought shy of men in their anger, and was of that prudent disposition that prefers flight to fight.

On going to town this afternoon, he left half the money he had got from his wife behind him. One hundred pounds was quite enough for one night; one hundred pounds was quite as good as two. Playing for certain stakes, one hundred pounds would last him the whole night, even if luck were dead against him. Two hundred pounds would enable him to play for stakes of double the amount: that was all. He would rather play two nights for small stakes than one night for stakes of double the value.

William Crawford was a cautious, not to say cowardly, man. This talk of the artificers engaged in making a machine for him was not wholly illusory. From time to time he ordered inexpensive portions of machinery at a mechanical engineer's in the Blackfriars Road. He never took the parts of the machine away; but left them in the workshops, saying he would not remove them until it was all ready to be put together. He had no fear that he might one day be driven to make good his words about this wonderful machine in course of construction; but if he were, there lay the wheels and racks and drums in the workshop. Of course the manner in which they were to be put together remained his secret. It was not likely he would divulge that until he had secured his patent, and, for aught you could know or should know from him to the contrary, he might have other portions of the machine in course of manufacture for him in other workshops.

When he arrived in town this early day in June he went first to the Blackfriars Road and gave an order for two cog-wheels of peculiar make. He handed in a paper with the specification, paid a bill of a couple of pounds, and then betook himself to the Counter Club.

Here he dined, and from the dinner-table went to the card-room, which he did not leave until seven o'clock the next morning. He breakfasted at the club, and after breakfast fell asleep in a chair in the deserted smoking-room, and did not wake for a couple of hours. Then he went out, and, turning into Bond Street, did a little shopping, and got back to Richmond at about noon.

He found his wife in the drawing-room with some fancy work in her hand. After an affectionate greeting, he sat down beside her and took her hand as usual. Contrary to his custom, he had brought no book, or flowers, or basket of fruit.

"And how did you get on in town, William?" she asked, giving no time for him to notice, if he had not already noticed, the omission of his customary little present.

"Very well indeed, Nellie. Better than I could have hoped. Better than I deserved."

"Not better than you deserved, surely, dear," she said fondly. "That could not be."

"Well, better than I could have hoped. I am afraid, Nellie, I got on so splendidly that success has turned my head."

She looked at him in surprise and pressed his hand. "I know you better than to think success could turn your head."

"Nevertheless, my success has had such an effect on me that I have not brought you any flowers, or fruit, or a book. Does not that look like being spoiled by success? Should I not be spoiled by prosperity when I forgot you?"

"It does not follow," she said tenderly, as though she were excusing herself, not him, "that because you did not bring me something that you forgot me."

He put his hand in his pocket, took something out of it, and before she knew what he was doing she found a gold bracelet, having a circle of pearls round a large diamond, clasped upon her arm.

She gave a little cry of wonder and pleasure. "Why, what is this? Where did you get it? Whom is it for?"

"It is for my own wife Nellie. I bought it for her in Bond Street to-day, to show her that I did not forget her when away. And I did not buy it out of the money she lent me yesterday--for, look!" He threw into her lap a lot of gold and notes. "There's the hundred pounds I took with me to town--and look!" He held out towards her more gold and notes. "Here is another hundred I have got over and above what she lent me, and the price of the bracelet."

"Wonder upon wonder!" she cried with a laugh and a simple childlike joy in her husband's success. "Tell me all about the affair. Have you met fairies?"

"No, dear. Only a good angel, and you are she," he said, and kissed the hand below the gleaming bracelet.

"But I did not give you this. You got this yourself."

"No, you did not give me this money directly, but you gave me the means of getting it."

"But tell me all, dear. I am dying to hear."

"You must know, then, that in designing some machinery for preparing my fibre I hit upon an immense improvement in the scutching machine now in use. I patented my improvement, and sold my patent last evening for two hundred and fifty pounds."

She was overwhelmed with gratitude and joy. This was the first-fruit of his genius, the earnest of his great triumph.

For half-an-hour they sat and chatted, he telling her his schemes for the future, and she listening, full of delight and pride and love. Then he said he had some writing to do, and went to his room.

The fact was that he could hardly keep his eyes open. It had been a very hot night at the Counter Club, and he had come away the winner of close upon three hundred pounds. He locked the door, drew down the blind, threw himself on a couch, and was fast asleep in a few minutes.

Mrs. Crawford always breakfasted in her own room, and had her other meals brought to her in the drawing-room. She had gradually sunk back almost to the helpless condition in which she had lived so long before the fire. She suffered no pain, but she was nearly as helpless as a year ago. If necessity required it, she could creep about the room by resting her hands on the furniture, but as a rule she went from one place to the other by means of her invalid's chair. She never ventured down-stairs now. She lived upon the first-floor. Here were her bedroom, the drawing-room, her husband's study--which he called his own room--and the dressing-room where he slept, so as to be within call if she needed assistance in the night.

The doctors told Crawford that his wife was, if anything, rather worse than she had been before the fire, and that any other such shock would in all likelihood kill her.

"Is there no chance of it producing an effect like the former one?" Crawford had asked.

Well, there was no saying for certain. This, however, was sure, that if she sustained another shock and by chance she once more regained the use of her limbs, the relief would be only temporary, and the reaction would leave her in a very critical condition indeed--the chances were ten to one she would die.

A shock, then, was to be avoided at any cost.

With Mrs. Crawford's life all William Crawford's interest in the property would pass away. This property brought in more than Ned Bayliss, or Jim Ford, or Matt Jordan, or any of the other loafers on Welford Bridge imagined. The income was nearer to two than one thousand a year, and Mrs. Crawford's savings exceeded three thousand pounds. These savings would become Crawford's absolute property upon his wife's death. She had practically put them at his disposal already. They were his own, she told him, and he took her word for it. But that was a good reason why he should be moderately careful of them. As long as she lived he had not only these savings at his disposal, but the lion's share of the income as well. If he did not blunder, nothing could take the savings away from him; if she died he would lose all participation in the fine income.

A shock was to be avoided at any cost.

One morning after breakfast, in the middle of June, Crawford came into the drawing-room, and said to his wife:

"I have slept so badly! I do not know when I had so little sleep, and the little I got so disturbed."

She looked at him anxiously. "You are not unwell? You don't feel anything the matter, do you?"

"O, no! I am quite well. But I have had such horrid nightmares. What you said to me a fortnight ago about the want of gates on that ice-house all came back to me in sleep last night, and I had the most awful visions of that young Layard drowning in it while I was looking on, unable to stretch out my hand to save him." He made a gesture as though to sweep away the spectacle still haunting him.

"I am so sorry, William, I said anything about the place. I am, indeed. I spoke foolishly, no doubt. You are not so superstitious as to fancy anything dreadful has happened?" she asked, losing colour and leaning back in her chair.

"Dear me! No. And I don't think you spoke foolishly at all. I now see that what you said was quite right. I own it's very selfish of me, but I do not feel disposed to go through another such night as last. That brought home to me the danger you saw at once, and instinctively."

She could not help smiling and feeling gratified at these candid and gracious words from so clever a man--from a man who got two hundred and fifty pounds the other day for the pure brain-work of a couple of hours.

"And what do you think of doing?"

"Well, I feel that the surest way to lay the ghost that haunted me last night, and provide against all danger, would be for me to go down to Welford and get these gateways boarded up."

"Indeed, indeed! I'm sure that would be the best thing to do. When did you fancy you would go?"

"I could go to-day. I am not doing anything particular. Do you want me for anything?"

He asked the question in a soft submissive voice.

"I!" she cried, flushing with pleasure at his deference to her. "Not I, William! I am all right, and feel as well as usual. You could do nothing that would please me more."

"Very well, then; I'll go at once. I shall not want more than an hour or so there. I need not wait to see the thing done. All I shall have to do is to get hold of a carpenter, and put the job into his hands."

And so he set out for Welford.

The fact is he had dreamed last night of Hetty Layard's bright face and wonderful golden hair, and he was getting tired of Richmond and--the house.

It would be very pleasant to go down to Welford, knock at the door, and find Hetty alone. Her brother would be at the gasworks. Philip Ray was in some public office or other, and could not come to make that tow-path horrible with his presence at that hour of the day. He should be able to reach Crawford's House at about eleven, and get away at about one or two. Thus he would run no risks, and he should see again the prettiest girl he had now in his memory.

CHAPTER XXII
WILLIAM CRAWFORD'S NIGHTMARE

"Hetty," said Alfred Layard to his sister at breakfast that same morning, "you know I am not a discontented man."

"Indeed, I know that very well, Alfred. See how you put up with me!"

"Hetty," said he severely, "in this house jokes are *my* prerogative."

"I am not joking in the least, Alfred. I know I am not anything like as good as I ought to be to you. But I'll try to be better in future, Alfred. Indeed I will!"

Her tone was full of sorrow.

"Hetty," said he sternly, "in this house pathos is *my* prerogative also. Mind what you're about. If you make me laugh or yourself cry you will oblige me to do something I should be extremely loath to do."

"And what is that?" she asked, struggling to repress a smile.

"Hold my tongue. Bad as my loquacity is, my silence would be a thousand times worse. How would you like me to sit at the table and only point at the things I wanted? Suppose there was some one here, how would you like me to make a motion for a slate, and write on it with a squeaking pencil, 'Hetty, your hair is down!' You would not like it a bit. No, Hetty; I was not thinking of you when I said I was not a discontented man. I was thinking of Crawford, our landlord-tenant."

"Of Mr. Crawford! O, what were you thinking of him?"

"I was thinking that I am not too well satisfied with our arrangements about this house. I fancy I am almost sorry I entered into the agreement at all."

"But why? Surely we are saving money: twenty pounds a year or more by the house, and Mr. Crawford is no trouble, or next to none."

"He's very little trouble in the house, I own. But he troubles me in my mind. There is something about the man I don't like. I can't tell you for certain what it is, but I think it is because he is a coward."

"A coward, Alfred! A coward! Good gracious! is it the man who saved Mrs. Crawford from the burning house at the risk of his own life? Don't you think you are very unjust?"

"Perhaps. But for goodness' sake, don't say anything about Bayard!"

"It was you who called him a Bayard."

"I don't think it was; and if it was, I meant it sarcastically. That man is in good bodily health, and yet he is afraid of something or some one. Now, when a man in good bodily health goes about in fear you may be certain he has good cause for being afraid, and you may be equally sure that whatever he is afraid of is not to his credit."

Layard rose to go. Freddie was in the kitchen with Mrs. Grainger.

"Isn't a good deal of, or all, this fancy?" asked Hetty, as she too rose.

"It may be fancy that he is afraid of something discreditable; but I am certain he is afraid."

"How can you tell that?" asked the girl, in incredulous wonder.

"By his eyes and the motion of his hands. That man could not for a thousand pounds sit in a room the door of which had opened at his back without turning round."

"Upon my word, you are growing quite fanciful, Alfred. And did you notice that he was very much afraid of us?" she said in a bantering tone.

"He is afraid of every one until he is assured of what that person is."

"Of Mrs. Grainger and me, for instance?"

"Yes, he would be afraid of you until he saw your face and discovered who you were."

"Alfred, I never felt so proud in all my life before. To think that a strong man like him should go about shaking in his shoes at sight of me is quite romantic. I must cultivate all kinds of dark and forbidding looks. I feel that I could act the bravo if I only had a cloak and a dagger and the divided skirt."

"Well, good-morning, Hetty. I am glad you will have no chance of terrifying him for a fortnight, anyway;" and off he went.

"That brother of mine," thought the girl, as she prepared to remove the breakfast-things, "is the very best man in the world. He is the most kind-hearted and generous fellow that ever breathed. But with respect to this Mr. Crawford, he has some strange prejudice which I cannot understand. I never knew him absolutely dislike a man before. He has not gone so far as to say that he absolutely dislikes him, but I feel sure he does."

As soon as the breakfast-things were removed and washed up, it was time to go out on the wharf and hand Freddie to Bramwell. This was now so well-established a custom that it created little excitement even in Freddie's mind. At about half-past ten Bramwell pushed the floating-stage across the bay, went over, said a few words to Hetty, took the boy, and returned with him. Then he hauled the stage back to its moorings on the Ait, put Freddie into the timber-yard, where Frank was already, fastened the gate, and went to his work in his study. At half-past two he restored the boy to Hetty. The Layards breakfasted late, and had not their midday meal till three. For the convenience of the children, Bramwell adopted the same hour for his midday meal.

"Mr. Bramwell," said Hetty that day as she handed the boy to him, "I am sure I do not know how we are to allow this to continue longer. Freddie goes over to you every day, and you will not let Frank come over to us once even. I am afraid either of us is selfish."

"Selfish? How, selfish?" He smiled as he looked up from the stage into the girl's face.

"Well, we seem to give you all the trouble of these two boys, which makes us seem selfish in one way, and you seem to wish to take all the trouble of them, which is selfish in another way. I am afraid we are both very bad. I give you one more chance," she said, shaking a warning finger at him. "To-morrow I am going to a toy-shop a little bit down the Welford Road, and I intend to take Freddie with me to buy him a Noah's ark in place of the one he lost----"

"The cat flew away with it and ate the elephant and lion," said Freddie.

"And, of course, Freddie can't go over----"

"Not even after dinner?" cried the boy.

"No. Nor must you go over again unless Frank is allowed to come with us to the toy-shop."

"I'll bring him," said the boy confidently. "Frank will come with me. We'll play Frank is a canal boat, and that I'm a horse, and I'll tow him all the way."

"But if his father won't give him leave?" said Hetty.

"O, he'll come!" said Freddie, with decision. "Frank always plays what I ask him. And will you get a Noah's ark for Frank too, Aunt Hetty?"

"Of course. Mr. Bramwell, you will let the child come? You will, won't you?" She held both her hands out to him pleadingly.

His eyes were still upon her face. She looked so bright and strong and full of spirits, it appeared as though the touch of her hand upon his boy must benefit the child. He hesitated for a moment, and said, "Very well, and thank you heartily, Miss Layard," and so the interview ended.

Bramwell carried the boy along the stage and put him into the yard, where Frank was impatiently waiting. Then he came back, drew the stage to its position alongside the islet, and moored it to the ring in the ground. After this he went back to the cottage and buried himself in his work. Unless something unusual occurred in the yard he might count on three-and-a-half uninterrupted hours. From where he sat he could hear the voices of the children at play. If anything went amiss he would be at once apprised by his ears.

As Hetty got into the small back hall from which the door opened on the quay there was a sound at the front-door. A key had been thrust into the latch and was being turned.

"Alfred coming back for something he has forgotten," thought Hetty, hurrying to meet him.

The door swung open and Mr. William Crawford pulled out his key, took off his hat, and bowed.

Hetty stepped back with an exclamation of surprise.

"You are surprised to see me, Miss Layard. Of course you are surprised; but I hope you are not displeased?"

He bowed with grave deference to her.

"Displeased?" she said, with a gallant attempt at a smile. "O dear, no! Why should I be displeased? When I heard the key in the door I made sure it was my brother coming back for something he had forgotten; and you know I had no reason to expect you." She now smiled without effort. She had recovered self-possession. "Will you come in here, or would you prefer going to your own rooms?"

"I do not want to go to my own lair to-day, Miss Layard," he said, as he followed her into their own sitting-room. "In fact, I am here by the merest accident, and I do not know that you will not laugh at me when I tell you why." He thought, "By Jove! what a contrast to some one in Singleton Terrace, Richmond! She is much more lovely than I thought her. I never saw her look so beautiful. Exquisite, exquisite Hetty!"

"Why do you think I shall laugh?" she asked.

"Because I came here owing to a dream I had last night. A most horrible dream! I am not superstitious, but this dream impressed me." Crawford did not act on the principle that all women are alike. He always considered every woman who interested him as a being the like of whom he had never met before, one requiring special study and special treatment. When he wooed his wife he always kept before him the idea that she was tender and affectionate. Of Hetty he said to himself, "She is imaginative and ardent."

"A dream? It must have been a very remarkable dream that made you come so far."

"Yes, a most remarkable and unpleasant dream. I thought in my sleep that some one--I knew not whom at first--had wandered out of the house through the door on the Bay by night, and, turning to the left, went near the open door of that flooded ice-house. There are two doorways to the ice-house and no door. I thought I was standing at the further one from this. The figure drew close to the nearer doorway, and I saw that the wanderer was a somnambulist, and was quite unaware of any danger. I thought I tried to cry out, but could not utter a sound. I thought I tried to rush forward, but could not move. I was half mad with terror, for as the figure drew near me I recognised who it was. The figure kept on until it reached the raised threshold of the ice-house. It stepped upon the sill of the doorway, and all at once I heard a scream and a splash; and I looked in and saw the figure struggling in the water. I strove with all my might to wrest myself free from the leaden weights that held my feet. The face of the figure was turned up to me, and I could see the golden hair and the lovely cheek and the wonderful blue eyes, and I heard a voice, the sweetest and dearest voice I ever heard, cry out in agony, 'Save me! Save me! O, Mr. Crawford, won't you try to save me?' and I wrenched and struggled, and at last I tore myself free, and with a great shout I awoke, terrified and trembling, and in a cold perspiration. And I could not sleep again."

"What a horrible dream!" cried the girl, with blanched face, and eyes wide open with dismay.

"It was terrible, indeed. But, Miss Layard, all I have told you was to me nothing compared with what I have yet to tell."

She drew back trembling, and feeling faint.

"Do you know who the drowning person that I could not succour was?"

"No," whispered the girl.

"You."

"I?"

"Yes; you!"

The girl drew back another pace, and shuddered; she seemed about to faint.

"It was your face I saw, and you were in peril of death! and I--I was looking on and could not help you. Great heavens! fancy my finding you in want of aid in my view, and I not able to help you! All the horrible dreams of my life put together would not equal the anguish, the insupportable agony, of that."

He took out his handkerchief, breathed heavily--as though the memory of his nightmare was almost as bad as the nightmare itself--and then wiped his forehead laboriously with the handkerchief. After this he sat for a while, leaning back in his chair with a hand resting on each knee, as though to recover himself. In a few seconds he rose with the affectation of an affected briskness, intended to convey that he was struggling against emotions that overcame him. He said, with a wan smile:

"So I came straight here to have doors put on those hateful doorways. I knew you would laugh at me."

"Indeed, I do not laugh at you! That dream was enough to upset any one."

He shook his head, conveying by the shaking of his head and the expression of his face the idea that, great as might be her power of realising his sufferings, they were infinitely greater than she could imagine.

Then he shook the whole of his body to rouse himself out of his lethargy, and establish himself in her mind as a man of action. He begged of her to get him a piece of string, and when she had found him some he asked her to favour him by accompanying him to the ice-house, and aid him in taking measurements for the doors to block up the yawning death traps, as he called the doorways.

He could not reach the lintel of the doors without something on which to stand. He asked her to hold the string for him till he came back, and went to the kitchen and fetched a chair. He mounted on the chair, and asked her to draw the string taut to the ground, and knot the point at which the string touched the raised threshold.

"There were double doors here once, but single doors will do now," he said.

When he had completed his measurement he said:

"I shall go from this to the carpenter and leave orders for the doors. I shall come back in a week to see them put up."

For a few minutes he seemed to fall into a profound reverie, and then, waking up all at once, looked at her with eyes full of terror, and, pointing into the flooded ice-house said hoarsely:

"Hetty, it was in there I saw you drowning! Do you know what that sight meant to me, girl?" He bent close to her ear and answered his own question in a whisper:

"Madness!"

Then, without another word, he hurried away, leaving her amazed, breathless, not knowing what to think of him, and all he had been saying, and not able to think of anything else.

CHAPTER XXIII
"MAN OVERBOARD!"

When Hetty recovered from the astonishment into which Mr. William Crawford's words and manner had cast her, the first fact which struck her memory was that he had called her Hetty. That might, no doubt, be excused in a man of his time of life to a girl of hers (she considered his thirty-six years entitled him to be considered quite middle-aged). But she would have felt more comfortable if the question had not been raised at all. It was, she urged in mitigation, to be taken into account that he spoke under great excitement and in haste. But, after all, the thing was not worth a moment's thought.

There was, however, a fact worth considering. This man, sleeping or waking, did seem to have a special care of the lives of others. Had he not rescued his wife from fire?--and here now was this dream, this dreadful dream about the odious old ice-house. No doubt some men were born with a natural taste for encountering risks, but her inclination did not lead her to plunge into burning houses or flooded ice-houses. For her part she would rather run away twenty miles.

And then what were these words he had said about herself? Now that they came back to her they seemed foolish, impertinent, and she ought to have been angry with him for laughing at her. But no; he had not been laughing at her. He could not laugh at anything on earth after having such an awful dream, and no doubt what he had said of herself was only his exaggerated way of describing how terribly hard he had wanted to save the drowning woman. But there was no person really drowning, and it would be nonsense not to forget the whole interview with him.

Yet it could hardly be got rid of in that way, for how would Alfred take it? The whole affair was very provoking and horrible, and she felt disposed to cry. Perhaps Alfred was right in his first estimate of Crawford, and he was a little mad.

Yes, clearly the man ought to be in a lunatic asylum, and not allowed to go about the country dreaming and terrifying people.

She had no doubt that in a few minutes a procession of men, carrying planks on their shoulders and bags of tools in their hands, would arrive and make the place unbearable with noise and chips.

Hetty would have made her mind quite easy on the last score if she could have seen into the mind of William Crawford as he left the door. For he had no more notion of going to any carpenter that day about the job than he had of flinging himself off Welford Bridge into the South London Canal. What he did intend doing was, to come back in a week and say he found the wretched carpenters to whom he had given the order had wholly misunderstood him and botched the job. This would be economical as far as the doors were concerned, and would give him another interview with Hetty.

He had no notion of keeping his promise to his wife either. What could be easier and more pleasant than to enjoy a few hours' freedom in town, and tell her on his return to Richmond that the difficulties to be overcome at the ice-house were much greater than he had anticipated, and that he had been most grievously delayed against his will.

From a map he had discovered, since his former visit, that he could come or go by water. At the end of one of the Pine Groves lay the Mercantile Pier, and Crawford turned in that direction, resolved to get to town by river.

It pleased him to know that there were two ways of approaching his office, and the line from Crawford's House to the Mercantile Pier was directly away from Camberwell, whereas the route by road was only at right angles to it.

"I think what I said to Hetty must create some effect," he thought, as he walked with brisk footstep and alert body. "It did all I intended anyway. She may, when she gets over her surprise, be either pleased or indignant; but she cannot be indifferent, she is too imaginative for that."

He passed by the Neptune public-house, and entered the Pine Grove leading to the Mercantile Pier. He had no need to ask his way: he carried the map of the place in his head.

Here on either side of him rose the tall black palings. The path between them was only a footway, and wound along sinuously for half a mile between the great docks on either side. The path bent so acutely that it was impossible to see further than a hundred yards before or behind.

To Crawford, who was always expecting to find Philip Ray spring forth, feel a burning sting, hear a report, and know that vengeance had overtaken him at last, this characteristic had one great advantage: it left both his sides protected. He could be approached only from the front or rear.

The place was very secret and retired. There was not a sound beyond the far-off hum of the city. Spying through the chinks in the palings one could see nothing but broken dark grey ground littered with all kinds of odds and ends of timber and metal objects, looking as dreary and deserted and forlorn as a locked-up and deserted graveyard. Overhead spread the faint blue sky, with the sun behind a dull grey cloud, and above the paling to right and left, and, as it were, rising from hulls lying far off inland, the lofty motionless spars of great ships in the stillness of the upper air.

From the time Crawford entered the Pine Grove until he had got more than half-way through he encountered no one. Then all at once he became aware that he was gradually overtaking a woman who was walking in front, and that footsteps which he had heard for some time behind him were gradually gaining upon him.

With him every unknown woman was an object of curiosity: every unknown man Philip Ray. The woman in front was poorly clad, and walked with lagging step and dejected head. She did not promise to interest him. He turned round. The man was not Philip Ray. Without further thought of either he continued his walk.

Presently the man was level with him, and said, "Beg pardon, sir, but I saw you pass the Neptune, and I thought I'd ask you if you had any odd job hereabout on your property."

Crawford started and looked sharply at the man out of his dark furtive eyes. The speaker he recognised as the man who had acted as his guide, and explained to him the means of Philip Ray's mysterious disappearance from the tow-path.

"No," he said sharply, "I have no job," and turned away to show he did not wish to be spoken to again.

"Perhaps, sir, you don't know the stage is off?"

"What!" cried Crawford, stopping and confronting the man. "What do you mean by the stage being off?" He remembered that Red Jim had told him about the floating stage at Boland's Ait. Could it be that the floating bridge had been removed, and that Ray's visit to the islet and its idiotic owner had ceased? or that the owner had taken himself away?

Jim pointed down the Grove. "The stage that goes from the land to the pier had to be taken away for repairs, and you have to get from the shore to the pier in a small boat, and when the tide is low, as it is now, you have to go down a long ladder so as to get to the bed of the river, and from the bed of the river to the small boat; and people with plenty of money don't care about doing that. So when I saw you turn into the Grove I thought I'd come and tell you, as I felt sure if you knew you wouldn't think of going by boat, and I remembered you gave me two tanners a fortnight ago."

"Then I won't give you anything now," said Crawford sharply, as he resumed his way. His anger had been aroused by the hopes raised and cast down by Red Jim's two speeches about the stage.

"Not as much as a tanner?"

"Not as much as half a farthing. I made a very bad bargain the last time, and this must be given in with what you did before. Besides, this is no use to me, for I intend going by boat all the same. Good-day. If you beg again I shall call the police."

The man abated his pace with a malediction, and Crawford went on, Red Jim followed him slowly, cursing his own luck.

The delay caused by the dialogue with Red Jim had given the woman a good start, and by the time Crawford reached the head of the ladder the woman was in the act of being handed into the small boat.

When Crawford looked down he was very sorry he had not given Red Jim sixpence for his news and advice, and gone back by land. But it was too late to retrace his steps. He felt a dogged determination not to give Jim anything or be jeered at by him.

Half the descent was easy enough, as it was by rude wooden stairs; but the other half had to be accomplished by means of a broad ladder of very muddy, slippery, and rotten looking steps. The foreshore, too, looked muddy, slimy, uninviting, and here and there was steaming in an unpleasant manner under the influence of the sun, now shining clearly between vast plains of pale grey clouds.

Crawford hated boats for two reasons. First, he couldn't pull; and, second, he always felt nervous in them, and he could not swim.

However, there was not much time for liking or disliking, for the men in the small boat beckoned him to come on. There were already in the boat the crew of two men, the woman who had preceded him down the lane, and six other women.

With repugnance he descended to the foreshore, and with repugnance and difficulty got into the boat. All the passengers except one were aft.

Crawford took a seat on the starboard side, next to the woman who had preceded him down the Grove.

She took no notice of his coming aboard. She appeared unconscious of everything round her. She wore a thick black veil, and kept her head bowed upon her chest, giving him the idea that she suffered from some deformity, or disease, or dire calamity. She clasped her elbow in one hand, her arm across her chest, and her other hand across her eyes. The moment she entered the boat she had assumed this posture, and had not moved since.

Her attitude was the result of two causes: her eyes were weak from recent illness, and she was suffering from incurable sorrows.

Her clothes were worn and betokened poverty, her purse penury. Under her thin frayed dress her shoulders bore marks of recent scratches; under the bosom of her dress her heart bore open wounds of anguish. She was on her way to a free hospital about her eyes.

Disease had lately threatened her life, but even Death refused to have her. At what she believed to be her last hour she provided for her only child, the apple of her eye, her solitary joy, by placing him in safety, but beyond the power of a recalling cry from her lips. She had then put aside money for her sepulchre.

Death had disdained her, and she was now wandering about alone with the vast world as a tomb and a solitude, and a broken heart and the fate of an outcast, and the undying gnawing remorse for company, with for the sustentation of her living body the money she had devised for its decay. An illness had taken away her voice, which was her bread.

Just as the boat shoved off, Red Jim reached the head of the stairs, and stood there regarding the progress of his patron. He noticed that the ebb tide was running very fast, and that the men kept the boat heading a little up stream to make allowance for leeway. He noticed that Crawford was the last passenger on the starboard side, and that, therefore, he would be on the inside when the boat got alongside. "I hope," thought Red Jim, "that there's some nice fresh paint or a nice long nail waiting for him when he's going up the side."

He saw the boat touch the side, and Crawford stagger instantly to his feet. He saw him sway to and fro, and then suddenly fall back against the hulk, boom the boat off with his legs, and drop overboard between the boat and the hulk.

Red Jim uttered a loud shout of triumph, and then began shouting and dancing like mad for joy.

"He'll shoot in under the hulk and be drowned!" cried Red Jim exultingly.

Then an oath:

"That ---- woman's got him!

"Catch him! Hold him!" cried the boatmen. "Hold on for your life or he'll be sucked under!"

The veiled woman had seized the sinking man and thrown herself on her knees--was holding on with all the power of her enfeebled arms.

"Trim the boat! Trim the boat, ---- you, or she'll capsize! On deck, there!" shouted the boatman to the hulk.

By this time aid had come from the deck, and the submerged man had been seized by the hooks and had hold of a line. Up to this the boatmen had been completely powerless, for all the women had crowded to the starboard side, and bore down the boat's gunwale until it washed level with the water, and if the men attempted to get near the starboard side aft the boat must have gone over at once. And now the passengers went on board the hulk.

When the woman who had saved him was relieved of his weight, she gave a loud cry, and fell back fainting in the boat.

CHAPTER XXIV
REWARD FOR A LIFE

Two men came down from deck and carried the fainting woman up, and brought her into the pier-master's little room, and left her to the kindly offices of some sympathetic women; while the two boatmen dragged the half-stunned, half-drowned Crawford out of the river over the stern of the boat, and then, after allowing some of the water to run out of his clothes, helped him up the accommodation-ladder to the deck of the hulk.

Here men squeezed his clothes and rubbed him down, and told him how thankful he ought to be that he had not been drowned, as he was within an ace of being drawn under the hulk, and if once that had happened his chance of ever seeing daylight again would have been small indeed. Was he a good swimmer?

No, he could not swim a yard.

Well, then, he had better for the future keep out of the water. Yes, of course he had lost his hat; but a sou'wester of the pierman's was at his service temporarily. No? He wouldn't have it? Very well. Better any day lose one's hat than one's life. He was very wet indeed; but, then, when a man has been in the river one must expect to turn out wet upon fetching port.

Why had his position been so very dangerous? Was it more dangerous than that of a man falling overboard under ordinary circumstances?

A thousand times. For he had fallen against the hulk and boomed off the boat, and in booming her off his back had slid down the side of the hulk until his heels were higher than his head, and as he left the boat his heels, driven by the force of the tide on the sheer of the boat, would thrust him inward and downwards and so under the bottom of the hulk, and then good-bye to him, particularly as he could not swim.

And how then came he to be saved?

Why, by the woman laying hold of him just as he slipped out, and sticking to him; for, owing to the list to starboard the passengers gave the boat, the boatmen durst not move, or she'd capsize for certain.

The woman laying hold of him? It was all dark to him.

Of course it was all dark to him, and a good job it had ever come light to him again. Why, the woman who had sat beside him! A poor sorrowful-looking creature, who wore a veil and kept her hands across her eyes.

He had noticed her. And where was she now?

In the master's room in a dead faint. She had fainted the moment they told her she might let him go. She looked a poor soul that had had her troubles, and if he thought well of doing such a thing, perhaps he might do worse than give her a trifle by way of reward.

A trifle! A trifle for saving his life! He could and he would reward her most handsomely. Had she recovered yet?

It was believed not. And now they had squeezed all they could out of him--unless he'd like to give them something for their trouble, for they had to go back at once.

He handed a wet and clammy five-pound note to be divided as they thought best among themselves.

He was generous, for had not a great life been at stake?

Was he going ashore, or going on? He had better get dry clothes.

He should stay until that woman was well enough to receive the reward for the great services she had rendered him.

The boatmen descended the accommodation-ladder, and Crawford, partly to keep off a chill and partly to prevent the people on the pier from accosting him, began walking up and down the deck at a brisk rate.

He had two reasons for not going to Welford for dry clothes. First, he did not wish to weaken the effect of his visit and words of that morning by so early a reappearance; and second, he did not care to present himself to Hetty in his miserable and undignified plight.

When he had money he liked carrying large sums about with him, for he never felt so sure of the possession of it as when he could tap a pocket-book containing a sheaf of notes.

He made up his mind to give this woman fifty pounds, for had she not done him the greatest service any man, woman or child ever performed towards him? had she not saved his life, and was she not worthy of the highest reward he could pay? He had no more than fifty pounds and some broken money.

In a few minutes the pier-master, who had heard him speak of the reward, came and said the poor woman had fully recovered, and asked if Crawford would wish to see her.

"By all means. I must get these wet clothes off as soon as possible. When is the next boat up?"

"In about five or ten minutes." The pier-master moved off, and returned immediately to say the woman was ready and willing to receive him. Adding, "It's a kind of thing we'd like to see done, as we saw her save your life, and know you are open-handed and have a good heart; but she says she'd rather there was only you two."

"Alone!" said Crawford in a tone of surprise. "It is a kind of thing generally done openly. Did you tell her I wished to give her a reward?"

"Yes, sir. She said you would know before you left her why she preferred no one should be present."

"Well," said Crawford, who felt that this was an attempt to keep the generosity of his gift from the eyes of others, "I am going to give her these five tenners." He held out the notes in his hand and turned them over, and then, still keeping them in his hand lest some one might suspect a trick, stepped into the pier-master's private room or cabin.

It was a very tiny room, with a small table in the middle, a writing-table in one of the two windows, and three chairs. There seemed to be no space for moving about. Even if the chairs were out of the way, two people could not walk abreast round the centre table.

Standing with her back to the second window Crawford found the woman who had saved his life less than half-an-hour ago. Her veil, which had been disarranged in the struggle, was now close drawn.

With the notes in one hand and holding out the other to grasp hers in his gratitude, he was about to advance, when she held up her hand and said in a hoarse dull voice, "No nearer. I have been very ill. It is safer our hands should not meet."

He sprang back as far as the walls would allow. He had the most intense horror of contagious diseases. He was now in the most fervent haste to bring the interview to an end. He would freely have given another fifty to be out of that room.

"I merely wished to thank you from the bottom of my heart for the noble manner in which you snatched my life from death, to offer you this fifty pounds as a small token of the esteem in which I hold the services you have rendered me;" he shook the notes, but did not advance his hand any nearer to the centre of contagion; "and to say that my everlasting gratitude must be yours." He could always make a little speech.

"There was a time," she said in her peculiar hoarse, dull voice, "when I should have been very glad to take those fifty pounds--ay, as many shillings--from you, but I cannot take them now."

"There was a time!" said he, surprised, and interested notwithstanding his fear of disease; "surely I could not have had the privilege of offering them to you longer ago than an hour."

"You could," she said, "and you ought."

"May I ask," said he, fairly carried away by curiosity, "if the disease of which you speak was of a nervous character?"

"You mean, was my mind affected?"

"Yes, if you choose to put it that way?"

"It was, but unfortunately I have not been in an asylum; even the grave that they told me was gaping for me closed of its own accord. It was the last door open to me, and it is shut now."

"But if your disease was mental, I cannot understand why we might not shake hands; why I might not shake the hand of my rescuer."

"Because she could not touch yours. It is in *your* hand the contamination lies."

"Poor creature!" he thought, "mad!--quite mad! To say such a thing of me, who am never ill--of the soundest man in London! I, who take such care not to be ill!" He laughed one of his short sharp laughs, and said aloud, "Contagion in my hand! And who am I?"

"I do not know who you are *now*." At the emphasised word he sprang into the air off the ground as though he had been shot, and then took a pace towards her, and paused and looked furtively at the door.

Was she, too, armed?

She also took a pace forward. They were not now two yards apart. With a scornful gesture she tore the veil from before her face and, looking into his, cried, "And who am *I*?"

The face was haggard and blotched.

He sprang back against the wall, crying:

"Good heavens, Kate, this is not you!"

"Yes, this is Kate. I saved your life to-day, and you offer me fifty pounds. How glad I should have been to get as many shillings when you left me and my child to starve in America! I saved your life to-day, and you offer me a reward. I will take it----"

He held out the notes to her.

She pushed his hand aside with a laugh.

"The reward I want you to give me cannot be bought for money--not even for your splendid fifty pounds. I saved your life to-day; give me for reward my husband and my child, and my innocence. It is a fair demand. You cannot give me less, John Ainsworth."

She thrust her hand suddenly into her pocket.

"She is armed!" he cried, and, bursting from the room, he leaped aboard a steamer then a foot from the pier on its way up to London.

CHAPTER XXV
A NEW VISITOR AT CRAWFORD'S HOUSE

When Red Jim saw Crawford hauled out of the water and aided up the side of the hulk his interest in maritime affairs was over. He had gone down to the end of the Pine Grove in the hope that Crawford would change his mind, and adopt the land route when he saw how uninviting the means of getting to the steamboat looked. In case Crawford came back he might fairly count on getting sixpence, surly as the other had been to him. But now there was no chance of anything good, not even of Crawford being drowned. Red Jim looked up at the sky as though reproaching heaven with doing him ill-turns, faced right about and began retracing his fruitless steps.

As he walked he reflected that it was not every day one saw a gentleman fall into the river and rescued. He had seen this sight to-day, and, moreover, as far as the shore was concerned, he had had the monopoly of the spectacle. Then after a long pause he asked himself was it not possible to convert his unique position into a little money?

Once more he turned those vacant blue eyes of his up to the sky, not this time, however, in reproach, but in appeal for light.

Suddenly he shook his head with the quick short jerk of determination, and quickened his pace. "Why, of course," he said out loud, "I'll go to Crawford's House, and tell them about it, and they'll give me a tanner for my kindness." So he hastened along until he arrived at the shabby green door, and then he knocked.

Hetty opened the door, and seeing a strange man, who looked as though he had a right to come there, concluded he had called about the ice-house. "O!" said she, "you've called about those gates, have you?"

"Hallo!" thought Jim, "there may be another tanner in this. Let's see." All Jim's thoughts ran on tanners. A shilling was two tanners, half-a-crown five, a sovereign ever so many. In the case between him and the young lady at the door caution was the great thing. He must take care not to commit himself. So he said nothing, but looked round as though in search of the gates.

"Come this way," said Hetty, observing the glance of search, "and I will show you the place."

"Yes, ma'am," said Red Jim, entering the house and following Hetty through it to the little quay beyond.

"These are the doorways that Mr. Crawford wishes to have boarded up," said Hetty, pronouncing the name with an effort, for she was still in tumult and perplexity about his visit and words.

"Yes, ma'am," said Red Jim with extreme deference, and looking full at her with his wide, open expressionless blue eyes, but moving no muscle, showing no sign of taking action.

The girl was highly strung, and his impassive stolidity irritated her.

"Well, what are you going to do?" she asked briskly.

"Whatever you like, ma'am," he answered with gallantry and impartiality.

"Whatever *I* like!" she cried impatiently. "I have nothing to do with it. What did Mr. Crawford say to you about this place. There can be no mistake, I suppose--you saw him to-day?"

"I did."

"And what did he say to you about this?" pointing to the gaping gateway.

"Nothing."

The girl stared at him in angry surprise. "Then why did you come here?"

"To tell you, ma'am, that Mr. Crawford fell in the river. I thought you'd like to know that."

"Mr. Crawford fell into the river! You thought *I* would like to know *that!* What do you mean?" Hetty was beginning to get confused and a little frightened. There was first of all Crawford's visit, then his account of his horrible dream of her drowning, then his strange, impudent words to her; now came this dreadful-looking man to say that *Crawford* had fallen into the river, and, last of all, she would be glad to hear he had fallen into the river? "Why do you think I would be glad to hear that Mr. Crawford fell into the river?"

"Well, he lives here, and when people fall into the river the folk they live with are mostly glad to hear of it."

"O," thought the girl, with a feeling of relief at finding that no mysterious net was closing round her, "so you only came to tell me the news?"

"And to tell you more news."

"What is it?"

"That he was got out again."

"Of course."

"But you didn't know until I told you."

"Certainly I did. If he hadn't been taken out you would have said he was drowned."

This was a sore blow to Red Jim. It had occurred to him as a brilliant idea to split up his news into two parts. First, that Crawford had fallen in; second, that Crawford had been dragged out. He had a vague hope that, treated in this way, the news might be worth two tanners, as it consisted of two items. It now occurred to him that in future he ought to say a man was drowned, get his reward, and then, as a second item, say that it had been for a long time believed he was drowned, but that it was at last found out he wasn't. In the present case, however, he thought he had better make the best of things as they were. He told her then exactly what had happened as far as he had been able to see, and assured her he had run every step of the way and was mortal dry, and he hoped she'd consider his trouble and good intentions.

She gave him sixpence.

"And how much this job, ma'am? he asked, pointing to the gateways.

"I have nothing to do with that. When you knocked I thought Mr. Crawford had sent you."

"Well, he as good as sent me. Only he fell in, I'd never have come here."

"But you have done nothing, and you are to do nothing, and I have nothing to do with it," said the girl, a little apprehensively. They were alone on the quay at the back of the house, and there was not a soul in the house but herself and this ragged, rugged, red-bearded, rusty-necked man, who was asking her for money he had no claim to, and asking her for it on, no doubt, the knowledge of their isolation.

"There's my time, though, ma'am," said Red Jim firmly. "You call me in, and you say there's the gate, and I do all I can for you."

"But you have done nothing at all. Why should I pay you for doing nothing? I thought you were Mr. Crawford's man."

The girl was now becoming fairly alarmed. Suppose this horrible man should become violent?

"Some one must pay me for my time, ma'am. I'm only a poor labouring man trying to earn his bread, and if people go and take up my time, how am I to earn my bread by the sweat of my brow, or any other way? That's what I want to know."

He stood in front of her: between her and the door of the house.

The girl now became fairly frightened. She was by no means timid by nature. But here was she hidden from the view of any one, alone with this rugged, threatening, desperate man. No one on the tow-path could see them, because Boland's Ait intervened. Worst of all, she had not any money. The sixpence she had given him was the last coin in her possession; still, she tried to look brave.

"If you want any money for this job as you call it, go to Mr. Crawford for it."

"How do I know where to find Mr. Crawford?"

"He lives at Richmond."

"He lives here, and my principle is cash--no tick. A nice thing, indeed, to expect a poor labouring man to give his time and anxiety of mind to jobs, and then tell him to go to Richmond for his money! Is that justice or fair-play?"

"Well, I tell you that you must go to him. I have no money." She was beginning to feel faint and giddy.

"No money, and live in a house like that!" he cried, pointing up to the old dilapidated habitation to which the late owner of the place had given his name. "Why, how could any one keep up a house like that without lots of money?"

Red Jim's notion of the probable financial result of this interview had enlarged considerably since it had begun. He had talked himself into the conviction that he had an honest claim for compensation for loss of time, and he saw that they were in a lonely place, that this girl was frightened, and that there was no succour for her near at hand. He now put down the result of his inspection of the ice-house at four tanners.

"I tell you I have no money," she repeated, feeling sick, "and you must go away at once."

"Look here, ma'am; what am I going to do with the rest of my day if I get nothing for this?" He hadn't done a day's work for months. "The rest of my day is no sort of use to me. I own I haven't been here half a day, but half a day is gone, all the same, and I couldn't think of taking less than two shillings; it's against the rules of my Society to take less that two shillings for half a day, anyhow."

"I tell you once for all, I have no money."

She began to tremble. She had never before been in such an alarming situation as this. She was afraid to threaten lest he should at once seize her and fling her headlong into the ice-house, where there would be no William Crawford or anybody else to rescue her. She could have borne the thought of death with comparative fortitude, but the girl's dainty senses revolted from the notion of contact with this foul and hideous being. She felt that if he touched her she should die.

"Nice thing for you to say!" cried the man angrily. "Take a poor man in here and steal--yes, steal--half a day from him, and then say you have no money!"

Up to this he had been importunate, then angry, but he had not threatened. Now he advanced a step, and shaking his fist at her, said:

"Look here, if you don't just pay me what you owe me I'll----"

The girl screamed, and at the same time, as if by magic, Red Jim disappeared from her sight.

She looked down.

Red Jim was rolling and writhing on the ground, felled by a blow from behind.

She looked up. Francis Bramwell stood before her, pallid with indignation.

"This blackguard has been annoying you, Miss Layard," said he, spurning the prostrate man with his foot.

"O, thank you, Mr. Bramwell! I thought he was going to kill me."

"I came out to fetch Freddie back, but found it wasn't quite time, and then I heard your voice and this wretch's angry words, and came round and crossed. He hasn't *touched* you?" asked Bramwell fiercely. The whole man was roused now, and he looked large in stature and irresistible in force.

"O, no! He has not touched me, but he threatened me, and I felt as though I should die."

"What shall I do with him. Give him to the police?"

"Don't do that, guv'nor," said the prostrate man. He had made no attempt to rise. He did not want to have his other ear deaf and the inside of his head at the other side ringing like a sledge-bell. "Don't do that, guv'nor, for they have something against me about a trifle of canvas and a few copper bolts I never had anything to do with."

"Very well. Now, Miss Layard, if you will go into the house, I'll attend to this gentleman. I shall take him across my place to the tow-path, and then come back to see how you are."

"But you won't harm him, Mr. Bramwell?" asked Hetty in a tremulous voice as she moved away.

"You hear what the lady says?" whined Jim. "Good, kind lady, don't go away and leave me to him. He has half killed me already, and if you leave me to him he'll murder me. Do let me go through your house. I was only joking. Indeed, it was only a little joke, and I only went on as I did to make your beautiful face smile. That's all, indeed."

"I promise you, Miss Layard, not to hurt him in the least. He shall be much better off when he leaves me than he is now."

Hetty went into the house.

"He's going to pay me the half day's wages," thought Jim, as at Bramwell's bidding he rose from the ground and crossed over to Boland's Ait. Bramwell led the way to the canal side of the islet.

"How much did you claim from that lady?" asked Bramwell, who knew nothing of the justness of the demand.

"Two shillings, fairly earned and fairly due," answered Jim, his heart expanding under the hope of tanners. "You will not keep a poor working man out of his own?"

"I'll pay you. But first you must answer me one question: Can you swim?" He took a two-shilling piece out of his pocket.

"I can, sir," said Jim eagerly. "I can do almost anything."

Bramwell flung the coin across the canal to the tow-path, crying, "Then swim for that."

"But, sir----"

"In you go, clothes and all, and if ever I find you here again I'll hand you over to your friends the police. Don't keep standing there, or I'll heave you in. Do as you are told, sir. The washing and cooling will do you good."

And seeing there was no chance of escape, and fearing some one might come by and steal the coin, Red Jim dived into the dark turbid waters and crossed to the opposite shore.

When Bramwell saw the man safely out of the canal he turned away, and, having crossed by the stage, entered for the first time Crawford's House--the house of the man who had wrecked his home and his happiness and his life three years before.

CHAPTER XXVI
A BRIDGE OF SIGHS

When Bramwell entered Crawford's House the first sight that met his eyes was the form of Hetty Layard lying prone on the floor of the passage.

With a cry of dismay he sprang to her and raised her. He looked round for help and called out, but there was no succour in sight; no response came to his cry. He took her up and carried her into the sitting-room, and laid her on the couch.

"I might have guessed she would faint," he moaned; "and now what am I to do?"

There was water on the table laid for dinner. He sprinkled some on her face. "What am I to do? Shall I run for help?" he cried, looking frantically round the room.

At that moment there was the sound of a latch-key in the door. Bramwell rushed out eagerly into the passage, saying to himself, "This must be either her brother or Mr. Crawford; Philip told me there are only two keys."

If instead of going up the river in the steamboat Crawford had come back to Welford, he would have arrived at about this time.

The front door opened, and a man with a remarkably long beard entered, and for an instant stood looking in speechless amazement at the other man.

"My name is Bramwell. Your sister has fainted. She is in the front room."

"Fainted!" cried Alfred Layard in alarm, as he dashed past the other.

At that moment Hetty opened her eyes and sighed.

"Hetty, Hetty, dear Hetty! what is this. What is the matter?"

Bramwell remained in the passage. He walked up and down in great agitation.

"I don't know what happened," said the girl, in a weak, tremulous voice.

Her brother got some wine, and made her drink a little.

"Try and remember, dear," said Layard with passionate tenderness. "Did any accident occur? Drink just a little more. Did you get a fright, dear? Has anything happened to the boy?"

"No, Alfred. O, I am better now. I remember it all. A dreadful man terrified me, and Mr. Bramwell came to my assistance, and I ran into the house; and I can remember no more."

Bramwell, hearing voices, knew that Hetty had recovered, and that he could be of no further use; so he stole quietly out of the house, and returned to his own island domain.

He did not seek the boys, who were playing in the timber-yard that the old barrow was a Punch-and-Judy show. He took the canal side of the wharf, and began pacing up and down hurriedly.

His condition was one of extreme exultation; he knew not, inquired not, at what. He trod the clouds, and surveyed below his feet a subjugated and golden world. The air was intoxication, and life a dream of jocund day. He did not pause to ask a reason for these feelings and sensations; they were his; that was enough.

Of late the hideous gloom in which he had lived for two years, a solitary upon that lonely and unlovely islet, had been leaving him as darkness leaves a hill at the approach of day. Now from the summit to the base, his nature seemed bathed in an extraordinary midday splendour. His soul was shining among the stars. He was a blessed spirit amid the angels. He was the theme to which all the rest of the world answered in harmonious parts.

It was not passion or love, but a spiritual effulgence. It was like the elation induced by a subtle perfume. He would have been satisfied to be, and only to be, if he might be thus. He was in clear air at a stupendous height of happiness, and yet did not feel giddy. He could think of no higher earthly joy than he experienced. It was a joy the very essence of which seemed of the rapture of heaven. It was a kind of ecstatic and boundless worship from a self-conscious and self-centred soul. It idealised the world, and restored Paradise to earth.

In his mind was no thought, no defined thought, of love for his beautiful neighbour, Hetty Layard. He was in the delicious spiritual experiences of that hour merely celebrating his emancipation from bondage. The note from Kate which had come with Frank and the subsequent announcement of Kate's death in the newspapers had left him no room to doubt that he was free. That day he had struck a man an angry blow for the first time in all his life. And he had struck that blow in defence of this beautiful girl, who was so good and so devoted to the little orphan boy, the son of her brother. He had an orphan boy too, and she was very gentle to his son. He had known for some time that he was a free man, free to look upon the face of woman with a view to choosing another wife; but until this day, until this hour, he had not realised what this freedom meant.

The notion that he might take another companion for life had not taken concrete form since Frank's coming, and now the only way in which it presented itself to him was that he might smile back to Hetty's smile, and glory in her beauty.

He was startled by hearing a voice saying behind him, "Mr. Bramwell, I have taken the liberty of coming over uninvited to thank you from the bottom of my heart for your timely and much-needed aid to my sister."

Bramwell coloured, and became confused. He was unaccustomed to new faces, unaccustomed to thanks, unaccustomed to pleasant thoughts of woman.

"I--I did nothing," he said. "It was merely by accident I knew about it."

To be thanked made him feel as though he had done something shameful.

"However it happened," said Layard, taking his hand in both his own and shaking it cordially, "you have placed me under a deep debt of gratitude to you."

"If you do not wish to make me very uncomfortable, you will not say another word about it. I hope Miss Layard is nothing the worse of the affair?"

"My sister is all right. Of course it gave her an ugly turn. It isn't a nice place to encounter a bullying rowdy alone. Since you ask me to say no more about your share in the business, I shall be dumb."

The two men were now walking up and down side by side along the tiny quay of the tiny islet.

A thin film of cloud dulled the glare of the afternoon sun. The whole expanse of heaven was radiant with diaphanous white clouds; a barge laded with wood indolently glided by to the clank-clank of the horse's hoofs on the tow-path; the sounds from Welford Bridge, which in the mornings came sharp and clear, were now dulled by the muffled hum of larger noises from afar. There was an air of silence and solitude over Boland's Ait. Notwithstanding the griminess of the surroundings and the dilapidations of the buildings on the holm, there was an aspect of peace and retirement in the place.

Hetty had not told her brother anything of Crawford's visit save as much as was necessary to explain the admission of Red Jim to the house and quay.

After a few sentences, Layard said, "You must know, Mr. Bramwell, I don't think I shall stay in this house a minute longer that I can possibly help."

"Indeed!" said Bramwell, feeling as though the sunlight from the sky had been suddenly dulled, and the things upon which his eyes fell had grown more squalid.

"To be candid with you, I don't care about my landlord. He is, to say the least of it, eccentric; and after the affair of to-day I shall never be easy. You see, the house is quite isolated, and no one ever by any chance passes the door."

"It must be very lonely for Miss Layard," Bramwell said, forgetting in his sympathy for the girl his own two years of absolute seclusion.

"She says, and I believe her, that she does not feel the want of company; but after to-day she will, I am afraid, dread the place. Of course, I must get some person to stay with her all the time I am out of the house. Could any one have been more helpless than she was to-day?"

"What you say has a great deal of force in it; but," said he, trying to restore the full complement of sunlight to the sky, "don't you think with a second person in the house all would be safe?"

"Well, I should imagine so; but one does not like to be continually saying, 'all is safe.' One likes to take it for granted, as one takes the sufficiency of air or the coming of daylight with the sun."

They walked for a few seconds in silence, and then Bramwell said, "No barge ever comes through the Bay now, but, owing to my habit with the floating-stage on the canal, I moor the second stage to the Ait every afternoon when Freddie has gone home, and haul it across in the morning. For the future I shall leave it across permanently, so that Miss Layard may feel I am as near to her as some one living next door. I hope and trust, and believe, she will never have any need of my help, but it may give her a little confidence to know that I can be with her instantly in case of need."

"It is extremely kind of you to think of that. It seems you are determined to place me under obligations I can never discharge. The worst of it is that when I came over here I had it in my mind to ask you a favour, and now you have offered to do one unasked."

"If what you came to ask is anything in the world I can do, you may count on me, Mr. Layard. For, remember, that although this is the first time we have met, I am quite well acquainted with you through Philip Ray."

"And I with you, through him also, or I should not speak so freely."

"Isn't Ray a fine fellow?" asked Bramwell enthusiastically.

"The finest fellow I know," answered Layard cordially.

"He is a little enthusiastic, or hot-headed, or fierce, I know, but he will calm down in years. Indeed, I find that of late he is calming down a good deal. As I said before, I treat you as an old friend. I suppose I have been so long an eremite that once I come forth and open my mouth I shall never stop talking. What I have in my mind about Philip, who was the only friend of my solitude, is that if he got a good sensible wife it would be the making of him."

"I have no doubt it would."

"But the worst of it is that I don't think he ever once regarded one woman with more favour than another. In fact, I have always put him down as a man who will never marry."

"Indeed!" said Layard. "I wonder does Ray himself share that notion. If he does, he is treating Hetty badly," he thought.

"And the pity of it is, that if he would only marry he would make the best husband in England."

"It is indeed a pity," said Layard, but he did not say what constituted the pity. To himself, "I don't think anything has been said between them yet, but it seems to me Hetty or he will have some news for me very soon." He said aloud, "The little favour I told you I had to ask----"

"Of course; and I told you if it lay within my power I'd do it."

"Yes; and it does lie easily within your power, and I will take no excuse. Come over and spend an hour with us this evening."

"But I cannot!" cried Bramwell.

"But you must. We will take no excuse."

He wavered. His views of all things had greatly altered since he was first invited to Crawford's House. "Still the boy. I cannot leave him alone." He felt half inclined to go.

"The boy will not be alone. Why, now that you have decided to leave the stage across all night, your house and ours may be looked on as one."

What a pleasant fancy it was that Crawford's House, where she lived, and Boland's Ait, where he lived, might be looked on as one!

"If," went on Layard, "you are uneasy about your boy, at any moment you can run across and see him. You really have no excuse. Our sons have been friends some time, and now you have placed me under a great obligation to you, and you refuse to make the obligation greater. Is that generous of you?"

Bramwell smiled. "I am conquered, fairly conquered."

"Very well; and mind, not later than eight o'clock. Now, where's this young savage of mine? His aunt will imagine you have sold the two of us into slavery."

CHAPTER XXVII
A LAST RESOLVE

"Good gracious, Mrs. Mellor, you don't mean to say you have been to the hospital and got back again since! But why do I say such a thing? If you had wings you couldn't do it," exclaimed kind-hearted Mrs. Pemberton as Kate Mellor walked into the greengrocer's shop in Leeham, hard by Welford, the same day William Crawford jumped aboard the moving steamboat after his immersion and scene with the invalid woman at the Mercantile Pier.

"No," answered Mrs. Mellor wearily. She did not remove her veil on entering the shop. "I hadn't the heart to go to-day. I got as far as the pier and then turned back." She did not care to enter into any further explanation.

"Hadn't the heart, dear child! And why hadn't you the heart?" said the sympathetic woman, raising her ponderous bulk with deliberation from the chair, and going quickly with outstretched hands to her unfortunate lodger.

"I didn't feel equal to it, and so I came back."

"Well, dear if you didn't go to the hospital I'm very glad you came back here straight, for the house seems queer and lonesome when you're not in it. You don't feel any worse, do you, dear?"

"No worse, thank you, Mrs. Pemberton, but I think the heat tired me a little, and that I'll go up and lie down awhile."

"The very best thing you could do, dear. There's nothing to freshen you up when you're hot and tired like a nice quiet rest in a cool room; and the sun is off your room now. I was just saying to Mrs. Pearse here, that I was sure you'd come in half-dead of the heat. Is there anything I could get you, dear, before you lie down?"

"No, thank you, Mrs. Pemberton," and Kate Mellor passed out of the shop and up to her bedroom on the first floor.

"That's just the way with her always," said Mrs. Pemberton to Mrs. Pearse. "She never complains of anything but being tired, and she never wants anything. If ever there was a broken heart in this world it's hers. She has said to me over and over again it was a mistake that she recovered. What makes me so uneasy about her is that I am afraid her money won't last her much longer, and that when it's gone she'll run away. Though, goodness knows, she's welcome to stay as long as she likes, for she's a real lady, and it's almost as easy to keep two as one, particularly as she isn't a bit particular about what she eats or drinks; and I don't want to let her room unless I could get some one as nice as she, and I'd go far before I could find her equal."

"The loss of the child is preying upon her mind," said Mrs. Pearse. "I remember when I lost my little Ted, I thought I should never be able to lift my head again."

"Ah, but you lost your little Ted in a natural though a sad way; but poor Mrs. Mellor lost her boy by an accident, as it were, and by her own act, too. You know, she is very close, and although she's as friendly as can be, she never says anything about the past. Whoever she sent the boy to will not give him back to her again."

"And you don't know to what person she sent the child?"

"He went first to Boland's Ait, but of course not to stop there. Why, there's no woman on the Ait to look after a child. The boy must be gone to some of his father's people. O, it's a sad, sad case! and I have a feeling--you can't help your feelings--that she's not long for this world, poor thing; and it breaks my heart to think of that, for I do love her as if she was my own child, though it was never given to me to know the feelings of a mother. I expect that private detective knew all about the case."

Meanwhile Kate Mellor had taken off her bonnet and cloak, and lain down on her bed, to rest and think. Up to that day she had lived hour by hour, since the loss of her boy and her recovery, with no definite purpose. At first she had been too ill and weak to consider her position or determine upon any course of action. She had drifted down to this hour without any plan or purpose. She knew the law would not enable her to recover her child, and she felt certain that her husband would see the child dead rather than restored to her arms. She had inserted the announcement of her death partly that her husband might not be fettered in anything he might design for the welfare of their child by considerations of her, and partly out of a pathetic craving for pain and self-sacrifice. She had bought the paper, and had cried a score of times over the bald, cold intimation that the world was over for her: for her the once beautiful and beloved bride of Frank Mellor, now the deserted, marred outcast of shame. She had wept that she, Kate Ray, Kate Mellor, was dead and buried before thirty--when she was not twenty-five. She had wept that she was poor. She had wept that her voice, her only means of earning a living, had been destroyed. She had wept longest of all that her beauty was gone from her for ever. Her beauty had been her greatest gift, her greatest curse, and she wept for it as though it had been an unmixed blessing.

Lying on her bed here to-day, she had no tears to shed. The scene on the pier had in some mysterious way calmed her spirits. She had read the announcement of her death in the paper, and now she was dead in verity. Why should she live? What had she to live for? Everything woman could hold dear was gone--husband, child, reputation, beauty. In material affairs her destitution could scarcely be greater than it was at this moment. She had a little money still left, but when that was gone where should she find more? *He,* the betrayer, had been overjoyed to get his life back from the jaws of death that day; she, the victim, would enter those awful jaws freely, But she must see her child, her little Frank, the sweet baby she had held at her breast and cherished with the warmth of her embraces.

She was afraid of only one person in the world, and that was Frank Mellor, who had changed his name to Francis Bramwell for shame of her. If he found her he would kill her, and she owned that at his hands she deserved death; she had robbed him of everything he held dear.

She had resolved upon death, but she could not take it at his hands. It was too awful to think of a meeting between them. That would be ten times worse than the most painful form of quitting life. That would be an agony of the spirit ten thousand times transcending any possible agony of the body.

Frank, her husband, had always been a man of strong feeling. At times this strong feeling had exhibited itself to her in profound taciturnity, at times in overwhelming ecstasy. If she should encounter him now, he would be possessed by the demon of insatiable revenge; he would strike her to the ground and murder her cruelly, and mangle her dead body. While he was beating the life out of her he would revile and curse her. He would heap coals of fire on her head, and crush out of her the last trace of self-respect. And in all this he would, perhaps, be justified--in much of it certainly.

How good and indulgent he had been to her! She had not understood him then. She had eyes for nothing then but admiration and finery. To-day she had nothing to call forth admiration--no finery; and yet, if she had not hearkened to that other man, could she believe that Frank would not love and shield and cherish her now as he had then? Frank was the very soul of honour. He would not hurt a brute or wrong any living being. She had not known, had not understood, him then as she did now, judged by the light of subsequent experience.

She must see the boy once more--just once more before she died. She would not look upon another day. By some means or other she would see her child, and then bid good-bye to the world. When she saw her child, there would be the canal close at hand. But that would not do. It would not do to pollute with the last crime of her life the presence of her child. No; the river of which that other man had stood in such terror would be the fitting ending place for such a wicked life as hers.

"O, how different would all have been if only that man had not tempted her with lies, and she had not listened through vanity! Frank would have been good and kind to her, and by this time she should have grown to love him as she had never loved the other; and her boy, her darling, her little Frank, her baby, would be with her, his arms round her neck, his soft, round, warm cheek against her own!

"But, there, there, there!" she moaned, putting her hand before her blotched, disfigured, worn face. "It is all over! I have lost everything, and no one is to blame but myself and the other. Only I must suffer all. Yet it will not be for long. I *will* see my boy to-night, even if I die there and then. I don't care about dying. Death has refused me once, but it shall not this time. O, my little Frank! my little innocent Frank! my baby that I warmed against my breast!"

She lay in a kind of torpor for a few hours; then having got up and made some small arrangements, she wrote a note for Mrs. Pemberton, placed it in her trunk, and, putting a lock of hair and an old worn glove of her boy's in her bosom, went down-stairs and slipped out by the private door beside the shop.

CHAPTER XXVIII
WILLIAM CRAWFORD'S LUCK

When William Crawford found himself safe aboard the moving steamboat, he uttered an exclamation of intense relief and satisfaction. He looked quickly behind him, and noticed with a laugh that pursuit was out of the question. He was safe! His life had been twice imperilled that day, and he had escaped with nothing worse than a wetting. He had been in imminent danger of death from drowning, had been saved by a woman whom he had ruined, and then escaped from her deadly demoniacal, maniac wrath. After all this, who could say that there was not luck in the world? and who could deny that luck had befriended him in a phenomenal manner?

Yes, he was lucky; he had been lucky all his life up to this, except at cards, and he should be lucky to the end. If Fate had meant ever to do him an ill turn, surely it would not have let slip two such remarkable opportunities. No, he was born to good fortune; and the saying was true that it was better to be born lucky than rich. And, thinking of riches, this day's mishaps had not even cost him the fifty pounds, for he still held the notes in his hand. What a fool that woman was not to take them! But then she had always been a fool.

And with this generous thought of the woman who had sacrificed everything for him, he dismissed her from his mind.

He was hatless, and his clothes were all rumpled and creased; and the water dripped from the ends of his trousers, making a wet patch on the deck wherever he stepped.

The people on the steamboat had noticed the hasty manner of his coming aboard, his rush out of the pier-master's room, and his leap from the hulk. They also observed that his clothes were wet, and that he was without any covering for his head. They were observing him with interest and curiosity. Becoming conscious of this, and feeling a slight shiver pass through him, he turned to one of the crew and said:

"In coming from the shore to the pier I fell into the water. Is there any brandy aboard?"

"Plenty, sir, in the fore-cabin."

To the fore-cabin he went forthwith, and drove off the chill with brandy, and escaped the curious eyes of the passengers.

He remained below until the boat arrived at Blackfriars Bridge. Here he went ashore, and, hailing the first hansom, drove to a tailor and outfitter's, where he got everything he wanted except boots, and these the obliging shopkeeper procured for him.

It was now four o'clock. He had had two great shocks that day, each of which was more severe than any other he had endured in his life. He felt that something in the way of compensation was due to him. Play went on all day long and all night long at the Counter Club. What better could he do with himself than have a few quiet games before going back to his dull Richmond home? He did not like appearing at the club in a suit of ready-made clothes, but, then, all kinds of men, in all kinds of costumes, went to the Counter; and he had never been a great dandy.

Accordingly to the Counter he drove, with four of the damp ten-pound notes in his pocket and some broken money. It was not as much as he should have liked, but then, he had no intention of making a night of it. He would get back to Richmond about dusk.

He left the club just in time to catch the last train for home. He found an empty compartment, and, as he threw himself into a corner, cried softly to himself:

"Luck! Why, of course, there never was such luck as mine! I used to be unlucky at cards. Unlucky at cards, lucky in love, they say. Well, I have been more lucky than most men in love, and here now are cards turning in my favour. I have now won twice running. I have a hundred and twenty pounds more in my pocket than when I came to town this morning. There seems to be absolutely no end to my luck. If that fool Kate had taken the fifty, of course I could not have played, and, of course, if I had not played I could not have won. My good fortune is almost miraculous. If any other person but Kate had rescued me, he or she would have taken the money, and there would have been no play; and if I had not fallen into the water it is very likely I should not have thought of treating myself to a game. Upon my word, it *is* miraculous--nothing short of miraculous."

His eyes winked rapidly, and he stroked his smoothly-shaven chin with intense satisfaction.

"But," he went on, "the whole thing is due to that delightful Hetty, for if I had not wanted to see that charming girl again I should not have gone to Welford to-day, and, of course, should not have played this afternoon.

Like all other gamblers, I am a bit superstitious, and I do believe that she has brought me luck. Now twice out of three times that I have played since I saw her I have won, and that never happened in all my life before. Yes, she has undoubtedly brought me luck. Suppose this luck continued, I should be a rich man in a short time. I should be quite independent of Welford and Singleton Terrace, Richmond, and although I am good at private theatricals, I am getting a bit sick of Singleton Terrace, Richmond. A man gets tired of a goody-goody part sooner than of any other kind. I do believe, after all, that if I had that three thousand pounds for capital and Hetty for luck, I should be better off without Singleton Terrace, Richmond. That is an aspect of the future well worth thinking over."

When he got home he found to his surprise and disgust that his wife had not yet gone to bed. He put his arm round her and kissed her tenderly, and chid her gently for sitting up. She said she was anxious about him, as he had said he should be back early.

"The fact of the matter is, Nellie, I had a great deal more trouble about those gates than I anticipated. You have no notion of how stupid workmen can be. They always want to do something or other you have said distinctly you do not want to have done. I told the creature I went to as plainly as I am telling you that I did not wish to have ice-house doors, but simply gates sufficiently strong and well secured to prevent anyone falling into the water. I told him to go see the place, and that I should come back in an hour to hear what he had to say about price; and would you believe it? the animal had made out an estimate for double doors! I could hardly get him to adopt my views. He said an ice-house ought to have ice-house doors, and that to put up any others would not be workmanlike, and would expose him to contempt and ridicule in the neighbourhood! Did you ever hear anything so monstrously absurd in all your life?"

"It was very provoking, William, and I am sorry that my foolish fears caused you so much trouble," she said in a tone of self-reproach, softly stroking his hand held in both hers.

"Not at all, dear! Not at all! I am very glad I went. But of course the work about the gates did not keep me till now. I have had a little adventure."

She looked up at him in alarm, and glanced in fear at the unfamiliar clothes he wore. "A little adventure?" she cried faintly.

"Yes," he said, with one of his short quick laughs, "but you need not be uneasy; I am not the worse of it, and there was no fair lady in it to make you jealous."

"Jealous!" she cried, with a rapturous smile of utter faith. "Not all the fair ladies in the world could make me jealous, William. I know you too well."

"Thank you, Nellie," he said in a grateful, serious tone, raising one of her hands and kissing it. "No. The fact is, as I was waiting on the pier for the steamer, a little boy, about the age of the one I saw in my dream, about the age of young Layard, fell into the river, and as he was beyond the reach of the poles and too young to catch a line or lifebuoy, and was in great danger of drowning, I jumped in and got him out."

With a sigh of horror she lay back in her chair unable to speak.

"It was a strange fulfilment of my dream. As you know, I am not in the least superstitious, but it seems to me that the nightmare I had last night was sent to me that I might be on the spot to save that poor little chap from a watery grave. Don't look so terrified, Nellie. There was great danger for the little fellow, but not the slightest for me. I am as much at home in the water as a duck, and you see, being stout, I am buoyant and swim very high."

"O, but 'tis dreadful to think of you, William, in the water!" she whispered in a voice breathless with a combined feeling of dread of the peril he had been in and thankfulness for his present security.

"Well, it's all over now, and you needn't be afraid of my doing anything of the kind again. When I got out of the water I went and bought a dry suit of ready-made clothes, and I think you must admit I am quite a swell in them."

She forced a smile. He went on:

"Well, even all this wouldn't account for my being so late. You must know there is nothing I hate so much as notoriety, and I had absolutely got to Waterloo on my way home when it suddenly occurred to me that as two or three hundred people saw the rescue some one might go to the newspapers with an account of it. Nothing could make me more shamefaced than to see my name in print in connection with this affair. I had experience of something of the kind at the time of the fire--you remember, dearest?"

She pressed his hand and said, "My own, my own, my own!"

"So I took a cab and drove round to all the newspaper-offices to bar a report going in. That was what kept me till this hour."

They sat talking for a little while longer, and then she rang for the maid and he went to the dressing-room.

The anxiety caused by his unexpected delay in town, or by the tale he had told her, may have had an injurious effect on the invalid, or it may be that, without any exciting cause, the aggravation would have taken place; but at all events, that night, or, rather, early in the morning, Mrs. Crawford rang her bell, and upon her husband coming to her he found her so much worse that he set off at once for the doctor.

As he closed the front-door after him he whispered to himself, "I wonder is this more of my luck?"

CHAPTER XXIX
AN INTRUDER UPON THE AIT

When Kate Mellor found herself in the streets of Leeham that evening the light was beginning to fail. The clouds, which during the day had been thin and fleecy, had, as the hours went by, grown in extent and mass. They now hung above, fold over fold, dark, gloomy, threatening. The air was heavy, moist, oppressive. Not a breath of wind stirred.

The woman turned to the left, and, taking the tow-path, as she had one night before, set out in the direction of Welford. She wore her veil closely drawn over her disfigured face. Her step was more firm and elastic than in the afternoon. Then she had been on her way to seek physical relief; now she was on her way to alleviate her heart.

She left the tow-path by the approach at Welford, and gained the bridge. The usual group of loungers and loafers were there, but they took no notice of her. They could see by a glance at her that she was poor and miserable, and to be poor and miserable at Welford Bridge insured one against close observation or inquisitive speculation--it was to wear the uniform of the place.

She leaned against the parapet, and gazed at the canal side of Boland's Ait. Everything there was as usual: the floating-stage being moored by the side of the islet, as it had been on the night she tried to draw it across the water.

She turned her eyes on the other side of the island, and started. She saw what she had never seen before: the floating-stage stretching across the water of the bay, making a bridge from one bank to the other. This discovery set her heart beating fast, for if one could only get on Crawford's Quay one could cross over the stage to the Ait.

Hitherto all her hopes had been centred on the stage lying along the islet on the canal side. Now the best chance of gaining the holm lay on the side of the bay.

Crawford's Quay was not used for purposes of trade now, all the buildings being vacant except the house in which Layard lived.

The daylight was almost gone, and the heavy banks of cloud shrouded earth in a dull deep gloom--a gloom deeper than that of clear midnight in this month of June.

Kate Mellor turned again to her left and walked to the top of Crawford Street. She looked down it. All was dark except the one lamp burning like an angry eye at the bottom. As she was perfectly certain no one could recognise her, she went into Crawford Street without much trepidation. She kept on the left-hand side: the one opposite to Crawford's House.

The window of the sitting-room was fully open for air. In the room were four people: a man with a long beard, whom she did not know; a girl with golden-brown hair, whom she had more than once seen take Freddie from her husband at the end of the stage; and a second man whom she could not see, for his back was towards her. And her husband. They were all just in the act of sitting down to supper.

She knew the place and the ways of the people thoroughly. She had studied nothing else for days and days.

"There is no one now on the island but the child, and they will be half-an-hour at supper; they will not stir for half-an-hour! Now is my chance, or never!"

Her heart throbbed painfully; she was so excited that she tottered in her walk. She was afraid to run lest she should attract the attention of people passing along Welford Road at the top of the street.

Everything depended on speed. She had been down here twice before, and found that one of the staples of a padlock securing a gate had rusted loose in the jamb. Without the floating-stage for a bridge, this discovery was useless; without the absence of her husband from the island, or unless he was sunk in profound sleep, the loose staple and the stage-bridge would be of little avail. But here, owing to some extraordinary and beneficent freak, all three combined in her interest to-night!

Not a second was to be lost. Already she was working fiercely at the loose staple. It was rusted and worn, and the wood was decayed all round it, but still it clung to the post, as a loose tooth to the gum.

She seized it with both her hands, although there was hardly room for one hand, and swayed it this way and that until her breath came short and the blood trickled from her fingers.

No doubt it was yielding, but would it come away in time? She had not hours to accomplish the task. She had only minutes, and every minute lost was stolen from the time she might bend over her darling, watching, devouring his lovely face, and listening to his innocent breathing, and feeling his sweet baby breath upon her cheek!

O, this was horrible! Break iron! break wood! break fingers! break arm! but let this poor distracted outcast mother into the presence of her child for the last time, for one parting sight, one parting kiss, in secret and fear!

At last the staple yielded and came away in her hand, and in another moment, after a few gratings and squealings, which turned her cold, lest they should be heard, the unhappy mother forced open the door and passed through.

In another moment she was across the bridge and on the land which her love for her little one had made dearer to her from afar off than ever Canaan was to the desert-withered Israelites of old.

There was light enough to walk without stumbling. She knew the lie of the place as well as it could be learned without absolutely treading the ground. She took her way rapidly round the wall of the old timber-yard and then across the little open space to the cottage. She observed no precaution now, but went on impetuously, headlong.

The door of the cottage was shut. She opened it by the latch, and, having entered, closed it after her. She did not pause to listen; she did not care whether there was any one in the place or not. She knew she was within reach of her child, and that she should be able to see him, to touch him, before she died. She was within arm's length of him, and she would touch him, though he was surrounded by levelled spears. The spears might pierce her bosom, but even though they did she could stretch out her hand and caress his head before the sense left her hand, the sight her eye.

She knew where to find the door of the room in which he slept, for the light she had seen the other night through the eye of Welford Bridge as she came along the tow-path was burning, much dimmed, on the same window-sill now.

She opened the door and entered the room.

In the middle of the bed lay the child, half-naked. The heat of the night had made him restless, and he had kicked off the clothes.

With a long tremulous moan she flung herself forward on the bed, and, penning his little body within the circle of her arms, laid her disfigured face against his head and burst into tears.

CHAPTER XXX
HETTY'S VISIT TO THE AIT

"And so we have got you at last, and here is Mr. Ray, who will hardly believe you are really coming," said Layard that evening, as Bramwell knocked at the back door and entered Crawford's House. "It is very good of you to make an exception in our favour."

"All the goodness is on your side in inviting one who has been out of the world for so long a time. I know you will believe me when I say that now we are known to one another I am very glad to come."

"There is nothing like breaking the ice, and let us hope for a phenomenon that the water below may be warm. You have no notion of what it is to be at the works all day long and never exchange a word with a congenial soul. Then when I come home I do not think it fair to my sister to leave her alone. So my life is a little monotonous and dull; but now that I have made the acquaintance of you and Mr. Ray I mean to lead quite a riotous existence."

"You will, I know, excuse me if I do not stay long tonight. I must go back to the boy."

"You may go back now and then to see that all is well. But, after all, what is there to be afraid of?"

"Well, you know, I made an enemy to-day, and it might occur to him to revenge himself upon the child."

"But he can't get near the child. Your stage on the canal side is moored, Mr. Ray tells me, and we are here at this end of the other stage, and I don't think there is a small boat he could get on the whole canal. Besides, how is he to know but you are at home? I am sure you may make your mind quite easy."

"Still, if you allow me, I shall go early."

"You may go early to see that all is safe, but we will not let you say good-night until you are quite tired of us. Come in: Mr. Ray and my sister are in the front room."

Layard had purposely delayed a little while in the passage. He was a most affectionate and sympathetic brother, and he did not know but that the two people in the front room might have something to say to one another.

They had, but it did not seem matter of great interest or importance.

"Miss Layard," said Philip Ray when her brother had left the room, "you told me you never were on Boland's Ait."

"Never," she answered.

"Mr. Bramwell is certain to be anxious about the boy, and it would be a great kindness if you would go over the stage and see that all is well."

"I! what? Do you mean in the dark?" she said, looking at him in astonishment.

"Well, Miss Layard, I thought you had more courage than to be afraid of a little darkness; but if you did feel anything like timidity, rather than that Mr. Bramwell should remain uneasy, I would go with you and show you the way. What do you say to that?"

She said nothing, but, bending her head over her stitching, blushed until her bent neck grew pink under her golden-brown hair.

He did not insist upon an answer. Apparently he felt satisfied. In a moment the door opened, and Layard and Bramwell came in.

Although the lamp-light in the room was not particularly strong, for a moment Bramwell was dazzled and confused. He had not been in so bright a room since his retirement from the world. Although the furniture was faded and infirm, it was splendid compared with that in his cottage. Then there were a few prints upon the walls in gilt frames, and curtains to the window, and pieces of china and an ornamental clock on the chimney-piece, and a square of carpet in the middle of the floor, and a bright cover on the table, not one thing of the like being on Boland's Ait.

There was, too, an atmosphere of humanity about the place which did not find its way to the island; here was a sense of human interest, human contact, human sympathy wholly wanting in his home. Bramwell had come from the cell of an anchorite to a festival of man.

But above all else and before all else was the tall, lithe, bright-faced, blooming girl, with plenteous hair and blue eyes, in which there were glints of gold, and the ready smile and white teeth that showed between her moist red lips when she spoke. This was the first lady Bramwell had spoken to or met since his exile from the world, and she was beautiful enough for a goddess--a Hebe.

Was this, he asked himself, the dream of a captive, and should he wake to find himself once more mured between his white washed walls, environed by silence and bound by the hideous fetters of a bond which was a horror and a disgrace? Should he wake up as he had awakened every morning for three years, to think of his ruined home, his blighted life, and his wife, who, though living, was dead for ever to him, and yet with her dead and infamous hand held him back from taking a new companion, to be to him what he had hoped she would be when he took her in all love and faith?

No--all this was true. The talk and the laughter were true. His own talk and laughter were true; and, above all, this radiant girl, with her quick wit and beautiful intelligence and sympathy, was true. All true--and he was no more than thirty years of age! A young man. A man no older than the youngest girl might marry. Philip had told him that this girl was twenty. Why, twenty and thirty were just the ages for bride and bridegroom!

And how different was this girl from the other! Here was no vanity, no craving for admiration, no airs and graces, and, above all, here were the swift responsive spirit, the keen sympathy, the aspiring spirit, the exquisite sensibility!

Ay, and it was all true, and it was allowable for him to dream, for he was free. Free as he had been when, carried away by the mere beauty of face and form, he had asked nothing but physical beauty, believing that he could inform it with the soul of a goddess, until he found that the physical beauty was clay, which would commingle with no noble essence, which preferred a handful of trinkets or an oath of hollow homage to all the stirring tumults of the poets or the intense aspirings of the lute! Yes, he could be a poet under the influence of such a deity. He could sing if those ears would only listen; he could succeed if those lips would only applaud!

He took no heed of time; it slipped away like dry sand held in the hand. He never could tell afterwards what the conversation had been about, but he knew he was talking fast and well. Never in all his life had he spoken under such an intoxicating spell as that of new hope springing in the presence of this girl. It was intoxication on an intellectual ether. His blood was fire and dew. His ideas were flame. The human voices around him were the music of eternal joy. There was in his spirit a sacred purpose that defied definition. He seemed to be praying in melody. He was upheld by the purpose of an all-wise beneficence now revealed to him for the first time; he was transported out of himself and carried into converse with justified angels.

Philip Ray sat in amazed silence at the transformation. It was more wonderful than the miracle of Pygmalion's statue: it was the enchantment of emancipation, the delirium of liberty. He had known and honoured--nay, worshipped--this man for years, but until to-night he had never suspected that he was a genius and a demi-god. He had known him as a martyr, but until this night he had never realised that he was a saint.

"I must go," at length said Bramwell, rising. "I have already stayed too long."

"No, no," said Philip Ray, springing up, "you must not stir yet. This is doing you all the good in the world. I have asked Miss Layard to have a look at the island, and she will see to the boy. You cannot deny her this little gratification. We arranged it before you came. You are here now, and you must do what you are told. I will take her safely over the bridge and back, and then we shall have another chat."

Hetty rose with a heightened colour.

"Pray sit down, Mr. Bramwell; we will bring you back news of the boy. It is much too early to think of leaving, and we are afraid that if once you went across to-night you would not come back again. Now that we have got you we will not let you go."

Layard passed his hand over his bearded mouth to conceal a smile. He guessed the object of Ray's proposal.

"Mr. Bramwell," he said earnestly, "you must not think of stirring."

He rose, and, placing his hands on the other's shoulders, gently forced him back on his chair.

"I am giving you too much trouble, Miss Layard," Bramwell said, with a smile; "but if I must stay and you will go, there is nothing for it but to submit."

His real reason for yielding so readily was the intense pleasure it gave him to find that she took such an interest in his boy.

"Put the lamp in the kitchen-window, Miss Layard," said Philip, when the two found themselves in the back passage. "The light will be useful in crossing the stage."

She did as she was bidden, and rejoined him on Crawford's Quay, just outside the back door, which they left open so as to get the benefit of the hall-light.

"Give me your hand now," said he, and he led her across the floating bridge. "You had better leave me your hand still," he said when they were on the Ait. "It is very dark, and I know the place thoroughly. What do you think of Mr. Bramwell?"

"I think him simply wonderful. I never heard anything like him before. Does he always talk as he did to-night?"

"No; still he usually talks well. But though I have been very intimate with him for many years I never heard him talk so well. As a rule he speaks with great caution, but to-night he threw reserve to the winds and let himself go."

"I think I can manage now without your help," she said, endeavouring to withdraw her hand.

"I should be very sorry to believe anything of the kind," said he, preventing her. "You had better leave me your hand for a little while."

She bent her head and ceased her effort.

"Miss Layard," he said, after a moment's pause, "I want you to do me a great favour. Will you?"

"If I can," she said in a very low voice, so low that he had to bend towards her to catch it.

"In the dark and the daylight leave me your hand. Give it to me for ever."

"But the boy?" she said. "We must go see the boy."

She made a slight attempt to release her hand. He closed his fingers round it.

"We shall go see the boy presently." They were now standing at the tail of the Ait "I have your hand now, Hetty darling, and I mean to keep it. I have loved you since the first time I saw you, and I never loved any other woman. You will give me your hand, dear, and yourself, dear, and I will give you my heart and soul for all my life. You will give me your hand, dear?"

She did not take it away.

Then he let it go himself, and, putting his arms carefully round her, folded her gently to his breast, and said, with a broken sob:

"Merciful Heaven, this is more than any man deserves. May I kiss you, dear?"

"Yes."

Her head was leaning on his shoulder. He bent down and kissed her forehead.

"I'm glad there's no light, dear."

"Why?"

"Because if I saw you I could not believe this is true. Hetty."

"What?"

"Nothing, dear. I only wanted to hear your voice, so that I might be sure this is you."

He put his hand on her head.

"Is that your hair, dear?"

"Yes."

"I can't believe it. And do you think you will grow fond of me?"

"No fonder than I am, Philip. I could not be any fonder than I am."

"This is not to be believed. So that when I come into the room where you are it makes you glad?"

"It gives me such gladness as I never knew before, nor ever thought of."

"This is not to be believed."

"And when you go away I feel so lonely and desolate."

"Do not tell me any more, or I shall hate myself for causing you pain."

"But I would rather feel the pain than be without it. And I'd give you my life, Philip, if you wanted it. I mean I'd go to death for you, Philip; and I'd follow you all round the world, if you wanted it--all round the world, if you would only look back at me now and then."

"You must not say such things, child."

"But they are true."

"I had hoped, dear, but I had not hoped so much as this--nothing like so much as this, and I cannot bear to hear you say so much. Listening to it makes me seem to have done you an injury."

"And I'd do everything that you told me. I'd even go away."

"Hush, child, hush! It is not right to say such things."

"But they are true. I'd go away and live alone with my heart if you told me, Philip. Now don't you see that I love you?"

"I do, dear. But now I see how much less my love is than yours, for I could not go away and live alone with my heart."

"I could. Shall we see to the boy now?"

"Yes."

CHAPTER XXXI
BY THE BOY'S BEDSIDE

Kate Mellor, lying beside her child on the bed, suddenly became aware of footsteps approaching the cottage along the canal face of the island. She had been fondling and talking to Frank, and he was now half awake.

Between the bed and the wall there was the space of a foot. The mother slipped down through this space to the floor, and there lay in terror, trying to hush her breathing and still the beatings of her heart. She could not tell herself exactly what it was she dreaded more than discovery. Her fears took no definite form.

The footsteps came up to the cottage, and then stopped. Through the open window sounded voices, the voices of a man and a girl. As the concealed woman listened her heart stood still, for she recognised the male voice as that of her brother.

"Go in, Hetty," said the male voice, "and I'll wait for you here. The room is on the left-hand side."

"You won't come in?" asked the girl.

"No. Of course all is right. If you speak in the room I shall hear you."

The girl came into the cottage, opened the door of the sleeping-room, and approached the bed.

"Mother," said the boy, who was now covered up.

The concealed woman grew cold with fear.

"Are you awake, Frank?"

"Yes, mother," said the boy, stretching himself, yawning, and rubbing his eyes. "Are you going to take me away again? If you do, take Freddie too."

"I'm not your mother, Frank. Don't you know me?" said the girl.

"You said you were my mother, and I know you are, though you have spots on your face."

"Rouse up, Frank," said the girl in a tone of alarm. "Look at me. Who am I? Don't you know me?"

"You're mother, and you said you'd take me away to Mrs. Pemberton's, only father wouldn't let you," said the boy, with another yawn.

There sounded a tumult in the ears of the mother, and she thought she should go mad if she did not scream out.

The visitor went to the window and spoke to the man outside. "The child has been dreaming, and fancies I'm his mother."

"Heaven forbid!"

"Why?"

"His mother is not to be spoken of. His mother was the basest, the worse woman that ever lived. She, fortunately for herself and every one else, died a little while ago. You are not to mention her name, dear. It sullies wherever it is uttered."

The hiding woman shrank into herself as if struck by an icy blast. Was it thus she deserved to be spoken of by her only brother? Yes--yes--yes! As the basest, the worst woman who ever lived? whose name sullied the place in which it was uttered? O yes--yes--yes! It was true! Too true.

The boy's eyes were now wide open, and he was looking at the tall slender figure of the girl standing out black against the lamp in the window.

"Aunt Hetty."

"That's my own boy. Now you know me," said the girl in a soothing and encouraging tone as she went back to the bed.

"Aunt Hetty, where's mother gone?"

"She wasn't here, Frank. You were only dreaming." "O, but I wasn't. I saw her. She lay down beside me on the bed, and she had red spots on her face."

The girl shuddered.

The woman gasped and felt as if her heart would burst through her ribs.

"Philip," said the girl, once more going to the window, "I don't like this at all. I think the child must be a little feverish. He says his mother was here, and that she lay down beside him on the bed, and that she has spots on her face. What do you say ought to be done?"

"Nothing at all. Get the child to sleep if you can. As you say, he has been dreaming."

"But, indeed, I don't like it. He's so very circumstantial. He says his mother told him she'd take him back to Mrs. Pemberton's, only his father won't let her. Who is Mrs. Pemberton?"

"I don't know. Some lodging-house keeper, no doubt."

"Well, I don't know what ought to be done. There is no chance of the child going to sleep soon, and either he is raving or--or--or--" the girl's voice trembled--"something very dreadful indeed has occurred here. The child cannot certainly be left alone now." She looked around her with apprehension. She was pale and trembling.

"You seem uneasy, Hetty."

"I am terrified."

"I assure you the child has been dreaming, that is all. It is quite a common thing, I have read, for children to believe what they see in dreams has real existence."

"O, talking in that way is no use. I am miserable and frightened out of my wits, Philip."

"What would you wish me to do?"

"I think you had better go for Mr. Bramwell."

"Very well."

"But no--no--no, I should die of fright. What should I do if *that* came again and lay down on the bed beside the child?" moaned the girl in terror and despair.

"You really ought not to think of anything so much out of reason. There was nothing in it but the uneasy dream of a child."

"Indeed, indeed I shall go frantic. Can nothing be done?"

"Well, you know, I could not think of letting you cross over the stage by yourself. Nothing on earth would induce me to let you attempt such a thing. And you do not wish me to go away, and you will not have the two of us go. I cannot see any way out of the difficulty."

"O dear, O dear, O dear!" cried the girl. "I shall go crazy! Stop! I have it. Didn't we leave the back door open?"

"We did, so as to have the benefit of the hall-lamp."

"Well, you stay here and watch the boy, and I'll go and call for Mr. Bramwell across the bay. They will hear my voice easily in the dining-room. That's the best plan, isn't it."

"Yes, if any plan is wanted, which I doubt."

The girl ran out of the room with a shudder.

The concealed woman had fainted. She lost consciousness when it was decided to summon her husband without watch being removed from the room.

As Hetty passed Ray he caught her for a moment and said, "Mind, on no account whatever are you to attempt to cross the stage by yourself. If you cannot make yourself heard, dear, won't you come back to me?"

"O, I promise; but please let me go. I am beside myself with terror."

He loosed his hold, and in a minute she disappeared round the corner of the old timber-yard. Philip Ray went up to the window, and with his face just above the sill kept guard. He heard her call eagerly two or three times, and then he caught the sound of a response. After that he knew a brief and hurried conversation was held, and then came footsteps, and the form of Bramwell hastening along the wharf.

"You are to go to Miss Layard at once and take her over. She would not come back. She is fairly scared. She told me all that has happened here. Run to her, and get her away from this place quickly. Good-night."

"It is nothing at all. The boy has had a nightmare."

"Nothing more? Do not delay. Good-night."

"Good-night."

The father then went into the cottage, and, having bolted the outer door, stole softly to the room where little Frank lay.

The child was wide awake.

"Well, my boy," said the father, kissing him tenderly, and smoothing the child's dark hair with a gentle hand. "So your Aunt Hetty has been to see you."

"Yes, and mother too."

"That was a dream, Frank, and you mustn't think any more about it."

The boy shook his head on the pillow. "No dream," he said. "She lay down on the bed there beside me, and put her arms round me like at Mrs. Pemberton's, where we lived before I came here; and she cried like at Mrs. Pemberton's, and I asked her to take me back to Mrs. Pemberton's, and she said she would, only you wouldn't let me go. Won't you let me go?"

"We'll see in the morning."

"And won't Aunt Hetty let Freddie come too? for I had no little boy to play with at Mrs. Pemberton's."

"We'll talk to Aunt Hetty about it."

"And mother has spots, red spots, on her face now, and there used to be no spots. And why won't you let me go? for I love my mother more than I love you."

"We'll talk about all that in the morning; but it is very late now, and all good little boys are asleep."

"And all good fathers and mothers asleep too?"

"Well, yes; most of them."

"And why aren't you asleep?"

"Because I'm not sleepy. But as you have had a dream that woke you I'll tell you what I'll do. I'll move the stretcher away, and sit down beside you and hold your hand until you go to sleep again." He did as he said, and when he had the little hand within his own he said, "Now, shut your eyes and go to sleep."

"Father."

"Yes, my child?"

"Didn't you know mother once?"

"Yes, my boy."

"A long time ago?"

"A long time ago."

"And when you knew her she had no ugly red spots over her face?"

"No, child."

"Well, she has now--all over her face."

"Go to sleep like a good boy. I will not talk to you any more. Good-night."

"Good-night;" and with one little hand under his cheek and the other clasped lightly in his father's, little Frank lay still awhile, and then fell off into tranquil slumber.

For a long time the father sat motionless. He was afraid to stir lest he might wake the little fellow. His mind went back to the evening he had just spent. How bright and cheerful it had been compared with the loneliness and gloom of those evenings with which he had been so long sadly familiar!

What a charming girl that was, and how she had brightened up the whole evening with her enchanting presence! What a home her presence would make! He had admired her as he had seen her on Crawford's Quay with little Freddie, but then she was bending her mind down to a child's level. That night he had seen her among men, the perfect complement of them, and the flower of womanhood. He felt his face, his whole being soften when he thought of her. Even to think of her was to feel the influence of a gracious spirit.

She was twenty and he was only thirty--who knows!

And then his head fell forward on his chest, and he slept. But Hetty followed him into his sleep--into his dreams.

He was walking along a country road in May, dejected and broken-spirited, thinking of the miserable past three years, when suddenly at a turning he met Hetty holding his boy by the hand and coming to meet him. And then, with a laugh, he knew that all these three years which tortured him so cruelly had been nothing but a dream, and that this sweet and joyous and perfect Hetty had been the wife of his young manhood. With outstretched arms and a cry he rushed to meet her.

The cry awoke him, and he looked up.

Between the bed and the wall rose a thin black figure sharp against the white of the wall, and above the figure a pale haggard face dabbled with large red spots like gouts of blood.

With a shriek of horror he sprang to his feet and flung himself against the wall farthest from this awful apparition.

"In the name of God, who or what are you?"

"Nothing to you, I know, except a curse and a blight, but *his* mother," pointing to the child.

"Living?"

"I could not die."

He thrust both arms upward with a gesture of desperate appeal. "Merciful God! am I mad?"

CHAPTER XXXII
BRAMWELL FINDS A SISTER

The sound of the voices had awakened the child, and he sat up in the bed, looking with wide-open eyes from father to mother, from mother to father.

Bramwell stood with his back against the wall, staring at his wife and breathing hard. He was stunned, overwhelmed. He felt uncertain of his own identity, of the place around him, and of the child. The only thing of which he felt sure was that he stood face to face with his wife, who had risen from the tomb.

"I did not come," she said, moving out from her position between the bed and the wall, "to see you or to ask mercy or forgiveness of you. You need not reproach me for being alive; because only I fainted, you should not have seen me to-night; you should never have seen me again, for I was on my way to my grave, where I could not go without looking on my child once more. The announcement of my death came only a little while before its time. I shall not see another day."

Her voice was dull and hoarse, the features wasted and pinched, and mottled with marring blotches of scorbutic red.

"This is no place for us to talk," he said, pointing to the child on the bed. "Follow me."

She hesitated.

"I do not want to talk with you; I wish to spare you. I know you would be justified in killing me. But I would not have you suffer because you wish me dead. I shall not trouble you or the world with another day of my wretched life. Cover your face, and let me kiss the boy again, and I will go. I know my way to the river, and I would spare you any harm that might come to you of my dying here--at your hands."

"This is no place, I say, for such a scene or for such words. Follow me."

"You will not kill me?"

"I will not harm you, poor soul."

"Your pity harms me worse than blows."

"Then I will not pity you. Come."

"May I kiss the child once more before I leave the room? You may cover your eyes, so that you may not see your child polluted by my touch."

"You will be free to kiss him when we have done our talk. I shall not hinder you."

He held the door open for her, and with tottering steps and bent head, she went out into the dark and waited for him.

"Lie down now, my child, and try to go to sleep. Mother will come to you later."

The child, overawed, covered himself up and closed his eyes. Bramwell took the lamp off the window-sill, and led the way into the sitting-room.

He shut the door behind them, put the lamp on the table, and, setting a chair for her by it, bade her sit down. She complied in silence, resting her elbow on the table, and covering her face with her hand.

"You said you fainted," he said, "do you feel weak still?"

"A little."

"I keep some brandy in case of sudden illness, for this is a lonely place." It was a relief to him to utter commonplaces. "And there are, or at least were until lately, no neighbours of whom I could borrow."

He poured some out of a pocket-flask, and added water, and handed the glass to her. "Drink that."

"What! you will give me aid under your roof?"

"Under the roof of Heaven. Drink."

She raised the glass to her lips, and swallowed a small quantity.

"All. Drink it all. You have need of it."

She did as she was told.

He began walking up and down the room softly.

"You sent me the boy when you believed you were dying, and when the crisis turned in favour of life you inserted the announcement of your death in order that I might believe myself free of you for ever?"

"Yes. I intended you should never see me or hear of me again."

"That I might be free to marry again if I chose?"

"That was my idea."

"And then you came to bid good-bye to your child before going to the river?"

"Yes; they never would have found out who I was. I left all papers behind me, and cut the marks off my clothes."

"But the love of your child was so strong, you risked everything to bid him a last farewell?"

"I am his mother, and all that is left to me of a heart is in my child. I do not ask you to forgive me for the past. I do not ask your pardon for what I did three years ago; but I do entreat you, as you are a just and merciful man, to forgive me for coming to see my innocent little child!"

"She took her hand from before her face, and, clasping both her hands together, raised them in passionate supplication to him as he passed her in his walk. Her thick, dull voice was full of unutterable woe.

"I forgive you the past and the present utterly. Say no more in that strain. My head is very heavy, and I am trying to think. Do not excite yourself about forgiveness. I am endeavouring to see my way. This has come suddenly and unexpectedly, and my brain seems feeble, and it will not work freely. In a little while all will be plain to me. In the meantime keep quiet."

He spoke very gently.

She groaned and covered her face again. She would have preferred the river to this, but the manner of the man compelled obedience as she had never felt obedience compelled before, and it was obvious he did not wish her to go to the river--yet, at all events.

"It was a terrible risk to run--a terrible risk. Suppose I had married?"

"But I never would have interfered with you, or come near you, or let you know I was alive. You were the last being on earth I wanted to see." She took her hand down from before her face and looked at him earnestly.

"I am sure of that, but you see what has fallen out to-night."

"O, forgive me, and let me go! My lot is bitter enough for what has happened, without reproaches for something that has not occurred. You have not married again? Have you?"

He shook his head, and said with a mournful smile, "No. I have not married again. Well, let that pass. Let that pass. Mentioning it helps me to clear up matters--enables me to see my way."

"May I go now?"

"Not yet. Stay awhile."

"I would rather be in the river than here."

"So would I; but I must not go, for many reasons. There is the child, for example, to go no Higher."

"But I can be of no use to the child. Your coldness is killing me. Why don't you rage at me or let me go? Are you a man of stone? or do you take me for a woman of stone?" she cried passionately, writhing on her chair.

He waved her outburst aside with a gentle gesture. "Nothing can be gained by heat or haste."

"Let me say good-bye to my child and go," she cried vehemently.

"The child and the river can bide awhile; bide you also awhile. It is a long time since we last met."

She grasped her throat with her hand. She was on the point of breaking down. His last words pierced her to the soul. With a superhuman effort she controlled herself and sat silent.

For a minute there was silence. He continued his walk up and down. Gradually his footfalls, which had been light all along, grew fainter and fainter until they became almost inaudible. Gradually his face, which had been perplexed, lost its troubled look and softened into a peaceful smile. It seemed as though he had ceased to be aware of her presence. He looked like a solitary man communing with himself and drawing solace from his thoughts. He looked as though he beheld some beatific vision that yielded heavenly content--as though a voice of calming and elevating melody were reaching him from afar off. When he spoke his tones were fine and infinitely tender, and sounded like a benediction. He saw his way clearly now.

"You risked everything to-night to get a glimpse of your child, a final look, to say a last farewell. You were willing to risk everything here; you were willing to risk hereafter everything that may be the fate of those who lay violent hands upon their own lives. Why need you risk anything at all, either for the boy's sake or in the hereafter, because of laying violent hands upon your life?"

"I do not understand you," she whispered, looking at him in awe. His appearance, his manner, his voice, did not seem of earth.

"Why not stay with your boy and fill your heart with him?"

"What?" she whispered, growing faint and catching the table for support.

"Why not stay with your boy and fill your heart with ministering to him?"

"What? Here? In this place?" she cried in a wavering voice, still no louder than a whisper.

"In this place. Why should you not stay with your child? There is no one so fit to tend and guard a little child as a mother."

"And you?" she asked in a wild intense whisper. "Will you go to the river to hide the head I have dishonoured?"

"No. I too will stay and help you to shield and succour the child. Mother and father are the proper guardians of little ones."

"Frank Mellor, are you mad?" she cried out loud, springing to her feet and dashing her hand across her face to clear her vision.

"No; there isn't substance enough in me now to make a madman."

"And," she cried, starting up and facing him, "Frank Mellor, do you know who I am? Do you know that three years ago I left your house under infamous circumstances, and that I brought shame and sorrow and destruction upon your home and you? Do you know that I have made you a byeword in Beechley and London, and wherever you have been heard of? Do you know that I am your *wife?*"

She had raised her hoarse voice to its highest pitch. Her eyes flashed. She brandished her arms. Her face blazed red in the undisfigured parts, and the red spots turned purple and livid. She was frantically defending the magnanimity of this man against the baseness of her former self, against the evil of her present reputation, against contact with the leprosy of her sin.

"All that needs to be known, I know," he said, in the same calm, gentle voice. "Years ago I lost my wife. I lost sight of her for a long time. To-night I find a sister."

"Sister!" she cried in a whisper, sinking on a chair, and losing at once all her fierce aspect and enhanced colour.

"To-night I find a sister who is in despair because of the loss of her child. I restore her child to her empty arms, and I say, 'My roof is your roof, and my bread is your bread.'" He lit a candle, and handed it to her. "Go to your room where the boy is, and take him in your arms, for it comforts a mother to have her child in her arms. I shall stay here. It is dawn already, and I have work to do. Good-night."

CHAPTER XXXIII
"I MUST GO TO FETCH HER HOME"

When Philip Ray left Crawford's House that night he felt anything at all but the elation supposed to be proper in the accepted suitor of a beautiful girl. He had, indeed, a great many troubles in his mind, and as he walked home to his lonely lodgings in Camberwell he was nearly a miserable man. It would not be true to say he was out and out miserable, but he was perilously close to it.

In the first place, he had to leave Hetty behind him, a thing almost beyond endurance. Then, when removed from the intoxicating influence of her presence and undistracted by the magic of her beauty, he began to turn his eyes inward upon himself, and investigate his own unworthiness with brutal candour--nay, with gross injustice.

What on earth was he that a faultless, an exquisite creature like Hetty should give herself to him? That was a question he asked himself over and over again, without being able to find any reason whatever for her sacrifice. More than once he felt inclined to go back, make a clean breast of it by telling her that as a friend he would recommend her to have nothing whatever to do with himself. The words of love and devotion she had spoken to him on the island were a source of intense pain to him. A nice kind of fellow *he* was indeed for her to say *she* would follow round all the world! He was obtaining love under false pretences, that's what he was doing. And such love! and from such a perfect creature! It was simply a monstrous fraud! There was something underhand and dishonourable about it; for if she had only known him for what he was, she would flee out of the very parish away from him. He must have been mad to ask her to marry him.

It had all come on him suddenly. When he suggested that she should go to the island with him on the excuse of seeing how the boy got on, he had no intention of proposing to her; and, nevertheless, no sooner had he set foot on the Ait than he must retain her hand and ask her to give it to him for ever! Could he have meant the whole thing as a joke, or was the Master of all Evil at the bottom of it?

But the full turpitude of his act did not appear until he considered ways and means. At present his salary was barely enough to keep himself in the strictest economy. He could not, after paying for food, lodgings, and clothes all on the humblest scale, save five pounds a year. It is true he had a yearly increase of salary, and by-and-by would have the chance of promotion. But at the most favourable estimate he could not hope to have an income on which he might prudently marry sooner than between twenty and thirty years. Say, in twenty-five years, when his salary would be sufficient, he would be fifty-two and she forty-five! If he had any hair left on his head then it would be snow-white, and he would be sure to have rheumatism and most likely a touch of asthma as well. He would have confirmed bachelor habits and exacting notions about his food and an abject horror of the east wind. He would tell old stories as new, and laugh at them, and the younger men in the office would laugh at him for laughing at these old tales, and mimic him behind his back, and call him an old fossil and other endearing names, indicative of pity in them and senility in him! What a poor idiot he had been to speak to the girl!

It was true the Layards were not very well off themselves now; but they had once been rich, and naturally Hetty ought to be raised by marriage far up above their present position. She was a lady and a beauty, and the most enchanting girl that ever the sun shone on, and ought to wear a coronet if such things went by charm; and here was he, a pauper junior clerk in one of the most miserably-paid branches of the Civil Service, coolly asking her to be his wife! His conduct had been criminal, nothing short of it.

What on earth would Frank say when he told him of it? If Frank was an honourable man he would go over to Layard, and advise the brother to forbid the suitor his house.

Suitor, indeed! Pretty suitor he was to go wooing such a girl as Hetty!

But then Hetty had told him she loved him and would follow him to the ends of the earth, and he'd just like to hear any man in *his* presence say Hetty wasn't to do what she pleased, even if her pleasure took such a preposterous form as love for him. Now that he came to think of it in that way, if it pleased Hetty to love him she should love him, in spite of all the Franks and all the brothers in Christendom; for wasn't Hetty's happiness and pleasure dearer to him than the welfare of empires? And if he hadn't quite a hundred a year, he could make it more by coaching fellows for the Civil Service and in a thousand other ways.

Philip Ray having arrived at this more hopeful and wholesome view of his affairs went to bed, and lay awake some time trying to compose a poem in his sweetheart's praise. Having found, however, that he could not keep the lines of equal length, and that the rhymes came in now at the wrong places and anon not at all, he abandoned poetry as an occupation with which he had no familiarity, and took to one in which he had experience--sleep.

When he awoke next morning all his troubles and doubts had cleared away. The lead of the night before had been transmuted into gold by the alchemy of sleep. He seemed to himself really a fairly good fellow (which was no egotistical over-estimate, but a very fair appraisement of his value). No insuperable difficulties presented themselves in his mind to the making thirty, forty, fifty pounds a year more than his salary. He knew Hetty loved him, and he simply adored his exquisite jocund Hebe with the rich heart and frank avowal of love. A fig for obstacles with such a prize before him! If any considerable sum of money was attached to the setting of the Thames on fire here was your man able and willing to undertake the feat.

When the afternoon came, and he found himself released from the drudgery of his desk, he hastened to Welford. Alfred Layard did not get home in the evening until eight o'clock, and, of course, Ray could not call at Crawford's House until after that hour. But he could go to the Ait, and who could say but Hetty might appear at the window, or even come out on Crawford's Quay? In any case he wanted to see Frank and tell him what he had done, for he would as soon have thought of picking a pocket as of keeping a secret from his brother-in-law.

Philip Ray hastened along the canal with long quick strides, swinging his arms as he went. Now that the prospect of seeing Hetty again was close upon him he had not only lost all his gloom, but was in a state of enthusiastic hopefulness. He hailed the island three times before Bramwell answered.

"I thought you were never coming," said he, as the two shook hands upon his landing.

"I was busy when you hailed," said Bramwell, "and I could not believe it was you so early." Then noticing the excitement of his brother-in-law, he said, "What is the matter? Has anything happened?"

"Yes. Let us go in. I want to talk to you most particularly," said Ray. Then in his turn noticing the appearance and manner of the other, he said, "What is the matter with *you? You* too look as if something had happened."

"I have been up all night at work," he answered, as they entered the cottage.

Ray's sister had gone to Mrs. Pemberton's to get the luggage she had left there.

They went into the sitting-room. Frank was playing by himself in the old timber-yard.

"Now, what is your news?" asked Bramwell, feeling sick at the thought that it must be something about Ainsworth.

Ray fidgeted on his chair. He found it more easy to say to himself, "I must tell Frank at once," than to accomplish the design now that the two were face to face. He hummed and hawed, and loosed his collar by thrusting his finger between his neck and the band of his shirt, but no words came. At last he got up and began walking about nervously.

"What is it, Philip? Can I do anything for you?" asked Bramwell, in a placid voice and with a quiet smile.

"No, thank you, Frank, I've done it all myself. I've done all that man could do."

Bramwell turned pale; seizing the arms of his chair, he said apprehensively, "You don't mean to say have met Ainsworth, and----"

"No--no--no!"

Bramwell threw himself back, infinitely relieved.

"The fact is I have made a fool of myself."

"In what way, Philip?"

"You know my income?"

Bramwell nodded.

"Well, it may as well come out first as last. I--don't start, and pray, pray don't laugh at me--I've fallen in love."

Bramwell nodded again and looked grave.

"And I have proposed."

Bramwell looked pained.

"And have been accepted."

"There is no chance whatever of my knowing anything of the lady?" said Bramwell in a tone implying that the answer must be in the negative.

"There is. You do. I proposed last night on this island to Miss Layard, and she has accepted me."

"Merciful heavens!" cried the other man, springing to his feet.

Ray paused and stared at his brother-in-law. "Why, what on earth is the matter with you, Frank? There is nothing so very shocking or astonishing in it, is there? I know for a man in my position it was rash, almost mad, to do such a thing. But there is nothing to make you look scared. Tell me why you are so astonished and shocked? If I told you I had shot Ainsworth you couldn't look more alarmed."

"I'll tell you later--not now. Go on with your story, Philip. When you know all you will see why I was startled. It has nothing to do with you. I wish you and Miss Layard all the happiness that can fall to the lot of mortals; but I need scarcely tell you that, my dear, dear Philip."

"I know it, Frank. You need not tell me you wish me well. You're the most-generous-hearted fellow alive. You have suffered cruel wrong through my blood, but never through me personally. Yet I believe if I had done you a personal wrong you would shake my hand and wish me well all the same. I believe if you yourself had thought of Hetty, and she chose me, you would be just as cordial in your good wishes as you are now."

"I should indeed," said Bramwell, with a strange light in his eyes. "And now tell me the rest of your story."

Again he shook his brother-in-law warmly by both hands, and then sat down.

"There is nothing else to tell. When we came over here to see about the boy last night I asked her to be my wife, and she consented. By the way, how did he get on after I left?"

"For a while his rest was broken," said Bramwell, with a wan smile, "but after that he slept perfectly till it was time to get up."

"I knew the child was only dreaming. But Hetty"--yes, he had called her Hetty to his brother-in-law: how incomparably rich this made him feel!--"but Hetty was fairly terrified, and I thought it better to give way to her. It was nothing but a nightmare or a dream."

"Do you know, I am not so sure of that, Philip?"

"So sure of what?" asked the other man, drawing down his straight eyebrows over his eyes, and peering into Bramwell's face, looking for symptoms of incipient insanity.

"That it was all a dream," answered the other, returning his gaze.

"Are you mad?" cried Ray, drawing back, and regarding his companion with severe displeasure.

"That is the second time I have been asked the same question within the past twenty-four hours. Do you know who the other person was who asked me that question?"

"Who?"

"Kate."

"O, he is mad!" cried Ray, stopping in his walk and surveying Bramwell with pity and despair.

The other went on, quietly looking his brother-in-law in the face steadily.

"The crisis of that disease went in her favour. She inserted that announcement of her death in order that I might feel myself free to marry if I chose. On her way to the River she came to this place to get one more sight of her child. I found her here----"

"And you forgave her?" said Ray, in a breathless voice.

"Yes."

"Why?" fiercely.

"Because I thought it would be well for her to be near her child. And she is to stay here----"

"Here? With you? You do not mean to say you will meet her day after day for evermore?"

"Why not? She had nowhere else to go to--except the River."

"But he will come again, and she will leave you."

"No, no. He will not come again. Her beauty is gone for ever."

"Her beauty gone for ever! How came that to be?"

"The illness marked her for life."

"And yet she may stay?"

"Why not? Will it not comfort her to be near her child?"

"O, Frank, you make all other men look small!"

"I said I would tell you why I started and cried out a while ago. Last night, when I believed myself free, I thought I might speak to Miss Layard----"

"O, my brother! O, this is the cruellest blow that ever fell on man! My heart is breaking for you."

"I did not know last night that your mind was set on Miss Layard."

"Do not speak of me."

"Boland's Ait!" cried a voice from without.

"Hark!" said Bramwell, holding up his finger. "That is Kate's voice. I must go to fetch her home."

CHAPTER XXXIV
CRAWFORD'S PLANS FOR THE FUTURE

Dr. Loftus pronounced Mrs. Crawford's condition to be very serious. He told her husband he did not expect a fatal termination immediately, but that in such cases there was no knowing what might happen, and it would be prudent that all preparations should be made for the worst. Above all, any violent shock was to be guarded against. There was now, he thought, absolutely no hope of improvement. If she felt equal to it, she might get up, and be wheeled about in her chair. In reply to Crawford's inquiry, the doctor could not tell how far off the end might be--hours, days, weeks.

"Months?"

"Scarcely."

When the doctor was gone Crawford sat a long time in deep thought. It was daylight now, and he lay down on a couch in his own room to ponder over the whole affair. The income of the property would be lost to him on her death. The three thousand pounds of savings would come to him. But how, and after what delay? There would be legal formalities and bother, and he hated both. That fool the doctor either could not or would not say how long the present state of things was likely to last. Yet, as he had said, it was wise to be ready for anything, for everything. Plainly, the best plan for him to adopt would be to induce his wife to make him a deed of gift of the three thousand pounds. That would diminish trouble in case of her death. There was no need of cruelty in asking her to do this. The only thing absolutely necessary was success. He need not even hint to her that he was taking the precaution because of the fragility of her life. He could manage to make the deed of gift seem desirable because of some other reason. One should seldom tell men the truth, and women never. The truth was too strong for women. Their delicate natures were not constructed to bear it with advantage to themselves, and if you told the truth to men they were likely to use it to their own advantage. Quite right: truth was a jewel, but, like any other jewel, it was fit only for holiday wear.

As soon as he got that deed of gift executed there would not be much more for him to do at Singleton Terrace. Viewed as a place of mere free board and lodgings, it was not of much consequence. With three thousand pounds and his present turn of luck he should be well off. Viewed as the home of a confirmed invalid who doted on him, Singleton Terrace was distasteful.

There would not be the least necessity for brutality or unkindness. Unkindness and brutality were always cardinal mistakes. He believed he could manage the whole matter with his wife, and appear in it greatly to his own advantage. He'd try that very day to arrange matters, so that at any hour he could quit Richmond for ever. What a merciful deliverance that would be for him! During the past few months he had scarcely dared to call his soul his own. Yes, if that deed could be got ready and executed in twenty-four hours, there was no reason why he should not shake the dust of Richmond off his feet in twenty-five.

Whither should he go? Ultimately back to the States, no doubt; but in the first instance to Welford. The latter place would be perfect only for two circumstances: first, that infernal Philip Ray visited Boland's Ait close by, and, second, Hetty--that charming Hetty--had a brother, a most forbidding and ruffianly-looking man, who might make himself intensely disagreeable. But it would be delightful to be under the same roof with that beautiful girl and saying agreeable things to her when they met. In all his life he never saw any girl so lovely as Hetty; and then look at the luck she had brought him! He would try Welford for a week or two--try the effect of Hetty's luck by playing every night for a fortnight. If he had won a good sum at the end of his trial, he should then be certain it was owing to Hetty. It would be easy to avoid Ray. He was engaged at his office until the afternoon. Every afternoon Crawford could leave Welford, go to the Counter Club, dine there, and not come back till morning. The affair was as simple as possible.

Then he thought of his escape from drowning and his meeting with Kate. But these were unpleasant memories, and he made it a rule never to cherish any reminiscences which could depress him, so he banished them from his mind and fell into a peaceful sleep.

It was late when he awoke. Some letters had come for him, and, after reading them, he went to his wife's room, and put them down impressively on a small table by the bedside. His inquiries were exhaustive, sympathetic, affectionate. He kissed her tenderly, and sat by her, holding her hand in his, and patting it. He said all the soothing words he could think of, and assured her of his conviction that in a few days she would be as well as she had been when they were so happily married.

She smiled, and answered him in gentle words, and in her soft sweet voice. She thanked him for his encouraging sayings, but told him with a shake of her head that she felt certain she should never be better--that this was the beginning of the end.

"But, indeed, you must get well," he said. "You must get well for my sake. Look, what glorious news I have had this morning! Here is a letter from my place in South America. It is, unfortunately, full of technicalities. Shall I read it to you? or tell you the substance of it?" He held up a bulky envelope, with several foreign stamps on it.

"O, tell me the substance, by all means! I am not clever like you over technicalities."

"It is, in effect, that my manager there has himself invented a machine quite capable of dealing with the fibre, and that we are now in a position to set about manufacturing."

"What splendid news, William!" she cried, with gentle enthusiasm, pressing the hand she still retained. "You did not expect anything of this kind?"

"No. But excellent as the news is, it has a drawback; and that drawback is one of the reasons why you must get well at once."

"Why, what has my recovery to do with the affair, and what is the drawback?"

"Well, the fact of the matter is we cannot get the machinery made without some money, and the little I have isn't nearly enough."

"But I have some. Take the savings. I have told you over and over again that they are yours. Would what I have be enough?"

"Well, with what I have and what I can raise I think it would; but you must get well first. It is only sentiment, no doubt; but I could not bear to take your money while you are not as well as you were a little while ago. The only interest or object I now have in this discovery is that you may share the great benefit of it with me."

"Indeed, indeed, you must not think of me in this way. It is like your dear kind self to say what you have just said; but it is not businesslike, and you must take the money. I am only sorry it is not ten times as much."

"No, no! Not, anyway, until you are as well as you were a couple of months ago, dear Nellie."

"But you must. I will listen to no denial. Fancy, allowing my illness to stand in the way of your success!"

For a good while he resisted, but in the end she prevailed, and he reluctantly consented to accept the money, and settle about the transfer from her to him that very day.

Accordingly, he went to town after breakfast, armed with a letter from his wife to Mr. Brereton, Mrs. Crawford's lawyer.

He came back early in the afternoon somewhat disappointed: it would take a day to complete the business.

"After all," he thought, "I must not grumble about the delay. The direct transfer of the money will be better for me than the deed of gift. In the one case I shall have the money, in the other I should have only a document."

He had abstained from going to the Counter Club that day for two reasons: first, he did not wish to risk discovery of his taste for play while the three thousand pounds were hanging in the clouds; and, second, he wished to believe the luck born of his acquaintance with Hetty prevailed most on the days he saw her, and should, to operate daily, be daily renewed by sight of her.

"When all is settled I'll write for Mrs. Farraday to come back and stay here. She promised she would in case of need. Then I'll tell my wife that my personal presence is absolutely necessary in America, and I'll say good-bye to her and go down to Welford. I must arrange with my wife that Blore, the former agent, is not set to work collecting for a month or six weeks, so that I may have time to get out of the country, or away from Welford at all events. I don't think I shall require more than three weeks at Welford. I can get those gates put up and taken down again, and stay there on pretence of superintending the work."

CHAPTER XXXV
HUSBAND AND WIFE

The meeting between Philip Ray and his sister was full of pain and shame to him and the acutest agony to her. Few words were spoken. Bramwell was not in the room. He tarried behind on the pretence of mooring the stage, so that the two might not be restrained or embarrassed by any consideration of him. But the presence of the husband seemed to haunt the place, and was felt by both as a restraining influence.

"If he can forgive her and take her back, what have I to say in the affair?" asked Philip of himself.

"No matter how much he may reproach me, I will not answer," thought the unhappy woman. "Anything Philip could say to me would not hurt me now."

So beyond a few formal words no speech was exchanged between the two, and shortly after Bramwell came back Philip went away.

"May I stay in this room? This is your room, I know," said Kate meekly, when they were alone. "I do not wish to intrude. I know you have writing to do, and that I may be in the way."

There was no tone of bitterness or complaint in her voice. She simply wanted to know what his wishes were.

"While you were out," he said, "I arranged the room I had intended to be a play-room for the boy as my own. Yours will be the one you used last night, and this will be common to all of us. I shall shift my books into my own room and write there."

"And the boy?" said she, with a tremble in her hoarse, dull voice. "Which room will be the boy's?"

"Yours, of course."

She moved towards him as if to catch his hand in gratitude. He stood still, and made no responsive sign.

"When I came here two years ago," he said quietly, "I changed my name from Mellor to Bramwell. I shall retain the name of Bramwell, and you will take it."

He did not request her to do it or command her to do it. He told her she would do it.

"As no doubt you are aware, I am very badly off now compared with the time--compared with some years ago." He was going to say "compared with the time I married you," but he forebore out of mercy. "I have little more than a hundred a year and this place rent-free; it is my own, but I cannot let it. I hope soon to be able to add to my income. If my anticipations are realised I may double my income; but at present I am very poor."

"And I am bankrupt," said she with passionate self-reproach, "in fortune, in appearance, and in reputation."

He held up his hand in deprecation of her vehemence.

"Understand me clearly. Mrs. Bramwell may not have any money, and may not be as remarkable for beauty as some other women. But recollect, she has no reputation, good or bad. She did not exist until this present interview began. The past can be of no use to us. I shall never refer to it again; you will never refer to it again. There may have been things in the life of Kate and Frank Mellor which each of them contemplates with pain. No pain has come into the life of Francis Bramwell during the two years of his existence. No pain can have come into the life of Kate Bramwell during the few minutes she has existed. It will be wisest if we do not trouble ourselves with the miseries of the Mellors. Do you understand?" he asked in his deep, full, organ-toned voice.

"I think I do," she answered. "You mean that we are to forget the past."

"Wholly, and without exception."

"And you will forget that you ever cared for me?"

"Entirely."

His voice was full and firm, but when he had spoken the word his lip trembled and his eyelids drooped.

He was walking softly up and down the room. She was sitting by the table in the same place as she had sat last night. Her arms hung down by her side, her head was bowed on her chest, her air one of infinite, incommunicable misery.

"And you will never say a kind word to me again?" she said, her voice choked and broken.

"I hope I shall never say any word to you that is unkind."

"That is not what I mean. You will never change towards me from what you are now this minute? You will never say a loving word to me as you used--long ago?"

She raised her face and looked beseechingly at him as he passed her chair.

"I shall, I hope, be always as kind-minded to you as I am now."

"And never any more?"

"I cannot be any more."

"Is there--is there no hope?" She clasped her hands and looked up at him in wild appeal.

He shook his head. "I loved you once, but I cannot love you again."

"You say you forgive me. If you forgive me, why cannot you love me? for I love you now as I never loved any one before."

"Too late! Too late!"

"Is it because my good looks are gone? Why, O, why cannot you love me again, unless it is because my good looks are gone?"

"No; your good looks have no weight in the matter. I could not forgive you if I loved you in the old way."

"Then," she cried, rising and stretching forth her arms wildly towards him, "do not forgive me; revile me, abuse me, yes, beat me, but tell me you love me as you did long ago; for I love you now above anything and all things on earth. Yes, ten thousand times better than I love my child! I never knew you until now. I was too giddy and vain and shallow to understand you. I have behaved to you worse than a murderess. But, Frank, I would die for you now!" She flung herself on her knees on the floor, and raised her clasped hands above her streaming face to him. "On my knees I ask you in the name of merciful Heaven to give me back your love, as I had it once! Give it to me for a little while, and then I shall be content to die. You are noble enough to forgive me and to take me back into your house. Take me back into your heart too. Raise me up and take me in your arms once, and then I will kill myself, if you wish it; I shall then die content. Refill my empty veins with words of love and I will trouble you no more. I have been walking blindfold in the desert all my life, and now that the bandages are taken off my eyes and I can see the promised land, am I to find I can never enter it? I am only a weak, wicked woman. You have extended to me forgiveness that makes you a god. Have for me, a weak woman, the pity of a god."

"I am no longer a man," he said, leaning against the wall. "I am smoke, an abstraction, a thing, an idea, a code. You are my wife and I will not cast a stone at you. You are my wife, and you are entitled to the shelter of my roof and the protection of my name. I make you free of both. But when you ask for love such as once was yours, I fail to catch the meaning of your words. You are speaking a language the import of which is lost to me. It is not that I will not, but that I cannot, give you what you ask. There would have been no meaning in the love I offered you years ago if I could offer you love now. Get up. It was with a view to avoiding a scene I spoke."

"I will not get up until you tell me there is hope--that some day you may relent."

"There is no question of relenting. When you left me you destroyed in me the faculty of loving you. Now get up. We have had enough of this. We must have no more. I have been betrayed into saying things I determined not even to refer to. Get up, and, mind, no more of this." With strong, firm arms he raised her from her knees.

She stood for a moment, leaning one hand on the table to steady herself. Then in a low quavering whisper, she said, "Is there any, any hope?"

"There is none."

She raised herself, and moved with uncertain feet to the door. "It would have been better I went to the river last night."

CHAPTER XXXVI
TEA AT CRAWFORD'S HOUSE

When Philip Ray left Boland's Ait he crossed over to the tow-path, and not to Crawford's Quay. It was still too early to call at Layard's. There was nothing else for it but to kill time walking about. Under ordinary circumstances when greatly excited he went for a very long walk. If nothing else but the startling and confounding affairs at Boland's Ait had to be considered, he would have dashed off at the top of his speed and kept on straight until he had calmed himself or worn himself out. But there was Crawford's House to be thought of. That must not be left far behind. Even now when he intended circling it he could not bear to think he was turning his face away from it, although he knew it was necessary to make a radius before he could begin his circle.

His mind was in a whirl, and he could see nothing clearly. The astounding return of his sister from the grave, and the still more astounding pardon extended to her by her husband, threw all his ideas into phantasmagoric confusion. Images leaped and bounded through his brain, and would not wait to be examined. Of only one thing was he certain: that Frank was the noblest man he had ever met. Although he repeated over and over to himself Bramwell's words about Kate, although over and over again he called up the vision of Kate in that room on the islet, he could not convince his reason that forgiveness had been extended to her. In his memory he saw the figures and heard the voices, and understood the words spoken, but a dozen times he asked himself, could it be true? or had his imagination played him false?

The affairs at the Ait dwarfed his own concerns, and made them seem tame and commonplace. That a young man should fall desperately in love with a beautiful girl like Hetty was the most natural thing in the world; but that a hermit, a young man of scrupulous honour like Frank, should take back an errant wife, whose former beauty had now turned almost to repulsiveness, transcended belief. It was true, but it was incredible.

As time went on, and the walking allayed the tumult in his mind, his thoughts came to his own position in the circumstances. He had not told Layard or Hetty any of Frank's history beyond the fact that it was a painful one, and a subject to be avoided. He had not told them that he was Bramwell's brother-in-law. He had never said a word about Bramwell's wife.

Now all would have to be explained. Of course, he had intended telling when he spoke to Layard about Hetty; things had changed beyond anticipation, beyond belief, since last night. Had he known what was going to happen on the Ait last night, what had absolutely happened when Hetty and he landed there, he would not have said a word of love to the girl. He would have told her the facts about Kate before asking Hetty to marry Kate's brother, before asking Hetty to become the sister of this miserable woman.

He knew he was in no way responsible for his sister's sins, but some people considered a whole family tainted by such an act in one of its members. Some people believed conduct of this kind was a matter of heredity, and ran in the blood. Some people would ask, If the sister did this, what could you expect from the brother?

Would the painful tale he had to tell Layard influence Hetty's brother against his suit? There were thousands of people who would consider that he himself was smirched by his sister's fault. Was Layard one of these?

The best thing for him to do was to relate the story at once; the most honourable and straightforward way for him to proceed would be to speak to Layard before he again saw Hetty. If Layard raised an objection, and that objection was insuperable, the most honourable course for him to pursue would be to give up all pretensions to Hetty.

Yes, but could he? And would he be justified in renouncing her now that he knew she loved him? It would be all very well if he had not made love to her and gone so far as to ask her to marry him. If only his happiness were concerned the path of duty would be plain enough. But Hetty and he were now partners in love, and had he the power or the right to dissolve the partnership without consulting her? Clearly not. However he looked at the situation doubts and difficulties arose before his mind. There was only one matter clear--he ought to speak to Layard at once.

It was now half-past seven. Layard left the gasworks at eight. Why should he not intercept him on his way home and put him in possession of all the facts? Upon what Layard said, the course to be adopted could be based.

He got to the gas-house, and was walking up and down impatiently when Alfred Layard came out of the gateway and saw him.

"Anything the matter?" asked Layard apprehensively when Ray came up to him.

"At your place? O, no! I wanted a few minutes' talk with you, so I came to meet you."

"All right," said Layard, with a smile. He thought he could guess what the talk would prove to be about. He was the incarnation of unselfishness, and it never occurred to him for a moment to consider how awkward it would be for him if Hetty married and left him.

"I want first of all to tell you a very painful piece of family history," said Ray, anxious to get the worst over as soon as possible.

"But why should you, Ray? I am the least curious man alive."

"You will know why I wish to tell you before I have finished."

Then, without further preface, he narrated the history of Kate, her marriage, her flight, her supposed death, her appearance last night at the Ait, and her husband's forgiveness.

Layard was greatly interested and excited by the story. When it was finished, he said:

"There is enough Christianity in that man Bramwell to make a bishop."

"To make the whole bench of bishops," cried Ray enthusiastically. "I always knew he was a hero, but I was not prepared to find the spirit of a martyr as well. And yet I ought to have been prepared for anything noble and disinterested in him. He does what he believes to be right without any view to reward here or hereafter. He has had his wild days when he plunged, under his great trouble, into the excitement of gambling, but even in that he was unselfish; he injured no one but himself. Once he pulled up, he stopped for good and all. And now I come to the reason for taking you into confidence and telling you what you need never have known only for something which concerns myself more deeply than all else which has happened to me in my life."

Then in a few words he explained his position, his feelings towards Hetty, and his belief that his feelings were reciprocated.

"You have three matters to weigh," he said, in conclusion; "first, the family history I have told you; then my financial position, taking into account the chance of my getting the tuitions; and, last, whether you would object to me personally. In the short time I have known you, I have taken to you more than to any other man I ever met except Frank. I am speaking to you as much as a friend as Hetty's brother. If I did not look on you as a friend, I should not care greatly to take you into my confidence and defer to you. But the notion of doing anything underhand or behind your back would seem to me intolerable treason."

"I'll be as straightforward with you as you have been with me. I have liked you from the first moment of our short acquaintance. The way in which you have spoken to me this evening strengthens ten thousand times my good opinion of you. The miserable family history you have told me has no bearing whatever on you, and I see nothing to stop you but the getting of those tuitions. Why, I married on little more than your salary; and during my short married life I never for one moment repented, nor did my poor girl. Contented and willing hearts are the riches of marriage, not money."

Ray was too much moved to say more than "Thank you, Layard;" but he stopped in his walk, and, with tears in his eyes, wrung the hands of the other man.

"And now," said Layard, as they resumed their way, "let us get home to tea."

That was his way of telling Ray that there was no need of further words either in explanation or of thanks.

"I thought we were going to have a thunderstorm last night, and to-night it looks like it too. I always feel a coming storm in the muscles of my arms, and they are tingling this evening."

Layard opened the door with his latch-key. The two men went into the front room, and in a few minutes Hetty appeared with the tea-pot. She coloured deeply on seeing Ray with her brother. She had not heard the footfalls of two people, and was not prepared to find him there. He had never before come in with Alfred, and a suspicion of what had occurred flashed through her mind.

She did not speak to Ray. She felt confused, and half-pretended, even to herself, that she did not know he was present. Her brother went to her and put his arm round her waist and kissed her cheek, and then drew her over to the chimney-piece, where Ray stood, feeling somewhat like a thief.

"You forgot to say good-evening to Ray," said the brother.

"Good-evening," said she, in a low voice, holding out her hand.

Ray took the long slender hand, feeling still more dishonest and shamefaced and miserable.

When the fingers of the lovers touched, Layard caught the joined hands in both his, and pressed them softly and silently together; then, turning away, he stepped quickly to the window, and stood a long time looking at the dead wall opposite through misty eyes.

"I don't think we shall have that storm," said Ray at length.

Layard turned round. Hetty was pouring out the tea, and Ray was standing with his back to the chimney-piece.

"No," said Layard, "I fancy it is passing away. My arms feel easier."

Hetty was smiling, but looking pale.

"Do you take sugar and milk, Mr. Ray?" said she.

"Dear me, Hetty," said her brother, "what a lot you have to learn yet!"

She coloured violently, and shook her head at him.

"I wish you would sit down, Alfred. You are keeping all the light out of the room; I can't see what I'm doing."

"No," said he, looking meaningly from her to Ray; "but, bad as the light is, I can see what you have done."

At this Hetty and Ray laughed a suppressed laugh, and looked at one another with joyous glances.

CHAPTER XXXVII
CRAWFORD WRITES HOME

The morning after Mrs. Crawford's relapse and Crawford's visit to town about the three thousand pounds, the husband was sitting by his wife's bedside. He was in a particularly cheerful and hopeful humour, and insisted that she had already begun to mend, and would in a week be better than she had been for months.

She shook her head with a sad smile, but said nothing. She did not wish to sadden the being she loved above all other living creatures by the thought of a final separation between them, a separation which she felt was inevitable, and to which she could not reconcile her mind. When alone she would cry out in despair to her gentle heart, "To be so loved, and to be so loving, and to be separated so soon!"

He went on affecting undiminished confidence in her recovery. "I tell you, I am certain you must, you will, get well, and that much sooner than even the doctor thinks." (The doctor had told him again that day there was little hope of her rallying.) "What good would my luck be if you were not by my side to share it? My Nelly comforted and sustained me in my days of doubt and difficulty. Do you mean that she is not to share my triumph? I will take very good care she shall. And now I want to tell you what I insist upon doing. I will take no denial, for I look on it as essential to your recovery."

"I will do anything you tell me," she said with meek devotion. "I will do all I can to get well. For, William, I am the happiest and most blessed woman in England, and I do not want to leave you, dear."

"That's my own brave wife," said he, winking his eyes quickly and patting her arm. "I don't think you will raise much, if any, objection to what I am about to do. I am going to write to Mrs. Farraday to come back and stay with you. She promised she would come if you needed her, and she will be a great source of comfort and confidence to you."

"But her brother?"

"Oh, her brother can do without her for awhile. You will be all right again in less than no time, and then, if she wishes, she can go back to her brother. And now I am off to write to Rochester for her by this very post, for a good thing cannot be done too soon, and I am sure this is a good thing for you."

He left her, went to his own room, wrote the letter, and posted it immediately himself. Then he came back to the house, and having entered the dining-room on the ground-floor, began walking up and down with brows lowered in deep meditation.

"I had better get it over me before Mrs. Farraday comes," he thought as the result of his cogitations. "I can't stay here any longer. I am not a sick-nurse to philander after an ailing woman, and dally in an invalid's room. She was a fool to marry me. Did she think for a moment I fell a victim to her ancient charms? If she did she ought to be in a lunatic asylum. Of course I told her I wanted to marry her for love, but is there in the history of the whole human race a single case of a man saying to a woman, 'I want to marry you for your money'? Not one.

"I can't stand this house any longer; it suffocates me. The doctor says there is no hope. Why should I wait to see the end? The approach of death and the presence of death are abhorrent to all healthy people. I can do no good by staying, and I have to think of myself. There are very few men living who would have been as good to her as I have been. She cannot expect me to do more, and," with one of his short laughs and a quick winking of his eyes, "my affairs in South America urgently demand my presence. I'll get the business over me at once. Brereton told me I could have the money early this afternoon."

Here his mind became so intensely occupied that his legs ceased to move, and he stood in the middle of the room lost in thought. He was contemplating scenes in his imagination: not proceeding by words. Presently words began to flow through his brain again, and he resumed his pacing up and down.

"If there should be any hitch about that money I should be in a nice mess." He shook his head gravely and repeated this contingency to himself two or three times. "That would never do. It would look weak and foolish. When I act I must act with firmness and decision. No, I had better make sure of the cash first."

He put all the money he had in his pocket, left the house, and took the first train to town. At Waterloo he jumped into a hansom and drove straight to the office of Mrs. Crawford's solicitor. He found Mr. Brereton in, and everything ready. The solicitor handed him an open cheque for £3,270, saying gravely as he did so:

"And you are fully resolved to put this money in that South American speculation?"

"My dear sir, there's a vast fortune in that fibre of mine; and now that the machinery has been perfected, it is only stretching out one's hands to gather in hundreds of thousands of pounds."

Brereton shook his head.

"The best place in which to put money is English Consols."

"What, less than three per cent.! For you can't buy even at par now. Why, my dear sir, it's letting money rust."

"It's keeping money safe."

Crawford shrugged his shoulders and made a grimace of dissatisfaction.

"Over-prudence, my dear Mr. Brereton. Who never ventured never got."

"A bird in the hand is worth two in the bush; and of all the uncertain things I know of there is only one worse than putting money in South American speculations, and that is putting it in Central American ones."

"Ah, but you have never been in South America!" said he triumphantly, and his eyes winked quickly, and he laughed a short unpleasant laugh, and thought to himself, "Nor have I either." Then he continued aloud, "I am aware that it is most unwise of any one who does not know the ground to dabble in South American speculations, but, you see, I am well acquainted with the place, and know the ropes."

"The last client I had who touched anything in South America blew his brains out. But, of course, it is no affair of mine. I have only to do what I am asked by Mrs. Crawford in her letter to me. The cheque is an open one, as you requested. They will pay you across the counter. I hope you will not think of keeping such a sum as that in your house?"

"O, dear, no! I am going to remit it at once to my agent. When you see me next, Mr. Brereton," laughing and winking his eyes, "you will congratulate me upon my spirit and success."

"I hope so," said the lawyer drily, and in a tone and manner which plainly said he believed nothing of the kind would occur.

Crawford said good-bye and went straight to the bank, where he got thirty-two one-hundred pound notes and seventy in fives.

He had never had so much money in his possession before. He had never had any sum approaching it. Once or twice after a good racing week in the old times he had been master of five or six hundred, but three thousand two hundred pounds! It was almost incredible! And it was all in cash! It did not lie in the cold obstruction of any bank. It was not represented by doubtful I.O.U.'s. It was not represented by shadowy entries in a betting-book. It was not invested in any shaky securities. It was not manifested by abstract entries in a ledger. The money was concrete and tangible, and lying safely in his breast-pocket under the stout cloth of his coat. He could take it out and count it now if he liked. That minute he could start for Monte Carlo or St. Petersburg, Australia or Norway.

As he walked along the streets he held his head high. He felt independent of all men, independent of fortune, of Fate. He had married for money, he had realised the prize, and it was now safe in his pocket. These notes were as much legally his own as his hands or his teeth. No one could take them from him except by force, and he took pride in thinking that few men who passed him in the street would be able to cope with him single-handed. He had as much thought of risking his money in anything so far off and tame as South American speculations as he had of buying a box of matches and burning it note by note.

Of course, Brereton had been right in saying it would be a dangerous thing to keep such a tempting sum in an ordinary house. There might even be danger in walking about the streets with it in his pocket. Some dishonest person might have seen him draw it out of the bank and might be following him. He might be a match for more than an average man, but he would be no match for two or three. Garrotting had gone out of use, but it might be revived even in midday in London by men who knew the prize he carried, and were bold and prompt. If in a quiet street he were seized from behind and throttled so that he could not cry out, and if a man in front cut the pocket out of his coat, the thieves might be off before passers-by knew what was going on or suspected anything being wrong. He had a horror of revolvers, but plainly he ought to be armed. He did not yet know where he should keep his hoard, but in any case it would be well to possess the means of defending it.

Crawford had by this time got out of the City and was strolling through Regent Street. He turned into a gunsmith's shop and bought a short large-bore revolver and some cartridges. The man showed him how to load the weapon. Crawford explained that he was about to leave the country for Algiers, and wished to have all the chambers charged, as he was going in a vessel with a crew of many nationalities, and was taking out a lot of valuable jewellery.

Lying was a positive pleasure to him, even when it was not necessary. "It keeps a man's hand in," he explained the habit to himself.

It was now about two o'clock, and he began to feel the want of luncheon. There was no place where better food could be got or where the charges were more moderate than at the Counter Club. He was only a short distance from it. What could be more reasonable than that he should go and lunch there? Nothing. So he turned into an off street on the left, and in a few minutes was seated in a luxurious armchair in the dining-room, waiting for the meal he had ordered of the obsequious waiter.

He was somewhat tired by his walk, and found rest in the well-cushioned chair grateful and soothing.

Could anything be more comfortable and cheering than to sit at ease in this well-appointed club, with a small fortune in notes under one's coat? Here was no suggestion of illness or approaching death. All the men present were in excellent health and spirits. They were talking of cheerful subjects--horses, theatres, cards, the gossip and scandal of the town. They spoke of nothing that was not a source of enjoyment; and though all they said ran on assumption that they did not contemplate the idea of any man denying himself pleasure or being unable to obtain pleasure owing to the want of money, they were not all rich men, but all spoke as if they were. It was so much pleasanter to sit here, listening to this talk and taking part in it, than to wander about that cold-mannered house in Singleton Terrace at Richmond, or to sit by the sick-bed of a wife ten years older than himself and whine out loving phrases and indulge in distasteful private theatricals.

Then the obsequious and silent-footed waiter brought in his cutlets, and whispered that his luncheon was ready. Everything was very nice at Singleton Terrace, but somehow cutlets there and here were two widely different matters. It was no doubt easy to explain the reason of the difference. In one place the cook got twenty, in the other a hundred, pounds a year. But though that explained the difference, it made the cutlets at Singleton Terrace no better.

He had had enough of Richmond. Why should he go back there? As he had always held, there was no advantage in being brutal, and he would not undeceive his elderly wife. He would not tell her in plain words that he had never cared in the least for her, that he had married her merely for her money, and now that she was dying and her income would, for him, die with her, and that he had got all the money she had, that his whole mind was occupied with the image of a beautiful young girl whom he was about to make love to and ask to fly with him on her (his wife's) money. No. It would be uselessly unkind to tell that middle-aged silly invalid any of these things. But why should he go back to Richmond?

If he went back to say good-bye he would have to play a long scene in private theatricals to which no salary was now attached, since he had all the savings in his pocket. Besides, he would find it hard, credulous as his elderly wife was, to make her believe there could be any urgent necessity for his immediate departure to South America. There would be a scene and tears--and he hated scenes and tears--and then if the surprise or shock made her worse, who could tell the consequences, the unpleasant consequences, which might arise?

In the next room were pen, ink, and paper. Why should he not write instead of going back? That was it! He'd write explaining, play at the club to-night, and go on to Welford in the morning. That was a better programme than crawling back to that silly old invalid and acting sorrow at parting when his heart was overrunning with joy.

He went into the next room and wrote his first letter to his wife. He used a sheet of unheaded paper, and did not date or domicile it.

My dearest Nellie,--Upon coming to town I found waiting for me a telegram from Rio Janeiro to the effect that if I did not reach that city at the very earliest moment possible--in fact, by a steamer sailing from London to-day--my title to the estate on which the fibre grows would lapse. Nothing but my personal presence could save it. So, much against my will, I was obliged to drive in hot haste to the boat without the satisfaction of bidding you good-bye. Indeed, I have barely time to write this scrawl, and shall have to intrust it to a waterman for post. Be quite sure all will go well with me, and that I shall telegraph you the moment I land. I am so glad I wrote for Mrs. Farraday before leaving home this morning. I know she will take every care of my Nellie while I am away, and I am sure my Nellie will take every care of herself, and be quite well long before the return of her loving husband,

William Crawford.

"Thank heaven that's the end of this ridiculous connection!" he said to himself as he dropped the letter into a pillar-box in front of the club. "My mind is now easy, and I can enjoy myself. I can play to-night as though I were still a bachelor with no thought of the morrow. Ah, but I have thought of the morrow! What delightful thought, too! delightful Hetty."

It was late in the evening when this letter was delivered at Singleton Terrace. Nothing else came by that post. Although Mrs. Crawford had often seen her husband's writing, this was the first letter she had got from him, and she had never before seen her name and the address of that house in his writing. She did not recognise the hand, and thinking the letter must be connected with routine business about the Welford property, she put it on the table by her bedside unopened. He attended to all such matters.

When the maid brought in her supper she took up the letter again and turned it over idly in her hands. All at once it struck her that the writing was familiar, but whose it was she could not guess.

With a smile at her own curiosity, she broke the cover and drew out the sheet of paper.

She looked at the signature languidly until she read it. Then hastily, tremulously she scanned the first few lines. When she gathered their import she uttered a low wailing sob and fell back insensible on the pillow.

CHAPTER XXXVIII
WILLIAM CRAWFORD FREE

When William Crawford had posted his letter to his wife he felt ten years younger than an hour before. He enjoyed an extraordinary accession of spirits. The day had grown heavy and cloudy, but to him it was brighter than the flawless blue of Mediterranean summer. Richmond and Singleton Terrace were done with for good and all. There were to be no more private theatricals played for board and lodgings. Instead of simulating love for an elderly woman, he was at liberty to make real love to the most charming young girl he had ever met. His notions of right and wrong were clear and simple: what he liked was right, what he did not like was wrong. Since he had come to man's estate he had acted upon the code, and it never once occurred to him to question it. He did not object to other men being pious or just or modest; he did not object to their even preaching a little to him about the merit of these or any other virtues. All he asked was to be let go his own gait unmolested.

He was now at liberty to take what path he chose and adopt what sport pleased his humour. He had played for a small fortune and won. He felt proud of his success, and sorry that the nature of it forbade him glorying in it. He was aware that the most disreputable and unprincipled blackleg in the Counter Club would scorn to get money as he had acquired his. But this did not matter to him. He was not going to tell any one at the club how he came by the money; that was an irksome self-restraint imposed upon himself out of deference to ridiculous conventional ideas. But he had the money in his pocket--that was the great thing.

As he intended playing all through the night, if the game were kept up, it was too early to begin at three o'clock in the afternoon. He should be fagged out before morning if he sat down now. He was neither so young nor so impetuous that he could not discipline desire to delay.

All at once he remembered that in abandoning Singleton Terrace so suddenly he had lost his kit. The value of his baggage was not very great, and with the sum now in his possession he would not for three times its value go back to Richmond for it. He had now no personal belongings but the clothes he stood in and a portmanteau at Welford. He would go to a tailor and an outfitter and order what he wanted. That would amuse him and help to kill time. He should get back to the club about seven, and devote the rest of the evening and all the night to cards.

He did not go to the tailor with whom he had dealt since he came to live at Richmond. He wanted to cut himself off from that place as completely as possible.

At the tailor's he ordered three suits of clothes to be ready in three days and forwarded to Crawford's House, Crawford Street, Welford. What he bought at the outfitter's were to be sent to the tailor's and to accompany the parcel of the latter. He paid in advance for all. Then he went to another shop, purchased a portmanteau, and directed it to be delivered at the tailor's, and sent a note with it, asking him to put the outfitter's parcel and the clothes into it and send it to the address already given.

Then he bethought him of a dressing-bag, and he bought a handsome one with silver-mounted bottle and ivory-backed brushes. The bag, being of leather, reminded him that he had no boots but those on his feet. So he purchased a couple of pairs and a pair of slippers, and the slippers put him in mind of a dressing-gown.

He directed all these things to be sent to the tailor's, and wrote to the tailor to let them all be forwarded at the one time--that is, when the clothes were finished, in three days.

He enjoyed this shopping greatly. He had never before spent so much money on himself in one day. It was so pleasant to buy these articles without worrying about the price, to be in doubt as to whether he should have a dressing-bag at thirty or thirty-five pounds, and to decide in favour of the thirty-five-pound one merely because it had prettier bottles and a greater number of pockets.

When he could think of nothing else which he wanted, he said to himself, "And now what shall I take Hetty? I must get the very handsomest present I can light upon."

This set him off calling Hetty up to mind. He looked into the windows of a dozen jewellers' and shops where fancy articles were sold. He failed to find an article to his liking. He could not realise Hetty accepting any of the costly gifts presented to his view. At length with a sudden start he cried out to himself, "What an idiot I have been! Of course, she would not accept any of these things from me now. A few simple flowers from Covent Garden to-morrow morning on my way to Welford will be the very thing."

It never once occurred to him during the day that the money he was spending belonged to his wife, and was being laid out in a way and under conditions not contemplated by her in giving it to him. When he decided on taking flowers to Hetty, it never once occurred to him that this would be spending his wife's money to conciliate a rival of hers, and that twenty-four hours ago he would have bought these same flowers for his deserted wife.

"Hetty," he said, formulating his theory, "is to be won through her imagination, not by pelf."

When he got back to the club he reckoned up what he had spent. It was an agreeable surprise to find that although he had treated himself with great liberality, all his purchases did not absorb the hundred-pound note he had changed at the tailor's. He had got a moderate outfit and a very handsome dressing-case, with cut-glass bottles silver-mounted, and ivory-backed brushes, for less than one thirty-second part of the money received from Mr. Brereton that afternoon. He sat down to an excellent dinner with the conviction that he had done a fair day's work, and that he was entitled to enjoy himself for the remainder of the evening, and as far into the morning as he chose.

The dinner was excellent; his shopping had given him zest for it, and when he stood up from the table he felt in the most excellent humour with himself and all the world.

He looked at his watch.

"She has my letter by this time," he said to himself, thinking of his wife. "If she is not a greater fool than I take her for, she will know from it that she has seen the last of me."

When he wrote the letter he had no intention of conveying any such idea to her, but his shopping and thoughts of Hetty had hardened his heart since then towards his unhappy wife, and now he wanted to believe that his letter would leave her no loophole of hope.

"Dr. Loftus said any shock might bring on the end. Perhaps my letter----" He paused and did not finish the sentence, but began another: "When a case is hopeless the greatest mercy which can be shown to the sufferer is, of course, to put an end to the struggle. She could not have fancied for a moment that I was going to spend all my life in the sick-room of a woman almost old enough to be my mother. Anyway, I need not bother my head any more about the matter. She cannot say that while our married life lasted I was not a kind and considerate husband. Turn about is fair play, and I am going to be a little kind and considerate to myself now. I'll put the past away from my mind. 'Gather we rosebuds while we may' is my version. Now to lose for the last time."

At the Counter Club there were men every night who did not mind how far into the morning they sat so long as they were winning. From the moment Crawford touched the cards until he rose at half-past six he had lost steadily. Though he had played for higher stakes than usual, he had been as careful of his game as if he had no more than a few hundred pounds with him. He had not been reckless. He had not plunged. Luck had simply been dead against him, and when, while eating his early breakfast, he counted up the cost, he found he was close on three hundred pounds the worse for his night's experience.

Mentally he cursed his bad luck.

"But I deserve no better," he thought. "I told myself that I should have good luck only when I had come from Welford. The luck I played with last night was my wife's or my own, and both have been invariably bad. I shall go to Welford to-day, and play to-night with Hetty's luck, and win back all I have lost and more besides. And now to get a bouquet for Hetty--for the loveliest girl in the whole of England. But the bouquet must not be too splendid. It must be simple and cheap, or it might do more harm than good."

At Covent Garden he bought some simple blossoms, and had them tied carelessly together.

"She will not value them for what they cost, but for my remembering her."

He was full of confidence in his power to fascinate and win. It never for a moment occurred to him that Hetty might not care for him or his memory of her. The notion of a rival had never entered his head, and if any one had suggested such a thing he would have laughed the consideration of it to scorn. He admired Hetty intensely, and he meant to succeed, and succeed he would.

He lounged about Covent Garden for a good while, for he did not want to reach Welford until Layard had gone to the gasworks. Of course he should say his visit to Crawford's House was made with the purpose of seeing what progress had been made with the gates for the flooded ice-house.

It was about eleven o'clock when he got to Welford Bridge.

"The coast will be quite clear till one or two o'clock," he thought, with a sense of satisfaction. "Layard has gone to the works and Philip Ray is in his office, curse him!"

When Hetty heard the latch in the door that day she came to no hasty conclusion that it was her brother come back for something he had forgotten. She was in the kitchen with Mrs. Grainger at the moment, and guessed immediately it was Crawford, although the week was not yet up. If Philip Ray had not spoken out to her, that sound at the door and the likelihood of the visitor being the landlord of the house would have thrown her into unpleasant excitement bordering on panic; but now she felt as calm and as much at ease as though certain it was Alfred himself.

"I shall say nothing of what that dreadful man said about his falling into the river," she resolved hastily. "If he chooses to speak of it, well and good; if he does not, well and good also. We are to leave this house as soon as Alfred can make arrangements for doing so. The quieter and the smoother everything goes in the meantime the better."

Crawford paused in the hall. Mrs. Grainger appeared "Is Mr. Layard in?" he asked, well-knowing he was not.

"No, sir, he's gone to the works."

"Then will you tell Miss Layard I should be glad to see her for a few minutes?" he said, taking off his hat and putting it on the table.

Hetty came at once, and held out her hand with a smile.

"She looks lovelier than ever," he thought, as he took the long slender hand and retained it. "I know I have come before my time, but I have been bothered again in my sleep about that ice-house and you. I will stay a day or so in order to see the gates put up--that is, of course, if you do not object?"

"Object!" she said, withdrawing her hand. "Why on earth should we object?"

"Well, I don't know," said he. "It may seem to you that I am unduly anxious about the matter. But upon my word, my anxiety about you has deprived me of all peace since I saw you last, and that scoundrel to whom I gave the order for the gates has not begun them yet. I assure you I had to exercise all my self-restraint to keep my hands off the fellow when I forced the truth from him. Will you accept a few simple flowers as a peace-offering and in lieu of the gates?"

"O, thank you," she said. "They are beautiful! But you give yourself a great deal of unnecessary anxiety and trouble about that ice-house. We never allow little Freddie on the Quay by himself, and of course there is no danger for a grown-up person, because no grown-up person ever goes near it. How on earth," she asked, with a laugh, "do you fancy a grown-up person could fall into such a place?" She wondered was he going up to his own room, or did he intend to remain standing there all day?

"I daresay I should not mind it if my dream happened to be about any one else. But the mere hint that any danger could threaten you is enough to drive me distracted. It is indeed," he said, looking at her intently, and with a pained expression on his usually passive face. "I assure you I did not sleep a wink last night; I could not, and I feel quite worn out and ill this morning. I have been wandering about, trying to kill time until I thought it was not too early to call here. I am hardly able to stand with anxiety, want of sleep, and fatigue."

"Would you not like to go to your own room and rest awhile? I will send Mrs. Grainger up with something nice for you."

"Mrs. Grainger could bring up nothing that I'd care for, and I hate the notion of going to that lonely room. I am quite nervous and unstrung." He sighed faintly and leaned against the wall for support.

"Well," she said, "will you come into our room and rest there?" Plainly, after his reference to the loneliness of his own place and the declaration of his exhausted condition, there was nothing but to offer him their front-room.

"Thank you," he said, "I shall very gladly accept your offer. I am thoroughly ashamed of seeming so weak and unmanned, but indeed I have had an awful time of it."

He sank on a chair as though completely exhausted. She stood by the door and said, "Cannot I send you something, Mr. Crawford?"

"If you would be so good as to get me a glass of water and then not leave me for a little while I should feel very grateful to you."

She hastened away and returned in a few seconds with the water.

"Miss Layard, I cannot tell you how ill I felt as I came along here. I really thought I should not have had courage to open the front door. I was full of the direst imaginings. I fancied that no sooner should I raise the latch than some awful form of bad news about you would strike me dumb with horror, paralyse me with despair." He took out his handkerchief and rubbed his forehead, which, however, was perfectly free from moisture.

"I am very sorry to be the cause of so much trouble to you, Mr. Crawford," said Hetty with some concern, though she had a vague kind of feeling that there was something wrong with the man--that he was either acting or of weak intellect. It never once occurred to her that he was thinking of making love to her. How could it? Was not he a married man? And did he not know that they were aware the owner of the Welford and Leeham property was his wife? She thought he had been a good deal too impulsive and a little impertinent on the former occasion when he told her of his dream, but now she was almost convinced that his violence of language on the former occasion and his physical collapse now were the result of a weak mind under strong excitement.

For a while after drinking the water he sat still and did not speak. Apparently he was gradually recovering, for he sighed once or twice, and once or twice straightened himself and sat upright on his chair. "I shall be all right in a few minutes. The sight of you is doing me good."

"Well, of course you know now nothing dreadful has happened?"

"To you--yes; I know that, thank Heaven! but to me, yes."

"Something dreadful has happened to you?" cried Hetty. "I am sorry to hear you say so. Nothing, I hope, that can't be mended?"

"Well, I do not know about that. If my condition were very desperate, Miss Layard, and it was in your power to mend it, and I asked you to help me, would you do so?"

"Certainly, Mr. Crawford, if I possibly could." He rose and went to her where she sat by the table, and bent over her, and said in a low, tremulous, tender voice, "Thank you--thank you a thousand times, my dear Miss Layard, my dear Hetty--may I call you Hetty?"

She coloured and looked uncomfortable, and this made her shine in his eyes with ineffable beauty. "It is not usual," she said at last.

"No, it is not usual, but I would deem it a great privilege. I of course would not call you by your dear Christian name when any one was by, but when you and I were having a little chat by ourselves I might, might I?"

Her colour and her confusion increased. "It is not usual," she repeated. "There is no reason why you should call me one thing now and another thing at another time." She raised her eyes, drew away a little from him, and pointing to the chair, said with steady emphasis which surprised herself, and showed him he must go no further--now, anyway: "I am afraid you are not yet rested enough to stand so long. Will you not sit down again?"

"You are right," he said with a deep sigh. "You are quite right. I am completely worn out, and my head is confused."

"There is no couch in your own room--perhaps you would like to rest on the one here? You will not be disturbed for some hours yet. My brother does not come in till three."

"Thank you very much, Miss Layard," he said, without any emphasis on her name. "But I think I'll go to my own room and lie down now. If I could get an hour's sleep I should be all right."

When he stood alone in his own room he said to himself, "I have not made much progress with her yet. I durst not go any further to-day than I went. Next time I ask her I'd bet a thousand pounds to a penny she'll give me leave to call her Hetty when we're alone. Once let her give me leave to call her Hetty when we are alone while I am to call her Miss Layard when any one else is present, and the rest is simple. My dreams"--he uttered his short sharp laugh and winked his eyes rapidly--"my dreams and my enormous solicitude for her welfare *must* tell in the end."

He went to the open window and looked out at the canal and the Ait and the tow-path. Then he turned his eyes downward.

With a cry of terror he sprang back, as though a deadly weapon or venomous snake in act to strike were a hand's breadth from his breast.

CHAPTER XXXIX
CRAWFORD IS SLEEPLESS

What startled Crawford and made him draw back in terror from the window was the sight beneath him of the stage reaching from Boland's Ait to Crawford's Quay across the murky waters of Crawford's Bay.

Involuntarily he put his hand behind and felt for the revolver in his pocket. It was reassuring to find it safe and within easy reach.

It had been bad enough to know that Philip Ray visited the idiotic recluse, Bramwell, on this accursed island; but to find a means of communication established between the Ait and the Quay was alarming in the extreme.

What could be the object of this floating bridge? Of course it was not there merely by accident. It was there with the consent of the Layards and the poor drivelling creature who lived on the holm.

William Crawford was not an intrepid man. Layard was near the truth when he called him a coward. Crawford never courted danger. His instinct was to flee from it. If he could not run away, he preferred thrusting his head into the sand to looking menace straight in the face. If a person or a place became obnoxious to him he simply went away or stayed away.

In the present case the thing he would like best was that Philip Ray might die, or be killed, or stop away from Boland's Ait because of some sufficient and final reason, death being the most satisfactory of all. After the cessation of Ray's visits to the Ait for fully sufficient reason, what he would have liked was his own absence from the neighbourhood. The latter means of terminating the difficulty lay in his own hands, but two considerations operated against his adopting it. In the first place, he could use the precaution of not being in the house, or even district, during the hours when Ray was likely to be free from his office; and, in the second place, he could not bring himself to abandon his pursuit of Hetty. He was willing to run a moderate risk for her sake.

"I think," he had said to himself that day on his way to Welford, "that if Nellie were to die, and I found Hetty continued to bring me luck, I should marry her."

He had never asked himself whether it was likely Hetty would marry him or not. He always considered that women should be allowed little or no voice in such matters.

From the shock of seeing the stage connecting the Ait and the Quay he recovered quickly. He went back to the window and looked out again.

There was not a cloud in the heavens. The noonday sun of mid-June blazed in the sky. There was no beauty in the scene, but it was looking its best and brightest. Under the broad intense light of day the waters of the Bay and the Canal shone like burnished silver, all their turbidity hidden from sight by the glare, as the darkness in the heart of steel is masked by the polished surface. Now and then a stray wayfarer passed along the tow-path. A barge, piled up high with yellow deals, trailed with slackened rope after the leisurely horse. The grass on the slope up from the tow-path was still green and fresh with the rains of recent spring. Beyond the wall at the top of the bank burned a huge vermilion show-van with golden letters naming in the light. The tiles of Bramwell's cottage glowed a deep red under the blue sky. Afar off factory chimneys, like prodigious columns of some gigantic ruined fane, stood up against the transparent air with diaphanous capitals of blue smoke uniting them to the blue vault above. From Welford Bridge came the dull sound of heavy traffic, and faintly caught from some deep distance came the faint napping beat of heavy hammers driving metal bolts through the stubborn oak of lusty ships. Sparrows skipped on the ground and twittered in the air. High up in the blue measures of the sky a solitary crow sailed silently by unheeding. All the world appeared dwelling in an eternal calm of vital air and wholesome light. All abroad seemed at peace under the spell of a Sabbath sky.

Suddenly he became conscious of voices near and beneath him. He looked out, but could see no one.

"They seem to come from the island," he thought, "and to be children's voices."

"It's a 'bus," said one of the young voices, "and I'm the driver."

"No," said another young voice, but a more resonant one than the former; "it's a tramcar, and I'm the driver."

"And I'm the conductor."

"No; I'm the conductor too."

"And what am I?"

"O, you're the people in the car. Fares, please. Here, give me this piece of slate. That's your fare. O, I say, there's a coal wagon on the line before us!"

The other boy uttered a shrill cry.

"What's that?"

"The whistle for the coal-van to get out of the way."

"But I am the driver, and you are not to whistle."

"Then I am the conductor, and the conductor rings the bell."

"No, you're not. I am the driver and the conductor, and you are the people in the tramcar, and all you have to do is to sit still and pay your fare. Fares, please."

"I am not to pay my fare twice. I don't like to be the people."

"O, but you are to pay your fare again, for we are coming back now, and you are different people."

"I don't like this game. Let us play something else."

"Very well. We'll play it's a boat, and that you fall into the river, and I catch you and pull you out, and----"

"Curse the brats, whoever they are!" cried Crawford fiercely, as he put his hand on the sash and drove the window down violently.

Freddie's words were purely accidental. For neither he nor any one else had heard from Hetty about Crawford's accident at the Mercantile Pier. She had said no more to her brother than that the landlord had come about the gates for the ice-house, and the subsequent alarming attempt at extortion by Red Jim had driven curiosity regarding Crawford's visit out of Layard's mind. Now that the latter had made up his mind to get out of this house as soon as possible, he cared little or nothing about the doings of the owner, so long as the owner kept his eccentricities within reasonable limits. The talk which Layard had with Bramwell on the subject of leaving Crawford's house had made no lasting impression on the brother. When he was by himself that night he made up his mind finally on two points. First, he would have Mrs. Grainger all day in the house; and, second, he would find a new home as soon as he could get rid of the present one.

The words of the child playing in the old timber-yard of the Ait had an unpleasant effect on Crawford. He did not know who the child was, nor could he bring himself to believe that this mishap at the Mercantile Pier had anything to do with the words overheard, and yet the coincidence vexed him. He told himself it was ridiculous to allow the circumstance to disturb him, but he could not help himself.

"I begin to think," he muttered, "that sitting up does not agree with me. I must be growing nervous. I ought to have some sleep if I am to try my luck again to-night--my luck and Hetty's," he added. "But if I sleep I must take care not to overdo it. I don't want to be here when that bearded ape of a brother of hers comes in to dinner." He went to the head of the stairs and called out to Mrs. Grainger to knock at his door and tell him when it was half-past two. Then he took off his coat, waistcoat, and boots, and lay down on his bed.

It was not quite as easy to go to sleep as he imagined it would be. The words of the child kept ringing in his ears. If by any chance the story of his fall into the water reached Hetty's ears, it would not improve his position in her mind. It might, in fact, cover him with ridicule. The bare thought of being laughed at made him writhe and curse and swear.

Well, if he wanted to get any sleep, he must put this nonsensical trouble out of his head. He ought to be very sleepy, and yet he felt strangely wakeful.

Then he could not say seriously to himself that he had made much progress with Hetty. Had he made any? He did not, of course, expect to find her in love with him all at once, but he had hoped she would show a little interest in him. If he must tell himself the truth, the only interest she showed in him was a desire to get him away from herself or to get away from him. In a week or so that would be all changed, but it was not pleasant just now.

"Confound it!" he muttered, turning over on his other side, "if I keep going on this way I shall not get a wink of sleep."

There was no more virtue in lying on one side than the other. He successfully banished from his mind any reflections that might disturb him. He thought of all the pleasant features of his present condition. He had for ever cut himself adrift from Singleton Terrace and the slavery to that infatuated old fool, his wife. He had now in his pocket, even after his losses of last night, four times more money than ever he had owned at one time in all his life before, and he had a weapon to defend himself and his money. He had never possessed a revolver or a pistol of any other kind until now. He was absolutely secure against all danger. No harm could come to him or his money. He was afraid of nothing in the world now, of no one----Curse that Philip Ray!

But he must remember that Philip Ray could have nothing more than a revolver, and that he himself had one, and at close quarters such a weapon was as effective in the hands of a man unaccustomed to its use as in those of one who had practised shooting hours a day for years.

No; sleep would not come. Perhaps if he put the revolver under his head the sense of security its presence afforded would soothe him into slumber.

He got up and took the weapon out of the back pocket of his coat. He poised it in his hand, and looked at it with mingled feelings of timidity and admiration. He cocked it, and took aim at spots on the wall paper a few inches above the level of his own eye. "If Ray were there now, and I pulled this trigger, he would be a dead man in less than a minute. I do not want to kill him. I should not fire except in self-defence. But if I thought he meant any harm, I'd save my life and put an end to his--the murderous-minded scoundrel!"

With the utmost care he lowered the hammer and, thrusting the revolver under his pillow, lay down again.

No; he did not feel any inclination to sleep. He counted a thousand; he watched a large flock of sheep go one by one through a gap; he repeated all the poetry he knew by rote, and found himself as wakeful as ever.

He tumbled and tossed about, and poured out maledictions on his miserable condition. He had not had experience of such a state before. Until to-day he had possessed the power of going to sleep at will. He had never lain awake an hour in his life. This was most tantalising, most exasperating. He should not be fresh for the cards to-night. He should be heavy and drowsy when he wanted to be clear and bright. How could he be fresh enough to play if he did not get rest?

Could it be the burden of this money was too great for him? Was he really apprehensive of being robbed? Brereton had told him it was dangerous to carry so large an amount in cash about with him. Had Brereton's words sunken into his mind, and were they now working on him unawares? No one could gainsay the wisdom of Brereton's caution. It was a dangerous thing to go about the streets of London with three thousand pounds in one's pocket. But there was nothing else for it. He would not put the money in an English bank, for he could not get an introduction without betraying himself, his presence in London, and telling more of his affairs than he desired. Lodging it in the Richmond bank was quite out of the question.

It was maddening to feel he could not sleep. Could it really be he was, unknown to himself, in dread of being plundered if he lost consciousness?

He opened his eyes and looked around him. Then, with an angry exclamation, he sprang up.

"What an idiot I have been," he cried, "to leave the door unlocked! My reason must be going when I could be guilty of such folly."

He turned the key in the lock. He looked around the room. He had shut the window to keep out the voices of the children, but he had omitted to fasten it down. He hasped it now. Then he went to the chair on which his coat lay, took the bundle of notes out of his breast-pocket, and thrust it under the pillow of the bed beside the revolver. He looked at his watch. "One o'clock," he muttered. "Now for an hour and a half's sleep. I shall wake fresh, and then be off to town."

Now and then he thought his desire was about to be realised. Now and then for a moment a confusion arose in his senses, and he lost the sharp outlines of reality, only to return to intense wakefulness and renewed despair.

"I shall go mad!" he cried in his heart. "Something tells me I shall go mad. Between Ray, and the Club, and Singleton Terrace, and Hetty, and the money, and this want of sleep, I know I shall go mad. Insomnia is one of the surest signs of coming insanity. O, it would be cruel--cruel if anything happened to me now that I have just won all! I am free of Nellie; I have the money; I have felt the influence of Hetty's luck, and will feel it again to-night. If Hetty would only come with me I should be out of the way of Kate's brother. Curse him a thousand times! And now I feel my head is going, my brain is turning. It isn't fair or just after all the trouble I have taken. It is horrible to think of losing everything now that I have so much within my grasp. I think that fall into the river and the meeting with Kate afterwards must have hurt my brain. And this sleeplessness, this wearing sleeplessness, will finish the work! O, it is too bad, too cruel! It is not fair!"

With a cry of despair he rose and began pacing up and down the room, frantically waving his hands over his head, and moaning in his misery.

Mrs. Grainger knocked at the door.

"It's half-past two, sir."

"All right."

The voice of the woman acted like a charm.

"What on earth," he asked himself, pausing in his walk, "have I been fooling about? I daresay that ducking and the fright of it, and the meeting with Kate, and the long repression at Singleton Terrace, and the cards, and finding myself so near Ray, and this bridge from the island to the Quay, and having the anxiety of the money on my mind, have all helped to put me a little out of sorts, and therefore, like the fool that I am, I must think I am going mad. The only sign of madness there is about me is that I should fancy such a thing. Why, the mere lying down has made me all right. I feel quite refreshed and young again. And now I must off. I don't want to meet that grinning bearded oaf."

Crawford put on his coat, waistcoat, and boots, replaced the money and the revolver in his pockets, and went downstairs. He could see Hetty through the open door of the sitting-room, arranging the table for dinner.

"I perceive," he called out to her in a blithe voice, "that you have opened up communications with your Robinson Crusoe. You have got a plank, or a stage, or something, from the Quay to the Ait."

"O," said Hetty, "Robinson Crusoe has a little boy the same age as our Freddie, and Freddie goes over every day to play with young Crusoe, and that's why the stage is there."

"I heard children's voices from my room. I suppose they belonged to Freddie and his young friend?"

"Yes. You couldn't be within a mile of the place without hearing Freddie's voice."

"Good-day."

"Good-day." Crawford went to the door and opened it. Suddenly a thought struck him, and he closed the door and ran upstairs. When he found himself in his own room he shut the door, and said to himself in a tone of reproach, "How stupid of me not to think of that before. Why need I carry all this money about with me when I can leave the bulk of it here?"

He counted out twenty-five one hundred-pound notes and locked them in a drawer. He turned the key in the lock of the door on the outside, and dropped it into his pocket. Then he slipped down the stairs noiselessly and gained the street without seeing either Hetty or Mrs. Grainger.

"I feel a new man now," he said to himself. "There is about as much chance of my going mad as of my being made Archbishop of Canterbury. And now we shall see if there is anything in my notion about Hetty's luck. Tonight will be the test."

CHAPTER XL
CRAWFORD SLEEPS

William Crawford was in a hurry away from Welford, not in a hurry to the Counter Club. His design was more to escape a meeting with Layard, than to pick up any of his gambling associates. "A walk," he thought, "will do me good." So, instead of taking the steamboat or any wheeled conveyance, he crossed Welford Bridge at a quick pace and kept on, heading west.

He felt that this day made an epoch in his life. He had bidden good-bye to his wife for ever. He had realised the fortune for which he had schemed. He had put himself under the tutelage of Hetty's luck. He would shortly cut the past adrift. If Nellie died soon--a thing almost certain--he would marry Hetty, leave the country and settle down. Of course, whether his wife died or not, Hetty must be his. That was settled, both because he admired her more than any other woman he had ever met and because she had brought him luck, and would bring him more. He knew, he felt as sure he should win that night as he did that the sun was shining above him. If he did not win that night he should be more astonished than if the sky now grew dark and night came on before sunset. O, how delightful and fresh would life be in the new world with Hetty and good luck present, and all the dangers and troubles and annoyances of the old world left behind here, and banished from his mind for ever!

He had not felt so light and buoyant for many a long day. What an absurd creature he had been half-an-hour ago, with his fears of going mad just because he had been a little upset and deprived of sleep for twenty-four hours!

He crossed the river by London Bridge and loitered about the City for a couple of hours. He felt that sensation of drowsiness coming on him again. He knew he could sleep no more now than when at Welford. Again his mind became troubled, and, shaking himself up, he exclaimed, "I will not suffer this again. There is nothing to rouse one up like the cards. Now to test my theory of Hetty's luck." He hailed a hansom and drove to the Counter Club.

The dinner at the club was excellent, but he had little or no appetite. As a rule he drank nothing but water. This evening he felt so dull and out of sorts he had a pint of champagne. It roused and cheered him at first, and after a cup of coffee he felt much better than he had all day. Not giving himself time to fall back into his former dull and depressed condition, he went straight to the card-room, where he found more men than usual, and the play already running high.

That night remains immemorable in the annals of the Counter Club. Play had been going on from early in the afternoon. Three brothers named Staples, members of the club, had lately come into equal shares of a large fortune left by a penurious old uncle. This was the first evening they had been at the Counter since they had got their legacies, and they had agreed among themselves to make a sensation. Up to this night they had been obliged to shirk high play, as their means were very limited and no credit was given at the card-tables. They were flush now, and had made up their minds to play as long as they could find any one to sit opposite them. When they came into the card-room an hour before Crawford they told a few friends their intention. The news spread, and the room filled to see the sport. Owing to the high stakes there were fewer players and a much greater number of spectators than usual.

"Now," thought Crawford, when he had heard the news, "this will be a good test. I am in no hurry, and I will give my luck, Hetty's luck, a fair trial. I have about five hundred pounds, and I'll play as long as they play if my money holds out."

There were six tables in the room, and at each of three one of the brothers sat. Crawford took his place at the table where the eldest was playing.

At midnight Crawford was ten pounds better off than at the beginning. This was worse than to have lost fifty. It was stupefying. It was more like earning money at a small rate an hour than winning money at cards.

As the men at Crawford's table had resolved to make a night of it, they adjourned for half-an-hour at one o'clock for supper. Crawford was still further disgusted to find that now he had eight pounds more than at starting. Eight pounds after five hours! Why, verily, the game did not pay for the candle. And worse than the paltriness of his winnings was this feeling of drowsiness which had come on him again. He now blamed the champagne for it. He drank water this time.

At half-past one play was resumed. The dull heavy feeling continued, and at times Crawford hardly knew what he was doing. The night flew by. By four o'clock all the lookers-on had left, and the room contained only players. All the tables but one were now deserted. At this one six men sat, Crawford, the three Staples, and two other members of the club.

By some extraordinary combination of luck no money worth speaking of had changed hands. All the players declared they had never seen anything so level in their lives. At this time there was a pause in the play for light refreshment. Five of the men had brandies and sodas, Crawford had coffee. He looked at the counters before him, and counted them with his eye. He had been making money at something like the rate of a day labourer. He had won two or three sovereigns! This wasn't play, but slavery.

The other men had nothing sensational to say; they all declared they were pretty much as they had started. No one had gained much, and no one was much hurt.

"Never saw such a thing in my life!" said the eldest Staples in amazement.

"Nor I," said Crawford.

"Shall we say seven for breakfast, and then, if there is no change, we'll chuck it?"

"All right," chorussed the others.

At seven, however, there was a very marked change: Crawford had won a hundred and fifty pounds.

"That's better," said the eldest Staples. "I vote we go on."

He was two hundred and fifty to the bad.

"Agreed," said the others.

"Is any one sleepy?"

"I'm not, at all events," said Crawford.

He could hardly keep his eyes open, and his head and limbs felt like lead.

At eight o'clock play was resumed, and Crawford's good luck continued. But he went on like a man in a dream. Now and then he lost all consciousness of his surroundings for a moment, and even when aroused he seemed only half awake; but though he was playing automatically, his good fortune kept steadily increasing the heap of counters at his left elbow.

At noon a few of the men who had been spectators the evening before came in to learn how the sitting had ended. They were overwhelmed with astonishment and envy when they heard that play had been continued all through the night and was still going on. They dropped into the card-room to see how the company bore the wear and tear of the night, and to gather how matters stood.

At one o'clock another halt was called for luncheon. The position of the players was then ascertained approximately. Two of the Staples and one of the other men had lost heavily, the youngest Staples had won a trifle, the other man was fifty pounds to the good, and William Crawford found himself in possession of sixteen hundred pounds, or eleven hundred more than when he sat down.

"Have we not had enough of it?" he asked of the eldest Staples; "I feel very tired."

"O," cried Staples, "let us go on till one of us gives in. If luck keeps on as it has been running I shall be dished soon. Then we can stop."

"All right," said Crawford. To himself he said, "If the play leaves off before midnight I know I shall increase my winnings, for Hetty's luck will be with me till then."

At seven o'clock young Staples said, "What about dinner?"

"O, hang dinner!" cried his brother. "Let us play until I'm cleaned out. I mean to stop at another hundred."

Crawford felt himself nod more than once between that and nine o'clock. He could no longer readily distinguish hearts from diamonds or spades from clubs. He heard noises in his ears, and every now and then he had to shake himself up sharply to make himself realise where he was.

"Crawford, you're falling asleep," said the eldest of the brothers, "and I've got beyond that hundred. Shall we stop? We've been at it twenty-four hours."

"I've been at it nearly thirty-six," said Crawford, rising. "I have had no sleep for forty-eight hours. I cannot see the cards."

"Shall we all dine together?" asked Staples. "This is an occasion which we ought to mark in some way or other."

"For my part," said Crawford, "I could eat nothing. I could not swallow a morsel until I sleep. I shall take a hansom and drive home."

As he stumbled stupidly into the cab that evening he carried away from the Counter Club two hundred pounds in gold, four hundred in notes, and sixteen hundred in cheques, making in all twenty-two hundred pounds, or seventeen hundred pounds more than he had brought into it the evening before. He directed the man to drive to Welford Bridge, and then settled himself comfortably in a corner to sleep on the way.

Before falling asleep he put his hand into his back pocket to ascertain if the revolver was there. "It's all right," he muttered. "After all, it's a great comfort to have it and to know I can defend myself and protect my money. But in reality, it isn't my money, but Hetty's. She brought me the luck. That's as plain as--" He started and stopped for a moment. A vivid flash of lightning had roused and stopped him for a second. "That's as plain as the lightning I have just seen." Before the long roll of the distant thunder died in the east he was asleep.

In little over an hour the cab reached the South London Canal. The driver raised the trap in the roof, and shouted down:

"Welford Bridge, sir."

"O, ay," said Crawford, half awake. "What is it?"

"This is Welford Bridge, sir."

"Very good; I'll walk the rest of the way."

He got out and paid the man. Rain was now falling in perpendicular torrents. Every minute the sky was filled with dazzling pulses of swift blue flame. The crash and tear and roar of thunder was almost continuous.

Crawford was conscious of flashes and clash and crash overhead, and rain descending like a confluence of waterspouts, but he did not feel quite certain whether all was the work of his imagination in dreams or of the material elements.

Dazed for want of sleep, and half-stunned by the clamour of the sky, and rendered slow and torpid by the clinging warm wetness of his clothes, he staggered along Welford Road and down Crawford Street.

"I shall sleep well to-night," he thought, grinning grimly at his present uncomfortable plight.

Arrived at the door, he opened it with his latch-key. He stumbled along into the back hall with the intention of shaking the rain off his clothes before going up to his room.

The door on the quay from the back hall was wide open. He stood at it and looked out. The light from the kitchen pierced the gloom, and the rain streamed across the wet and glittering floating-stage.

At that moment three pulses of fierce blue light beat from sky to earth, illumining vividly everything which distance or the rain did not hide.

William Crawford saw by the swift blue light from heaven the form of a woman advancing towards him across the stage. He saw that she held and umbrella open above her head. He saw that she had red spots on her thin and worn face. He knew that this woman was Kate Mellor of three years back, the woman who had rescued him from death a few days ago.

It was plain she did not recognise him, he standing between her and the light in the hall. She said, shaking the umbrella:

"I brought this for you, Philip."

Philip! Her brother! Philip Ray, her brother, who had sworn to kill him, must therefore be absolutely in the house under whose roof he now stood. Monstrous!

He turned swiftly round with a view to gaining the foot of the stairs and dashing up before he could be recognised.

Under the light of the hall-lamp, and advancing towards him, was Philip Ray, Kate's brother. For a moment Philip stood stock still, regarding the other fixedly. Then with a yell the brother sprang forward, crying:

"By ----, 'tis he at last! 'Tis Ainsworth!"

With a shriek of terror and despair Crawford bounded through the open door out on the narrow quay, and turned sharply to the left. In a second Ray sprang out on the quay in pursuit. The darkness was so intense he could not see which way Crawford had taken. For a moment he stood in the light coming through the doorway.

It was at this instant Kate Bramwell stepped ashore off the stage. As she did so two flashes in quick succession burst from the heavens. By this light she perceived Crawford standing half-a-dozen paces to the left of the back-door. She recognised him instantly. She saw that he had his right arm raised and extended on a line with his shoulder in the direction of her brother. She saw in his hand something metallic gleam in the lightning. With one bound she clasped her brother and strove with all her power to drag him down to the ground out of the line of the weapon. There was a snap, a loud report, and with a pang of burning pain in her shoulder, she fell insensible to the ground.

The thunder burst forth in a deafening roar.

The man who had fired the shot turned and fled headlong, he knew not, cared not, whither.

Suddenly he tripped over something and shot forward. He thrust out his hands to break his fall. They touched nothing. His whole body seemed to hang suspended in air for an instant. Then his hands and arms shot into water. His face was dashed against the smooth cold surface, and a boisterous tumult of water was in his ears, and his breathing ceased.

"The ice-house! No gates! Why do I not rise? If I do he will kill me. I cannot get out of this without help, and he is the only one near who could help, and he would kill me, would with pleasure see me drown a thousand times. When I rise I shall shout, come what may. I wonder is he dead? Why do I not rise? Yes, now I know why I do not rise. The gold, the two hundred pounds in gold; and my clothes are already soaked through. I shall never rise. I need struggle no more. I am going, going red-handed before the face of God."

That night William Crawford slept under ten feet of water, on the bed of ooze and slime, at the bottom of the flooded ice-house on Crawford's Bay.

The wounded woman never spoke again, never recovered consciousness. She passed peacefully away in the fresh clear light of early day.

It was not until the evening after the fatal night that, at the suggestion of Bayliss, the water of the flooded ice-house was dragged, and the body of William Crawford discovered. In the case of Kate Bramwell, a verdict of wilful murder was brought in by the coroner's jury against William Crawford. In his own case the jury said that he was found drowned in the flooded ice-house, but how he happened, to get into the water there was no evidence to show.

Mrs. Farraday, who came at once to Richmond on receiving Crawford's letter, was careful to let no newspaper containing any account of the Welford tragedy near Mrs. Crawford. The patient and gentle invalid was gradually sinking. She never complained to any one of his desertion. She never told a soul of the money she had given him. Whatever she thought of his letter to her she kept to herself. Her evidence, no doubt, would have been required at the inquest if her health had been ordinary. But Dr. Loftus certified that the mere mention of his death would in all likelihood prove fatal to her.

About a month after his death she said one evening to Mrs. Farraday:

"I should like to get one letter from my husband, announcing his safe arrival, before I go on my long journey. But it is not to be. I shall not be here when the letter comes. Let no one open it. Let it be burnt unopened. The letters between a husband and wife ought to be sacred."

She was afraid something in it might militate against the good opinion in which those who had met Crawford in Richmond had held him.

One morning, about six weeks after the inquest, Mrs. Farraday thought the stricken woman was sleeping longer than usual as she had not rung her bell by half-past nine o'clock. Mrs. Farraday went to the bed and found the poor sufferer had glided from the troubled sleep of life into the peaceful sleep of eternity.

"It is a mercy," said the good and kind-hearted woman, "that she never knew the truth."

It is now two years since that awful night. Once more Boland's Ait is uninhabited; once more no one dwells on the shore of Crawford's Bay. But in a very small but comfortable and pretty house in one of the leafy roads of the south-east district, and not far from the great Welford Gasworks, live in amity and cheerful concord two small families consisting of Alfred Layard and his little son Freddie, and Philip Ray, his wife Hetty, and their tiny baby girl, who is called after the mother, but always spoken of as Hesper by the mother, because of the great seriousness with which young mothers ever regard their first little babes. Hetty declares Hesper to be the wisest child in all the realms of the empire, for she never by any chance utters a sound during the two hours each evening that Philip is busy with his pupils.

Bramwell lives with his boy in a cottage at Barnet, where he is preparing for the press a selection from articles written by him in magazines during the past two years.